Espresso Shot of Charm

Book 1

G.M.ASMAU

Copyright Page

Espresso Shot of Charm
Copyright © 2026 by Asma'u Garba
All rights reserved.

Cover design by G. M. ASMAU
Imprint: Independently Published
First Edition: [February, 2026]

Dedication

For the women who placed their hearts in the hands of Allah
And the men who fear Allah enough to protect it

﴿ ...وَعَاشِرُوهُنَّ بِالْمَعْرُوفِ... ﴾ .

"... And live with them in kindness."

— Qur'an, An-Nisā' (4:19)

Prologue

BADR

فَبَعدَ لَحظِكِ لا أرنو لغانِيَّة
وَلَو تَحَلّت بِنورِ الشَّمسِ وَالْقَمَر

After your gaze, I shall never glance at any enchantress,
Even if she adorned herself with the light of the sun and the moon.

- ابن البراق الاندلسي

Past

I was flung terribly far back in my seat, my mouth widening into a yawn, eyes already soft with sleep. The teacher kept talking, a steady stream of words that stopped meaning anything the moment they reached me.

I hardly got two hours in last night. There was an itch in my skull that said *just one more, just one more.* I tried to focus, but without it I couldn't, and that thought sat on my chest like a stone. I have always been an A student, but without that edge, I would fail. I can't afford to fail.

My hand went into my bag. I felt the cool shape of the pill and felt the floor of my resolve set itself around it. Then a voice stopped me.

I sat up straight, as if posture could sharpen hearing. Instead my vision sharpened. My eyes landed on one bright thing in a room of gray: orange, so clean it looked lit from inside. A dress, a woman in an orange dress and a cream hijab. She was the only color that belonged where it was, like a little sun in a dim classroom.

I wanted to see her face, but she sat in front of me, turned away. I could, however, hear her, and the sound made me do a thing I had not done in weeks. I listened.

"Interesting observation Habiba, elaborate please." The teacher commented.

Habiba.

Beloved

The name drifted through my head, loose and unguarded. Beloved. Someone loved. Someone worth gentleness.

Her voice was not from anywhere I could name. It had the roundness of someplace warm, the crisp edges of someplace far. Jamaican? Arab? Indian? none of those fit. I tried to attach a label and only found a shape that would not submit. The mystery did something to the itch in my head. Trying to place the accent pulled me toward attention. Trying to hear her made thinking possible. For the first time in a week, a thought came that had nothing to do with the pill in my bag. *Who is she?*

My mind, which had been a single needle-point of craving, widened. The classroom detail came back into frame, softer and kinder. Her voice, when it came, was small and private, like a bell you have to lean toward to hear. I wanted to say something, anything clever or stupid enough to make her turn. I imagined questions and challenges and little provocations, nothing academic, everything stupidly human.

My fingers loosened.

The pill in my bag lost its brightness. She made me feel awake in a way a chemical never did, electric and strange.

I was, undeniably, better than I had been five minutes ago, but exhaustion is patient. My friends crowded around, laughing and thumping backs, dragging me back toward the same map of obligations. They kept pulling me into their noise while I only wanted a sliver of quiet to slip away and be honest with myself for a second.

As soon as the bell sounded, I was out the door. They called my name, but not now. I rummaged through my bag as I walked, fingers scrabbling. I had one more, I knew the exact weight of it. When my hand closed around it, I smiled at myself the way people smile when they think they've won a small war.

I was about to toss it into my mouth when someone collided with me. I reached to steady it and watched it escape, tumble from my fingers and roll, slow and traitorous, into a puddle of melted snow.

"Are you serious?" I snapped, whirling to see whoever the hell had just ruined my day.

The first thing my eyes caught was orange. The dress. Her again. Habiba. She was crouched on the ground, one hand clutching her ankle. The world narrowed again, but this time not to a craving. It narrowed to orange, to the remembered sound of her voice.

I was ready to unleash another snap, but then she looked up and I had to pause. Maybe rewind, maybe double-check reality. I'm not much of a ladies' man—truth is, I don't even remember the last time I saw a girl I genuinely thought was beautiful. And yet here I was, staring like an idiot.

"I'm so sorry. I was in a rush. Did you drop something?" she asked, climbing to her feet. She glanced around as if she could help me find whatever I'd lost. "Hello?" She waved a hand in front of my face.

I couldn't pin down what it was. Her brows? Her eyes? Her lips? Or just the harmony of her face altogether. Maybe it was the voice. It had to be the voice. Every word jolted me awake. My veins buzzed. Suddenly I wasn't angry anymore.

"Are you okay? I didn't mean to bump into you. Blame it on my heels, I wasn't expecting the paving to be so rough. So Sorry."

Definitely the voice.

"Hello?—"

"What accent is that?" I blurted.

"What?" Her brows drew in.

"Your accent. You have an accent. What is it?"

She stared at me, long enough for me to see the defences slide into place. "I don't have an accent."

I smirked, a scoff slipping out before I could stop it. "You might be confused, because if that's no accent, I'd hate to hear what counts as one."

She folded her arms. "I think you're the one who's confused. If I had an accent, I'd know."

"I'm not confused." I shook my head. "But I am fascinated. It's not every day someone makes me forget what I was about to do."

Her frown deepened. "Maybe you should go get a coffee. You look like you need it."

"What?"

"You heard me. Get a coffee. Or three." She glared.

"Fascinating observation. You're a regular Sherlock, aren't you?" I shot back, sarcasm dripping.

"Impossible," she muttered under her breath. Then she turned and walked away.

I wanted to follow, to stop her, to stretch this moment thinner and thinner until it wouldn't break. But I had a sibling to pick up from school. On the bus, I caught myself thinking not about the pill I'd lost, but about her.

While I waited for the last bell to ring, I slipped into the café across the road. Coffee had never intrigued me. Everyone was obsessed with it, swore by it, but I never cared. Now, suddenly, I wanted to try. Who knew, maybe this was the fix I needed.

"Good afternoon. What can I get you?"

"What's the strongest coffee you have?"

"The espresso."

"I'll have that."

When she set down a tiny cup, I thought it was a prank. I looked at her face, hunting for a smile, but there was none. So I lifted it carefully, let the steam rise, then leaned in for a sip.

My life shifted. That one sip peeled the film from my eyes. The streets outside sharpened, the sounds deepened, the air itself felt alive.

8

But even in that little awakening, it still wasn't the jolt I'd felt when she bumped into me.

The coffee was bitter and strong, something new on my tongue. But even then, all I really wanted was one more conversation with her.

1

HABIBA

أَي سِرٍ فِيكِ إِنِّي لَسْتُ أَدْرِي
كُلُّ مَا فِيكِ مِنَ الأَسْرَارِ يُغْرِي

What secret lies within you? I confess I cannot see,
Yet every mystery you hold lures and beckons me.

- إبراهيم ناجي

Present

"Jamila!" I snapped, my voice sharp and quick. Her little head snapped up. One glance at my face and she stilled, the splashing water falling silent.

I exhaled, rinsed the last of the soap from her tiny arms, and bundled her in a towel. The terry cloth swallowed her up, leaving only her round cheeks visible.

Normally, I would've kissed her forehead, and promised the world. But today, I was already running late. "Teeth. Now!" I instructed, pointing to the sink. She pouted but obeyed, clutching her toothbrush like it was punishment.

The smell of oil hit me before I even left the hallway. I rushed back to the kitchen, where the last golden-brown batch of fries sizzled in the pan, edges threatening to burn. I drained them, slid them into the cooler, snapped it shut, and set it on the table.

When I returned, Hadi was already there, dressed in his little button-up shirt, trying to wrestle Jamila into her jeans. At six, he was far too serious for his age, brows knitted in concentration as if this was a math problem and not a squirming three-year-old.

"Good job," I said, taking over before Jamila could topple. "Go eat. And don't make a mess."

He shot me a quick nod and darted out, leaving me to finish the job. Once Jamila was dressed, I took her to the dining room, seating her next to Hadi. The two of them bent over their plates like it was a mission.

I used that time to mop the bathroom, take the fastest shower imaginable, and pack my office bag.

Gogo, my step-grandmother, sat on the sofa, her laughter sharp and high-pitched as she doted on her grandchildren. Jamila leaned against her knee, Hadi perched at her side, both glowing under the warmth she reserved only for them.

I walked over quietly and bent down, lowering myself to my knees, my head bowed. "Ina kwana, Gogo," *Good Morning, Gogo.* I murmured.

She didn't bother looking at me. Just a flick of her wrist, a careless wave, like I was a fly buzzing too close. I didn't care enough to dwell on it, I needed to get to the office.

I rushed to where the children's bags were tossed, slinging them over my shoulder and crouching to slip Jamila's shoes on her restless feet. Hadi tugged impatiently at my sleeve, eager to leave.

Just then, Baba appeared at the top of the stairs.

He wore his usual off-white kaftan with matching trousers, his walking stick tapping steadily against the steps as he descended. His face lit up the moment Hadi darted forward, wrapping little arms around his legs. Jamila followed once I fastened her straps, squealing as she twirled around him in circles.

"Make sure you're the top in your class," Baba said with a chuckle, ruffling Hadi's hair before reaching down to Jamila. His smile was soft, eyes crinkling with pride.

"Baba, ina kwana," *Baba, Good Morning.* I greeted, standing straighter.

"Habiba," his gaze found me with that familiar fondness. "Ya naga baki tafi ba?" *How come you haven't left yet?*

11

"Walahi, I woke up late," I admitted, glancing nervously at my watch.

Baba's eyes swept the room, landing on Gogo like a hawk spotting prey. Gogo's smile vanished. She glared at him, sharp enough to cut.

I lowered my eyes quickly. I was already late, the last thing I wanted was to be caught in the middle of their endless war.

The car was already waiting. I got the kids inside, kissed their foreheads, and as soon as the driver pulled out, I sprinted the opposite way to the bus stop.

Ten stops.

My watch glared at me. The meeting must have already started, and today, Terrence was announcing who got the project. The project, the biggest project that our firm has scored. This project is exactly what I need.

When I finally arrived, the hallway was silent. Everyone was already in the conference room. I slowed down in front of the mirror because I couldn't go in looking like a sandstorm had caught me.

Fixed my hijab. Wiped the sweat glistening at my nose. Blotted the smudged kohl, retouched my gloss. Deep breath.

I pushed the door open and stepped inside. "Good morning," I announced.

A few people mumbled greetings. And of course—Badr. Never one to miss a moment.

"Nice of you to grace us with your presence," he said, eyes twinkling with mischief. "We were two minutes away from sending out a search party."

Every cell in my body begged me to ignore him. But I'm only human.

"Couldn't go ten minutes without me, Badr?" I walked to my seat, turning it slightly away from him but keeping him in my line of sight.

"Nah," he said, not even looking at me. "Just wanted you here when Terrence hands me the client."

"Wow. We're trusting mediocres with the big projects now?" I feigned surprise.

"Clapbacks mean nothing when coming from a woman who's been chasing my shadow."

"You're not that fast, Badr. I walk behind so I can watch you trip on your own ego."

That earned me a few chuckles.

Before Badr could fire back, Terrence cut in.

"Now that our power duo is reunited, can we proceed?"

Badr El-Idrissi. My personal migraine.

University? He was there. First job? Also there. Office cubicle? Directly across mine. Like a human shadow with a smart mouth. I'd get a promotion—so would he. I'd land a big client—he'd one-up it. The firm split everything between us because neither of us ever dropped the ball. It was maddening.

Terrence began the meeting. Updates, praise, the usual. But when he finally got to the point, my pulse sharpened.

"I've seen great improvement in all your performances this week," Terrence said, eyeing us all. "Good news is, I can't work with anyone in this project, I will need a duo rather. Bad news is, it has to be a reliable duo."

Here it comes.

They'll split it. Again. Badr and me, back in the ring. I fought the urge to tug at my hijab in frustration.

Terrence continued, "I'll be handing the project to… Gabe and Theo."

The names hit like cold water.

Gabe and Theo.

I blinked. Smiled. Even tried to appear gracious. Inside, my left

13

eyelid twitched.

Badr looked equally stunned. We locked eyes across the table, a silent truce in our shared confusion.

As if he could feel our protests coming, Terrence gathered his things and left.

Gabe and Theo cheered like toddlers with juice boxes. Theo tossed a jab our way. "Bet some egos were crushed today. About time."

Ever since Theo joined the firm, he seemed to appoint himself a shadow, turning me and Badr into his private finish line. He wanted to pass us, beat us, even though we barely spared him a thought. When Gabe arrived, Theo scooped him up like a sidekick, and the two of them built their own little corner, buzzing with self-importance. Theo threw words around like knives, but everyone knew they were rubber. The truth was obvious: he was scared of Badr.

Maybe it was the height difference, Badr stands just over six-two, muscles defined even under loose shirts, or maybe it was because Badr's confidence wasn't something he had to rehearse. Either way, it was almost entertaining to watch. As long as I wasn't caught in the middle, of course—which was very unlikely. Because, as much as I hated to admit it, Theo wouldn't even come near me when Badr was around.

The chair rolled back as I stood, the same instant Badr pushed his away. He gathered his notes with practiced ease, voice light, almost lazy, as he said, "Looks like you win the prediction game. Mediocres, big projects—check."

I slid my notebook into my bag and rounded the table, a smirk tugging at my lips. "Naturally. I'm never wrong."

By the time I reached the door, he was already there, holding it open for me, a teasing glint in his eyes. His smirk matched mine. "Oh, I know. Accuracy is your toxic trait."

I rolled my eyes, though I couldn't help the curve of my mouth. One last glance at Theo—still glaring, like he'd choke on his own pride.

14

He had the kind of grin that tried too hard to look harmless and instead curved into something almost sinister. Blonde hair, pale eyes, a smile just shy of evil. He wore a grey suit that might've been sharp if not for the crime scene of a tie—a garish shade of red that clashed with the stripes of his shirt and ruined the whole ensemble. He was all talk, no bite, the kind of man who mistook volume for presence.

I walked out. My pace quickened to catch up with Terrence, Badr's footsteps falling a beat behind mine. Terrence was speed-walking. So were we. "Terrence!" we called in unison.

"The decision is made," he tossed over his shoulder. "You won't change my mind."

He reached his office, tried to shut the door, but Badr was faster. He held it open and turned to me with a mock bow. "After you."

I stepped in. Badr followed.

Terrence looked like he aged ten years. Hand at his temple. Visibly regretting every life choice.

"Seriously? Gabe and Theo?" Badr started.

"They're all we've got left," Terrence said. "And they actually work well together."

"In that case, why don't we just gift-wrap the client and hand him to Rie Enterprise?" He threw his hands up in frustration.

"My original plan was to give it to you two, you know that." he said. "But you can't work together."

"We can!" we both said, horrified.

"You bickered over office lighting. You fought over pens. You couldn't even share an office without a wall built between you. You want me to risk our biggest client on your bickering?"

The memory burned. When Badr and I got promoted, they put us in the same office—two desks, two egos, and zero personal space. I spent 50 hours a week staring at his smug face, with his voice constantly ricocheting off the walls like an echo I couldn't escape. We argued about everything, lighting, air conditioning, the placement of the coffee machine. It got so bad, management gave up and installed a faux wall between us, like we were squabbling toddlers in need of a timeout.

Still. This was different. This was Franklin.

"Whether or not Badr and I get along is irrelevant. Franklin deserves the best. We are the best." I stated.

"I'd rather hand him a mediocre project than lose the client completely."

Silence.

Then Badr spoke again. "You can't take this from us."

"I already did."

I felt the anger brewing. I stepped forward, folder in hand, and dropped it onto his desk harder than I intended. The smack made him flinch. My voice cut sharp, too sharp, but I didn't rein it in. Not this time.

"I went to that ridiculous gathering," I snapped. "Sat through his wife's gardening lecture for two hours. I hate gardening. I hate small talk. But I did it. For this project. I convinced Franklin to even consider us." I leaned in, finger jabbing the desk. "You cannot take this away from me."

Terrence froze. The silence was heavy.

Then, from beside me, Badr's voice slid in. "Easy, Lalla. I think the man got the point." His hand hovered, undecided whether to comfort or tease. I whipped him a glare. He only smiled. "You heard her," he added smoothly. "She braved gardening talk. That's practically martyrdom."

I almost laughed—almost.

"We'll work together," I added. "I'll even consider his brainrot ideas."

"Brainrot is the new amazing," Badr quickly added. "New generation slang, you wouldn't understand."

Terrence groaned, rubbing his bald head, the universal sign he was out of arguments. Finally, he sighed. "Fine. The project is yours. But if I hear one complaint, one, you're both off it. Effective immediately."

Relief and triumph warred in my chest. I nodded. "You won't regret it."

Once Terrence finished instructing us on the next steps, Badr and I finally left his office. The click of my heels kept a steady, businesslike beat against the polished floor.

Beside me, Badr's stride was longer, slower. One step for him was two for me, but somehow we stayed in sync. His left hand was buried in his pocket, the other swinging a folder in an easy arc. His shoes made softer, slower thuds, matching my quicker taps in a strange, unspoken rhythm.

"We just scored a big client. How about a smile as a form of celebration?"

I didn't say a thing. I just kept walking.

"Come on, Habiba. Smile. It's sunnah."

I plastered on a grin so fake it hurt my cheeks, spearing him with a look. "There. Satisfied?"

He grinned. "That smile could bankrupt a man. No wonder you don't use it often."

"If a smile could bankrupt you, that sounds like a budgeting issue," I shot back.

He didn't miss a beat. "I wouldn't mention bankruptcy if it weren't worth the risk."

I rolled my eyes, struggling to hold back a real smile. "I just want us to survive Franklin without chasing him off."

Right on cue, his hand slid into my path, a folder snapping open in front of me as we walked. Two renderings stared up, same building, same angle—except one gleamed in soft cream tones, and the other carried a rough, stone-textured façade.

"Which one?" he asked, eyes fixed ahead like he didn't actually care.

I didn't slow down. One glance was enough. I pointed to the stone. "That one. Cream makes it look like a resort brochure."

"Textured it is," he murmured, tucking the folder under his arm.

We reached his office. He stopped. I didn't.

"When do you want to discuss our project?" he called after me, his voice easy, almost teasing.

I turned to look at him. He stood in front of his office, annoyingly unbothered as usual. His shirt was crisp white, but one of the top buttons was undone like he'd gotten lazy midway through dressing. I had an almost compulsive urge to fix it, to fasten it properly, for the sake of visual order if nothing else.

His curls had flopped forward slightly, the way they always did, one stubborn lock trailing close to his thick eyebrows. His skin was a warm, sun-fed brown, the kind that somehow always looked richer beneath office lighting.

Yes, I'll admit it. He was good-looking.

A shame he came with a mouth.

"I'll mail you my schedule," I said, my hand already on my door.

Our doors, side by side, shut at the exact same second.

 HABIBA

إِنِّي لَأَعْجَبُ مِن حُبٍّ يُقَرِّبُنِي
مِمَّن يُبَاعِدُنِي مِنْهُ وَيُقصِينِي

I am amazed by this love that pulls me so close,
Toward the very one who drives me off with a cold glance.

- أبو العتاهية

Past

Three weeks. I have been here three weeks and yet I still haven't made a friend.

Either there's a secret board where everyone's been warned to stay away from me, or I just don't look very approachable. Probably the latter.

I thought I'd at least make one friend by now, but clearly I'm terrible at it. Maybe I should've held on tighter to my old friends, but it's not easy being close to someone who's been through a loss. People don't want to feel weighed down by someone else's grief.

I knew there was someone behind me, I felt the presence of someone. Not to mention the shadow offering me shade on my back.

I put on my kindest smile and turned, ready to face whoever it was, but as soon as I met eyes with the person, my smile dropped. My brief flicker of excitement instantly died. Of course. It's just Badr.

Charming smile. Dark, mischievous eyes. Curls that look like they never misbehave. Tall. Broad. And the absolute, textbook definition of "pain in the ass."

Black high-neck shirt, sleeves casually folded to his elbows, cream trousers like he just walked out of a men's fashion spread. Pain in the ass with style.

Badr doesn't really count as a friend.

"Mukhtar," he said, dropping into the seat across from me, leaning forward with that grin that actually worked on 99% of the female population, including the teachers. "I have a proposition."

I didn't even bother looking at him again. My eyes stayed glued to my laptop screen and my geometry task.

"Pair up with me, I'll do all the work."

That made me look up. My brain froze somewhere between is this a compliment or an insult?

Out of all the people on this campus, why did I keep running into him? Coincidence? Or maybe he was following me, I can't tell.

I blinked at him. He blinked back. Then I went right back to my notes.

"No," I said flatly. "I'm perfectly capable of doing my own work."

The professor had given us the option: pair up or go solo. Naturally, I went solo. Or maybe it was not so much of an option for me.

"Exactly," Badr said smoothly. "That's precisely why I'm here. You're perfectly capable. My friends aren't very capable at getting the job done and I really need an A. So how about you direct me and I do the work, It's a win win."

"I got you one better " I smiled sweetly. "How about you find someone else to bother, and find new friends."

"But I enjoy bothering you, I thought that was obvious by now." He tossed his hands up like it was the most obvious thing in the world.

I breathe in deeply to absorb whatever spare atoms of patience flying in the air before speaking. "Why me, Idrissi?"

He flashed that irritating grin again. "How do I explain this…" He rubbed his chin, pretending to think. "You're… what's the word," he said, scratching his beard. "An Espresso Shot of Charm, concentrated chaos that somehow works. Also probably bad for me, but here we are."

I raised a brow. "Is that a racist joke?"

His eyes widened. "What? No! I would never use coffee to deliver racism. Coffee is sacred. Have you even tried an espresso? One shot, and you're alive. Like vodka, but halal." He waved it off. "Anyway, that's beside the point. The point is: Oggy likes you. Oggy hates me. Oggy won't fail you. Which means, by extension, Oggy can't fail me."

I frowned. "I don't know who Oggy is, but if he hates you, I'm sure it's for a good reason. Probably not far from mine."

The truth? I didn't really have a reason to hate Badr, I didn't even hate him, I just didn't like the fact that he was male, insufferably confident, and somehow always had a quick, cheeky answer for everything. Most people outgrow that energy after high school. Badr clearly packed it in his university backpack.

Oh and he's hell bent on the fact that I have an accent. Which I only now realized that I do, but I didn't need him to point it out.

"Look," he leaned closer, lowering his voice conspiratorially, "I just need this pass. And maybe, in exchange, I'll help you survive geometry."

"Maybe I can survive geometry on my own," I shot back.

He tilted his head toward my paper, tapped a line with one finger. "I don't think so."

I froze. Okay, so maybe geometry and I weren't friends. Baba could always get me a tutor, but he already wasn't thrilled about my choice of major. More struggling wouldn't help my case.

I sighed. Maybe I could use a partner.

"If saying yes means you'll leave me alone, then fine."

His smile stretched wider as he stood. "Pleasure doing business with you, Mukhtar. Text me." He dropped a slip of paper onto my notebook and walked off like he'd just closed the deal of the century.

Later that day, I sat in a café with a book, trying to read my way into becoming a better architect. But when I went up to order, my eyes snagged on the espresso in the menu.

I drink cappuccinos often, but I've never tried an espresso before. Maybe now was the time.

Once I had my order, I sat back down, staring at the tiny cup like it was a threat. I hated hot drinks, hated the tongue-burn, so I waited until it cooled down then eventually I braved it and took a sip. My entire face scrunched into a grimace. It was bitter. Unholy. I swallowed it down, resisting the urge to gag.

"Clearly, you hated that."

I whipped my head up. Of course. Badr.

"Next time you call me an espresso, try not to make it sound like a compliment," I snapped. "Why is it so bitter!?"

He smirked. "I never said you weren't bitter. I said you were an espresso. Bitter, but with exactly the kind of kick I need to get things done."

He slid a cold cup toward me, a matcha latte, condensation beading on the plastic. "Here. Have this." Then he picked up my espresso.

"I can finish it," I protested weakly.

"Don't worry, Mukhtar. I like to spice my day up with a little bitterness. Why else do you think I interact with you?" He grinned once more before turning away, but my question stopped him.

"What about the charm?" He turned back, brows slightly raised. "You said I'm an Espresso Shot of Charm. Why charm?"

"Oh, that." He paused, as if weighing whether it was worth explaining. "That was just a little touch. I had to tread lightly. I didn't know if you're an espresso fan. So I threw in *charm*. Figured one of the two would land."

That was the last thing he said before heading off to a corner table.

I tried to focus on my book, but it was useless. The one person who annoyed me most had just rescued me from my own curiosity.

3

BADR

قَليلٌ مِنْكَ يَكْفِيني ولكِن
قَليلُكَ لَا يُقَالُ له قَليلٌ

Just a little from you is enough for my soul's desire,
But your "little" is far from being lesser.

- الميكالي

Present

"Woah," I gasped as I stepped into Hana's room, clutching my chest like I'd seen a ghost.

She paused mid-pack, eyes scanning for danger. "What?" she asked, alarmed.

I smiled. "You're getting prettier by the minute. What's happening here?" I poked her cheek.

She swatted my hand away, but a smile curled at the corners of her mouth. "Stop, Badr." I grinned while she turned back to shove her pens and book into her bag.

"How's book club going?" I flopped down on her bed, sinking into the soft floral quilt as I watched her pack.

Hana was sixteen, our only sister, the only girl in a house of 3 brothers.

Her skin matched mine in tone, that warm, soft brown, but her features carried more gentleness. Her almond-shaped eyes were larger, framed by lashes that made them look perpetually bright, and her round cheeks hadn't quite thinned out, no matter how much she complained about her "baby face."

Today, she wore a flowy white skirt that brushed the tops of her feet and a blush-pink blouse that blended perfectly with her pastel hijab.

She always dressed like that, modest but sweet, the kind of softness that made her look like she had stepped straight out of spring. A walking cherry blossom.

She got a hard time from us constantly circling her, teasing, testing her patience. But the truth was, we liked it. Annoying her until she snapped, then laughing when she couldn't resist smiling a second later.

Protected… maybe too protected, but that was how we preferred it.

"Why? You planning on joining me?" She arched a brow at me, already knowing I couldn't stand the sappy stories she devoured.

"Depends. Are there boys there?" I narrowed my eyes in mock suspicion.

"Yeah. We have five of them, and they're all asking for my hand. Want me to give them your number?"

"Yeah, do that." I smirked. "I'll invite them all over for a baking match. Whoever makes a better cheesecake than Zain gets the girl."

She burst out laughing and tossed her pen at me. I caught it midair before it hit my chest.

"Don't you think you're setting the bar too high?"

Zain's voice cut in from the doorway. He leaned against the frame with his arms crossed, posture casual but presence sharp. Grey shirt, black sweats—his usual half-effort uniform.

Zain's skin was a few shades deeper than mine, darker like our father's, rich, warm, like burnt honey left in the sun. His features were all edges and shadows, intensity carved into him even when he wasn't trying. His hair fell in softer curls than mine, more like our mother's.

"Really? I thought that was quite low," I muttered.

"Yeah, if they were competing against you," he shot back. He crossed the room, bent down to kiss Hana's head, then reached into her bag to pull out the book she'd just packed.

She smacked his hand and snatched it back then shoved past him, bag over her shoulder, but paused at the door. "Who's dropping me off?"

We all exchanged looks. Of course it was me. Oldest child. Driver. Errand boy.

"Let's go," I sighed, pushing myself off the bed to follow.

"Where's Ma?" Hana asked as we made our way downstairs, her footsteps pattering behind me.

"She took Ahmed to the dentist," I answered, grabbing the keys.

The air outside was warm, late afternoon sunlight casting a golden sheen over the driveway. I opened her door for her, waited until she slid in, and shut it before circling to my side. By the time I settled into the driver's seat, she was already adjusting her hijab in the mirror, tugging at the fabric until it framed her face just right.

"Who are you trying to look pretty for?" I teased, starting the engine and reaching into the glove compartment for my rug so I could dust the dashboard.

"Allah," she shot back smoothly. I gave her a look. She smirked, smug and victorious.

As I tugged the rug free, a folded paper slipped out, and with it, a small photo fluttered into her hands. Hana held it up, studying it with raised brows.

"Well, well, look who's judging me," she drawled, flashing the picture at me.

It was of a girl with tan skin, green hijab, and a black abaya, smiling brightly. Another one of those. I snatched it out of her grip and tossed it into the backseat.

"Should I tell Ma you're hiding pictures of girls in your car?" she pressed, grinning.

I scoffed. "How about you tell Ma to stop hiding pictures of girls all over my room? That would be helpful."

Her eyes widened. "She's doing that? Seriously?"

I nodded.

"Wow." Hana laughed, shaking her head. "I can't believe she didn't let me in on it."

I shot her a glare. "Seatbelt." We both clicked ours into place.

The drive was short, the city alive around us with its evening hum. Her book club met close to the mall, which worked in my favor. As soon as I watched her walk safely inside, bag bouncing against her hip, I turned the car toward the mall parking lot.

I came here often, mostly to sit at a café on the top floor, where tall windows stretched across the wall. My favorite spot overlooked the street below. If that table wasn't free, I'd usually just leave. Something about it anchored me, cleared my head, gave me space to think through the next day's work.

But first, groceries.

I went straight to the supermarket on the lowest floor. I wasn't the one who cooked at home, but I was always the one restocking the fridge and knowing everyone's favorites by heart.

With no rush, I shopped slowly, the fluorescent lights humming above, the cool air a contrast to the warmth outside. Once done, I wheeled the bags to the car, stowed them neatly in the trunk, and finally headed upstairs toward my café.

I was on the escalator to the top floor when a familiar figure caught my eye. My breath hitched as I leaned forward, trying to stretch for a better look before the moving steps carried me past. Once I reached the top, I didn't think twice, I just circled around and rode back down, needing to be sure.

It was her. Habiba.

I rarely saw her outside of work, and whenever I did, I'd usually slip into the kind of humor she hated so much. But today, that lightness wouldn't come. Today, she wasn't alone.

A man walked beside her, holding a little girl balanced easily in his arms, while Habiba clasped the hand of a boy who trotted confidently between them. The four of them looked like a portrait.

She was wearing a soft blue hijab. The kind of blue that reminded me of cloudless skies in August. She had on a flower patterned skirt and blouse. I have always admired the way she dresses, nothing modern, since the first day I've known her, she's always dressed in their traditional Hausa clothes. Different colors, patterns, styles and she wears them all with confidence.

The man was tall. Pale. Brown hair. Seemingly blue eyes. Clean-shaven. Wore a button-up and tailored slacks like he came out of a minimalist fashion blog. He looked... safe. Predictable.

He didn't look like her type. Not that I ever knew what her type was, but still. I always figured Habiba would end up with someone bold. A little too intense. Definitely someone who could argue her into silence—which, let's be honest, isn't easy.

But this guy? He looked like the kind of man who apologized when someone else bumped into him.

Suddenly I felt out of place. Heavy in my own skin.

The realization landed like a stone in my chest, sinking hard. I never crossed a line with her. No touch, no inappropriate words. Still, something about the discovery unsettled me. Maybe it was the reminder that we weren't kids anymore. We were adults now—adults old enough to be married, to have children.

They were laughing at something when her eyes lifted. I froze, realizing too late that I'd been staring. Our gazes collided. Her eyes widened, just for a second. Then, in true Habiba fashion, she gathered herself quickly, expression smoothing into composure.

I turned fast, heat rising to my face, and stepped back onto the escalator to the top floor. My pulse thundered.

I've known Habiba since university, through both bachelor's and master's programs.

She was undeniably, devastating. Not just in the way she looked, but in the way she carried herself, always appearing untouchable. I became consumed by the chase, finding her snap entertaining and, more importantly, addictive. She quickly became everything I needed, the kind of energy that kept me moving.

I knew I would keep chasing that feeling. Keep chasing her. This rivalry, this intense focus, had become the structure holding my world together.

When our years in architecture ended, I told myself I was finally free of the act, of pretending that I enjoyed her company, that I needed her around. I'd long stopped needing her to get through the day, she wasn't my keeper anymore. She had done her part, pulled me out of the hole. Still, I couldn't let go. Maybe it was out of guilt, because I knew I'd used her like a lifeline. Or maybe because, even if she'd hate to admit it, she enjoyed my company. So, I kept showing up, annoying her, chasing that spark she gave me. Somehow, she'd become part of what clean felt like.

But as I watched the crowds thin out on the day of our graduation, a strange hollow feeling bloomed in my chest. I wasn't relieved. I was disappointed. The "espresso shot" that had kept me alert all these years was gone. The addiction I thought I'd beaten had only changed form. And for the first time, I realized that it was never about the wake. It was about her.

And then came my first day as an intern. She walked into the firm like she owned it, chin high, shoulders squared, confidence trailing her like a signature scent. I didn't want to notice, but I did anyway. One look, and I knew my life wasn't about to get easier.

After weeks of not seeing her, just the sight of her again hit straight to the veins—sharp, exhilarating, impossible to ignore. For the first time in a long while, I actually felt excited. Alive. But that didn't change the fact that she could crawl under my skin better than anyone else alive.

We both got hired and both got promoted so, we were assigned to share an office. I thought it was a blessing, daily doses of her, right across from me. My own personal shot of chaos. But working with Habiba was anything but easy. Every file had to be color-coded. Every pen in its place. She'd glare at my desk, clean it without asking, and then complain about my tie choices as if they were crimes against humanity.

It was infuriating. It was entertaining. It was... addicting. Every argument ended with me half-irritated, half-amused, wondering how someone could make me want to strangle them and smile in the same breath.

When we finally got paired on our first project, it was nothing short of a war zone—clashing presentations, creative sabotage, and one very traumatized client who nearly resigned mid-meeting. Terrence didn't fire us, though. He just separated us. Probably the smartest decision he's ever made.

Gradually, our rivalry evolved into something resembling friendship. Habiba would never admit it, but we both understood that our constant bickering and competition served as a means for us to connect. I couldn't just stroll into her office and strike up a conversation without a purpose; however, I could certainly provoke her, prompting her to come and engage in a spirited debate with me. She enjoyed it, and so did I.

At the café, I ordered a filter coffee, letting the bitterness ground me as I sank into my usual seat by the window. The city sprawled below, traffic crawling like red veins of light. I tried to clear my mind, to focus on work, but knowing Habiba was somewhere in this building made my thoughts restless.

The door chimed. My stomach tightened when I saw her walk in with him, and the kids.

Panic rooted me to the chair. I fixed my gaze on the window, as if ignoring them would make them vanish. But of course, fate laughed in my face. The little boy plopped himself in the seat right next to me. Of all the empty chairs, he chose that one.

I turned, and he was staring at me. Wide, curious eyes. Maybe five, six years old. My chest tightened. Had she really been married that long? My mind flickered through every heated argument Habiba and I had had, imagining her husband storming in to deck me for pushing her buttons.

I couldn't help myself, I pulled a silly face. The boy giggled, but the sound of his father's voice snapped him back.

"Hadi, come here."

The boy scrambled to his father, leaving the seat beside me empty until Habiba took it. Of course, she angled her body away from me, as if to cut me out of her air entirely. I smirked despite myself. That was exactly the Habiba I knew.

Their voices carried easily.

"Daddy, last night, Jamila threw up," Hadi said.

"Really?" His father cooed, voice softening. "Oh my little baby, are you okay?"

"Yes. Bibi made her soup," Hadi answered, while Jamila was busy trying to climb into Habiba's lap.

"Of course she did. Bibi takes very good care of you." His smile lingered on Habiba, his eyes warm, tender. So much love in that gaze it made my stomach knot. Jamila wrapped her arms around Habiba's neck.

His gaze slid to me. Something in my chest twisted. I turned my face away, but I could still feel the man's eyes on me, burning into my temple.

Habiba followed his gaze and looked at me too. I gave in and said the only thing that felt right. "Salam."

She looked away, but replied softly, "Salam."

"You two know each other?" her companion asked.

She hesitated. "Yeah, we work together." The edge in her tone nearly made me grin.

He extended a hand. "Pleasure to meet you, I'm Muhammed."

"Badr," I said.

His brows lifted, his smile dimming just slightly. "Oh. Badr?" He turned to Habiba.

She stiffened, irritation flashing across her face. My grin grew. She talks about me. "Yeah," she said flatly. The barista called their drinks, and she used it as an excuse to slip away.

"I'm guessing you've heard all the bad things," I joked.

"Some good things too," Muhammed said, then grinned. "That's a lie."

I laughed.

When Habiba returned, the kids pounced on their drinks. Muhammed took his, and I leaned back, unwilling to let the moment pass.

"So you're the husband?"

He chuckled. "Oh, no, no. I'm her brother-in-law."

Relief washed through me. My shoulders dropped, the weight in my chest easing. Wait, a brother-in-law in love with his sister-in-law. Interesting dynamic. I wonder how her sister feels about it.

"Cousin-in-law, actually. Ex cousin-in-law. Her cousin and I are divorced. These are my kids." He patted Jamila's head.

Oh. Ok

"Oh," I grinned. "I thought those were her kids. I was shocked she never mentioned them."

"You really find it hard not to stick your nose in my business, don't you, Badr?" Habiba cut in sharply.

I leaned back with a grin. "You barely have enough business to go around. When something does come up, I like to savor it."

"Let's go." She got up. Muhammed chuckled, but followed her lead. He shook my hand again before they left.

"I'll see you tomorrow, Habiba," I called, unable to resist.

"InShaAllah," she said, not sparing me a glance.

I sat back, smiling like a fool. For once, it felt like I'd learned something about her beyond her love for potatoes.

One time, I brought in a potato dish my mom made. Looked amazing. Smelled even better. I knew she loved potatoes. So I didn't give her any.

Petty? Absolutely.

She stole my client. I needed revenge.

4

فلا انا مفصح عما أعاني
ولا وجعي على صمتي يزول

I cannot give voice to all the pain I hold inside,
Yet keeping it within me does not make the torment heal.

- عبد الرزاق عبد الواحد

"Bibi?" Jamila's small voice rang out as she pushed my door open.

"Hmm?" I turned from my desk, watching her shuffle in. Her hair was wild, strands falling in her face, and she clutched a hairband in one hand like it was urgent. She thrust the band toward me while using her other hand to shove curls out of her eyes.

Jamila and Hadi carried their father's Canadian features more strongly than their mother's Hausa blood. Wavy hair, light brown skin, and his storm-grey eyes that always seemed too sharp for a child. Hadi, at least, had their mother's softer brown eyes.

I made Jamila turn around so I could gather her messy hair. My fingers worked carefully, parting strands, pulling them into place.

"Ina Mama?" *Where is Mama?* I asked in Hausa.

"Tana sleeping," *She's sleeping.* she mumbled, English and Hausa tangled on her tongue.

I smiled faintly at the mix, though it wasn't enough to mask the irritation simmering beneath. Sleeping, again. She gave birth to two children but hardly ever raised them. No wonder she was divorced.

Khadijah, their mother, my cousin, had insisted on marrying Muhammed years ago. Gogo didn't approve. But Khadijah always got what she wanted. Always.

At first, it worked. They had Hadi early in the marriage. But it didn't take long for Muhammed to see what kind of wife he'd married. She had charm enough to fool anyone, at least for a while. But charm doesn't cook, clean, or raise children. He learned that too late. He was a gentle man, too gentle for a woman like her. And now, years later, here we are.

Every weekend, I drop them off with their father because she can't be bothered to see his face.

The door creaked again. Hadi bounded in, a plate of rice in his hand. Without a word, he offered Jamila a spoonful, then stuffed one into his own mouth. Placing the plate on my bed, he attempted a backflip mid-chew.

"Hadi, what did I say about jumping while chewing?" I scolded.

He froze, cheeks puffed, then sank obediently to the floor to chew properly. That boy had his father's patience, his kindness. A better caretaker than their own mother ever managed to be.

Just as I tightened the last knot in Jamila's hair, Gogo's sharp voice sliced through the air.

"Habiba!"

"Na'am, Gogo?" I answered quickly, rising to my feet. The children trailed behind me, like ducklings, as I made my way to her room.

I knocked softly before entering. She was propped against her pillows, her eyes already narrowed at me as I approached and knelt by her bed.

"Kin kira Jacob?" *Did you call Jacob?* she demanded.

"Yes," I murmured, eyes fixed on the floor to avoid her piercing gaze. "He said they'll come by tomorrow morning to sort it out."

"Why didn't you come and tell me then?" Her tone cracked like a whip, accent thick.

"I came, but you were on the phone, then… I forgot."

I risked glancing up, only to be caught by her sharp and heavy glare, the kind that made your chest tighten with guilt even when you'd done nothing wrong.

Before I could say more, Jamila slipped next to me and plopped herself down on the floor.

"Jamila, my little girl, zo ki zauna tare da ni. Come sit with me," Gogo crooned, her voice softening like silk as she stretched her arms toward the child.

Jamila's face lit up. She climbed onto the bed without hesitation. Hadi joined her, and Gogo welcomed them both, drawing them close. Then, without even looking at me, she waved a dismissive hand.

"Go and make dinner. Baba ya kusa dawowa." *Baba is almost back.* she ordered.

I bit my tongue, nodded, and carried the plate away.

This was Gogo's rhythm. Honey for them, vinegar for me. She could smother her grandchildren in affection while reminding me that in her eyes, I was nothing more than the maid of this house.

She and Baba had raised me after my parents died, paid for my schooling, put food in my mouth, a roof over my head. For that, I owed them everything. And for that, she made it her mission to break me.

Khadijah woke up and drifted straight to the living room, eyes glued to her phone. She was beautiful—I could never deny that. Her sharp, almond-shaped eyes had a way of holding attention, her skin smooth and glowing, close to the same shade as mine. Her smile could brighten a room, though it never matched the sly, careless personality behind it. She wore a white shirt and green sweatpants, casual but perfectly fitted.

Unlike me, who had grown up mostly in Nigeria and still dressed like it—boubous, skirts and blouses, long gowns—Khadijah dressed like a Westerner. Effortless. Comfortable.

I walked past her into the kitchen, the smell of onions sizzling faint in the air as I stirred sauce on the stove. Minutes later, my name cut through the walls like a whip. I turned, wiping my hands. When I stepped out, I saw juice spilled across the tiles, a sticky trail dangerously close to the carpet.

"Go get something and clean that up," Khadijah ordered, her eyes never leaving her phone.

My stomach tightened. I hated when she ordered me around like I was her maid. I owed her nothing. But every time I tried to push back, she would run to Gogo, and I'd end up paying the price, except when Baba is present, but he's not right now, so I swallowed the anger rising in my throat and fetched a rag.

The spill barely touched the edge of the carpet. I crouched and wiped quickly before it could seep in.

"Goge da kyau mana," *Clean it properly.* she snapped, her sharp eyes cutting into me, watching like a hawk waiting for me to fail.

Heat rushed to my face. "To, ke ki zo ki goge dakanki," *Then come and clean it yourself.* I snapped back before I could stop myself.

Her head shot up, eyes blazing. "Ke! Wallahi ban san iskanchi pa." *Hey, wallahi I don't like disrespect.* She jabbed a finger dangerously close to my face.

"Me kika dauke ni ne? Wawiya che da zan zauna ki ta yi mani yadda kika ga dama?" *What do you take me for? A fool who'll just sit and let you treat me however you want?*

"Yes, you are a fool, what are you gonna do about it?"

"Leave me alone," I slapped her hand away, returning to the floor, scrubbing harder than I needed to. But she wasn't done.

"Or what?" she hissed, stepping closer. Suddenly, her hand shot out, yanking at my scarf. The choke of fabric against my neck startled me, and instinct took over. I bit her hand. Hard.

Khadijah screamed, jerking back. She stumbled, crashing against the kids, who seemed to appear out of nowhere. Jamila burst into tears, her small voice wailing in terror.

"Kai! Kai! Kai!" Gogo's roar shook the walls. My blood ran cold. Before I could even rise to my feet, her slipper flew across the room. I flinched and blocked it with my arm just before it struck my face.

Her voice cut sharper than leather. "What did I tell you about troubling the people of this house?" Her glare burned into my skin until I dropped my eyes. Tears pricked the corners of my eyes, but I forced them back. I bent, wiped the last of the juice, and fled to the kitchen with my head bowed.

Only when the door shut behind me did I let go. The rag slipped from my hand as I washed my hands, the sobs broke free. I crouched by the counter, my back pressed against the cabinet, chest heaving like it might split open.

It always hurt.

It always hurt to be here.

I pressed my hands over my face, muffling my cries. Ten seconds. That was all I allowed myself. Ten seconds to break before I forced the pieces back together. When the seconds passed, I washed my hands, wiped my face, and returned to the stove. Dinner wouldn't cook itself.

Later that evening, when Baba returned, I set his tray down in the living room. The TV flickered as he switched it on, the sound of the commentator rising just as I straightened from arranging his food. I was about to sit when his voice cracked through the room like a whip.

"How do you expect me to eat? Ina zan wanke hannuna?" *Where will I wash my hands?*

I froze, my chest tightening, before quickly jumping to my feet. Of course. I had forgotten the bowl, the soap, the jug of water. Normally I never did, but today my mind was elsewhere. My mistake.

"I forgot, Baba," I murmured, and hurried to fetch it.

This was Baba, sudden bursts of anger that scattered like sparks. I had grown used to them. Everyone in his orbit had, I think. But they didn't erase the man he was underneath. It didn't make him unkind. Not entirely.

I set the bowl before him and poured water over his hands as he scrubbed them with soap, his thick fingers working methodically, the veins prominent under his skin. Once clean, he crossed his legs before the steaming dish of tuwo and okra soup. Food always softened him; that much I knew.

I sat nearby, my laptop open on my knees. He tore into the meal with his hands, and I let the familiar sounds soothe me, the rhythmic dip of tuwo into soup, the satisfied slurp, the occasional clicking of his tongue. His eyes flicked to the screen where Franklin Starr was playing. Baba's shoulders eased, his face lifting with boyish delight. Basketball always did this to him; it was the only time he looked younger than his years, like the weight of his anger loosened its grip.

I watched him quietly, my heart tugging. For him, I wanted the Franklin project to succeed. For once, I wanted him to look at me with pride. My degree, my published designs, the magazines that praised my work—none of it moved him. But Franklin did. If I finished this hotel, if Franklin himself praised me… maybe Baba would finally see me.

"Gaskiya, Habiba," he said, licking his fingers, his voice softer now. "Ya chi ki yi aure. Abinci mai dadi haka?" *Honestly Habiba, it's time for you to get married. Food this delicious?*

I chuckled, "Na fi so in tsaya nan, in hada maka abinci mai dadi." *I prefer to stay here and make yummy food for you.*

He shook his head, firm as ever. "No. What you need is to stop wasting your youth with work. Find a husband."

I swallowed the groan pressing at my throat. The marriage lecture again. I knew better than to argue. With Baba, pushing back too hard only fanned his temper, and then I'd be branded disrespectful.

"Toh, Baba," I said lightly, forcing a smile. "Insha'Allah, miji zai fito." *Insha'Allah, a husband will come.*

The game on TV shifted, pulling his attention away. He leaned forward, eyes narrowing at the screen, muttering under his breath at a missed pass. I took my chance and rose quietly.

I didn't like being alone in my room. The silence weighed heavy there. But it was easier than staying for another round of that conversation.

The next day passed without much noise. Toward evening, Terrence came into my office with Badr trailing behind him.

Terrence had an emergency. His daughter had flown in unexpectedly for a quick visit before heading back to Italy that same night. He adored his family, always talked about them, and there was no way he was going to miss a chance to see her. But it also meant he couldn't attend the very important meeting scheduled for that evening— the one where he was meant to pitch a project to a client.

Instead, he asked Badr and me to represent the firm in his place. Luckily, we both knew the project well enough; he'd consulted us multiple times during its drafting. Since it was still early, we each took a copy of the proposal and stayed in our offices, familiarizing ourselves with every detail.

By five, we had gone home to change. The meeting was at six.

I slipped into an orange lace gown with butterfly sleeves—the prettiest thing I had that still carried the right weight for clients of this status. I wrapped a cream hijab around my head and, for once, put in more effort with my makeup: kohl on my eyes, mascara, lips lined with black and gloss to seal it. Normally I only brushed my brows and added lip balm, but tonight demanded more.

Baba wasn't home, and I slipped out quietly before Gogo or Khadijah could notice. I wasn't in the mood for new drama. Badr was parked a few blocks down. When he saw me step out, he drove closer and stopped right in front of me.

He'd told me earlier he would pick me up. The car was cool when I slid inside, his perfume filling the air, the same perfume he uses for every big event. He looked... devastatingly good. I'd seen Badr look handsome plenty of times, but somehow each time still caught me off guard.

Grey suit, crisp white shirt, his hair freshly styled, curls slick and dark, falling lightly over his forehead. He had shaved, but only just enough to leave his jawline clean and sharp. For a moment I could swear he stared at me, like really stared, in a way that made my chest tighten. I blinked, unsure if I was imagining it.

Then he broke it, reaching into the backseat and pulling out two ties. "Which one?"

I studied them quickly and pointed to the brown. It was warmer, better against the grey. He nodded, then reached into the center console, taking out two small boxes. He flipped them open, one held a pair of Tommy Hilfiger cufflinks, the other Montblanc. Without hesitation, I chose the Montblanc; they completed the look perfectly.

"Alright, here." He tossed the tie at me while slipping on the cufflinks. I shot him a glare, but he only answered with a quick wink before starting the car.

I looped the tie around my neck, straightened it, tightened it as best I could. When we stopped at a red light, I handed the tie to him. He slid it carefully around his collar then angled his body to me so I could check the knot.

When I finally nodded in approval, he muttered a low, almost absent. "Thanks" before shifting his focus back to the road.

5

BADR

موقعي عندك لا أعلمه
آه لو تعلم عندي موقعك

The place I hold within your heart, I do not know,
Oh, if only you knew your place within my soul.

- أحمد شوقي

The city had already softened into evening by the time we pulled into the restaurant's lot. Warm light spilled from tall glass windows, catching against the polished hoods of cars far more expensive than mine. I killed the engine, fingers drumming against the steering wheel longer than they needed to.

Habiba sat beside me, scrolling through her phone, her posture collected as always. She carried that rare kind of beauty that wasn't loud, but impossible to ignore—and tonight it pressed harder against my senses than it should have. Like I had no business sitting this close to her. Maybe it was the dress. The same one she wore the first time I saw her. One glance at it, and suddenly I was back there—back at the start, back before all this, before I even knew how much she'd come to mean to me.

It struck me all at once how far we'd come, how much she'd become the center of everything. The thought left my chest tight. I cleared my throat, forcing my hand toward the folder on the back seat. "Ready?"

She didn't respond and instead slipped her phone into her bag and gave a small nod. Her face was calm, composed. "Terrence sent another message."

"Let me guess. 'Show a united front.'"

Her lips quirked, though her eyes didn't leave the bag she was adjusting on her lap. "Word for word."

I chuckled, pushing the driver's door open. "I'm sure Stark won't mind a little banter. Might even help."

I spotted two men crossing the lot toward the entrance. Recognition clicked immediately; I studied their pictures enough. Jacob Stark, sixty if he was a day, walked with the kind of steady confidence money and experience layered into a man. His son Mark trailed just a step behind, his stride quicker, almost eager.

Jacob's handshake was firm, his palm warm, gaze steady. Mark mirrored him, less practiced, but enthusiastic. When he turned toward Habiba, extending his hand, I cut in before the pause could grow awkward. "She doesn't shake hands," I said smoothly.

Habiba inclined her head, calm as ever. "I'm Habiba. It's a pleasure to meet you both."

Mark's hand lingered a second too long in the air before he tucked it back into his pocket. His polite smile returned, but there was curiosity in his eyes now.

Inside, the hostess guided us to a corner table set for four. Habiba slid into the seat beside me, her focus absorbed as if she were immune to the weight of my glance.

We ordered drinks, slipped through the usual opening pleasantries, and soon enough, the conversation shifted to the project. I let Habiba handle part of the technical explanation; her voice was steady, articulate, weaving numbers and sustainability features with the kind of clarity that impressed even me. Jacob leaned in, listening closely. Mark, though, seemed more fascinated by her than the actual content.

I watched him angle his questions toward her, watched the small tilt of his head, the way his gaze lingered a second too long when she answered. And Habiba, oblivious, responded with her usual professionalism.

"Beauty and brains. Your firm is very fortunate." Mark commented, his eyes lingering on Habiba.

I cut in before she could respond. "Fortunate doesn't even begin to cover it. Habiba's work has carried projects that would've fallen apart without her brains. The rest," I gestured dismissively, "is just coincidence."

Dinner arrived, plates of seared fish and roasted vegetables, the conversation still circling back to projections and returns. Whenever Mark tried to slide in a line that sounded half like business and half like something else, I cut it off with a redirect, never sharp enough to seem defensive, but enough to steer him back to the project. He probably didn't even notice.

Jacob was sharp, though. His gaze flicked between us, taking in more than he said.

After the plates were cleared, Jacob leaned back, stretching slightly. "Shall we step outside for a bit? A stretch after the meal."

I agreed before I could think, pushing back my chair. But Habiba shook her head, amusement glinting briefly in her eyes. "I'd rather stay seated, if that's alright. You men go have fun."

I hesitated. The idea of leaving her alone didn't sit well with me. But then she smiled, the kind of smile that said without words: *I'll be fine.*

"We won't be long," I murmured, my voice lower than I intended.

I put on my trench coat and followed behind them but turned once more, just to make sure. She was already watching me. Our eyes caught and held longer than polite. And when she smiled again, softer this time, it slipped right past my guard. I felt my own mouth curve in answer, my chest loosening, heart tilting toward the warmth in her gaze.

The cold air bit as soon as we stepped outside, crisp against my face. I slid a hand into my pocket, posture steady, refusing to let the chill pull a shiver out of me. Jacob and Mark each lit a cigarette, the flare of orange briefly painting their features before the smoke curled into the night.

"You don't smoke?" Jacob asked, exhaling in a stream that caught the breeze.

I shook my head.

"Smart," he said with a rough chuckle. "Wish I'd done the same."

We fell into talk—business chatter, nothing that needed my full attention so my focus drifted. Through the glass, I caught sight of Habiba. She had risen from the table, drink in hand, and now moved toward the bar. She took a seat and said something to the bartender.

"You're watching her," Jacob said suddenly, his tone curious, not accusing.

I pulled my eyes away, forcing a small laugh. "Just making sure she's comfortable."

"Your girlfriend?" His brows lifted.

I chuckled, shaking my head. "No."

Mark smirked around his cigarette, smoke curling from his lips. "Shame, she's definitely my type."

Heat flared through me, sharp and unwelcome. I bit back the response that rose to my tongue, keeping my smile neutral. "She's a colleague. A valuable one."

They moved the conversation forward, something about contracts and timelines, but my gaze was pulled back again. A man had slid into the stool beside her. He leaned in, his body angled toward her in a way that made the hairs at the back of my neck stiffen. I waited, hoping he'd simply move on, but then I caught the flicker of discomfort on her face, the subtle stiffening in her shoulders, the uneasy shift of her fingers on her glass. She tilted her head politely, but her discomfort was clear to me, written in lines no one else would notice.

That was all it took.

"Excuse me a moment," I muttered, already moving.

The warmth of the restaurant wrapped around me as I stepped back inside. My strides carried me across the room before I could think twice. Sliding into the space at her side, I angled my voice just right, calm, casual, but with weight beneath it. "There you are," I said, my hand brushing the back of her chair. "Didn't mean to keep you waiting."

The man's eyes flicked between us. He read it in an instant. "Enjoy your evening," he muttered, retreating with his glass.

Habiba exhaled softly, almost too quietly to notice, then glanced at me with the faintest curve to her lips. "Now he probably thinks we're dating."

"That was the plan," I smiled. "You alright?"

The ring on her finger clinked against the glass, the sound sharper than it should've been. My eyes lingered on her hand, on the delicate motion of it, then watch her place the cup on her lips, until I caught myself staring. Heat crawled up the back of my neck. I turned away quickly.

"Why are you back already?" she asked instead, her voice light, controlled.

"They were smoking," I said. "Not a fan of the smell."

She nodded knowingly. "I figured as much." Then she pushed her glass toward me, the ice clinking. "Want it? I can't finish."

A smile tugged at me despite myself. "Feels like today is full of memories."

Her brows lifted slightly.

I reminded her. "Study sessions. You'd leave half your drink, and I'd end up finishing it."

Her composure softened into something warmer. She smiled, not her polite one, not the shielded one, but something smaller, real. "I guess some things never change."

I stared at the drink for a second, battling with myself whether it'll be appropriate to drink from right where her lips had been. Back then I never even used to give it a second thought, I'd down the drink without a care but now, now I wasn't so sure. I gestured to the bartender for a straw, slid it into her glass, and took a sip. The mint and lime were sharp on my tongue.

"Have you noticed?" she said quietly, a mischievous tilt at her lips. "We were civil tonight."

The words slipped out before I could stop them. "Or maybe you're too much for words tonight."

Silence stretched, her gaze locked on mine. I hated how good she was at holding eye contact. I used to think I had the upper hand there, but she had a way of making me blink first. Not tonight. Tonight I welcomed the excuse to keep staring.

At last, her head turned, lashes lowering. "So that's only tonight? Tomorrow I'll go back to being intolerable?"

My chest tightened. "No," I said quickly, shaking my head. "You've always been easy on the eyes, Habiba."

When I glanced back at her, she had one brow arched, lips curved the slightest bit.

"Don't act surprised," I added, letting the faintest smile tug at my mouth. "You're still bitter," Her lips twitched, though her gaze stayed lowered. "Espresso shot, remember?" I murmured.

For a heartbeat, the words lodged in my throat, heavier than they should've been. The joke was hers now—ours—but I couldn't stop the sharp pang that shot through me. Because I remembered exactly what it meant.

The first time I'd called her that, it wasn't about her spark or her stubbornness. It was the physical jolt she gave me when nothing else could cut through the fog, when I was clawing my way through a dark place and needed anything to keep me awake, sharp, alive. She didn't know that. She still didn't.

I forced the guilt back down, forced my smile to stay easy, casual.

And then she laughed. Low, genuine, unguarded. The sound slid under my skin, tightening something in my chest, an ache I couldn't name, one I wasn't sure I wanted to. In that moment, the guilt evaporated, replaced by the simple truth that I could live inside her laughter forever.

She shook her head, still smiling. "It's a good thing you still start your day with an espresso. Otherwise, I might've been offended." Her eyes flicked toward me, quick, sly. "Though I can't tell if it's my charm or just the caffeine talking."

For a second, the air between us felt smaller, pressing in and for the first time that night, I couldn't summon a comeback. She'd turned my own words against me, smooth as silk, and I hated how much I liked it. My pulse tripped, and I had to look away before she saw more than I wanted her to.

I forced a smirk. "I don't know… maybe I should cut down on the espresso anyway," I muttered, aiming for casual. "Between you and the work, I've got more than enough to keep my heart racing."

Before I could get a reaction out of her, movement caught my eye. Jacob and Mark were heading back in, smoke still trailing faintly from their suits. Habiba straightened, her expression smoothing back to its usual composure, and together we returned to the table.

As we wrapped, Jacob leaned forward, giving a firm nod. "You've got a sharp team. Sharp, and solid."

I thanked him, closing the folder as he stood. But even as we exchanged handshakes and farewells, my thoughts weren't on the client. They were on Habiba, on the soft curve of her smile at the bar, the sound of her laugh, the unspoken ease of sitting beside her again.

Outside, we waved goodbye to the clients, then I turned to face her. "Come on. I'll drop you home."

She blinked at me. "I can manage—"

"It's late," I cut in, my tone leaving no room for argument. "I'm not letting you take an Uber alone."

Even if she were just a colleague, I wouldn't allow it. But she wasn't just a colleague. She was Habiba, and that made it all the more impossible to let her walk away on her own.

She sighed, resigned, and followed me. I unlocked the Mazda, opened her door first, then tossed my jacket into the back before sliding behind the wheel.

I never really had the luxury of buying a car I loved—a flashy, personal kind of car. The Mazda's beautiful, sure, but it isn't a one-man ride; it's a family car. I chose something that could fit my family, not something that fit me. And that's fine. It's just a car.

Zain got the one he wanted—the fast, impractical kind. Sometimes I like watching him live out the kind of youth I never really had. It makes me happy. Almost feels like I'm living mine through him.

The hum of the engine filled the quiet between us. "You should know," I said finally, eyes fixed on the headlights cutting through the dark, "Theo's furious about losing the project."

"Of course he is," she muttered.

"I overheard him with Gabe," I added. "Same garbage as always. The cheap shots. Be careful."

She nodded, her voice flat but steady. "I've already been steering clear."

I glanced at her then, just a second. She looked unbothered, but I knew her well enough to hear the quiet edge beneath her calm. Gabe and Theo had been at it for years, whispering, disturbing, undermining. We'd both learned to tune it out, but that didn't mean I liked the idea of her being anywhere near their poison.

She fought too hard for her quiet, for the steadiness in her soul. And I owed mine to her. I couldn't, wouldn't let anyone endanger the peace of the woman who had given me mine.

Ten minutes later, I pulled up outside her gate. I leaned back slightly, smirking. "I finally know exactly where you live."

"Just so we're clear," she said, reaching for the handle, "this is not an invitation for surprise visits."

48

"Visiting uninvited?" I let a grin slip. "That's never been my habit. Don't worry."

She smiled despite herself. "Goodnight."

"Goodnight," I said softly, watching as she stepped out.

I stayed there, engine running, eyes following her until the gate opened and she disappeared inside. Only then did I let out the breath I hadn't realized I'd been holding.

And still... I didn't want to leave. Not yet. There was something about tonight, something that clung to me, that made it feel like we'd slipped backward in time, to university, to the days when rivalry had been our language, when every exchange was a duel but carried the faintest trace of friendship beneath it.

Except now it felt heavier. Quieter. Different.

I found myself wishing I could sit with her again. Just a little longer.

6

وَلَقَدْ ذَكَرْتُكِ وَالرِّمَاحُ نَوَاهِلٌ
مِنِّي وَبِيضُ الْهِنْدِ تَقْطُرُ مِنْ دَمِي
فَوَدِدْتُ تَقْبِيلَ السُّيُوفِ لِأَنَّهَا
لَمَعَتْ كَبَارِقِ ثَغْرِكِ الْمُتَبَسِّم

I thought of you while spears were drinking from me,
And Indian blades dripped with my blood.
I wished to kiss the swords,
For they flashed like the smile of your shining teeth.

- عنترة بن شداد

I woke up at 4 a.m. for my tahajjud and witr prayer, the room still hushed in its predawn stillness. My forehead pressed against the cool mat as I whispered duas until the first call for Fajr. Afterwards, I slipped back into bed for my short, treasured nap. The sleep between Fajr and waking always felt like a gift, deeper and sweeter than any other. Alhamdulillah.

As usual, I bathed the kids, sent them off to school and got on the bus to work. I had barely set my bag on the desk when my assistant, Tina appeared. "Terrence needs you in his office."

I smoothed my abaya and went. Inside, Badr was already there. I hesitated, then quietly stood near the chair, avoiding his eyes.

I didn't really want to face him, not after last night. Something about that dinner unsettled me in a way I couldn't name. Teasing and sharp comments had always been our language, a rhythm I knew well, but last night, it wasn't the same. His words lingered longer than they should have, tugging at places inside me I'd never let anyone reach.

"Have a seat," Terrence offered.

"I'll stand, thank you," I replied with a small smile.

He nodded and opened the folder in front of him. "Franklin Starr is coming in today."

Badr and I exchanged no words, only nods, while Terrence reminded us to be on our best behavior, to keep things professional, no arguing, no distractions. Badr stayed behind to discuss another project. I hurried back to my office to polish the designs I'd done, pouring everything into making them as sharp as possible.

Halfway through printing, I realized I was out of paper. With a groan, I pushed back from my desk and headed down to the storeroom.

The smell of dust and faint ink lingered as I flicked on the light. Shelves towered around me, stacked with supplies, but when I reached the spot for the printer paper, only an empty wrapper remained. I sighed. The heavy reams were kept on the upper shelf.

As I dragged a stool from the corner, I heard the door behind me open. I didn't jump. Not visibly, at least, then I turned my head, Theo.

He seemed to have come in with an agenda, but when he looked up and saw me, his eyes narrowed with that fake smile he wore whenever he was about to say something insulting dressed up as a joke.

"I guess congratulations are in order," he drawled. "You and golden boy managed to steal the project back."

I forced a polite smile and turned back to the shelf. "It wasn't theft, just taking what was ours to begin with." I wasn't sure if getting on the stool was a good idea anymore.

He chuckled, the sound low and bitter, and moved closer. His cologne, sharp and overbearing, filled the narrow space. My chest tightened, but I kept my posture steady.

"You know what I think?" His breath brushed hot against my cheek. I didn't flinch. Not outwardly. "I think you and Badr believe you're untouchable. That the firm owes you every big client because you walk around acting like you're God's gift to architecture."

I straightened, spine rigid, and turned my head to meet his gaze. "We act like that," I said evenly, "because maybe we are that."

His laugh was sharp, humorless. "You're just a pretty face with sharp words, Habiba. Let's see how far that gets you in—"

"You done?"

The voice sliced through the air like a blade dipped in ice.

Badr.

He stood at the doorway, expression unreadable, but I knew that look. It was the one he wore when he was one snide comment away from verbally skinning someone alive. I've seen it happen before.

Theo sneered. "Here comes the other half of the royal couple."

Badr raised an eyebrow. "If you're going to cry about our achievements, at least do it with some grace."

"I wasn't crying—"

"You were cornering my colleague in a storage room," Badr cut in smoothly. "That's a potential HR issue."

Theo's jaw ticked. "You two think you're untouchable."

"We're just competent," I said. Badr was beside me now, without even looking at Theo, his eyes scanned the shelf like this was a grocery run. "Which is apparently threatening."

"Don't be too harsh on him," Badr added, voice deceptively mild as he reached up. "Not everyone can handle being mediocre."

Theo bristled. "You think you're better than everyone."

"Not everyone," I shot back smoothly. "Just the ones who get handed projects and still manage to fumble them."

"Ah," Badr murmured, as if Theo weren't even there. He tugged a thick stack of papers free, balancing it easily in one hand while the other stayed tucked in his pocket.

I took it from him without hesitation. My arms dipped under the unexpected weight, forcing me to grab it with both hands. He let it go without protest, barely sparing me a glance.

"Thanks," I muttered.

He didn't acknowledge it.

Turning to Theo, I squared my shoulders. "Move." He didn't

budge.

Badr stepped forward. "She said move."

Theo shifted aside, silent now. As we passed, I added, "Next time, keep your tantrums outside the supply room."

"And maybe," Badr said, without looking back, "try working on projects instead of conspiracy theories."

We walked the hall in silence, climbing the stairs.

"You're welcome," he finally muttered.

I glanced at him. "For making one dramatic entrance?"

His lips twitched. "For rescuing you. Obviously."

"I didn't need rescuing. But I'll send you a thank-you card if your ego needs it."

He snorted. "Make it gold foil. Embossed. Maybe a trophy while you're at it."

We stopped at his door. I tilted my head, lips curving slightly. "You'd love that, wouldn't you? 'Best in Arrogance: Badr El-Idrissi, undefeated since birth.'"

He gave me a look, dry as dust. "Can I have that back?" He pointed at the papers.

I frowned, clutching them tighter. "I went to get these."

"So did I." He smirked. "You think I went there for you? Touch grass, Mukhtar."

Rolling my eyes, I tore the stack open and handed him half. He snatched it, disappearing into his office with an apology to whoever waited inside.

Soon, Terrence's message was waiting: Franklin had arrived.

I rushed to finalize the edits, sent the documents to print, and tucked them neatly into a file. As I stepped out, Badr exited his office too. He waited until I was close, then matched my stride.

"Don't start," I warned.

"I didn't say anything."

"You were about to."

He gave me a sidelong glance. "You sure you want to walk in there radiating this much hostility?"

"It's confidence. Not hostility."

"Mm."

We reached the stairs. He gestured for me to go first. I ignored the gesture, descending with a muttered, "Let's just make it through this without a scene."

"Of course. United front, remember? Boss's orders."

I arched a brow. "Can you fake that without rolling your eyes every five seconds?"

"I've faked enjoying your company for this long, haven't I? One could mistake that I might be in love with you."

I didn't answer.

A small weight lifted off my chest, we were back to our usual banter, the familiar rhythm I could handle.

We reached the bottom of the stairs, made the turn, and approached the conference room. Through the glass, I saw Franklin, already seated at the table, mid-laugh with our boss. The room brightened slightly when he saw us coming. Badr opened the door for me. I stepped in, head held high, my face sliding into a perfect smile, a mask I've worn a hundred times before.

"Mr. Franklin," Badr greeted, voice smooth.

"Pleasure." Franklin stood, wide smile, already extending his hand. "To finally meet the dream team," he said, shaking Badr's hand firmly. Then he turned to me and reached forward again without hesitation.

I offered a polite nod, keeping my hands clasped around my folder. "I don't shake hands, sorry." I said gently, but before the air could even shift awkwardly, Badr swooped in with a half-grin and caught Franklin's hand again.

"I'll take that one on her behalf. She's the brains, I'm just the handshake guy."

Franklin laughed, "Well, I'm honored either way."

I took my seat, smoothing my dress as I did. Badr adjusted his shirt again, rolling his sleeves up just a bit higher, like he was about to dig into something serious. My eyes betrayed me for just a moment. Now I could properly see his muscles, the fabric of his shirt straining as if threatening to split at the seams.

I yanked my gaze away, muttering, "Astaghfirullah," my heart doing a little extra thump for entirely the wrong reasons.

"Shall we begin?" I said, resting my hands lightly over my notepad.

"Let's," Franklin said, clearly pleased.

Franklin Starr was impossible to miss. Even seated, he towered over the conference table, his frame broad and commanding in a beige suit that shouldn't have worked but did. His skin was deep, rich as polished mahogany, and his honey-colored eyes had a way of holding a room without trying.

"So," Franklin began, adjusting his cufflinks. "A hotel."

"We read through the project brief," Badr replied smoothly. "But it would help if you described it in your own words so we can visualize it the way you see it. Bring it to life for us."

"Hmm…" Franklin said, leaning forward, like he'd practiced it a thousand times for cameras. "I want a resort. A place families can come to and actually breathe. Basketball courts, sure, but also something more, something you step into and immediately know it's not just luxury. It's peace. A getaway. I want it to make headlines."

Badr nodded politely, arms crossed, the model of calm. I, on the other hand, was already fitting his words into the site plan we'd reviewed. The land was generous, coastal, with plenty of open space that could cradle more than just buildings.

When he finished, I opened the portfolio I had prepared. "Given the plot you've chosen, I'd suggest a cluster of low-rise villas instead of one dominating tower. That way, you preserve sightlines and keep the scale more intimate. A central plaza could serve as the heart—restaurants, a play area, even a reflection pool."

"Actually," Badr interrupted, leaning forward. "May I?"

He reached for the paper, but I placed my palm over it, keeping my smile in place. "Why didn't you bring your own notes, Badr?" I asked through clenched teeth.

"Because I knew my very capable partner would bring hers," he replied just as sweetly, tugging at the page again.

"I didn't print these for you to scribble all over. They contain data."

"Data that could be communicated just as easily with a simple sketch."

Terrence cleared his throat, and I reluctantly lifted my hand, allowing Badr to slide the paper toward himself. Without hesitation, he flipped the page and clicked his pen open.

He sketched out an alternate concept, his pen moving effortlessly across the page. As much as I hated to admit it, Badr had an undeniable skill. His ability to translate ideas into sketches in real time was enviable. Meanwhile, I had to work twice as hard to impress anyone.

"Or—" he said smoothly, tilting the pad toward Franklin. "We take advantage of the slope and raise the main structure here, at the highest point. You'd get panoramic views, uninterrupted, and we can layer terraces down toward the water. Villas can wrap the base instead of competing for the horizon."

"That would block the sea breeze," I countered before Franklin could decide too quickly. I turned the plan toward me, tapping the spot he'd just sketched over. "Villas down here mean better airflow, natural cooling. Guests feel the sea in every room instead of just seeing it."

Badr's lips curved into that maddening half-smile. "Unless we design smarter, angled facades, cross-ventilation, shaded courtyards. We can have both."

I hated the way my pulse kicked, caught between irritation and admiration. He was good, too good. "Yes, but that means choosin-"

"Guys," Terrence warned, sensing the tension.

Franklin laughed. "No, no this is good. I love this. I like that you're both so invested in this."

Badr and I exchanged a glance. Neither of us was eager to continue the argument, but something told me this wouldn't be the last time we clashed.

"How about we let the client pick what he would prefer for *His* resort."

Franklin leaned back, steepling his fingers, gaze flicking between the two of us as if we'd just staged a private duel for his entertainment. Then his grin spread, wide and easy.

"Why do I have to choose?" He tapped Badr's sketch first, then gestured toward the area I'd pointed out. "The views from his design are unbeatable. But the intimacy she's talking about, family-friendly, connected to the water, that's what gives it heart. Why not marry the two?"

For a second, the table fell silent. I caught it, the almost imperceptible tightening in Badr's jaw, the subtle stillness in his hand. He didn't like it. He hated compromise when he was sure of his vision.

And I relished it.

"Brilliant," I said quickly, too brightly, turning to Franklin with a smile. "It gives the resort presence, but keeps it grounded. A balance of grandeur and intimacy."

Badr's gaze slid to me then, unreadable, and for a flicker of a moment, I wondered if he could see how smug I felt. But when he finally spoke, his voice was level, smooth as always.

"We'll refine the details to make sure the integration feels natural. It's not an easy blend, but achievable with the right zoning and elevations." Professional. Unshaken. But I saw it, the faint shadow of disapproval before the mask slipped back on.

We exchanged a few closing remarks with the client before Terrence stood to walk him out. The door had barely shut behind them when Badr snapped, "Are you happy now?"

I turned to him, eyes bright. "Am I happy?" I echoed, letting a slow smile stretch across my face. "Yes. Yes, I am."

He stood abruptly. "SubhanAllah, Habiba... You only smile when I'm on the verge of a stroke."

"There's just something about watching you shut up that... soothes me," I said sweetly.

His nostrils flared. "I had a perfect idea for this project. You knew it was good. What was the point of overcomplicating it?"

"You can always drop the project, Badr. No one's chaining you to it." I leaned back, folding my arms, calm and unbothered.

"You'd love that, wouldn't you?" He tilted his head, a sharp smirk forming.

"What? Me?" I said, gasping in mock horror. "I'd be devastated." I turned back to my stuff to pack up, murmuring, "Astagfirullah."

Just as I reached the door, Terrence returned. He had that look again, the one he reserved for when he caught Badr and me at each other's throats.

"What did I say about presenting a united front to clients?"

"I was united," I said with a pointed glance at Badr. "You should be having this conversation with him."

Badr didn't even flinch. "This isn't a village fairground, Habiba. Clients don't come to a coastal resort to admire how 'intimate' the scale feels. They want to be blown away the second they arrive."

"Excuse me for not being dazzled by theatrics," I shot back, keeping my voice level but laced with steel. "A resort isn't a monument, Badr. Guests don't live in panoramic views—they live in spaces that feel comfortable, accessible, and human."

His jaw tightened. "You're excused."

He said it so coolly—and turned on his heel. I blinked, stunned. He walked away? He never walks away first. "Did you see that attitude?" I barked at Terrence.

He raised an eyebrow.

"Have you seen yours?"

I huffed and stormed past him.

7

HABIBA

وجهت وجهي نحو بابك راجيا
والحال لا يخفى وانت عليم

I have turned my face toward Your gate, hoping and in need,
My state is not hidden, and You are All-Knowing indeed.

The air was heavy when I walked into the house, the silence broken only by Khadijah's sobs. She was on the ground, clinging dramatically to Baba's leg, her tears soaking the fabric of his trousers. My heartbeat spiked the instant I stepped in, the weight of their eyes crashing down on me.

Baba sat rigid in his chair, his expression unreadable, while Gogo's glare burned through me like fire.

I considered walking away, letting them drown in whatever new drama Khadijah had spun. But I knew her too well. If I left, she'd twist the story until somehow, it was my fault. I needed to stay and defend myself.

"Habiba, come here," Baba ordered.

With him, hesitation was a kind of defiance. His voice carried the weight of command, heavy and immovable. Gogo and Khadijah I could argue with, even snap at when pressed. But not Baba. Baba was law.

I crossed the room quickly, lowering myself onto the mat in front of his chair, my knees pressed together, eyes down. My heart hammered against my ribs. "Baba, lafiya?" *Baba Is everything ok?* I whispered, careful.

Khadijah's voice cut through before he answered. "Baba, look at her, pretending to be innocent. As if she didn't just try to ruin my life and embarrass me!"

I didn't move, didn't let my glare slip past my lashes even though I wanted to. Baba's eyes were on me, and his silence was sharper than shouting.

Then, suddenly, the whip-crack. "Didn't I tell you to shut up?" His voice slammed into the air. He pivoted toward Khadijah, his stick clattering once against the floor. "Da san shi kike, won't you be in his room now?" *If you loved him, wouldn't you be in his room now?*

Khadijah froze, lips trembling, eyes wide. The silence that followed was suffocating. My lungs stilled. I forced myself not to smirk. His rage was terrifying—but when it landed on someone else, it was also my shield.

"Habiba." His voice again, low now, steady, dangerous. "Two days ago, my friend told me he saw you at a restaurant. Sitting at a bar. With a man. Is that true?"

The floor tilted beneath me. I gripped my knees to stop my hands from trembling. Think. Stay calm. Choose the right words. "Baba, that was my colleague. We were at a business dinner."

"Why just the two of you?" His voice sliced through my explanation, suspicion heavy in every word.

"The clients were there," I blurted. "They stepped out for a smoke. He and I don't smoke, so we stayed back. I just wanted more ice in my drink. That's why I went to the bar."

He was silent. Silent was worse than shouting. Silent meant his anger was steeping, waiting for a crack in my story.

"Baba, walahi, he's only a colleague." I forced the words past a tightening throat. "Walahi."

"She's lying!" Khadijah sobbed, perfect tears sliding down her cheeks. "She seduces men, manipulates them—"

"Ke!" *Hey!* I snapped, breaking before I could stop myself. My chest heaved, anger flaring through my fear. "What does this have to do with you?"

Baba ignored me. His voice softened, almost casual. "Muhammad came here today. Do you know what he wanted?"

I blinked, caught off guard. "No."

"He came to ask for your hand in marriage."

My chest hollowed. "Muhammad kuma?" I choked out. My cousin's ex-husband. Father to her children. The thought alone made bile rise in my throat.

"Shegiya," Gogo spat from her corner. Her voice was sharp, venom-laced. "Just like her mother and grandmother. Born to steal people's husbands. Dama dai mahaifiyata ta ce, Iri da aka shuka, shi ne zai tsiro." *As my mother used to say, 'The kind you plant is the one that will grow.'*

The words stung deep, a knife in my gut. She never let my parents rest. I clenched my jaw so hard my teeth ached, forcing back the fire in me.

"Wallahi, Baba, I didn't know. I never encouraged him."

Baba leaned forward, eyes sharp, testing. "Are you interested?"

"No!" My answer was too fast, too desperate. But it was true.

Khadijah's voice rose to a shrill pitch. "My friends will laugh at me, Baba! My ex-husband marrying my step-cousin—"

The fury inside me cracked. "Maybe if you knew how to keep a husband, we won't be here!"

Gogo lurched forward, hand raised, and I flinched instinctively. But Baba's stick struck the floor, hard. "Hey! Sit down!" His roar shook the walls. Even Gogo froze.

I turned back to him, swallowing tears. "Baba, wallahi, I didn't ask for this. If Muhammad wants to marry me, it's not my fault."

His face softened suddenly, his voice dropping into something almost kind. "Habiba, I believe you. But, you're twenty-seven. Do you think people won't talk? You think they won't question me, mock this house? It's my fault for giving you too much freedom."

Relief trickled in—just for a second—until his next words fell like a hammer.

"I'm getting you married."

"What?" My heart lurched.

"That is my final decision. Since you can't choose, I'll choose. Idris has been asking."

The name sent a cold chill through me. "Idris? Baba, he's seventy!"

"Fifty," he snapped. "He'll provide for you."

"No!" The word burst out, loud, reckless.

"Ke!" He shot to his feet, the stick jerking up inches from my face. His eyes blazed. "How dare you raise your voice at me?"

"Because you're trying to ruin my life!" The words slipped out, my fear overridden by fury.

For a beat, the fire in his eyes dimmed. His voice softened, almost aching. "Why are you so against marriage, Habiba?"

"I'm not," I whispered. "I just want to find someone good. Someone like my father."

Something shifted in his gaze—something pained. "Men like your father don't come twice. Idris is mature. He'll take care of you. I will make sure of it."

"Baba, please." My voice cracked, desperate. "Let me find someone myself."

And just like that, the warmth vanished. Rage surged back, violent and unrelenting. "You will do as I say!" His shout thundered. "I know what's best for you."

He turned, storming away, his stick pounding against the floor with each furious step. I stumbled after him, crying, begging, shouting. But my voice was swallowed by the echo of his rage.

When I got back to my room, my brain felt jagged, like broken glass pressing against the inside of my skull. I shut the door firmly, twisted the lock, and dragged my old suitcase from the top of the wardrobe. My hands shook as I pulled clothes from hangers and drawers, shoving them inside without care. Tops tangled with scarves, skirts balled into corners. The more I packed, the more useless it felt. Halfway through, my hands stilled, and I sank to the floor. Hot tears spilled down my cheeks, soaking into my palms.

Running away wouldn't fix this.

Eventually, I did the only thing I knew to do. I prayed. I pressed my forehead to the mat, whispering to Allah through tears I couldn't hold back, begging Him to help me.

Somewhere between sobbing and reciting, I drifted into sleep on the prayer mat. When I woke, the room was dark, the clock blinking past midnight. The silence pressed heavy against me, and memories of the evening crashed back in. The tears came again. I curled into myself, wondering if there was anyone—anyone at all—I could call. But my contacts list was empty of real lifelines. That was when the truth sank deep: I had no one.

I thought, foolishly, about texting Muhammad, blaming him for the mess my life had become. But deep down, I knew it wasn't his fault. I considered quickly finding someone else to marry, then, unbidden, Badr's face slipped into my mind.

I couldn't possibly ask him to marry me—he and I were at each other's throats every single day. But... would it be that bad? The jokes, the quiet kindness beneath his teasing, the strength in his presence—everything about him screamed marriage material. Strong in his deen, respectful, steady... yet I couldn't even imagine looking him in the eyes and proposing such a thing.

But there was no one else. No one I could imagine marrying. I had never built those kinds of relationships. I hadn't even allowed myself the space to befriend men. It had always been just me. And as for women, most of my friendships hovered at arm's length. I was too busy, too buried in responsibility to make room for closeness.

Maybe I could ask Badr to have his sheikh come here, speak to Baba, persuade him this marriage shouldn't happen. Baba wouldn't like it—he'd probably explode—but what choice did I really have?

"Rabbi inni lima anzalta ilayya min khayrin faqeer." My whispered du'a cracked with desperation.

I wept some more, my mind tumbling over reckless ideas, but none of them stuck. I prayed again, then read Qur'an until fajr came. My voice was raw when I made my final supplication before sunrise.

Exhausted, I staggered to the kitchen. My body was hollow, drained by crying. I searched for food, though eating felt mechanical. Normally, I carried the weight of the housework alone. Baba refused to hire help, always repeating, "There are three women in this house. We don't need another."

This time, I didn't clean. I deliberately left the mess. Let them see what the house was without me. Maybe that would make them think twice before trying to marry me off like livestock. I could live like a maid in the maids' quarters for the rest of my life if it meant I didn't have to marry that man.

A strange, reckless thought struck me: What if I married someone random? Just temporarily, just to escape Baba's choice. But that was dangerous too. Baba would pounce on it, hold it up like proof of my foolishness. Another broken marriage in the family. Another scar on his pride.

The morning slipped past faster than I realized. An alarm on my phone blared—it was time to get the kids ready for school. But I didn't move. Normally, I would wake them, dress them, pack their bags. Today, I left them. It was their mother's job. One missed day of school wouldn't hurt them. Let Baba and Khadijah see what life was like without me. Maybe then Khadijah would finally speak up on my behalf.

In the bus, my heart pounded as I rehearsed what I would say to Badr. Over and over, I turned the words in my mouth. How I'd bring up the sheikh. How I might even confess my situation. Maybe he would have a solution.

I had to talk to Badr today. I knew as soon as Baba wakes up, he'll start plotting my demise, especially after the way I spoke to him last night.

The bus lurched to a stop, jerking me forward. I nearly missed my stop, but jumped off at the last moment. The air was cool against my face as I walked the rest of the way to the office. My feet slowed in front of the door.

Once I step in, I should go straight to his office and talk to him. This is time sensitive.

Or... maybe I should wait until lunch. I could ask him for a sheikh's number, maybe even ask him to take me to the Masjid that he goes to every Friday. I needed someone to speak to Baba for me, to help him understand why this is wrong, he wouldn't disrespect a sheikh.

Maybe I should just wait for any chance that comes.

"I hope you're not planning on burning the building down."

The voice startled me so badly I stumbled back as I spun around, hand flying to my chest.

Badr.

He stood behind me, casual as ever, and yet the sight of him set heat rushing through my body. Warmth spread under my skin, my pulse thundering in my ears. My mouth opened, but words refused to form.

Who was I kidding? All my life I'd thrown sharp words at him, cold dismissals, little jabs. And now that I needed something, here I was—sucking up. A hypocrite.

"Are... you ok?" His brow furrowed, his gaze intent.

"I—I'm fine," I stammered, eyes darting anywhere but his. "I have—I got—I was jus—"

"Ok..." he said slowly, studying me. "I'm starting to worry.

Were you actually planning to burn the building down?"

It was a joke, but there was something behind his tone—an edge of real concern. He leaned down slightly, lowering his head until we were eye to eye.

And that was when I made the mistake of looking directly into his eyes.

Dark brown, but in the light, I could see the hazel glinting beneath, honey-gold threads shimmering under the morning sun. His curls caught the light too, the strands deepening into rich brown with golden tips. It fascinated me every time—how Allah could craft such beauty in something so simple.

And I stared.

And stared.

Astagfirullah.

My chest tightened. I broke away abruptly, spinning toward the door. My hand shoved it open, and I walked fast—too fast—my footsteps loud on the tiles. I nodded and gave quick greetings to those I usually greeted, but didn't stop, didn't slow, until I reached my office.

Once inside, I slammed the door shut behind me, pressed my back to it, and squeezed my eyes shut. My body slid down the wood until I sat on the floor. My breaths came uneven.

Brilliant. Charming. I totally nailed that.

I groaned, smacking my wrists against my forehead in frustration.

"Maybe I should come back another time."

The unfamiliar voice jolted through the room.

I screamed, jerking back against the door. My eyes flew open.

A man sat casually on my desk. Someone I had never seen before. I didn't know who he was, or what he was doing in my office. He stood, stepping toward me. Dark skin, sharp suit, short coily hair—and a British accent when he spoke again. "Are you ok?"

Before I could react, my office door slammed open, trapping my finger painfully between the door and the floor. Another scream tore out of me as I yanked it free.

Fantastic. What a great day.

Badr stormed in, intercepting the man before he could reach me. He stepped in front of him. I scrambled to my feet, brushing at my dress.

"Who are you?" Badr demanded, holding him at bay.

I didn't stop him—I wanted to know, too. Bag in hand, I edged closer.

Terrence rushed in next, "What's going on here?" he snapped, a small crowd now gathering at the door.

"Who is he?" Badr asked again, voice clipped. "What's he doing in her office?"

"He's a client, for God's sake—"

"Doesn't explain why he's in here," Badr cut him off.

The man finally answered for himself, his tone calm, accent thick. "I was asked to wait here."

I looked down at my throbbing finger—the skin peeled but no blood.

"Oh God, are you alright? Can I look at your ha—" He started toward me.

Badr's arm shot out, blocking him. "She's fine."

The two men squared off, standing in line with each other, their stares sharp.

"No, she's not," the man said, irritation bleeding through. "You crushed her hand when you barged in." His jaw clenched, teeth grit.

Badr turned to me quickly, stepping closer but careful to keep space. His eyes softened, apologetic. "I did?"

I nodded.

"I'm sorry." His voice gentled—then, just as quickly, hardened again as he faced Terrence. "But don't you think it's a bit weird to have someone in your office without invitation?"

"It's fine," I cut in, sighing. "I was just... startled."

The stranger finally smiled faintly. "I'm sorry I startled you, Ms. Mukhtar."

I nearly swooned. My last name had never sounded so elegant—his British accent wrapping around it like silk.

Terrence filled in quickly. "This is Mr. Hussein Rashid. He came here specifically to discuss a project with Mukhtar, so I asked him to wait in her office."

"Next time, have him wait in the lobby like everyone else," Badr said evenly, though strain coiled under his voice. "You heard her scream—I thought it was an intruder."

I hurried to calm things, ushering everyone out except Mr. Rashid. He was, after all, a potential client—and I couldn't afford to lose one now.

"Can I get you some coffee or tea?"

"I'm fine, thank you."

I avoided his eyes, keeping my gaze on my desk, my computer, my notepad. But he watched me intently, and that wasn't helping.

"I'm sorry for the chaos," I said finally.

"No, I'm sorry for interrupting your... private moment." His words were careful, curious. "I hope you're alright?"

"I'm fine," I laughed nervously. "I just get... overwhelmed sometimes."

"Happens to the best of us." He smiled.

I forced myself back on track. "So—you wanted to discuss a project?"

He leaned forward. "You were the architect behind Mr. Delator's vacation home, yes?"

I nodded.

"Absolutely gorgeous. He recommended you, and I had to see you myself."

"Thank you. I'm glad you liked it."

"It's exactly the style I want. With a few personal touches, of course."

We spent the next half hour reviewing his vision. A simple villa, one I could handle alone. Yet his budget was generous—more than generous. It should have thrilled me.

Instead, part of me drifted, imagining Baba marrying me off to Idris. If that happens, none of this would matter. I'd lose everything, there is no way Idris will let me keep working.

I can't let that happen.

"I'm boring you," Hussein said, catching my far-off look.

"What? No!" I snapped back. "I just... have a lot on my mind. Please, continue. You have my full attention."

He chuckled. "It's fine. That's all for now. I'll wait for your feedback. I can take you to the site myself, if you're available."

"You don't have to. I can go alone."

"I insist." His voice was firm, his gaze holding mine. For a moment, it felt like he meant more than just business—but I let it pass with a polite smile.

"I'll think about it.."

We wrapped up, and I walked him out.

"I'll get back to you, Mr. Rashid. Thank you for coming."

"It was a pleasure."

I smiled. "Have a good day."

I needed to talk to Badr. I couldn't just sit by and let Baba decide my life for me. Sure, I could handle this on my own—drive down to the nearest masjid, ask the questions, get the information I needed. But for some reason, I wanted to go through him. With Badr, things always felt simpler. He always got things done.

Confidence surged as I walked down the hall, up the stairs, straight to his office door. I knocked without hesitation—then instantly regretted it.

My heart pounded, my legs trembled.

"Come in," Badr called from inside.

I froze.

His voice called out again.

I reached for the handle, stopped, turned to leave. But before I could, the door opened.

Badr stood there, frowning. "Habiba?"

I turned slowly, sheepish. "Hi…" I gave a pathetic little wave before realizing how ridiculous it was. I dropped my hand immediately. *What am I doing?*

"Habiba…" His voice was low, careful. "You're starting to worry me. Are you okay? You've been… off. Since this morning."

"What do you mean I'm off? You're off." I scoffed. "Your hair is off. I'm kidding, I just needed something to say, haha. You're not actually off, you're perfectly fine." I wish he would just slam the door shut on my face.

He stared at me flatly for what felt like forever, then nodded slowly. "Okay… Do you need something?"

"Yes. The project designs. We should finalize them. Could you come with me so we can go over them?"

"Can you come back at maybe 5pm? I'm in the middle of something."

I nodded, forcing a smile, then walked back to my office. Once I closed the door behind me, I looked around to make sure I was alone in the office before I slid to the ground with a groan, burying my face in my hands.

Disaster.

8
BADR

أن تحظى بالأحنّ هذا
هو الفوز الدافئ

Winning the affection of the most caring soul,
That is life's warmest victory.

- سيرين

"Weird," I muttered, though a small smile tugged at my lips.

I shook my head, holding back a laugh as I closed my door.

The image of her wiggling her fingers in that shy little wave replayed in my mind, and I couldn't help the quiet chuckle that followed. Who would've thought Habiba could ever be that... cute? She's fierce, mesmerizing, tough, but seeing her slip into something so unguarded, so silly and soft, felt almost strange.

SubhanAllah.

Leaning back in my chair, I tried to focus on solving the batch delivery problem for my project. But even as I worked, I was smiling.

After about an hour or two of working, I got up, stretching and grinning faintly, when the door to my office creaked open and Ayaan walked in. He shut it behind him and extended his hand before I even reached him. I met him halfway, our handshake melting into a quick, familiar hug.

Ayaan, my best friend, and I usually meet for lunch—sometimes at his office, other times at mine—depending on who's more buried under work.

He wore a black polo shirt, it's sleeves snug around his biceps, paired with beige pants. Taking off his shades, he settled into the chair across from me while I circled back to sit behind my desk.

"So, what's new?" he joked, reaching to steal a paper from the stack on my desk. He skimmed it lazily.

I reached into my bag and slid a photo across the table. Another girl. One of many my mother thought would make a suitable wife for me.

She went back home to Morocco for her niece's wedding and somehow returned with a roster of "perfect candidates." But she didn't dump them all on me at once; she's smarter than that. She doles them out weekly, slipping photos where she knows I'll find them, hoping one will catch my eye.

Eventually, I got tired of the game and told her I already loved someone. A lie, but it bought me breathing room. She believed me—barely. Asked to meet her, but I told her we weren't ready for marriage. Since then, she's been trying to dig, but of course, there's nothing to find. Because there's no one.

That was two months ago. I think she's catching on.

Ayaan glanced at the photo, smirk tugging at his lips. "You didn't think that lie would stick forever, did you?"

I let out a long sigh. "It gave me a month of peace. Worth it."

"Maybe it's time to stop running," he said, leaning back. "What's the harm in choosing one and leaving the rest to Allah?"

"Where's your wife, then? Maybe I should tell Ma to get you one instead. I've got another photo in my car if you're interested."

Ayaan just chuckled, stretching before standing up. "Why are you so against marriage?"

"It's not that I don't want to marry," I added as I got up and pulled on my jacket. "It's that I haven't found the one yet."

He arched a brow. "And how do you know she's not one of the girls your mom is dangling in front of you?"

"I just do." I responded flatly.

73

"Or maybe," He leaned onto the wall that is separating my office from Habiba's "you're just addicted to a certain dynamic that seems to have spoiled you rotten."

"What's that supposed to mean?" I stopped in my tracks.

He sheepishly scratches the side of his neck with his index finger while clearly pointing his thumb towards Habiba's office. I just watched him with the blankest expression I could make before heading for the door. "Real mature," I muttered.

Ayaan, born and raised in Canada, but his roots are Senegalese. His skin is a deep, rich brown that gleams under light, his hazel eyes sharp and catching. Despite us hitting the gym together, his muscles have always been more defined, his frame naturally sculpted. Back in the day, women trailed him wherever we went. I kept my distance, though occasionally I got swept up in his chaos.

One incident—serious, life-altering—snapped us out of that lifestyle. It rattled us both, pushing us toward faith. Toward Islam. I was already Muslim, but not practicing. Ayaan was stuck between Atheism like his mother and Islam like his father. It was after we started our religious journey that he chose Islam and took his Shahadah.

Now Ayaan gives the best advice. Even if I dodge it half the time because he tells me what I don't want to hear.

We stopped by Habiba's office so Ayaan could say Hi and maybe invite her along, but she wasn't in her office, so we left. Once break was over and Ayaan went back to work, I slipped back behind my desk and worked on some corrections while waiting for her to come back. At half past 5, I heard a knock.

It creaked open, and Habiba stepped in.

"Are you done?" she asked, her usual crisp tone back in place.

"Please, sit," I gestured toward the small seating area in the corner. "I'll join you in a bit."

She nodded, sat, and opened the folder of documents while

I finished up. Even with my eyes fixed on the monitor, I caught her sneaking glances at me. That's when I knew something was off.

We had spent countless hours working together in the same office. Habiba was always focused, almost to the point of pretending I wasn't there. For her to keep stealing looks at me now? Something was wrong.

She's been hovering around me in this odd way, as though she wanted to say something but couldn't figure out how. And Habiba—who prides herself on confidence—wasn't one to hesitate without reason.

Once I finished, I joined her at the small table. She was laying out printed designs for us to sort through. The plan was simple, she'd print out the images she likes out of the inspiration options that the client provided, I'd pick from there, and we'd narrow it down together. It was easier than me choosing alone and fighting her inevitable counterarguments.

"I like this one. And this." I slid two designs forward.

She removed another. "This won't go with either of those."

I nodded, continuing to sort. I picked five designs total—and to my surprise, she didn't argue once. Not even a little.

Arguing with Habiba was half the fun. She usually raised strong points that sharpened my work, forcing me to think critically. If she wasn't pushing back, everything feels rather boring.

"So… you go to the masjid every Friday, right?" she asked suddenly, her voice softer than usual.

I froze for a beat. Odd question. Still, I nodded.

"Do you trust the Sheikh there? Do you stay for the khutbah? Do you think he can answer questions?"

I set the designs down, giving her my full attention. "What do you mean?"

Her eyes flickered with something—hesitation, maybe hope. "If I asked him a question… do you think he'd be able to answer?"

75

"I believe he'd answer to the best of his knowledge," I said. When she stayed quiet, I added gently, "Is everything okay?"

She nodded slowly. "I just... have some questions I need answers to. I don't go to the masjid here except for Tarawih. Do you know the best time to go? When I could actually speak to him?"

"I can find out for you on Friday."

She shook her head. "I need answers now. It's... urgent."

Her tone made my chest tighten.

I thought for a moment. "If it's not too private, maybe you can tell me. I can stop by the masjid later today and ask for you."

She picked at the skin under her nails—her nervous habit. When she finally spoke, her voice was low.

"I have a friend... she's facing problems at home. She wants to leave. I told her to stay, but the problems are bad enough that she might have to leave the house. Is it permissible for her to leave?"

I wanted to assume this "friend" was really her. But the way she spoke—steady, not panicked—made it impossible to be certain. Then again, this was Habiba. She would rather swallow fire than show weakness.

I thought, but didn't feel qualified enough in that to give her an answer so I simply nodded. "I'll ask."

She nodded, then added quietly, "And about marriage... what are the grounds for a forced marriage to be haram?"

This time, I didn't hesitate. "There are none. The moment either person is unwilling, it becomes haram and invalid. As simple as that."

Her shoulders slumped slightly—not relief, but not despair either. Something in between.

"She has this... stupid idea," she continued, "to find someone she could marry temporarily. Just until her grandfather backs off. Then they'd divorce."

I was already shaking my head before she finished. "That's wrong.

It's called Mut'a—"

"I know Mut'a. But this isn't that, right? She's not doing it for selfish reasons. She just wants to protect herself."

"Wanting protection isn't wrong," I said gently, "but marriage isn't a tool we bend for convenience. Allah made it sacred. It's an amaanah—a trust. Not just between husband and wife, but between them and Allah." I softened my tone. "When someone enters marriage already planning to end it—even if they don't say it out loud—they're playing with something holy. Even if it's not Mut'a, it's still deceptive. It pretends to be permanent, while both hearts know it's not."

She angled her body toward me, eyes sharp. "But isn't intention everything? Isn't it about why they're doing it?"

I smiled sadly. "Intention matters—but so does honesty. The Prophet ﷺ warned against this. Scholars across madhhabs agree: a premeditated divorce, kept hidden, is deceit. It's not just about what you do—it's what you mean by it."

She sat in silence, absorbing my words, her brows furrowed.

Finally, she whispered, "She's just scared."

Those three words carried more emotion than I'd ever seen from Habiba. Vulnerability was foreign on her face.

"Then tell her she doesn't need a fake husband," I said gently. "If her family is forcing her, she should marry someone she trusts—for the sake of Allah. Not for escape. For truth."

She nodded. "Do you think you can get me his number?" I nodded again.

"I'll get it to you as soon as possible."

Habiba nodded as though she'd gotten what she came for, she suddenly rose, dusted her gown, and headed for the door.

"Thank you. So much," she said before slipping out, leaving her papers scattered on my desk.

I didn't move. Just stared at the door.

This wasn't about a friend.

The thought of Habiba carrying something so heavy made my chest tighten. I wanted to shield her from it, to fix it. Marriage isn't a small matter—it's everything. Just weeks ago, I could hardly stomach the idea of her marrying at all, and now she might be forced into it. The thought alone burned.

I packed up my things quickly, my mind too clouded with thoughts to focus on anything else. The drive to Ayaan's hotel blurred past me—streetlights streaking across my windshield, my fingers drumming on the steering wheel in restless rhythm. I would prefer to go there with him, we might even catch maghrib there together.

When I arrived, Ayaan wasn't in his office. I asked his secretary to let him know I was outside, so I leaned against my car, arms folded, staring blankly at the horizon. The evening air was heavy, warm, the kind that clung to skin. My thoughts ran in circles until the sound of footsteps approached, and a shadow fell across the ground beside me.

"Bad day?" Ayaan asked, leaning against the car next to mine.

"Something like that," I muttered, my eyes still fixed on the distance.

He studied me for a moment. "Want to come inside and talk? Or should we grab coffee?"

I shook my head. "We need to go to the masjid."

He frowned. "The masjid?"

"Habiba came to me today… she asked some questions. I answered what I could, but I think she's in trouble. I don't want to waste time."

Ayaan's expression shifted—serious, concerned. He gave a short nod. Fifteen minutes later, we were both in our cars, trailing each other to our usual masjid.

The masjid was quiet when Ayaan and I slipped inside, the sun dipping low enough that the call for Maghrib would come soon. A few men sat in hushed circles, murmuring Qur'an. The air smelled faintly of oud, the carpet cool under my feet as we walked toward the imam's small office.

Sheikh Mahmood was there, sitting cross-legged, a Qur'an still open in front of him. He greeted us warmly, his voice carrying the calm weight of someone used to listening more than speaking.

I explained quickly, careful not to give away too much. First about leaving home when the situation grew unbearable, then about forced marriage, then the matter of temporary marriage.

The sheikh listened without interruption, only nodding slowly, his gaze steady. Then, with the clarity of someone pulling weeds from tangled ground, he laid it out.

Leaving home is permissible only if there is genuine harm or fear of oppression. Forced marriage, he said firmly, has no place in Islam—consent is the foundation of nikah, and without it, the bond is void. As for temporary marriage, he shook his head. "Marriage is not a shield for convenience. It is amanah. To enter it planning to leave is deception—no matter the reason."

I asked more because I wanted no cracks, no doubt left hanging. The sheikh answered each patiently, with examples from Qur'an and sunnah, his words wrapping around me like iron and mercy at once.

I took his number before shaking his hand, grateful for his time, then he led the maghrib prayer and we left.

Before I even reached the car, I was already typing, fingers quick against the screen. I told her I had her answer and sent his number in case she needed it urgently.

Ayaan and I said our goodbyes and headed to our cars. The drive home was quiet, only the hum of the engine filling the night. My thoughts circled Habiba. By the time I pulled into the driveway, the house was alive with noise and movement.

The savory scent of onions frying hit me first. Inside, the kitchen buzzed with chatter—Hana and Ma cooking together, their voices rising and falling in rhythm with clattering pans. From the sitting room came the roar of football on TV, Ba's laughter mixing with Ahmed's commentary. Outside, the rhythmic bounce of a basketball echoed— Zain and our neighbor, Frank, playing in the yard.

For a moment, I tried to shake Habiba from my mind and joined them outside. The ball thudded into my hands, the pavement rough beneath my sneakers. But my head wasn't in it, I tripped, stumbled, sweat plastering my shirt to my back until I tapped out with a laugh that sounded emptier than I meant.

After a shower, dressed in sweats and a tank top, I found Ahmed and Hana sprawled on my bed, mid-conversation. Normally, I'd tease them, join in—but tonight, I clipped my nails in silence, my thoughts elsewhere.

Eventually, we all gathered downstairs for dinner. The table was full, as always—each of us in our usual seats, plates of steaming tajine between us. Spoons clinked against plates, laughter echoed off the walls, but I barely ate.

"Kulshi mzyan? habibi?" *Is everything ok, habibi?* Ma's voice cut through the noise. She didn't even need to call my name—everyone knew she meant me. All eyes turned in my direction.

"Just… you know, long day," I muttered, forcing a sigh.

"What happened?" Hana asked softly, her eyes searching mine.

"Nothing, ya Rooh." I reached over and tugged her cheek with a small smile. "Too many clients. Feels like I've talked enough for a week."

"Do you wanna talk about it?" Ahmed, our 12 year old brother spoke, looking up from his game. I couldn't help cracking a smile. Normally, I was the one asking him that whenever he felt down.

I shook my head at him before returning to my plate. "I'm okay. Don't worry about me." I quickly turned the attention away. "Zain, how are your courses going?"

His face lit up, then he launched into updates about his IT program, two more years, the projects he loved. I smiled faintly, pride swelling in me. I often thanked Allah for parents who let us pursue what we loved. Too many people never had that chance.

But Ma's gaze stayed on me. I felt it, sharp and knowing, even as I avoided her eyes.

After dinner, once Zain and I had washed the dishes, Ma followed me upstairs. She sat beside me on the bed, her presence warm, grounding.

"What's wrong?" she asked gently.

"I'm fine, Ma. You worry too much."

"I'm your mother. I have to worry." Her eyes softened. "Is it the girl?"

I hesitated, then sighed, leaning into her shoulder. "Something like that."

She stroked my cheek, patient, waiting.

"I can't tell you," I admitted before she could ask, meeting her gaze with a small smile.

She smiled back, though her eyes were both warm and strict. "Don't do anything foolish. I trust you."

The words eased something in me.

Just then, Ahmed padded in, tablet in hand. He settled on my bed while tapping away at his game. He didn't speak—Ahmed rarely did—but his presence was constant, comforting. Wherever Ma was, Ahmed was. And when she wasn't around, it was me.

Ma got up to leave and I got busy with my bedtime routine while Ahmed stayed sprawled across my bed like he owned it, half-buried under my blanket. His skinny legs kicked against the mattress, restless, too much energy for the hour.

"I think I'm moving in here." he announced, stealing my pillow too.

I snorted, folding my arms. "And where exactly am I supposed to sleep?"

He grinned, a flash of braces. "Floor's plenty big enough."

I threw a balled-up T-shirt at him, and he laughed, ducking. Typical. Always loud, always pushing.

Then, in that same breathless way he always shifted topics, he said, "So… who's that girl you have a problem with?" His eyes gleamed, curious, mischievous.

My jaw tightened. "Why are you asking?"

He shrugged, kicking at the blanket. "Just wondering. You look worried. You like her?"

I groaned, dragging a hand down my face. "You're twelve. You don't need to worry about that."

"But you didn't say no," he sing-songed, a smug little grin plastered on his face.

I grabbed the pillow he'd stolen and smacked him with it. He yelped, laughing so hard he nearly rolled off the bed.

And then, just as quick as the teasing came, his voice softened. "You're always out. I barely see you anymore."

That caught me. I sat down on the edge of the bed, ruffling his messy hair until he swatted at my hand. "I'm here now, aren't I?"

He leaned into me, the weight of him small but steady. For all his noise, for all his teasing, he was still just a kid. My kid, in a way.

Later, when he left my room, I prayed, then stretched out on my bed. Sleep pressed heavy on me, but I forced myself to wake for Tahajjud. I often did—those quiet hours gave me peace, clarity. But tonight, my heart wrestled with unease.

Because as long as someone I even remotely cared for was in trouble, true peace would not come.

9

HABIBA

بروحي فتاة بالعفاف تجملت
و في خدها حب من المسك قد نبت
و قد ضاع عقلي و قد ضاع رشدي مذ أقبلت

My soul yearns for a girl adorned with chastity,
On her cheek is a beauty mark, like a grain of musk that grew there.
My sanity, my balanced mind, all vanished in a trace,
The moment she approached and stood before my face.
- unknown

When I woke up the next morning, I was restless with anticipation. Habiba still hadn't responded to my message, which only worried me more so I couldn't wait to get to the office to see if I could help her piece together the rest.

But when I arrived, her office was empty.

At first, I thought little of it. Maybe she was running late, she gets late occasionally. But she's also the kind of person who never missed a single day of work. That small fact about her had always fascinated me.

By noon, her chair was still untouched, so I typed out another message.

Me: Hey, I hope you managed to solve your friend's problem

I told myself not to overreact, but unease began to creep in, coiling tight in my chest. What if yesterday's questions weren't for a friend after all?

The universe seemed determined to hold me back. A mix-up with a batch order kept me tied up for nearly an hour. Then, as though on cue, one of my clients showed up unannounced and drained another two. By the time I glanced at the clock, it was almost four.

Still no response. Enough waiting.

I made my way to Terrence's office. Beatrice was already in there, bent over blueprints, so I waited by the door, pulse drumming, until she finally left.

"Badr, can I help you?" Terrence asked, looking up.

"Habiba didn't come to the office today," I said.

He blinked at me, confusion flickering across his face, and for three solid seconds he just stared—then his brows lifted as if he'd misheard. "You want to open a bottle of champagne?" He asked, his tone unsure.

I stepped closer, my voice harder. "Why didn't she come?"

"Why do you care?" he asked, setting his pen down and watching me with sudden interest.

The question made me hesitate. What was I supposed to say? That I was worried she was being forced into a marriage she didn't want? That I couldn't focus on anything else until I knew she was safe?

Instead, I deflected. "Did she call in sick?"

"No. I tried her phone earlier—no answer. Her client came by too, but she wasn't here."

The pressure in my chest tightened. My mind scrambled for reasons, but every possibility circled back to the same gnawing fear: this wasn't a coincidence. Not after the things she asked me yesterday.

As soon as I left his office, I grabbed my stuff and left.

I parked a block away from her house, palms damp on the steering wheel. My chest had been tight the entire way.

I walked slowly to the front door, every step louder in my head than it should've been. I didn't know who lived here—grandparents, uncles, all of them? The not-knowing made my pulse race. Just as I raised my hand to knock, muffled voices drifted through the door. Sharp. Heated. An argument.

For a moment I froze. Should I even be here? Should I turn back? My hand hovered over the bell. But then the voices rose, jagged with anger, and something inside me hardened.

I pressed it.

The sudden silence on the other side was deafening. Then a lock clicked. The door opened.

A girl stood there. Soft eyes, headscarf draped neatly. She looked irritated at first, but when her gaze fell on me she straightened instantly, lips curving into a practiced smile.

"Hi," she said sweetly, batting her lashes. "How can I help you?"

"I'm here for... Habiba." My voice came out slower than I intended.

Her brows pulled together, then smoothed again. A smirk tugged at her mouth before she turned to call something over her shoulder in Hausa.

Hausa. The accent that took me weeks to place.

When I first heard Habiba speak, it drove me crazy. I asked her over and over, but she never told me. It wasn't until I started digging— Googling her style of dressing, narrowing it down to the Arewa tribe— that I found it. One YouTube video of an Arewa woman, and there it was.

The same lilt. The same softness.

"You're here for Habiba?" Her smile widened. "Come in."

Something about her tone prickled at me, too smooth, too knowing. My gut told me this was wrong, but stepping away wasn't an option. Not when Habiba might need me.

The moment I crossed the doorframe, I felt it—the air itself pressed down on me, heavy and suffocating, thick with judgment.

An old man stood in the center of the hall, clad in a brown kaftan with matching pants, a handwoven cap perched on his head, stick resting firmly in his grip. His frame was slight, almost frail, but his eyes... sharp, predatory. They pinned me where I stood, like a hawk fixing on prey.

My gaze slid past him—and stopped.

Habiba.

But not the Habiba I knew. Not the composed, razor-edged woman who matched me blow for blow in the office. She was on the ground, shoulders trembling, her face streaked with tears. Her eyes were swollen and bloodshot, lowered, as though even looking up had become too heavy a burden.

An older woman hovered over her, dressed in a blouse and wrapper—similar to Habiba's usual style, only messier, almost careless. That had to be Gogo. Habiba had told me about her—how mean she could be, how cruel. The malice was written all over her face, the twist of her lips, the faint tremor in her hand, like she was seconds away from striking.

By the couch stood another man, his kaftan pale blue, his frame sturdier than the old man's but his expression eerily calm. He looked to be in his fifties, maybe sixties. And while the room seethed with tension, he only watched me curiously, as if this cruelty was routine, a performance he had long grown used to.

Something inside me clenched hard. I'd never wanted to protect someone so badly.

"What do you want?" the old man demanded, voice clipped.

Before I could answer, the woman barked something at Habiba, her hand snapping up mid-accusation. I jerked forward without thinking, but stopped myself just in time. My chest burned.

"What do you want?" the old man repeated, harsher now.

"Habiba," I said, forcing my voice steady. "I need to speak to her." My heartbeat thundered, but I didn't let it seep into my tone.

"You can speak another day. She is busy now." The dismissal was cold, final.

My gaze went back to Habiba. Her shoulders shook. Her hands twisted in her lap. She looked so small.

"With all due respect, sir…" My voice dropped lower, firmer.

"I'm not leaving her like this."

"And what is it to you whether she's like this or not?" He stepped forward, slow and deliberate, his anger measured like a blade being drawn.

"She's my colleague. And we look out for each other."

It was true enough. And if it wasn't, I'd make it true.

Habiba stood up, her movements shaky, and my eyes followed as she wiped at her face with the back of her hand. Her voice was small but steady. "We can talk in my room," she whispered.

The words had barely left her lips before her grandfather snapped, his whole body jerking like a whip. "Dan uban ki, ba ki da hankali?" *Damn you, are you out of your mind?*

His hand shot out, fingers spread wide, the threat in the gesture so sudden that both she and I flinched. My chest tightened. I wasn't used to seeing her—Habiba, the woman I thought of as fierce and unshakable—cower like that.

"In front of me? In front of your soon to be husband?" He jabbed a finger toward the old man seated by the chair, his eyes blazing. "You would invite this boy to your room? Yer iskar banza, Yer iskar wohi!" *You worthless brat, useless fool!*

"Baba—" she tried, her voice trembling.

"Shut up!"

The words cracked through the air like a gunshot, and she fell silent instantly.

I felt my stomach twist, disbelief clawing at my insides. My ears rang. He had pointed at that man—the one old enough to be her father—as he soon to be husband. My heart lurched. I couldn't believe it. Her own family, turning against her like this? I had heard of things like this, seen it in movies, but watching it unfold before me—seeing her shoulders shake, her eyes red and swollen—was something else.

The silence stretched, thick and suffocating, before he finally broke it.

"Leave my house," he ordered, each word heavy, final.

"Why?" The word slipped from me before I could stop it. My voice shook at the edges, but I forced it steady.

His glare could have burned through steel. "Habiba is busy. She will only return to the firm with the permission of her husband." His tone was sharp, unapologetic, like a gavel striking down.

My pulse hammered in my throat, but I refused to look away. "It doesn't look to me like that's what Habiba wants."

"Look here, young man," he barked, his accent thick with fury. "I can get her married to whomever I wish."

The room tilted, like the air itself had dropped in temperature. My palms were damp. If he was forcing her into marriage with the man's son or even a grandson, maybe I could have found a twisted sense of logic in it. But no—this. This was different. This was cruelty parading as family honor.

I wasn't sure if what I was doing was right. My knees were trembling, and my body screamed at me to leave, to get out of that suffocating room. But another thought anchored me. If Hana—my Hana—were left alone in this world, and someone tried to force her into the arms of a man three times her age, I would go feral. I would burn the world to protect her. And right now, I am ready to burn the world for Habiba.

"If you don't leave my house, I'll call the police," the grandfather spat.

My chest rose and fell fast, but I took a step forward anyway. "Call them," I said, voice low but firm. "I'd love to file a complaint against you forcing her to marry an old man."

His jaw tightened, but he didn't back down. "Go ahead. She is my granddaughter. I raised her. I have every right to choose her husband. I don't care about your western nonsense. This is family business. Leave now before I make you."

88

I swallowed hard, fighting the urge to shrink under his words. My father's voice echoed in my head, lessons he drilled into me about the law. I clung to them like a rope.

"If you don't care about western nonsense, maybe you shouldn't have moved here," I countered, pulse racing. "Because here, there are protective laws that stop people like you from doing this. Section 293.6 of the Criminal Code—forcing someone into marriage is a crime. You could be arrested." I drew a breath, steadying my voice. "Forget the law—Islam forbids forced marriage."

Ok, so maybe the numbers I just pulled were complete BS, but such a law still existed anyway.

He stiffened, caught off guard. I'd struck a nerve. His fury boiled over, spilling in the way his face contorted, the way his chest rose and fell. He stepped so close I could see the veins pulsing in his temple.

"Leave. Now!" His spit hit my cheek, hot, rancid.

I wiped it away slowly, refusing to break eye contact. My heart wanted to bolt, but I anchored my voice in calmness. Calmness was the best weapon.

"If I leave now," I said, quiet but unyielding, "I'll be back—with the police."

For a long moment, he just stared at me, fuming. Then something shifted. His rage cracked, and a slow, sinister smile stretched across his face. It rattled me more than his yelling.

He didn't look like much—thin frame, silver beard, tired eyes—but power clung to him like armor. He didn't need to shout. His presence itself cut sharper than a blade.

When his gaze slid to Habiba, she shrank, shoulders folding inward, lips pressed tight. She couldn't even meet my eyes. That told me everything I needed to know about the grip he held over her.

Finally, his voice dropped, quiet and measured. "And who are you to speak for her? You work in an office together. You think that gives you the right to tell her family what's best?"

"No," I said, forcing air into my lungs, fighting the quake in my knees. "But I'm Muslim. And I am looking out for a fellow Muslim. She has the right to say no. And she clearly—"

"You're in my house." His voice sliced through mine. "You came here uninvited, stirring up matters that do not concern you."

I didn't blink. "They do concern me. Because she's scared."

His eyes sharpened with amusement—dark, cruel amusement. "Young men today, always running their mouths. But when it comes time to act like a man…" He scoffed. "You think you're brave? That you've done something noble here? Then go ahead—marry her."

The words dropped like a stone into water. The room went utterly still. Habiba's head snapped up. Her lips parted. I felt my stomach twist into a knot.

"What?" My voice cracked, too loud in the suffocating silence. Surely, I'd misheard him.

"You heard me." His smirk stretched thin, cruel. "Since you're so righteous—be the hero you claim to be. Marry her. Right now. Or get out."

I froze. The room seemed smaller, the walls pushing in. My throat was dry, but I forced myself to swallow.

The old man in the corner began, "Alhaji—" but he slashed his hand through the air, silencing him with a glare so sharp he shut up without another word.

He thought he had me cornered. That I'd fold. That I'd stumble over an apology and leave with my tail between my legs.

And for a second—part of me wanted to.

But then I looked at Habiba. The tears clinging to her lashes. The way her hands trembled in her lap, her knuckles white. She looked lost, like she was holding herself together with threads too thin to last.

"If you marry her," her grandfather sneered, his voice trembling with both rage and triumph, "then she won't have to marry him. You'll be the noble savior you pretend to be."

His words were sharp, mocking—but they landed differently in me. Because I thought about what I knew of her. She prays. She wears hijab. She's kind—even when stubborn. Strong. Loyal. And yes, infuriating sometimes, but principled.

The words of the Prophetﷺ came to mind: "A woman may be married for her wealth, her lineage, her beauty, or her religiosity. Marry the one who is religious." My heart tightened at the reminder. I didn't care about wealth, looks, or family connections. I cared about her faith. About her character. About the woman she was in the sight of Allah.

And I thought of years ago—when I was clawing my way out of the haze, when I would've drowned if not for the fact that she was there. Not knowing it, not meaning to, but she kept me steady. Just by being herself. She never knew how much she saved me, and I never had the courage to say it.

Maybe this was Allah giving me the chance to repay what I owed.

Could I marry her? Not out of love, not out of romance, but for Allah's sake—for her safety, her dignity. And maybe, quietly, to finally return even a fraction of what she'd unknowingly given me.

I closed my eyes and whispered a silent du'a: *Ya Allah, if this is good for me, for her, for our deen, then make it easy.*

When I opened them, the old man was watching me, grinning as though he'd already won.

"Leave," he said coldly.

"I'll marry her," I heard myself say.

The grin faltered.

"I'll marry her," I repeated, louder this time. My voice didn't feel like my own, but it held steady. "You want a man who'll take responsibility? Fine. I'll take responsibility. You want to test my courage? Test it."

I turned to Habiba. My tone softened. "Only if you agree."

Her lips trembled. She looked at me as though I was someone she'd never seen before. Tears rimmed her eyes, her whole body quivering.

Her grandfather made a noise with his mouth, a mocking click. "You think I'm bluffing? You think this is a game? You don't need a hall, or your family, or a fancy suit. Islam doesn't need that. All it takes is for me to say, 'I marry her to you,' and for you to say, 'I accept.' With two witnesses—it's done." His voice dropped, sharp and deadly. "So decide. Because if you don't walk out that door now, you're her husband."

He was right. He could do that.

I thought of my mother. How she'd dreamed of my wedding. The celebration, the family, the joy. This would shatter her. It would turn my whole family upside down.

But leaving? Walking away? Leaving Habiba to an old man who'd strip her future bare?

No. I couldn't.

And maybe it wasn't only about her. Maybe part of it was me— the selfish part I couldn't deny. I didn't need her to stay clean anymore. But the thought of her being taken away—of never seeing her again, never hearing her sharp comebacks at work, never watching her stride into a room like she belonged there—it burned me worse than any craving ever had.

She wasn't my antidote anymore. She was something else entirely. And I knew admitting it was selfish, but it was the truth: I couldn't survive the office without her. I didn't want to survive this without her.

"Let me call my father—" I started.

"You're a man." He snapped. "Speak for yourself."

My chest felt heavy, but I forced the words out anyway. "Then fine. I'm ready to marry her. "

His smirk returned, sharp and victorious but I could see the hesitation, he hadn't expected me to agree. "You will marry her right here, right now."

Habiba spoke this time.

"Baba—" Her voice was small at first, but when he lifted his hand to silence her, she didn't back down. She stepped forward, past her fear, until she stood toe to toe with him. "Baba, I understand you're angry at me, but you cannot do that to him." She turned sharply to me. "Badr, leave. Right now. This does not concern you. Don't do this to yourself. Please."

Her words carried a boldness, but her voice betrayed her. It trembled at the edges, her hands quivering so badly she twisted her scarf just to hide it. Her eyes shimmered, not from defiance but from the strain of holding herself together.

I wanted—desperately—to reach for her, to wrap her in my arms and promise her she was safe. But I couldn't move. I didn't understand why it affected me this much, why seeing Habiba cornered and breaking felt like a fist closing around my chest.

"You can't punish him like that, Baba," she pressed, her voice cracking as her resolve wavered. "You can't just keep tossing me from one man to another."

His hand trembled at his side, whether from fury or age, I couldn't tell. "Then he should have thought of that before coming to my house, pretending to be brave." His words dripped with scorn. "You're ready to marry her, you say?"

I forced myself to nod, though my stomach knotted. My confidence was more costume than truth, but I wore it anyway.

"Badr, please," Habiba whispered now, the steel in her voice finally giving way. "Please stop. Please leave." Her lips quivered as though each word tore her apart.

I softened, meeting her gaze. I wanted her to see I wasn't backing down, not this time. If no one else in her family would stand for her, then I would.

I spoke, my voice steady though my heart pounded in my throat, "I know this isn't the marriage you dreamed of. And it isn't what I imagined either. But if you want me to stay, I will. I won't walk away. If I stay, it will be with full intention, with honesty, and with the fear and love of Allah in my heart. That will be my promise—before Allah, before His angels, before you, and before your family. I will honor your rights, guard your dignity, and protect your peace."

Her eyes filled, lips trembling as if each word I spoke pushed her closer to breaking.

"Oh, spare me this nonsense." The old man's voice cut like a whip, his face contorting with contempt. "You young men are so good with words." He sneered at Habiba, his lip curling. "Look at her. Foolish girl. She's already fallen for it."

"Alhaji, maybe we—" Gogo's voice fluttered nervously from the side, but he cut her off with a snap, his words crashing over hers.

"Khadijah!" He muttered something sharp in their language, and Khadijah jumped to obey. She rushed to the main door, pulling it open with an eagerness that felt wrong.

Moments later, a man stepped in, wiping his hand down his jeans as though he'd just finished some chore. "Yes, sir?" he greeted politely.

Habiba's grandfather's expression shifted—his mouth curling into a smile that was colder than his anger. "Come here, Habib. Today, you'll serve as the second witness to my granddaughter's wedding."

Habib froze mid-step. The smile drained from his face, and though he tried to mask it, his hesitation showed. His next step forward faltered, heavy with the unease that had settled in the room like smoke.

"Tell me, Habiba," he demanded, his hand shaking now as he jabbed a finger toward her, "do you want to marry this young man?"

The air thickened. No one moved. I watched her, praying for her eyes to meet mine. When they finally did, I tried to tell her without words: *I mean this. I want this. I want you safe.*

At last, she nodded, and I exhaled.

"Your nod means nothing!" he barked, his voice rising until it cracked. "I need to hear you say it. You were so bold in arguing with me minutes ago, and now you go silent? Speak! Say you agree!"

"I agree," Habiba whispered, her voice dry and cracked, as if her throat were made of sand.

"Good." His grin was jagged, triumphant. He snapped his fingers at his wife. "Give me a pen. A pencil. Something to write with." She hesitated, frozen in her chair, until his glare cut into her like a blade and she scrambled to obey. "How much do you want for your mehr, Habiba?" he pressed.

Her silence stretched, heavy and suffocating. I could almost hear the way her breath shuddered in and out, see her chest rise and fall too quickly.

"Habiba, I don't have time for this." His voice trembled now with impatience. "I'll give her to you for 5000." He slammed his hand down, the table rattling. "WHERE IS THAT DAMN PAPER?" he roared, his voice cracking with fury.

"She's not an object you can just sell!" The words slipped out of me before I could stop them.

"You're right," he hissed. "How could I marry her off so cheap?"

I stared at him, my hands curling into fists at my side. He was her family, her grandfather, her supposed guardian. But the urge burning in me—to strike him down, to wipe that smug cruelty from his face—was so strong it startled me.

I hated him. I hated the way he treated her, the way he reduced her to nothing, the way he made her believe she was worthless.

She wasn't. Not to me.

"Habiba, name your price. But before you do—" her grandfather's voice quivered with barely contained fury, though he forced it into something resembling control, "—as your grandfather, let me give you a piece of advice."

His wife finally returned with a pen and paper, but before she could even steady her hands, he snatched them away, his fingers trembling as if the anger inside him had nowhere else to go.

"Name a good price. Take as much as you can. Because once this is done, once I marry you off, you will never step foot in this house again. So get the money, save it," his voice dipped low, cold and sharp, "because you're going to need it when he decides to leave you."

My throat tightened. I wanted to tell him to stop, to stop looking at her like she was a burden to be traded away. But I knew if I opened my mouth, I would only pour fuel on his rage. So I stayed silent, swallowing the shame that burned my tongue.

"Fine! Fifteen thousand." His words burst out like a gunshot, his hands restless, his chest heaving as if each breath was a battle. "That should keep her afloat when she's abandoned. Do you agree, Habiba? Answer me!" His voice cracked with impatience. "Goddammit, stop wasting my time!" He flung the notebook in his hand across the room, the sound of it hitting the floor making Habiba flinch.

She squirmed, tears trembling on her lashes, and nodded far too quickly, far too desperately. "Yes, it's fine. I—I'm fine with that," she whispered, though her voice betrayed her.

"Perfect. Fifteen thousand." His gaze swept the room until it landed on Khadijah. "Get me that paper."

She scampered to where it had landed, her footsteps quick, almost gleeful. When she returned, there was a curl of amusement tugging at her lips, as though she delighted in watching Habiba's suffering. My stomach twisted at the sight.

The old man scribbled furiously while standing, then thrust the pen and book at Habiba. "Sign."

Her hand shook as she obeyed, her signature scratching faintly over the paper like a surrender. Then he shoved the pen at me.

I forced my hand to steady, tried to wear a mask of bravery I didn't feel, and signed. My signature looked bold, though my insides quaked.

He ripped the paper from the book and tossed the rest aside as if the weight of marriage could be reduced to a single sheet. He yanked Habiba forward, forcing her beside me, pried open her fist, and slapped the paper into her palm.

"I pronounce you husband and wife. You may leave my house."

The last words were not a blessing. They were an execution order.

I froze. My mind couldn't process it. Just like that—we were married. No warmth, no prayers, no joy. Just fury and exile.

His eyes darted again until they landed on Gogo. "Where is her bag?" he barked. Even she trembled under his gaze. "Bring it," he snapped again, and her hand shook as she gestured for Khadijah.

Khadijah rushed off, dragging a bag moments later. He snatched it from her grip without so much as a glance and stormed toward us, his steps quick, face blotched with rage, as if he couldn't bear this sight a moment longer. Dropping the bag at Habiba's feet and her phone in her hands, he stabbed a finger toward the door. "Leave."

I glanced at the man who was supposed to marry her. For someone who had just watched his future wife handed off to another, he looked disturbingly calm—almost statue-like, unmoved by the chaos around him. But when our eyes met, I caught it—the rage he was burying deep, simmering just beneath his stillness.

"I'll leave," he announced flatly.

"Stay," Baba ordered, his voice clipped, iron-hard. "We have other business to discuss." Then he turned back to us, the sharpness in his eyes returning, cutting through the air like a blade.

I bent down and gripped the handle of the luggage, its cold metal biting into my palm. My other hand twitched with the urge to reach for Habiba's, to anchor her through this storm, but I hesitated. This was her

97

home. I couldn't drag her out of it.

She stood frozen, tears streaming unchecked, her body trembling as though her spirit refused to move.

"Leave my house!" His roar thundered again, jolting her forward. She stumbled toward me, sobbing, her breaths broken and raw.

And so, just like that, with tears and silence, we walked out.

This was not how a wedding was supposed to happen.

10

HABIBA

رُبَّ خَيْرٍ أَتَاكَ مِن
حيثُ تأتي المكاره

Often, good comes to you from the very place,
From which misfortunes show their face.

- معن المزني

When I got home from the office yesterday, it was like they had been waiting for me. Everything was already set in motion—my bag packed neatly in the corner, my clothes folded, my bedroom mostly cleared out, as if I'd agreed to it. As if I had chosen this.

I argued, of course. My voice cracked from shouting, but it was pointless. Gogo snatched my phone, and when I lunged for it, she shoved me back with surprising strength for a woman her age. I begged, I yelled, but she only shook her head, lips curled in that way she always does when she's watching me suffer.

So I ran. I locked myself in my room—or thought I did. Minutes later, I heard the click of the key from the outside. They locked me in like a prisoner. I pounded on the door until my fists ached, screamed until my throat burned, but no one answered. Exhaustion dragged me under, and when I woke up the next morning, it was already afternoon.

The air outside was alive with movement—feet shuffling, voices overlapping. Preparations. For my wedding.

I tried again, banging until my palms stung, but it was useless. My only escape was prayer, so I prayed. Over and over, sometimes in tears, sometimes in whispers, sometimes just letting my forehead rest on the mat, too weak to speak.

Then I heard it. A car pulling up. Doors slamming. Male laughter filling the living room. Baba's voice blending with another's. The man's. The one I was supposed to marry. My stomach turned. Did he know? Did he know I didn't want this? Did he care?

When they finally dragged me downstairs, I fought, clawed, shouted. A scene, yes—but what else was left to me? Baba came to me, his voice kind and soft, I thought he would change his mind but he said. "I'm doing this for you Habiba, he will keep you happy, and right here in Canada and I can visit you as much as I want. This is good for you."

I resisted again and his anger returned.

I argued harder, my voice raw, but Baba only shouted louder, spittle flying, veins straining in his neck. Every word was another chain, another wall pressing me into place.

And then—Badr.

He came, cutting into the madness like air in a suffocating room. My lifeline. My chance. I hadn't planned it, hadn't even dared to imagine it. But in that moment, with Baba's stick hovering above me and the man's calm, predatory eyes watching, I knew.

I didn't want to ruin Badr's life. I didn't want to drag him into the storm that was mine. But I also couldn't marry that man. Between two wrongs, I reached for the one that gave me hope. Selfish, yes. Maybe unforgivable. But in that moment, I chose the only chance I had left.

I chose Badr.

Now I was curled up on the ground, leaning against his car as sobs wracked my body. The cool metal pressed into my back, grounding me, but every breath still burned in my chest. I felt bad for him—he crouched beside me helplessly, his shadow falling over me under the evening sun. He didn't know what to do, and I couldn't believe I was crying like this in front of him. Out of all people—Badr. But then again, that wasn't the worst thing that had happened today.

I couldn't bear to see pity in his eyes. My guilt clawed at me; I should have stopped it. I could have refused, could have saved him from throwing his future away. But I didn't. Because deep down, I was selfish. I would rather be married to Badr than be handed to that man as his third wife.

"Everything is ruined," I choked through sobs. "It's all my fault."

"Nothing is ruined, Habiba," Badr said, his voice steady, low. "You'll be okay."

"No." I shook my head, pressing my face into my hands. "No, it won't."

He tried again, his tone carrying a flicker of warmth, of reassurance. "At least you didn't marry him."

I finally looked up, my face blotchy with tears. "You make it sound like marrying you is any better," I snapped, before immediately lowering my face again, ashamed. My voice cracked. "How am I supposed to live with you, knowing I'm the reason your life got ruined?"

I could barely look him in the eye, he didn't get to marry the woman he loves because of me.

He sighed, long and heavy, and the sound of it made my chest ache.

"Habiba, look at me," he said.

I didn't move.

"Look at me." This time it was an order—firmer, carrying a weight I couldn't ignore. Reluctantly, I forced myself to lift my head. My sobs slowed, though my throat still burned, and I wiped my cheeks with trembling fingers.

The second I met his gaze, his eyes softened. He reached forward, unflinching, and brushed the dampness from my face. His touch was careful, as though afraid I might break.

"I told you everything I needed to say back there," he murmured, lowering his head to meet my eye level. "I'll stand by you. I won't leave, unless you look me in the eye and honestly tell me you want me gone."

101

I stayed silent. Because I knew damn well that I didn't want him gone. He chose to stand beside me instead of turning away. He felt like a lifeline—a mercy Allah had sent me when I needed it most. How could I tell him to leave?

He went on, voice firm with conviction. "I don't expect perfection, and I won't promise it either. But I promise sincerity. I want us to move forward—not as two people chained by circumstance, but as two souls fulfilling a sacred trust together. For Allah. For something that, one day, maybe, could grow into love."

He didn't rush me. Didn't pressure me. He just held my gaze, waiting. The quiet strength in his eyes steadied me more than any words could.

I swallowed hard, and slowly, I nodded. A strange courage welled up inside me, lifting me from the floor. I wiped at my face, shaky but determined. "You're right. I shouldn't be crying," I whispered, though my nose still stung. "But your family—how are you supposed to explain this to them?"

"Leave that to me." His voice was certain.

I glanced back at the house one last time, fear biting at me. Had I made a mistake? My chest tightened, but I forced myself forward. I opened the car door, slipped inside, and shut it behind me.

The silence weighed heavily. My body still trembled, heart still hammering.

"You have quite the family, Habiba," Badr muttered finally, almost to himself.

"I know…" My voice cracked, the word heavy with shame.

He started the car, his expression unreadable, and soon the road stretched before us. I didn't know where he was taking me, but his steady grip on the wheel made me trust that he had a destination in mind.

"I'm sorry you had to see that," I whispered.

"I'm sorry you had to live it," he replied quietly.

My throat tightened. I turned away, my eyes stinging again.

The car slowed, then stopped. I blinked through the blur of my tears and saw where we were—parked in front of a police station. Panic jolted through me.

"I—I don't want to press charges," I stammered, shaking my head. "Baba… he raised me, gave me a home when I had no one. I can't do that to him."

Badr gave a small smile, almost reassuring. He turned off the engine, then shifted fully to face me. "We're not here to press charges. Relax."

Air rushed from my lungs in relief. I didn't want to betray Baba like that, no matter how cruel he had been the past few days.

"My dad works here," Badr continued. "I need to tell him everything. Don't worry—he won't arrest your grandfather. But he will know what to do."

I looked down, twisting my hands in my lap. "Ok…" I whispered.

The evening air was sharp as I opened my door and stepped out. I pulled my hijab into place with the side mirror, wiped the traces of grief from my face, and forced a smile. Badr was waiting patiently. He gave me that small, steady look before gesturing for me to follow.

Inside, the air smelled faintly of paper, ink, and old wood polish. Fluorescent lights buzzed overhead, illuminating officers shuffling through stacks of files, typewriters clacking somewhere in the background. The place felt stiff, but alive.

"This way," Badr said, guiding me toward the staircase. His presence was steady, like an anchor.

Behind the upstairs desk sat an older man with silver hair, his uniform slightly faded but his presence commanding. A warmth radiated from him, his grin splitting his lined face as soon as he looked up.

"Walter!" Badr called out, smiling as he extended his hand.

"Badr! My boy!" Walter boomed, practically leaping from behind the desk. His voice filled the room, rich and gravelly, but cheerful. He rounded he table and wrapped Badr in a hug, clapping his back. His cologne smelled faintly of tobacco and pine, a comforting scent.

I stepped back, awkward, watching their reunion.

"Been too long," Walter said, still grinning. "How are the kids? Your mother?"

"Alhamdulillah, all good," Badr chuckled.

Walter's eyes fell on me then, sharp but kind. He moved around Badr, his heavy boots thudding against the floor, and stopped in front of me with a polite nod. His smile softened, eyes kind.

"How can I help you, ma'am?" he asked warmly.

Before I could answer, Badr stepped in. "She's with me, Walter. We're here to see Ba."

Walter's brow rose, his eyes flicking between us. Then, realization sparked, and his face broke into a grin. He leaned closer to Badr and whispered—not very quietly—"Is she the missus?"

Heat crept up my cheeks.

Badr's grin widened, and he nodded. "InShaAllah."

"Oh!" Walter threw up his hands, his laugh booming through the hall. "I can't believe it. I live to see you married!" He clapped his hands together, turning to me with eyes brimming with genuine joy. "And you—such a beautiful young woman. You are very lucky, Badr. No—you, young lady, are lucky too."

For the first time in what felt like forever, I laughed softly. His joy was so infectious it lifted the heaviness from my chest. For a fleeting moment, my burdens felt lighter.

Walter gestured toward a door down the hall. "Your father stepped out. You can wait for him inside."

I murmured a small 'nice to meet you' before following Badr into the office.

"I'm sorry about him," Badr said with a faint smile. "He's...

enthusiastic."

"That's alright," I replied, a small smile tugging at my lips. "I think he's very sweet."

He pulled out a chair for me, the gesture steady, thoughtful. I sat, my body still trembling faintly, but my heart calmer than it had been in hours. For once, I wasn't completely alone.

We sat in silence, waiting for his father. The air between us was heavy, my thoughts noisier than the ticking clock on the wall. I wanted to say something—anything—but every word that came to mind felt like it would ruin everything. I didn't dare ask Badr if he was sure. What if he said no? What if he changed his mind? The thought of Baba saying I told you so burned in my chest. I wanted this to work.

The door creaked open, and we both turned.

A tall man entered, the resemblance to Badr unmistakable—his same sharp eyes, though his curls were tighter, and skin darker. A gentle warmth touched his face when he saw his son, though his brows quickly knit with curiosity when he glanced at me.

"Walter said you came here with a girl," he teased as Badr stood to hug him. "I thought he'd finally lost his marbles. Now, I'm thinking maybe you have."

Badr laughed nervously. "After I tell you what I'm about to, you might actually think I did."

I rose out of politeness, but his father motioned quickly with a kind hand. "Please, stay seated." His voice was calm, almost melodic, but with an undertone of authority I couldn't ignore. He rounded the table and sat across from us. "How are you?"

"I'm fine, thank you. And you?" I smiled.

"I suppose I'm about to find out." His tone was unreadable, serious but not unkind. He chuckled softly, and I forced myself to smile back. Still, dread weighed on me—the moment his smile faded, so would mine.

"So?" he said at last, folding his hands neatly on the table. "What can I help you with?"

Badr shifted uneasily, cleared his throat twice, then finally spoke, "Habiba works with me." My body stiffened, wishing the ground would swallow me whole. "And…" Badr swallowed hard. "We're married."

His father's brow furrowed. "You want to get married?"

"No," Badr said firmly. "We are married. Already."

The man's gaze sharpened, his silence pressing down on us like a weight. Badr squirmed under it.

"And how, exactly, did that happen?"

"Her grandfather got us married," Badr admitted.

At that, his father turned to me, his voice gentle. "Forgive me, I don't mean to sound disrespectful, but I must ask—"

"She's not pregnant," Badr cut in quickly.

My breath caught. I hadn't even realized that was an assumption anyone would make.

His father nodded slowly. "Then explain. Properly."

So Badr did. Every detail. His voice stumbled at first but grew steadier as he spoke, though my heart hammered the whole time. I was terrified of the man's judgment, certain that he thought I was trapping his son.

But when Badr finished, his father turned to me. "I'm sorry you had to endure that, Habiba." Relief washed over me, though it was fleeting—because the very next moment he faced Badr with quiet sternness. "I understand you acted to protect her, but there were better ways. You shouldn't have gone alone. You could have called me. Ayaan. Anyone."

Badr leaned forward, stubborn. "If I had waited, she would already be tied to that man. It would've been too late."

His father shook his head firmly. "No. It would not have been valid. No marriage forced upon her would stand before Allah. Your marriage on the other hand is valid because she gave her consent—but it could have been handled with more wisdom." His voice was strict, words cutting, but there was no anger—only discipline laced with care.

Badr fell back into his chair with a sigh.

His father leaned closer. "Right now, I'm more concerned about your mother's reaction. That's why we must handle this properly. We will go to her family together. Speak with them. Ease into this instead of forcing it further. Habiba shouldn't lose her family because of this. What do you say, Habiba?"

I swallowed the lump in my throat, my voice hoarse. "I'd like that."

And so we drove to my house. My stomach twisted tighter with each turn of the car. Could this man fix things? Could he soften Baba's heart? I wanted to believe. I wanted to hope.

But the moment the door opened and Baba's glare burned into me, that hope wavered.

"What new shame have you dragged into my house, Habiba?" His tone was harsh. "Did I not tell you never to return?"

Badr's father stepped forward, lowering his head slightly in respect, his tone calm but firm. "As-salamu alaykum. I am Ilyas, Badr's father. Please, let us sit and talk."

Baba's nostrils flared. "No. I am done with people coming here only to insult me."

"We have not come to insult you," Ilyas replied evenly. "Only to speak. Please."

Miraculously, Baba turned away and strode toward the living room. That was his way of conceding. Khadijah's smug grin flickered as she followed him, relishing my humiliation.

She'd been enjoying all this far too much. Ever since it started, she'd been grinning like a fool, tailing Baba everywhere, probably whispering poison into his ear whenever she got the chance. Maybe she thought my leaving the house was her victory.

What she didn't realize—what she was too blind to see—was that my absence wasn't good news for her. The housework would all fall on her shoulders, every bit of it. Because one thing I knew for certain: Baba wasn't going to hire a house help. Not for her.

I almost smiled at the thought. Let her taste it. Let her see what it's like for once. I can't wait for it all to turn on her—her carrying the weight, her breaking under it. For once, I'd be the one watching.

We all sat—Badr and his father on the couch, Baba stiff in his chair. I stood behind them, too restless to sit.

"First," Ilyas said gently but firmly, "Badr should apologize."

Badr bristled but obeyed. His words were sincere, and I could see Baba's eyes soften slightly before hardening again.

Then Ilyas spoke, carefully respectful but unwavering "I understand she is your granddaughter, and I apologize if it seems I am overstepping. But forcing her to marry a man against her will is wrong."

Baba snapped. "I let my sons marry who they pleased, and both ruined themselves. I let her marry for love once," He pointed at Khadijah, "and look where she is now—back under my roof! I gave Habiba over 4 years to bring forward a husband, but she didn't. Idris is a good man. He provides. He has wives, yes—but they are cared for. She doesn't need love. Love is the result of a successful marriage."

Ilyas leaned forward, his tone still calm but edged with conviction. "Love is not the point. Consent is. A marriage without it is no marriage at all. Let her live her life, make her own mistakes if she must. Allah's decree will unfold regardless."

Baba's jaw tightened. "I have a reputation to protect. She destroyed it."

"Your family should matter to you more than your reputation," Ilyas said softly.

"Don't tell me what should matter to me."

Silence hung heavy. Then Badr's father nodded. "You are right. Forgive me. But let us at least ease into this marriage properly—for her sake. For yours. For the family's dignity."

But Baba's decision was carved in stone. "She is not my responsibility anymore. I married her off. She belongs to your son. And she is not welcome back here."

Hope shattered in my chest. Ilyas tried once more, but Baba's final "No" cut off any chance.

We left.

Outside, Badr's father exhaled heavily. "I thought you exaggerated when you said he was difficult."

Badr only shrugged.

"I'm sorry, Habiba," He said gently. "I couldn't do more."

"It's alright," I whispered, though my throat burned.

Badr turned to me, his voice quiet but steady. "Habiba... I can't promise perfection. But I can promise my home will be a lot more peaceful than this."

I smiled faintly.

11

HABIBA

وَإِذا تَشاجَرَ في فُؤادِكَ مَرَّةً
أَمْرانِ فَاعْمِدْ لِلْأَعَفِّ الْأَجْمَلِ

If two choices ever struggle in your heart,
Then choose the one that is more chaste and more beautiful.

- عبد قيس البرجمي

Badr drove in silence, his hands steady on the wheel. The faint creak of leather sounded each time he shifted his grip, too deliberate, too controlled. We stopped by the station again, where his father brought a marriage certificate which we signed and discussed the Mehr before leaving the station.

I sat in the passenger seat, my hands tucked beneath my thighs so I wouldn't pick at my nails. My stomach was a knot, my chest tight. Each streetlight we passed flickered briefly across Badr's profile, carving shadows on his face, making his jaw look sharper, more restless. Every turn of the wheel felt like a step closer to something I wasn't sure I was ready to face.

When we pulled into their driveway, I nearly told him to keep driving. A tall two-story with neat brickwork and a gabled roof, it looked Canadian on the outside, ordinary even. A basketball net clung above the garage, the kind of detail that whispered family, laughter, home. But all I felt was dread.

I wasn't here for a visit. This wasn't a favor. My grandfather had married me off to Badr—I was his wife now. The only way I'd leave this house was if Badr divorced me. And deep down, though I hated myself for it, I didn't want that.

We walked up the driveway. I followed silently behind them, letting their shoulders block me from view, from what was ahead. My heart hammered harder when I saw Badr's face as he glanced back at me—tight with nerves.

Badr rarely got nervous. If he was nervous now, knowing his mother better than me, then what chance did I have?

His father rang the bell. The air thickened, as though even the night was holding its breath.

The door swung open to reveal a young man—Badr's younger brother. Zain. I recognized him from pictures, Badr speaks about him a lot. He was like Badr carved in leaner lines: slightly shorter, his frame slimmer, skin a warmer brown. A thin scar ran down the side of his neck, disappearing into his shirt. His eyes flicked between his father and brother with curiosity, and a voice edged with suspicion.

"You two came together?" He asked, one eyebrow arched.

Badr's father stepped past him into the building, and I followed quickly before the door shut in my face. Zain caught it just in time, muttering, "Oh—sorry."

The moment I stepped inside, I was swallowed by a different world. The sharp scent of mint tea lingered in the air, mixing with the faint smoke of incense. Woven Berber rugs covered polished wooden floors, soft underfoot. Carved furniture gleamed faintly under the warm yellow lights, brass teapots catching glimmers on a side table, patterned cushions thrown across low couches.

Zain's eyes darted to my suitcase in Badr's hand, curiosity bright in his expression. "Where's Ma?" Badr asked.

"Kitchen," Zain replied, still studying us like a puzzle. "I'll call her."

My heart lurched. Meeting her was inevitable, but I wasn't ready.

She came out a moment later, wiping her hands on a towel. The sight of her hit me like a memory. A scarf was loosely tied over her hair, and she wore a worn house gown that still looked graceful on her. She reminded me of my mother—the exact way she'd dress at home, unbothered and warm. For a fleeting second, I smiled at the thought.

But then I remembered why I was here.

Her face lit up when she saw her son and husband. She said something to them in Darijah, her voice carrying laughter—smile easy and natural. Then her gaze fell on me.

Her smile widened. I smiled back.

"Salam," she greeted warmly.

"Salam," I managed, my voice soft.

Her eyes flicked between them, her tone still light. "Who's she?"

For a beat, no one answered. Both men hesitated, waiting for the other to speak. I held my breath, knowing it wasn't my place. Zain reappeared from the kitchen, spatula still in hand, leaning against the doorframe like he was watching a play unfold.

Her brows rose suddenly, then she turned to Badr, her lips curving into a teasing smile as she said something to him, and to my surprise, Badr blushed.

Seeing him like this—flustered, caught off guard—was strange. A different Badr than the one I sparred with at work. But the warmth of the moment was brief.

Badr's father cleared his throat, stepping forward with steady authority. "Husnah," he said, and at the sound of her name my stomach knotted. "This is Habiba. Badr's wife."

The air froze.

Her smile faltered. She blinked. "Ya'ni… they will be married?" she asked slowly.

His father didn't flinch. "Ya'ni, they are married."

The warmth drained from her face, like a flame snuffed out. Her eyes narrowed, settling on Badr, sharp, searching, almost accusing. "Badr… shno hadshi? What is this?"

112

The softness in her tone was gone.

Badr shifted slightly, his voice steady, polite.

"There was a problem at her home. Her grandfather gave me no choice but to marry her. I did what I felt was right."

Her face tightened.

"That's not how it works," she snapped. "You don't just—just do such a thing without your family knowing."

The weight of her disapproval pressed against my chest. I stood still, my hands clasped together in front of me, feeling like an intruder in my marriage.

"Husnah," Badr's father interjected, his tone firm but calm. "He made the right decision. The circumstances—"

"Right decision?" she cut in, switching briefly into Darijah, her voice rising. I didn't understand the words, but the tone was clear: disbelief, outrage.

Badr's father replied "Yes. You think badly now, but you don't know what was at stake."

She turned toward me briefly, her gaze assessing, almost too direct. I lowered my eyes, unsure if I should speak or just disappear into the floor.

"Badr you know this, you know that this is not the way!" she snapped, taking a step forward. "You don't let someone force you like this. You should have come to me. We talk, we—" She waved a hand as if brushing off the idea that there could be any justification.

I stood there, every word felt like a stone dropped between them, and I hated that I was the cause of it.

"Husnah," his father cut in firmly, stepping closer to her. "He did what he thought was right, and I respect him for that. You should too."

She turned to him, eyes flashing. "Respect? He makes a decision like this, big like this, and you say respect?"

"Because I know him," his father said, his voice low but unyielding. "He wouldn't take a wife without good reason. He works with Habiba, I'm sure he thought it through,"

The air felt thick. I could hear the faint hum of the fridge, the clink of a spoon in the sink from somewhere earlier, even my own heartbeat.

Upstairs, there was a sudden thump, and then light footsteps. A girl about fifteen, sixteen appeared in the doorway, her hair wrapped in a scarf but loosely, home-style. She took one look at her mother's face and frowned. "What's going on?"

Her mother pointed at me, exhaling sharply. "Look at this. Your brother—Ya Latif—your brother has gone crazy." She stood next to her mother, eyeing me.

"Who is this? What is going on?"

"Hana, go back to your room," Badr said, still even-toned but firm.

She blinked. "What? Why? I want—"

"Go," he said, sharper this time, the first hint of command.

She opened her mouth again, but Zain stepped forward. "Hana, it's none of your business. Go upstairs."

"It is my business—" she began.

"It's not," Zain cut her off. "It's Badr's business, not yours. Not mine either."

"So you get to be here and I don't?" She snapped.

"Why are you trying to make her leave? Because you want to, gang on me?" His mother argued.

"Because you are going to make her overreact the same way you are," His father responded "Hana, leave." that was all it took for Hana to have to leave, his command. She shot me a glare—quick, sharp, almost childish in its heat—then turned and stomped upstairs, her footsteps echoing until they faded.

The tension in the room didn't ease. If anything, it deepened.

His mother's voice softened, but only in volume, not in meaning. "This is not right. Something is wrong here. Wallah, this…" She pressed her hand to her forehead. "This has to be sihr. This is Black magic. There's no other reason."

I felt heat crawl up my neck. My eyes dropped to the tiled floor, tracing the intricate pattern while my chest squeezed tighter.

Badr inhaled slowly. "Ma—"

"Enough, Husnah," Badr's father said firmly, stepping closer. "Hshuma."

"Things like this don't happen without reason—"

"The reason," Badr interrupted, still respectful but sharper now, "is that I made a choice. I don't need you to agree, but you will respect her."

I wanted to tell him not to defend me, to keep the peace, but my voice stayed locked in my throat. My chest ached with the guilt of being the wedge between him and his mother.

Zain's voice joined in, quieter than the father's but carrying weight. "Ma… there has to be a good reason. He wouldn't do this just like that."

Badr's father nodded in agreement.

"You're making her uncomfortable, Husnah. Look at her—Is this how you welcome your son's wife?"

For a moment, she didn't respond. Her eyes moved between all of us, unreadable. Then she exhaled sharply, muttering *La hawla wa la quwwata illa billah* under her breath, and turned away.

"I don't want to do this right now." With that, she turned and walked upstairs, rubbing her head. The silence that followed was almost heavier than the argument itself.

His father sighed, rubbing his head, the sound of something boiling over sounded from the kitchen, causing Zain to jog there quickly.

"You two don't worry, I will take care of this." He patted his son on the shoulder.

After pathetically standing through all that, I finally decided to force myself to speak. "I'm sorry" I squeaked out, keeping my eyes down. "I know it's all happening because of me-"

"Please Habiba, don't let anything she said go to heart. This was just shocking for her, but I promise you in a few days she will start to think properly again." His father said, then he reached to pat my head before heading upstairs.

Badr and I quietly watched him go upstairs, then we glanced at each other and both looked away quickly. "Let's go up, I'll show you the room," He said, taking my bag in his hand. "I'm sorry about the drama, I know you've had enough of it for one day."

"Please don't apologize."

12

BADR

شَكَوْتُ إِلَيْهَا حُبَّهَا فَتَبَسَّمَتْ
وَلَمْ أَرَ شَمْسًا قَبْلَهَا تَتَبَسَّمُ
فَقُلْتُ لَهَا جُودِي فَأَبْدَتْ تَجَهُّمًا
لِتَقْتُلَنِي يَا حُسْنَهَا إِذْ تَجَهَّمُ

I complained of my love for her, and she smiled,
Never had I seen a sun that smiled before.
So I asked her for kindness, but she frowned instead,
As if her beauty, when it frowns, wishes me dead.

- صريع الغواني

I shut the door behind me and caught the way she looked around my room, slow and deliberate, like a cautious cat entering new territory. Her eyes lingered on the bed, the desk, the wardrobe—as if cataloging everything in silence. I bit back a smile.

For the first time in years, my own room felt foreign to me. The frames on the wall, the faint musk of my cologne that lingered in the air, the stack of books by the bedside—all of it suddenly seemed strange. Clean, organized, familiar to me, yet with her standing there, it felt... exposed.

She isn't family, my mind whispered.

But she is now.

Habiba is family. My wife.

I needed to keep that in mind, even if my chest tightened with every reminder.

I wasn't prepared for this—not for her, not for the weight of sharing this space. I had always imagined moving out, starting fresh in an apartment with my wife when the time came. Not this. Not bringing her here, into my boyhood room. But everything had happened too fast, and it wasn't as if I could conjure an apartment overnight. Besides, part of me feared waking up tomorrow and finding she'd changed her mind.

This all felt like a lucid dream I couldn't shake.

I cleared my throat, forcing a grin. "Welcome to my lair," I said, with mock grandiosity, trying to lighten the air between us.

Her lips quirked, but her eyes were still clouded. "Not exactly how I imagined your room to be."

I raised a brow, teasing. "So you think about me outside office hours?"

She rolled her eyes and looked away, but I saw the corner of her mouth twitch. "You know what I mean." Then she glanced back at me, and this time, sadness tugged her expression downward, her eyebrows softening into something that broke me a little inside.

I wasn't used to seeing sadness in Habiba. Hatred, yes. Annoyance, often. That sharp, cutting glare she always saved for me at work, everyday. I had learned to decipher each one, even laugh them off. But this—this wasn't sharp at all. It was fragile. It was real.

"On the bright side, I won't have to bring my ties to the office anymore. We can do that from right here." I joked.

She smiled, but it didn't last long. "I'm sorry, Badr," she murmured, her voice uneven. "I shouldn't have involved you in all this. I shouldn't have accepted this."

I sighed, stepping closer but careful to keep the respectful distance. "Habiba, I told you already. I did this because I wanted to. Please, stop apologizing."

My chest tightened. The truth was heavier than I could ever admit aloud: this marriage wasn't only for her. It had saved me, steadied me, given me something I'd been too blind to see. Without her, my life would've unraveled long ago. Every careful word I spoke, every soft reassurance, was a shield—protecting her from the selfish part of me that had benefited far more than she could ever know. If I confessed that, it would shatter the foundation of trust she had in me.

She nodded faintly, her gaze darting away. She tried to be composed, but her shoulders sloped under the weight of thoughts I couldn't reach. I held mine in check, letting her believe she carried the burden alone, when in truth, it was I who had been saved.

"Can I... use the bathroom, please?"

"Of course." I quickly pointed to the door.

Once she disappeared inside, I ran a hand through my hair, restless. Not knowing what else to do with myself, I started clearing the wardrobe. Shirts I never wore, jackets I refused to throw out, the clothes I'd bought but never touched—all of it went into a pile on the bed. I shifted things around until there was actual space for her. I didn't know how much she'd brought, but at least she'd have a place to put it.

A knock came at the door. Zain peeked in, balancing a tray of food. "I'm not hungry," I muttered, but told him to leave it anyway in case she was.

When she stepped out again, her face was freshly washed, her scarf adjusted neatly. But her eyes... her eyes were red, rimmed as if she'd cried.

"What are you doing?" she asked, eyeing the mess of clothes.

"Making space. For you."

Her lips curved, faint and unsure. "You don't have to do that."

"Well, it's either I make room, or watch you claim it all eventually. Might as well surrender with dignity."

She shook her head, a real flicker of amusement softening her sadness.

"Besides," I added, lowering my voice, "the excess is going straight to Zain's couch. That's what little brothers are for—free storage and emotional damage."

She chuckled.

My chest warmed. After the day she'd had—after everything— she still managed to laugh. It wouldn't erase the hurt, I knew that. But for that fleeting moment, she'd forgotten. For that second, she smiled. And that was enough, for now.

"Adhakal Lahu Sinnaki," I said. The words slipped straight from my heart to my lips before I could catch them.

No.

I didn't want to catch them.

I meant them. Every syllable.

She blinked, a crease forming between her brows, curiosity softening her expression.

I hesitated—for a moment, I considered keeping the meaning to myself. Letting it hang there like a secret only I knew. But if she were anyone I loved—and she's supposed to be—I would tell her.

"It means," My voice dropped, just for her. "May Allah always keep you smiling." Her eyes crinkled lightly, her lips curled upwards. But almost immediately her smile wavered into something sadder. A smile fighting with sorrow. I wondered what storm brewed inside her head—what thoughts dragged her back down.

"Do you have a prayer mat?" she asked.

"Yeah." I hurried to the corner, pulled the curtains aside, and laid out the mat, showing her the Qibla. "There's food, too—Zain brought it."

She gave me a small, polite smile and a nod before settling into her prayer.

I sat back, watching her. It wasn't the first time—we used to pray in the same office when we had to share—but tonight felt different. When she lowered into sujood and stayed there, still, longer than usual, I knew this was her sanctuary. A moment of peace in a storm. I gave her privacy, scooping up the pile of clothes and slipped out, closing the door with my leg.

The hall was dark, though the house wasn't asleep. Thin slits of light leaked from beneath every door, a reminder that no one had quite found rest tonight. I shifted the pile of clothes in my arms, tempted to dump them on the living room couch, but I could already picture Ma's face in the morning. Another reason for her to scold me, another weight on her disappointment. No, better to deal with Zain.

I knocked on his door with my elbow before nudging it open. The blue glow of his monitor painted his face, headset clamped tight as he mashed buttons.

I set the clothes on his chair and shut the door. On impulse, I flicked him on the neck. He jolted, swore under his breath, then twisted around with a frown that quickly melted into a smile.

"I didn't think I'd see you tonight."

"Why? I'm literally next door."

"Yeah, well…" He spun back toward his screen. "Figured you'd be busy with… married people things."

I slapped the back of his head, not too hard, then rubbed the spot before pressing a quick kiss to his hair. "And what exactly do you think married people things are?"

He wrinkled his nose. "Don't know. Don't wanna know." He finally paused his game, pulling the headset off. "How's she settling? She didn't take anything personal, did she?"

The concern in his voice tugged at me. I exhaled. "I'm not sure yet. I just… hope they don't keep treating her that way."

Zain's eyes softened. "Yeah… If it helps—" he leaned back, folding his arms, "—I think it's actually pretty cool of you."

I raised a brow. "You do?"

"Yeah. You stood up for someone you love. That's inspiring."

The words landed heavier than he knew. Someone I love.

I forced a grin. "Well, don't let it inspire you too much. Ma's already disappointed enough—I don't want her going through this twice."

The guilt pressed down again, thick in my chest. I hated the shadow in her eyes tonight, hated knowing I put it there. And yet—I still couldn't regret helping Habiba. Not for a second.

Zain's gaze flicked to the pile of clothes. His eyes lit up. "Wait—you're giving me your clothes!?"

"No." My voice was flat. "Just keeping them here until we figure out the wardrobe situation."

He groaned, rolling his eyes, "Wanna go for a round?" He asked, extending the headset to me. I shook my head and with a slight nod, he pulled the headset back on. Conversation over.

I stayed anyway, sitting with him in silence as my eyes traced the framed puzzle on his wall with a missing piece. Only he knew where the piece is and no matter how much I try, he's refused to tell me where it is. I moved around the room, letting the minutes stretch long enough to give Habiba her space. Long enough for her to breathe in the room without me hovering.

When I finally pushed myself up and headed back, I slowed at the sound of voices behind my door and opened it carefully.

Habiba was still on the prayer mat, the plate of food beside her, but now Ahmed sat cross-legged on the floor next to her. He looked up at me first, his small grin bursting into life as he scrambled over and wrapped an arm around my waist.

"Badr!" His voice was hushed but bubbling with excitement.

"You're not in bed," I said, ruffling his hair.

"I came to tell you good night."

That tugged at me. Normally I was the one making the rounds, pressing kisses to each forehead before lights out. But tonight, the air in the house was too heavy, and I'd skipped it. Of course Ahmed noticed. He always noticed.

I glanced down the hall. Hana. Today was the first time I dismissed her like that. I saw seen the hurt in her eyes before she turned away. I knew she'd be offended, especially since we all told her to leave. Being the only little girl in the house, she hardly ever faced rejection.

But this one? This one would cut deeper, because it came down to me having a wife now. Still, I didn't go to her room. It felt better to wait until morning, when I'd have the energy to answer her questions.

I crouched down to his level, kissing the crown of his head. "Good night. Go on, tell Habiba too."

He turned, shy all of a sudden, and whispered, "Good night."

Habiba's smile bloomed soft at the edges. "He's adorable."

I shut the door behind Ahmed, watching as she folded the mat and set the half-eaten plate back on the table.

"Yeah," I said, my lips twitching into a smile. "Just wait till he decides he owns the whole house."

Her smile deepened, a quiet warmth in her eyes that made the air shift between us. "Where do I take this?" she asked, nodding toward the plate. "Sorry, I couldn't finish it all."

"Leave it right there," I told her gently. "You're good."

The exhaustion of the day pressed down on me, heavier than any blanket. All I wanted was to collapse into bed, maybe fool myself into thinking that by morning things would feel lighter. Habiba was still standing where she had folded the prayer mat, her eyes skimming over every corner of the room—everywhere except me.

"I'll change first," I said quickly, grabbing my pajamas. "Then you can go in."

I shut myself in the bathroom, grateful for the barrier. Normally I'd sleep in just the pants, bare-chested, but tonight I buttoned the shirt too. She was my wife, yes, but we were strangers in so many ways. I didn't want to add another layer of awkwardness to the mountain already between us.

When I stepped back out, she was perched stiffly on the edge of the bed, waiting. I decided to leave that side for her, closer to the wall, safer. I'd take the side by the door.

She slipped past me with her change of clothes and disappeared into the bathroom. The silence she left behind was thick. My eyes drifted to the bed. How would she feel, lying there beside me? Was it too soon? Too much? My chest tightened with guilt—I hadn't even thought this part through.

She's my wife, I reminded myself. We are supposed to share a bed. But knowing that didn't erase the unease building in my stomach.

When she came out, she wore a loose gown, her scarf tied so carelessly it slipped down her neck. The sight made heat rush to my face—I turned away too quickly, fumbling with my watch, pretending to be busy. It felt strange, seeing her like this, casual, without the shield of her hijab. Too intimate for a first night that already felt unbearably fragile.

She folded her clothes neatly, then walked back toward the bed. We stood there, one at each end, two hesitant statues.

"Uh… I'll take—" I started, but she cut in fast.

"I'll sleep on the ground."

I blinked. "You want to sleep on the ground?"

"Yeah," she said quickly, almost too quickly. "I don't mind. I do it a lot—it's nice."

"I can't let you do that," I said, sighing as I set my watch on the dresser. "I'll sleep on the ground. You take the bed."

"No, no—it's your room."

"It's our room now." I turned back to her, her scarf slipping again as she avoided my gaze. "It's either we both take the bed, or I sleep on the ground. But I can't let you sleep on the floor."

Her face softened, but not with relief, with guilt. She looked lost in her own thoughts before murmuring, almost reluctantly, "Then… we both take the bed."

Guilt twisted in my chest. I'd backed her into that answer. I should have insisted she take the bed alone and should have taken the ground myself. Now she was agreeing because of me.

"No," I tried again, voice low. "Take the bed. I'll—"

"Please don't do that." Her eyes lifted to mine for the first time all night, wide, pleading. "I can't make you sleep on the ground in your own room. You've already done so much for me."

I rubbed a hand over my face. "I just want you to be comfortable."

"I will be," she whispered, then forced a tight smile. "If we both share the bed."

I gave a slow nod, then pulled the covers back, trying to make it feel less intimidating. She hovered for a beat, hesitant, as if waiting for me to move first. So I did. I sat down, deliberately, hoping it would make it easier for her.

She slipped off her ring, placed them gently on the table, dusted the pillows and sheets like she needed something to do with her hands. Then, finally, she sat down.

"Wait." I held out my hand, trying to lighten the moment. "Do the honors, turn off the light." I smiled.

She followed my gesture, rose, and switched it off. Darkness swallowed the room whole.

I heard her careful steps on the carpet, the small bump of her shin against the bedframe, then the mattress dipped as she climbed in beside me. The covers shifted. Two bodies lying stiffly, not touching, breathing too loud in the silence.

"Habiba?" My voice was low, almost hesitant.

She answered quickly. "Yeah?"

"I'm sorry," I said, the words tumbling out. "For my mom. I'm sorry."

She was quiet for a moment, long enough that I thought she'd fallen asleep. "I can't blame her. She had every right to react that way."

"Maybe," I sighed, staring into the dark. "But she was angry at the wrong person. I'm the one who married you and brought you here."

"My grandfather forced you," she whispered, so soft I almost missed it.

"No one forced me," I said firmly. "I made a choice that felt right at the time."

Silence again. Then her voice. "And now?"

The question struck harder than I expected. Did I regret it? Was I even sure of myself? The truth tangled in my throat, heavy, so I reached for levity instead.

"As long as you don't steal any of my clients," I joked, "my decision stands."

She made a sound—half a laugh, half a sigh—and I smiled in the dark. It was too dark to see her face, but I knew she was turned towards me.

"Good night, Badr," she whispered.

"Good night," I said back, though disappointment pricked at me. I didn't want the conversation to end. I wanted more. I wanted something to prove this wasn't a mistake.

She drifted first, her breaths evening out into a soft rhythm. I lay there listening, restless.

I'd always liked my room dark—the heavy curtains, the absolute stillness. But tonight, I hated it. Tonight I wanted light. I wanted to see her face as she slept, unguarded, at peace. To memorize it. To know if I could ever be the reason she looked like that.

When my eyes faltered open, moonlight was pouring into the room. I blinked until my eyes settled on the figure sitting on the floor.

Habiba.

She was on the prayer mat a few steps away, palms raised, head lifted—not in distraction, but in devotion. Her lips moved in whispers I couldn't hear, but I didn't need to. It was a prayer. A conversation between her and the Lord of the Worlds.

She looked... untouched by this world. Like light. Like a soul suspended between earth and heaven. That image did something to me.

Allah commanded us to marry the believing. And now, I understand why.

I realized how little I'd ever considered what I truly sought in a wife. I was ready to accept anyone—their flaws, their quirks—but one thing I could never compromise on was devotion to prayer. I knew Habiba wasn't selfish, nor a backbiter; I'd seen her guard her five daily prayers. Yet until now, I had never witnessed her in the intimacy of Tahajjud and the sight alone softened my heart.

I often woke a moment before my alarm, an odd habit but when the alarm finally rang, it startled her. She glanced my way, quick as lightning, but I was quicker—shutting my eyes and pretending to be asleep. Then came the act: a lazy stretch, a groggy reach for the alarm.

When I opened my eyes again, she was already standing, moving to silence her own phone by the window before returning to the mat. She began praying once more, fajr.

I left quietly to make wudu. When I returned, she was finishing her salah.

I slipped out again to wake everyone for Fajr. Zain was already setting his mat. Ahmed stirred awake at my call. Hana, however, needed a gentle nudge.

"Salah, Hana," I whispered.

"Mmm, I can't pray," she mumbled, pulling the blanket over herself.

"Okay," I kissed her head softly before leaving. Ma and Ba were already awake; the light spilling from under their door told me enough.

When I got back, Habiba was still on the mat. She rose so I could pray. I focused entirely on my salah—first the sunnah, then the

127

Fajr. At the end, as I raised my hands for dua, I stole a glance. She was on the bed, her phone glowing against her face, but I turned back quickly, finishing my supplication.

Her voice broke the quiet while I folded the mat. "Do you have some sort of schedule here?"

"Meaning?" I asked.

"Like… does everyone stay awake after Fajr? Or sleep? Or… does someone make breakfast?"

I slid under the covers, shrugging. "Everyone does their own thing. I usually go back to sleep till 7. By then, the kids are ready for school, Ba's dressed for the office, Ma's made breakfast. Zain's routine depends on his classes, sometimes he's up, sometimes not."

She nodded, thoughtful, then went quiet again. Truthfully, all I wanted was to sleep, and that's exactly what I did.

13

HABIBA

تَتَوقُ إِلَيْكِ النَّفْسُ ثُمَّ أَرُدُّها
حياء ومثلي بالحَيَّاء حَقيق

My soul yearns deeply for you, yet I hold it back with grace,
For one like me should, with all dignity, keep pride in place.

- قيس بن ذريح

I stayed on the bed, pretending to scroll through emails, though my mind wasn't really on them. A few sites, a meeting, some pending tasks. Things I could have done better on my laptop. But truthfully, I was just stalling. I didn't have the courage yet to leave the room.

What if I bumped into his mother without him or his father around? I didn't want to make her angrier than she already was.

Still, if Allah had placed me here, then surely there was wisdom in it. I wanted to believe I could be a good daughter-in-law, that I could earn my place in this family. The house was bigger than ours, far too big for me to sit idle in. I liked to keep busy, to do something with my hands.

After fixing my hijab, I took a deep breath and twisted the doorknob quietly. The hallway outside was silent and dim, the first light of dawn barely touching the windows. Shadows clung to the walls as I shut the door behind me and tiptoed down the stairs.

In the kitchen, I flicked on the switch, wincing at the sudden brightness. It wasn't dirty, but it wasn't sparkling either. The counters bore faint crumbs, the sink a glass or two. Normal. Lived-in. But my father's perfectionism had rubbed off on me. I liked things spotless, polished.

I searched for cleaning supplies, hesitating when I found them. There were several rags, sprays, sponges, but I didn't know which was for what. What if I ruined something or used the wrong cleaner? Maybe it was safer to leave it alone. I sighed, shutting the cupboard.

The door creaked open.

I straightened, my heart skipping. For a terrifying moment I thought it was his mother. But it wasn't.

It was Zain.

He stood in the doorway with his messy curls still damp, glasses sliding down his nose, sweater loose over grey joggers. He looked surprised to see me, then broke into a grin.

"Caught ya snooping," he teased.

I chuckled nervously. "You did."

He shut the door behind him, heading for the fridge. "What are you doing down here?"

"I couldn't sleep," I admitted. "Thought I'd clean to pass the time, but... I don't really know how things work here." I shrugged, embarrassed.

"You clean to pass time?" He turned, eyebrows raised behind his glasses.

"Yeah."

He grinned and gave me a thumbs up. "I like you. When it's time to vote on whether you get to stay or not, You have my full support."

"Oh... we're voting?" I asked, half-cringing, half scared.

He chuckled, shaking his head. "I'm kidding."

I smiled but wasn't sure how to respond. My nerves buzzed, desperate to say the right thing.

He pulled out bread and mayonnaise, then sugar from the cabinet. "You normally wake up this early?" I asked, trying to keep the conversation alive.

"Fridays, yeah. I've got an 8 a.m. lecture. I leave before most of them wake." He began spreading mayo on the bread with practiced indifference.

"That's your breakfast?" I asked, watching the knife scrape.

"Yeah. Enough to keep me awake while driving."

"I can make you something," I offered quickly. My voice came out too eager, but I didn't care. This was my chance. "I make breakfast for the kids all the time. Give me ten minutes."

He paused, knife mid-air, then shrugged. "You don't have to—"

"I insist," I cut in, smiling as warmly as I could.

He studied me for a moment, then finally set the bread down. "Fine. But if Badr asks, you insisted."

"Don't worry," I said with a playful smile. "Our little secret."

He laid out the ingredients, even pointing out the right rags for the counters and floors before leaving me to it.

As soon as the door closed, I got to work. My movements were quick, deliberate. I wanted to impress him—show him I could fit here, that I wasn't the stranger who dropped into their lives unwanted. I chopped onions and tomatoes, sautéed them with eggs, the sizzle filling the kitchen with a savory warmth. I spread mayonnaise, layered the eggs, and pressed the bread together neatly. Then I tidied everything—wiping down counters, sweeping crumbs, leaving the place better than I found it.

That's when the door opened again.

I looked up, expecting Zain.

It was his mother.

My stomach dropped.

"Good morning," I said, forcing a smile. My voice sounded small, almost pleading.

She didn't answer. She just shut the door and walked away.

It hurt. Her silence weighed heavier than an insult. But at least she hadn't shouted. Winning her over would take time. I could be patient.

Zain returned shortly after, dressed now—navy sweater over a collared shirt, loose pants, his hair neatly brushed, glasses perched

131

comfortably. He looked like a younger version of Badr from our university days, casual but polished.

He grinned, grabbing the plate from the microwave. "Moment of truth. If this sandwich is good, I'll make you my special cupcakes."

"You bake cupcakes?" I asked, genuinely surprised.

"I bake everything. Ask Badr." He puffed his chest slightly, proud.

I watched him take a bite, my palms damp with nerves. His eyes lit up. He put the sandwich down and clapped, impressed.

I bowed playfully. "Thank you, thank you."

"If you make me this every Friday, I'll make you cupcakes every weekend. Deal?"

I crossed my arms, teasing. "Depends. I'll need to taste those famous cupcakes first."

He grinned. "You're a good addition to the family." The words warmed me more than I'd expected.

He wrapped the extra sandwich in foil, leaning against the counter as he finished the rest.

"When does everyone wake up?" I asked.

"By now, they're up and getting ready. Badr usually drives the little ones to school before work."

My heart jolted. Work. I have a job.

"What time is it?"

"Seven-thirty-five."

Panic shot through me. "I need to shower," I blurted, hurrying for the door. "Enjoy your day!"

"It started well, it'll end well," he said, grinning.

"InSha'Allah," I called back, climbing the stairs two at a time.

At the top, I nearly collided with Hana. She spotted me, frowned, then pretended to forget something and ducked back into her room without a word.

I sighed, my chest heavy. It seems the women of this house hate me.

When I entered the room, Badr was still in the bathroom. The sound of running water hummed faintly behind the door, a steady rhythm that made the room feel both occupied and oddly quiet. I set my suitcase on the bed, unzipped it, and pulled out my outfit for the day—a shin-length green blouse paired with a matching patterned full length skirt.

As I bent to place the suitcase neatly on the floor, the bathroom door unlocked.

Badr stepped out, towel draped around his neck, another pressed against his damp hair. Droplets of water clung to his skin and trailed down, disappearing beneath the waistband of his sweatpants.

And then I realized what I was looking at.

Muscles. His chest was broad, his shoulders wide, arms thick and powerful. My gaze slipped lower, unwillingly, to the firm definition of his abdomen, each ridge of muscle cut sharply beneath his skin.

Astaghfirullah.

My breath caught in my throat, and when his eyes met mine, the realization hit both of us at the same time. I snapped my gaze away, heat rushing to my face.

"S-Sorry," I stammered, fumbling with the weight of the suitcase. I almost tripped over it in my flustered attempt to turn away.

He froze, towel still in hand, equally startled. "I'm sorry," he said quickly. "I forgot you were here." Then, without waiting, he slipped back into the bathroom, shutting the door behind him.

I pressed my palm against my forehead and shook my head at myself. This is going to be a long year. I just know it.

When he emerged again, he was dressed in a loose shirt, the air between us weighted with awkward silence. I didn't dare meet his gaze, and he seemed just as unwilling to meet mine. Seizing the chance,

I hurried into the bathroom, closing the door with more force than I meant to.

Inside, I stripped off my clothes, only to realize I hadn't brought a towel. My stomach sank. I slapped my forehead once, twice—then kept going until the sting grounded me. How careless could I be? Finally, I mustered the courage to open the door a crack.

"Badr?" My voice was barely above a whisper.

"Yes?" His reply came instantly, followed by the soft thud of his footsteps.

"Do you happen to have… a towel?"

"Just a second." I heard him rummaging around, more shuffling, then he returned to the door.

"Here. Sorry—it's the one I used, a bit damp. I don't have a spare, but we can buy you one today after work."

I stretched out my arm through the narrow opening. "Thanks."

The towel was still warm, still damp with his touch, and though it wasn't ideal, it was better than nothing.

I stepped into the shower. The moment the water hit me, I realized everything smelled of him—the soap, the shampoo, even the cream on the counter. His scent wrapped around me, musky and clean, distinctly him. It lingered on the towel, filling the small space, surrounding me until I couldn't escape it. It unsettled me how much I noticed.

After washing, brushing with my finger and dressing, I wrapped my hijab neatly, tugging it tighter than usual. He was my husband, yes, and technically he had the right to see me without it—but I wasn't ready. Not when I wasn't comfortable, not when I still feared what his acceptance truly meant. My hair wasn't even prepared, unbraided, unkempt. Vulnerability wasn't something I could offer so easily.

When I stepped out, Badr was before the mirror, blow-drying his hair. His reflection caught mine in the glass, but he didn't speak. I busied myself with my bag, pretending to check for things I already knew were there. Then reality hit—I worked with this man. The office. Our colleagues. How would we tell them we were married? What if it didn't last? What if divorce followed and we had to face everyone every day afterward? We shouldn't have registered the marriage so early.

The thought twisted in my stomach.

"Are you okay?" His voice cut through my spiral. He was watching me, eyes sharper than I liked.

"I'm fine…" I forced a small smile.

"We'll leave together. I need to drop the little ones at school first, then we can head to the office."

I nodded, grateful for the practical direction, then he stepped out to check on his siblings. Left alone, I quickly tidied the room, smoothing the bedspread, straightening the dresser. When my eyes landed on the damp towel he had used on his hair, lying abandoned on the bed, I grimaced. I hated towels on beds. I carried it back into the bathroom to hang it properly.

When he returned, his gaze lingered on me. He did that often now—stared without explanation, like he was trying to read something hidden.

"You cleaned the kitchen?" His tone was unreadable—neither anger nor approval.

I hesitated before nodding. "Yeah."

He exhaled slowly. "You didn't have to do that, Habiba."

A frown tugged at my lips. "Why not? What's wrong with that?"

"Because that's not your burden," he said, voice quiet but firm. "That's my family's mess, not yours." His brows drew together in a sadness I hadn't expected.

I swallowed. His family. Not our. Just last night it was our bed

"It's not your duty to clean up after anyone," he added, almost scolding now.

Was it because he didn't like that I cleaned—or because he didn't want to feel indebted? Maybe he didn't want me to do things that could bind him to me, not when he wasn't sure if this marriage would last.

"Why are you scolding me for cleaning?" I muttered.

"I'm not scolding you," he sighed. "I just don't want you to feel like that's what you're here to do, to clean up after me and my family."

"Well," I said softly, "if it's any consolation, sometimes I clean and cook just to pass time."

Before he could respond, the door swung open and Ahmed bounded in, school uniform crisp, backpack slung high. "We're ready," he announced brightly.

Badr turned to me. "Let's go."

I nodded, glancing at the mirror one last time before following them out.

"Habiba, good morning!" his father called warmly from the hallway.

I grinned, relief flooding me at his kind tone. "Good morning. I hope you slept well."

"I should be asking you that," he chuckled. "I hope Badr didn't snore too loud."

I laughed lightly. "So far so good. Ask me again in a week, and I might have some complaints."

He roared with laughter, as though I'd told the funniest joke, and I found myself smiling with him. "You're funny," he said before disappearing into the kitchen.

I turned to find Badr standing before Hana, adjusting her hijab with careful hands before patting her cheek. She beamed up at him, and he grinned back. The sight warmed something in me. I hadn't known this softer side of him—the patient, nurturing one.

"Let's go. Ahmed, your laces," he said, crouching again to tie his brother's shoes. Then he herded the kids toward the door, ushering them

136

out with playful shooing.

When he looked up, his eyes briefly caught mine before drifting to his mother in the kitchen doorway. His expression softened immediately. He walked past me to her and kissed her hands, then her forehead, whispering something I couldn't hear. She nodded, smiling faintly, and then his gaze returned to me.

"Shall we?"

I nodded, following him out. He held the door open for the children first, then, without a word, opened mine as well.

I hopped into the car, fastened my seatbelt, and the engine hummed to life. The morning air was crisp, sunlight filtering through the windshield, throwing shifting patterns across the dashboard. Badr and Ahmed fell quickly into conversation, their voices a low rhythm of brotherly banter, while Hana sat in the back with a book propped in her hands, her lips moving silently over the words.

I stayed quiet the entire ride, eyes on the blur of passing streets. When we pulled up at the school, they all filed out. Ahmed waved, smiling as always. Badr raised a hand too. Hana didn't bother. She turned to Badr instead, her voice sharp and deliberate.

"Bye, Badr."

She didn't even glance at me. The car door slammed, her figure retreating toward the gates without so much as a flicker of acknowledgment.

I exhaled, shaking my head. "Your sister and your mother hate me, you know that?" My voice was flat, but the sting behind it was real.

Badr sighed, his grip on the wheel tightening before loosening again. "They don't hate you, per se. They're just... directing their anger. I'm sorry it's falling on you."

"Is there any way I can win their hearts?"

His eyes cut to me, startled. "You want to do that?"

"Why not?"

He shrugged. "Just give them time. I'll talk to them today. Don't worry, Ba and I will handle it."

I nodded, letting silence settle again. It was Badr who broke it this time.

"What about the office? How do you want to go about it?"

My throat tightened. "Should we tell them?"

Another shrug. "Let's just say it as it is, I guess."

"We filed the wedding, right?"

"Yeah. Ba took care of it."

"Do you think it's better to keep it a secret?"

He smiled—soft, certain. "This isn't a secret wedding, Habiba. I didn't marry you to hide it. We signed the papers, and we did it in front of your family. No secrets. No loopholes. You're my wife, in every way."

I sighed. "I'm not sure it'll do us any good. I'm sure there are HR rules about this that we've never even looked at. Let's give it at least a week. See how things go. That way, if anyone raises questions, we'll have proof it hasn't affected our work."

I didn't want HR breathing down our necks, forcing one of us to resign. And it would be me, of course. The woman. The easy one to push out. I refused to hand them that power, not yet.

Badr nodded slowly. "I understand. We can wait."

A beat passed before I asked, carefully, "Am I expected to take your last name?" I was already bracing myself for a fight.

He chuckled. "Why? Don't you like yours? Can't blame you—El Idrisi is a pretty cool last name."

I blinked, caught off guard, then smiled despite myself. It wasn't the answer I'd been expecting. I always smile a lot around him.

We neared the office building, but Badr didn't slow down. My chest tightened. If someone saw me stepping out of his car, it would raise questions.

"Stop here, please."

138

"Where?" He glanced around.

"Here's fine."

He eased the car to the side of the road. "You need to grab something?"

I shook my head. "No. I'll walk from here. You go." My hand was already on the door.

"Why?"

"It's not far. We shouldn't go in together."

"Why not?"

"You don't think that's suspicious? If we're not telling anyone and they see us together, they'll suspect."

He thought for a moment, then shook his head. "I can't just let you walk the rest of the way."

"It's thirty steps, Badr. You're overreacting. Maybe you're leaning into this husband role a little too much." I tried to joke.

He didn't laugh. His silence was thick, unreadable. Then he leaned back in his seat, shut off the engine, and crossed his arms. "I'll wait here. Once you're inside, I'll go."

I groaned. "You could just drive to the office. I'll be right behind you."

"Habiba, I'm staying right here. I'm watching you walk into that office."

I sighed, shaking my head, but climbed out anyway. Glancing around to be sure no familiar cars passed, I shut the door quickly and walked.

My steps felt clumsy under his gaze. Twice I tripped, my pulse hammering, until I finally slipped around the corner toward the office entrance. Inside, I tried to steady myself, tried to breathe normally.

"Habiba!" Tina's voice rang out, snapping me from my thoughts.

I turned, and she jogged up to me with her usual wide grin.

"Hey." I forced a smile.

"You didn't come yesterday, and you didn't respond to any of my messages."

"Yeah…" I sighed, lowering my voice. "Family emergency. But everything's fine now, Alhamdulillah."

"I'm glad." She set her bag on the desk. "Listen, Caden called. The client visited the site yesterday and tried to make some changes, but Caden told him he had to run it by you. I scheduled a site visit at 2 p.m, but we can adjust if needed."

"I'll review their requests first. Thanks, Tina."

The main door opened just then. Badr walked in, his presence commanding as always. He greeted everyone easily, but when his eyes found mine, he faltered.

"Good morning, Mukhtar."

"Morning,"

He turned quickly to Tina. "Morning."

She smiled politely. He moved past us and disappeared upstairs, his office door shutting firmly.

I tried to bury myself in work. Emails. Contracts. Client calls. For two hours, I tried not to think about him, but all I could smell was him. Every time I tried to fix my hijab, every time I took in a deep breath, every time I stepped into a room, all I could smell was him. His strong fragrance stayed with me–soft, patient, calming.

I returned from a particularly difficult meeting and saw a small package on my desk. I frowned, setting my folder down. A paper bag with warm grease spots at the corners. Beneath it, a note.

- Sorry, we missed breakfast. Have some of these—you'll love them. I'll see you after Jumu'ah.
Badr

I couldn't stop the smile that spread across my face. As if on cue, my stomach growled.

I opened the bag, and the smell hit me—warm bread, spiced

potatoes, comfort wrapped in dough. My heart leapt. Potatoes. My weakness. I didn't even know if he realized, but he'd chosen exactly what I loved.

I made tea, letting the steam rise into my face, the scent of mint calming my nerves. I snapped a picture of the food with my phone and typed *I love this, thank you…* deleted it. Too much.

You should know I love potatoes. Delete. Too arrogant.

Thank you. Boring. Delete.

I tossed my phone aside, frustrated, then took a bite. The bread was soft, the filling warm. My chest filled with something dangerously close to joy.

A knock at the door startled me. I quickly finished chewing before calling out. "Come in."

Badr stepped inside, and before I could stop it, my smile widened. On its own. Once, I scowled every time he walked into my office. Now it felt… different.

"Hey." He gestured toward the half-eaten pastry. "You like it?"

"Did I ever tell you how much I love potatoes?"

His grin widened. "Habiba, I'm sure everyone in this office knows how much you love potatoes."

I frowned, laughing. "No, that's not true."

"Every group lunch we've ever gone to, you order something with potatoes. Every. Single. Time."

"Oh." Heat rushed to my cheeks. I hadn't even realized. "Well… thanks."

He checked his watch. "I was about to head out when I heard you come in. I will head straight to a meeting after salah. So, I'll be out for most of the afternoon. Text me if you need anything, okay?"

I blinked. My first thought was—why are you telling me this? Then I remembered. We are married now. This is what it meant. To tell someone your plans. To share your day. To be around each other in every possible way.

I have someone to share my day with.

"I'll be visiting two sites too. I can push them earlier, so I should be back before you return."

"That's ok, I can pick you up from the site. Just text me the address." His tone was firm, but gentle.

"I'll take a cab, don't worry."

"I'd rather have you in my car."

I tried to hide my smile. "We'll see."

He nodded, then reached into his pocket. I watched as he pulled out a red tie, his smile deepening mischievously as he studied me.

"What?" I asked, frowning.

"I wear ties to meetings, remember?" He raised an eyebrow.

I thought about arguing, about refusing to tie it for him, but he'd been so kind lately. It felt only fair. With an exaggerated, deep sigh, I stood and took the tie from him.

I draped it over my neck, ready to start, but he stopped me. "Wait. You don't have to do that anymore." His grin lingered, teasing. I frowned, confused. "You can… just tie it directly on me now?"

Heat rushed to my cheeks as I realized what he meant.

He was standing close now, close enough that the faint scent of his cologne reached me. I hesitated, the silk of the tie slipping slightly between my fingers as I met his gaze.

Badr's expression didn't change; his smile stayed—light, teasing, as if he was quietly amused by the storm unraveling inside me.

"Right," I murmured, forcing my focus on the fabric. I lifted the tie and looped it around his neck, careful not to brush his collarbone. My fingers trembled anyway.

He didn't move, didn't even blink, just watched me. The weight of his gaze made me hyperaware of every breath, every accidental brush of my knuckles against his chest. His shirt was crisp, warm under my fingertips. I tied the knot as quickly as I could, though my clumsy fingers betrayed me; it took two tries before it looked decent.

"Done," I said, stepping back, too quickly.

He glanced down at the knot, then at me, his grin deepening, softer this time. "Not bad," he said. "I could get used to this."

I rolled my eyes, more to hide my nerves than to disagree. "You'll be late to Juma'ah."

He chuckled, low and easy, then picked his phone. "Keep me updated," he said, pausing at the door.

I nodded without meeting his eyes, as I rounded my table. The door clicked shut behind him, and only then did I exhale—slow, shaky—my heart still thudding far too fast for something as simple as tying a tie.

As I sat down and saw the pastry he got me, my heart burst with something I hadn't felt in a long time. Happiness. Pure, unguarded happiness. It made me want to dance. I never want to dance.

But as quickly as the warmth came, doubt slid in. What if I get used to this? What if it fades? What if he doesn't feel the same way, and one day decides it isn't working?

No. I couldn't let that happen. I'd kept my heart locked safe all this time. I couldn't risk it now.

Not even for him.

#

14

والود يظهر في العيون خفيه
إن الوداد سريرةٌ لا تُكتم

Love shows its face within the eyes, though its hidden deep
For genuine love is a secret that will not stay hidden from sight.

- ابن زيدون

I took a taxi to the site, only to find the workers on break and the client nowhere in sight. I used the quiet to walk the grounds, jotting notes on the small things that always slip through cracks until someone insists they're "big things."

Dust clung to my boots. The tang of wet cement and steel cut sharp in the air. Somewhere in the distance, a grinder screeched. Caden, the site manager, spotted me and jogged over, sweat soaking the collar of his shirt. His face was already apologizing.

"You're not going to like this."

I capped my pen. "What happened?"

"The client showed up. No call, no warning. Just walked in like he owned the place—which, I guess, he technically does. Told us to remove that column." He pointed toward the central support pillar in what would eventually be the living room. "Said it ruined his 'open concept vision.'"

I followed his finger and exhaled.

"That column is the backbone of the structure." The words came out half-sigh, half-statement, more for me than him.

"Tried telling him that," Caden muttered. "He didn't care. Said we should 'make it float.' His words, not mine."

Of course he did.

"Where is he now?"

A voice sliced through the dry air. "Ms. Mukhtar."

I turned. Mr. Quint approached, sleeves perfectly crisp, sunglasses tucked into immovable hair, carrying that kind of arrogant calm only money could breed.

"I asked for one small thing. One. A cleaner space. No column in the middle of my living room. That's not complicated."

I didn't waste a smile. "It's not complicated. It's impossible."

"Then shift it. You're the architect—be creative."

"We discussed this, Mr. Quint. You approved the plan. You approved the 3D. You saw the column."

"Well, now I don't want it there. Fix it."

I slipped my tablet from my bag, fingers already swiping. The structural model glowed to life on screen, a skeletal frame of beams and slabs. I held it toward him.

"That column supports the load of the second floor and redistributes it to the foundation. Moving it even a meter means redesigning the beam network, increasing the depth of the slab, reworking the foundation, and getting new permits." I zoomed in. Tapped. "You're looking at three months' delay and a fifty-thousand-dollar increase. Minimum. And that's if the city doesn't flag the entire redesign."

His jaw twitched. "There has to be another way. I don't like the look of it."

I tilted the tablet, flipped to an alternate draft I'd never bothered to show him.

"We don't remove the column. We reimagine it. Travertine wrap. A vertical light shaft. Make it the heart of the space, not the flaw. And I redesign the ceiling to pull the eye up. You get your drama—without compromising structure or timeline."

Silence stretched. He stared at the render, then at me, as if he hadn't expected a solution—only a fight. "That... actually sounds good."

I didn't smile. Not yet. Because I knew this was only another battle with Mr. Quint. And now I understood why Badr hadn't fought for him.

I turned, ready to go over a few tweaks with Caden, when another voice spoke. "I'm starting to understand why Delator keeps singing your praises."

A deeper voice. A familiar voice with that unmistakable English accent. Mr. Rashid.

He was leaning against a column, safety helmet sitting perfectly on his head. His beige polo clung to a frame that hinted at muscle beneath, brown trousers completing the picture of someone who looked both out of place on a construction site and entirely at ease.

"Mr. Rashid," I greeted, steadying myself. "I was headed for your site after this."

"I told you I would pick you up." He stepped closer.

"And I told you that wasn't necessary." I kept my smile light, my distance measured. "Why are you here?"

He raised a brow. "Do you think I followed you here, Ms. Mukhtar?"

"For all I know, you could be a stalker." I slipped my tablet back into my bag, trying not to flinch under the weight of his gaze.

He didn't blink. "Well, if I am, at least I have excellent taste."

And then he smirked—an expression that made him look less like a client and more like someone who'd been handed a puzzle he couldn't wait to solve.

He was charming. Disarmingly so. Attractive in a way that could make anyone's stomach knot. But all I could think was: I'm married. We hadn't told the office, hadn't told extended family. And yet, the way he was looking at me felt... wrong.

"He came with me." I exhaled in relief at the sound of Mr. Quint's voice. He was suddenly beside Mr. Rashid. "Ms. Mukhtar, if you could give him a tour of the premises, I'll catch up to you in a moment," Mr. Quint said.

My first instinct was to say no. It was within my rights to delegate, or have Caden handle it. But I was the site architect, and Mr. Rashid was also a client. What better way to secure his trust than to walk him through the progress myself?

"Sure," I said, a sigh hidden in the word.

Mr. Rashid followed as I began the tour, tablet outstretched so he could see the renderings. He kept a respectful distance—thankfully. I've dealt with clients who breathed down my neck, even some who tried to touch despite clear boundaries.

Everything felt suddenly more exposed. I was hyperaware of myself, of every glance. Married only one day and already terrified of giving Badr the wrong impression. I didn't want to jeopardize something still so new. I didn't want to hand him a reason to walk away.

When we reached the top floor, Mr. Rashid drifted to the window, a personal touch of strategic lighting. He stared out at the view—the sea spread wide like a canvas—silent for what felt like too long.

I stepped up beside him, the sunlight framing us both, and for a moment caught the same view through his eyes. "Tell me this wasn't just for daylight optimization."

"It was," I replied.

"Shame. I thought maybe you were giving Quint a place to stare wistfully out into the distance, thinking about the one that got away." He wore a half-smirk as he said it, staring out himself like he'd rehearsed the part.

I moved toward the stairs leading to the balcony, refusing to feed his theatrics. "If he lost her, he probably doesn't deserve the view."

His laugh rang across the hall, warm but uninvited. My attention stayed locked on the stairs. Something was off. I crouched, stared longer,

147

making sure it wasn't my eyes.

"Something wrong?" His voice was closer now—too close. I stepped away quickly, retreating to the window and scanning the workers below until I spotted Caden.

"Caden!"

He looked up, alert, and scrambled over when I gestured. Mr. Rashid stood to the side, watching with that same quiet intensity, while I pulled out my ruler and measured. When Caden came, I pointed to the discrepancy. "The fourth step is higher than the rest. Fix it."

He blinked, then nodded. "Oh. Right away."

That step was an accident waiting to happen—one distracted moment, and someone would fall. Caden jogged off to rally his crew, while Mr. Rashid stepped closer again.

"How did you even notice such a small detail?"

"It's not that small," I said, straightening. "When you've done this long enough, you know how a proper staircase should look." I pulled up my tablet, flipping to the fireplace design.

He leaned in, eyes lighting. "Now that's a fireplace. I can already picture my friend brooding dramatically in front of it after being rejected at every possible turn."

"He'll get over it. The insulation's solid—no room stays cold for long."

Mr. Rashid smirked. "You've got plenty of those up your sleeve, don't you?"

This time I turned to face him fully, my expression flat. "You joke a lot about rejection, Mr. Rashid. Maybe it's time you work on better analogies."

He grinned, unbothered. "What can I say? I'm an author. Tragedy is the genre—and your work inspires romantic tragedy."

I looked away. "Good thing I design structures, not love stories. You might want to change genres before the tour ends."

"What if I prefer slow burn?"

"Then pace yourself—we're nearing the end." I started toward the balcony stairs.

His laughter followed me, unshaken. If anything, my comebacks seemed to encourage him. He wasn't deterred—he was entertained.

My phone buzzed. While he admired the view from the balcony, I slipped it out.

Badr: Everything going well?

Pressure presses into my chest. Part of me wants to smile at his message, part of me wants to groan. This checking-in—it's thoughtful, yes, but it also feels like a weight on my shoulders. Because now... now I like it. I like the way he makes me laugh, how his presence doesn't feel as sharp anymore but soft, steady. I like this new life that's unfolding—but it isn't final.

Yes, he says he'll stay. But will he really? What if one day he sees someone else he'd rather marry? What if his mother finally convinces him to leave me? What if he simply gets tired? I'm standing on cracked glass, pretending it's solid ground. And even though I know, deep down, it's unlikely he'll just walk away, I can't help feeling like at any moment the floor might give way.

I just want everything to go smoothly. I want to breathe without wondering if the air will vanish. It's strange—how easy this all seems for him. He doesn't look the least bit unsettled by the fact that we're suddenly married, like we've been doing this forever. Like he wasn't forced into it. Like he wanted it all along.

"Shall we head back?" I asked, sliding my phone away.

"Lead the way," he said with a smile.

The walk back was quiet, his silence almost heavier than his banter. Mr. Quint was still on his phone when we reached. We waited under the shade together. "Will you really not come with me in my car? It'll be much faster. I can drop you at the office afterward," he said.

"That won't be necessary," I replied, reaching to fix the corners of my hijab. Suddenly, all I could smell was Badr. I looked around, half-expecting to see him nearby, only to remember the scent was coming from me. Mental note: no more of his products.

"You seem very against getting into my car. Do you think I'm going to kidnap you?" He raised a brow.

"If I got in, it wouldn't be a tragedy anymore—just a cliché. And you already peak in tragedy," I said, smiling sweetly.

He grinned, hands in his pockets. "True. But don't underestimate me—I can make even clichés unforgettable. Still, it's your choice. I won't force you; that might actually prove I'm a stalker."

I said nothing, turning my attention to Mr. Quint, who was heading our way. "So? How do you like it?" he asked, squinting in the sun.

"More proof that she's the best architect for the job," his friend responded.

"She is great," Mr. Quint agreed, smiling.

"Gentlemen," I interrupted. "I'm leaving." I turned to Mr. Rashid. "I'll have to stop by my office to get some documents, but I'll see you later today." Then to Mr. Quint, "My team and I would appreciate it if you called and scheduled your next visit. There are safety precautions to be followed, and we'd be grateful if you trusted the process and let us do our job." I said it as kindly as possible.

He squinted, looking away, sheepish. "Sure… I'll give you a call next time," he said.

As I waited for my cab, I realized I hadn't opened Badr's text yet. This marriage thing is going to take some getting used to—for me, at least.

Me: Just finished at the site. I'll stop by the office for some papers and then head to the next.

I sent the message just as my cab arrived. When we reached the office, I spotted Badr's car in the lot. The moment the cab stopped, I handed over the fare—and at the same time, the door opened. I saw his body first—broad shoulders framed in the doorway—then his face as he leaned down into the cab, smiling. "Salam, Lalla," he greeted.

My eyes widened. I quickly motioned for him to move. When I got out, I glanced around to make sure no one saw. We weren't supposed to be friends. "Hi, Badr," I said, walking past him toward the office, trying not to let my face give away the way he made me feel.

"So where's your next site?" he asked, falling into step beside me.

"Why? Don't you have anything better to do?"

He jogged ahead to open the door for me. "I became your personal driver last night, remember? After you."

I shot him a look before stepping inside. Lowering my voice, I answered, "I don't think having you drop me everywhere will look good." We were walking casually now, our faces kept strict—at least mine was. "I can go myself. It's less risky." I sighed.

"What's risky," he said, his voice dropping too, "is you taking a taxi everywhere. Why don't you have a car?"

"Because I don't need one." I quickened my pace, hoping he'd drop the topic.

I'd never really had anywhere to go—always home, always busy, always working. If Baba sent me somewhere, the driver took me. If I had to take Hadi and Jamila to see their father, the driver took me. The only time I ever used a taxi was for work. So honestly, owning a car just felt unnecessary, a waste. Besides, I never even got around to taking a driving test.

He didn't even have to jog, his long strides caught up easily. "Well, you can either get a car," he said, his voice a shade louder, "or you'll have to live with me taking care of you."

"Badr, lower your voice. Someone might hear," I hissed, suddenly aware of our surroundings. Luckily, Terrance's office was the only one up

151

here with ours.

"Let them hear, Habiba. I didn't say anything wrong," he replied, quieter now.

I pushed open my office door and stepped in. On a normal day, I would've slammed it in his face. But we were married now and I was trying to make better choices. He closed it behind him.

I set my bag on the table, dragged my palms over my face, and sat on the edge. "Badr, I know you want to be nice, but—"

"Habiba," he cut me off, stepping forward and stopping right in front of me. Too close. He towered over me, his voice strict and low, and I hated the way it made my heart race. "This has nothing to do with being nice, I know you're used to doing everything on your own. And I promise I won't get in the way of anything else. But I need you to shut up and let me take care of you. Let me do my duty as your husband."

I could smell him even more now—except this time, the scent was coming from him, not me. His eyes were soft yet intense, deep brown, almost dark; his beard framed his face perfectly, and his lips, I'd never noticed the subtle curve.

"The minute you became my wife, you became my responsibility. You became important in my life, and I take care of those who matter. So I don't care what grudges you hold against me; as long as you remain my wife, I will take care of you. Get used to it."

I didn't know what to say. My brain barely processed anything other than the fact that he was so close, and all I could smell was him. We simply stared at each other. I got lost in his eyelashes, mostly jealous of how long they were, before his gaze flickered down to my lips so fast I nearly missed it.

Some sort of realization must have hit him, because he suddenly stepped back, hands sliding into his pockets as he looked everywhere but at me. "I'm sorry. I know that sounded harsh," he added quickly, scratching his jaw, before looking back at me. "Look, taking care of you isn't a favor. It's a promise I made to Allah—and I will really appreciate if you let me get this barakah."

I sighed. "I'm sorry. It's just… it's all so weird."

He paused, watching me.

"I've spent most of my life alone. No one checking in, no one waiting up. Just… me. And now suddenly I'm expected to tell someone where I'm going, let someone drop me off, update someone about my day." My voice cracked slightly. "It feels strange."

His shoulders dropped, like something inside him softened, like he finally heard what I wasn't saying. He smiled gently. "I'm sorry, too," he said. "I should've thought about how much of a shift this is for you."

He stepped forward again, slow and deliberate. This time, when he was close, it didn't feel overwhelming. It felt calm. Safe. Like I could bury my face into his chest and never be alone again. I didn't, obviously. That'd be weird. Well, depending on who you asked.

"You don't have to update me about your day… but it would be nice if you did. To know you're okay, that your day didn't wear you down."

His smile deepened.

"I don't have to drop you off everywhere… but it would be nice to know you weren't in some stranger's car, that you got there safe and sound. And I'm not trying to control you. I'm just doing for you exactly what I'd do for my mother. For Hana. Because that's what you are now, someone I need to protect, someone I *want* to protect."

I smiled up at him, and he did that intense stare again. There was always something in his eyes I couldn't place, and not knowing what it was bothered me.

A knock on the door made him jump back, and I straightened instinctively. I regained my composure quickly and called out for whoever it was to come in as I rounded my desk. Terrence stepped inside, stopping in his tracks when he saw Badr. He looked between us.

"That's weird… I didn't hear any arguing from outside," he said, shutting the door behind him.

"Believe it or not, Habiba and I are capable of discussing without arguing," Badr shot back.

Terrence scoffed. "Could've fooled me." Then he turned to me. "Look into these for me. I need them by next week if possible. How are things going with Mr. Rashid?"

"Fine. I met him briefly some time ago, but I'm headed to his site now," I said. I didn't need to look at Badr to notice the shift in him.

Terrence nodded. "Take good care of his project. He's an important client."

"I will," I replied, and he left the office, leaving Badr and me alone again.

He cleared his throat, his expression stricter now, detached as he spoke. "I can go home now if you'd like, and we can meet there. I won't have to drop you off if that makes you uncomfortable."

I shook my head. "No, I just don't want you wasting your time on me," I admitted honestly.

"You know very well, Habiba, that doing anything for you isn't a waste of time for me," he said.

I wasn't sure how to respond, so I said the first thing in my mind. "I'd like it if you dropped me."

He nodded. "I'll meet you outside."

Knowing I was going to visit Mr. Rashid's site and that Badr might be nearby didn't make me feel any calmer, so I was more than thankful when he offered to wait in the car until I was done. It felt like a small comfort, knowing he'd be close but not hovering over my shoulder.

I walked across the plot, scanning the land for reference points, and only then did I spot Mr. Rashid at the far end, leaning against his car with a cup of coffee in hand. He waved, and I waved back, moving straight into professional mode, diving right into the site discussion.

154

I explained the areas that could accommodate structures, the drainage challenges, and what the zoning restrictions meant for design flexibility. "So here's where the main living area will face," I explained, pointing to catch the late afternoon sunlight. "You get plenty of natural light in the mornings, and the breeze from the northwest should keep it cool."

I walked him through each plot line, detailing possibilities and limitations. It was a serious, focused discussion, and I silently appreciated how professional and engaged he was being, it made my job easier.

"I like the way you've organized the north wing," Mr. Rashid said, glancing at the layout. "It's... impressive. You make it almost look effortless." His tone carried a subtle warmth, and I had to resist rolling my eyes at the faintly flirtatious lilt.

I was about to respond when Badr's voice suddenly cut through, sharp and calm from behind us. "She's yet to blow your mind, this isn't even the half of it." he said, his tone clipped but polite, entirely professional.

My cheeks warmed. Mr. Rashid blinked, startled for a moment, then laughed and extended his hand toward Badr. "Sorry, I didn't know you'd be here too," he said.

Badr shook it firmly. "Habiba is a very precious piece of our firm," he replied evenly.

Badr always praises me in public, always finding a way to slip in a compliment. I've wondered sometimes if he really means them, or if he's just trying to "show a united front," to be kind in front of others.

Still, his words always warm me. They make me feel like I'm doing something right.

"So sometimes someone comes along to make sure she's safe. Too many weird men out there," he added, the hint of a joke in his voice—but I could tell from the tautness in his jaw it wasn't entirely playful.

"That makes sense, rich men are the worst right." Mr. Rashid responded.

"You can't begin to imagine." He responded, stepping back, holding a folder. "I'll let you continue. You left this in my car."

I took it from him, thanking him quietly. It was the sketches I had prepared for this site. Once he headed back to the car, I used the plans to guide Mr. Rashid through my ideas and wrapped up the discussion efficiently.

I thought he would make a comment about me getting into Badr's car and not his, but thankfully he didn't say a thing about that.

After the meeting, he walked me back to the car and said goodbye to Badr before leaving.

15

HABIBA

أنتَ القتيل بأي من أحببته
فاختر لنفسك في الهوى من تصطفي

Your love will be the death of you, if chosen wrong,
So in affairs of heart, be wary, wise, and strong.

- ابن الفارض

His phone buzzed, so he picked it up, glancing at the screen.

"It's Hana. She wants me to grab juice on the way," he said, setting it back down.

An idea leapt into my mind, bright and sudden, and I turned to him with a smile that felt almost too wide for my face. He caught the look, brow furrowing. "What?"

"What if you don't buy the juice?" I asked, my voice too eager, too hopeful.

He side-eyed me, suspicious. "Why?"

"What if I make it instead?" I leaned forward, my heart thumping. "I make really good drinks at home. Everyone usually loves them. It could be… I don't know… a chance for me to do something."

His lips curved in approval, soft and encouraging. "Whatever you say, Lalla."

Excitement bubbled in me like soda fizzing in a glass. Maybe this was my chance.

At the supermarket, we bought pineapples, lemons, and new towel and toiletries for me. I held the bag like it contained hope itself.

When we got home, the house was busy. Hana and her mother were in the kitchen. When Hana asked where the juice was, Badr told her calmly that I'd be making it. Her shoulders sagged instantly, her lips pressed into a thin line.

My smile wavered. I rushed to explain, "I make a really good drink, I promise." She didn't respond.

Badr gave me a look, his eyes apologetic, heavy. I forced a small smile to tell him it was fine. I'd been through worse.

I changed into a light gown, then returned to the kitchen. The air was heavy with the warm scent of fried dough and spices. Hana was plating, scattering parsley over golden pieces, and I set to work on my juice.

My hands trembled slightly as I sliced lemons, the tangy citrus burning a small cut on my finger I hadn't noticed earlier. I've made this drink a thousand times, but now it felt as if the outcome of my entire existence depended on it. What if their taste was different? What if Moroccans didn't like it the way Nigerians did?

I glanced at Hana. She moved with easy confidence, shoulders relaxed, humming under her breath. She didn't look at me.

"Would you like to taste it?" I tried, my voice soft. "Maybe tell me if it needs more sugar? I don't know what everyone here prefers."

No pause. No glance. She sprinkled more parsley as though I hadn't spoken.

The rejection landed like a stone in my chest. At least she wasn't cruel, I told myself. At least there were no insults, no sharp words like the ones I'd grown up with. Silence could be survived, right?

I tried again. "What's the name of the dish you're making? Is it Moroccan?"

Nothing. She carried the plate out of the kitchen, and I was left alone with the sting of her absence. I stirred the juice harder than necessary, watching the sugar swirl into the golden liquid. My throat ached. Still, I whispered a dua under my breath and decided I'd keep trying. Family was worth effort—wasn't it?

158

When his mother came in, scanning the kitchen, I swallowed my nerves and tried once more. "Do you know how much sugar I should put in?" I asked, hesitant, searching her face for something, anything.

She grabbed a box from the storage room and left without a word.

I added sugar the way I always did, blinking back the burn in my eyes.

Hana, Zain and his mother were already gathered at the table, plates passing, spoons clinking, voices weaving into the warm hum of family. I slipped in quietly, the jug cool and heavy in my hands, and set it carefully on the table.

"That looks nice," Zain said, his smile easy.

Relief flickered through me, and I returned the smile. "Thanks. It's my favourite drink—my mother's recipe. Should I pour you some?"

"Of course." He held out his glass.

The sound of liquid splashing into crystal felt like music to me, a small victory. I handed it back, only to glance up and find Badr's father lowering himself into his seat with a satisfied sigh.

"Every day I sit at this table," he said, turning to his wife with eyes full of affection, "I only love you more."

She shook her head, shy, a smile tugging at her lips, then she said something in their language as her hand brushed Hana's back. Hana straightened instantly, grinning, and he turned toward her with mock surprise.

"Oh my God! When did my little girl grow so much? Cooking like a big girl already?"

Hana laughed, jumping up and looping her arms around his shoulders. "I'll be 50 soon Ba, you need to spoil me now. In fact let's go to the bookstore after this."

Her mother gave her a playful slap on the shoulder. "You've spoiled this one rotten."

159

"Hey," he said, tugging Hana's head down to kiss her temple, "she's my little girl. She's allowed to be spoiled."

The easy laughter, the soft touches, the warmth spread around that table like light. My throat tightened, and I blinked hard. I couldn't help but wonder what my own family might have looked like, had life given us more time. What would mornings have been like if we'd all lived long enough to sit together like this?

Alhamdulillah, I had sixteen years with them. For that, I whispered a quiet dua, smiling faintly to myself.

"She's not even the last born, yet she gets all the love," Zain leaned toward me and murmured.

I chuckled softly. "Perks of being the only girl, right?"

"Habiba?" Ba's voice pulled my head up. "Where's Badr?"

"He was in the shower, but he should be down soon," I answered.

"Well, sit. Have something." He gestured to the empty chair.

"I'll wait." I smiled politely. "But… I made a drink, if you'd like to try."

I felt like a street vendor pushing samples, desperate for someone to accept. Embarrassing, maybe—but necessary. This was my way in.

"Oh, great. Why not?" he said warmly, raising his glass.

Hope lifted me, and I rounded the table, pouring carefully.

"It…" Zain started, then lowered his voice as if ashamed. "It has sugar."

The glass in my hand wobbled slightly. I turned to Badr's father, whose expression was kind but apologetic.

"My doctor banned me from sugar for a while," he explained softly. "I'm sorry."

"That's alright." I smiled, though inside something folded in on itself. My chest felt tight, crowded with the sting of rejection.

He looked around the table. "Why aren't Hana and Ma having any?"

160

I glanced quickly at them, silently begging, maybe if he asked, they'd try. Maybe someone, anyone, would take a sip.

"I don't want any drinks," Hana mumbled, not even lifting her eyes.

I nodded, hiding the small fracture inside me.

Then Ahmed came running in, flinging himself into the chair beside Zain. "Careful," Ba scolded as he climbed onto his knees.

"You want some juice, Ahmed?" Zain asked, and my heart lifted in gratitude.

"Yeah, sure!" Ahmed beamed, holding out his cup. I grinned, rushing to his side, jug in hand. But before I could pour, he hesitated. His hand dropped, cup lowering to the table. "I don't want any juice," he muttered.

The words sliced through me.

I froze, staring. His eyes darted between me and his mother, flickering, guilty, unsure. That was it. That was the answer.

Of course he'd obey her. She was his mother.

And me? Who was I?

The lump rose so fast in my throat, it hurt. I set the jug down too quickly, the glass clinking louder than I meant.

"I'm coming, I'll check on Badr." I muttered, my voice tight, before slipping back. I didn't dare look at anyone.

I walked away quickly, my breath turning shaky in my chest, my fingers trembling from the effort of holding myself together. The familiar burn behind my eyes returned, unwelcome but unsurprising. Second day in this house, and already I was breaking.

I headed toward the stairs, desperate for solitude—but Badr was coming down the stairs. I froze, heart skipping. I couldn't let him see me like this. I turned sharply and veered into the kitchen instead.

The tears started before I even reached the kitchen. I stumbled into the corner and crouched down beside the cupboard, curling into myself as the first sob tore through my throat. I clamped a hand over my mouth, sobbing quietly.

I didn't realize how much I needed to be needed. And now that no one did, I felt like I was unraveling.

I would take the chaos of my old life over this quiet rejection—any day. Back home, I was the one everyone called for everything. I hated it then, the endless demands, the cooking, the caretaking, the way they leaned on me until I could hardly breathe. But at least my presence had weight. At least I mattered.

Here, it's different. They already have each other. They are already a family, complete without me. They don't need my juice, my help, my hands, or even my company. And realizing that I could vanish and nothing would shift—hurt more than all the burdens I once carried.

I heard footsteps approaching. Panic hit me like ice water. I wiped at my face, tried to swallow the sobs, hide the redness in my eyes, fix my expression, but he was already there. It was Zain

I couldn't meet his eyes. I didn't want him to see me like this. Small. Weak. Shattered. "Habiba," he breathed, his voice low and soft. "I'm so sorry."

Then he turned. His footsteps moved back into the hallway.

A beat of silence. Then his voice laced with fury. "Are you happy now? You made her cry."

"Made who cry?" This time, it was Badr's voice, sharp.

Then came the sound of more footsteps. I tried again to wipe my face, to gather myself, but the weight of everything, of trying so hard and still not being enough kept pressing down. The past few days had already stretched me thin, and this moment? It just snapped something inside me.

So much had happened. So much had changed. I pushed through all of it, carried myself with quiet strength. But now, here I was, curled up on the cold kitchen floor, crying over juice no one wanted.

"Habiba." His voice was soft, a low urgent call.

Then I felt him, his presence like a shield. A moment later, his arms wrapped around me. Firm. Steady. He pulled me against his chest, and my face found warmth in the space beneath his collarbone. I didn't resist. My arms found their way around him, holding on tight as though I might fall apart completely if I let go.

I hadn't cried like this in someone's arms in years.

And God—it felt so good.

To be held. To be comforted. To feel safe while falling apart. I hadn't realized how deeply I needed this. How much it meant just to have someone there. Someone who wasn't telling me to stop crying or to be quiet or to disappear into myself. Someone who stayed.

"What happened?" he asked, voice tight but not aimed at me.

Zain answered, explaining what had happened, word for word. Every sentence made me shrink deeper into myself. Hearing it out loud, it sounded so small, so silly. Like I was fragile.

Like I was a joke.

I pulled away, still shielding my face with the edge of my scarf, trying to laugh it off. "I'm sorry," I whispered, the sound broken and soft. "I can't believe I'm crying over juice."

No one said anything.

"Stay with her," Badr said, and I felt the absence of him before his footsteps even faded. The space he left behind seemed colder than it should've, as if the warmth had been pulled out of the room.

Then Zain lowered himself beside me. I didn't look up but I felt the weight of his presence settle into the silence, his quiet solidarity pressing against the edges of my shame.

"I'm so sorry they're doing this, Habiba," he murmured.

"No, I—" I started, but my voice was drowned by Badr's anger erupting from the living room.

"SERIOUSLY?" The sound cracked through the walls, loud

163

enough to rattle me. My stomach clenched. "SERIOUSLY, MA?"

A beat later, the sharpness in his tone dropped, but the fire remained, burning just under the surface.

"Is this really how you're going to treat my wife?" His voice was low, tight, restrained, but I could hear the hurt tangled in it. "After all those years of you telling me to get married?"

His mother's reply came swift, cutting. "Badr." Her scoff curled around his name, her accent sharpening the edges. "I told you to get married, yes. But not like this. This isn't how marriage works, our families are supposed to come together, we're supposed to learn about her first. I gave you girls, good girls."

There was a pause, the air weighted with his anger. I could almost hear him forcing his breath through his nose, steadying himself.

"And I didn't like any of them, Ma." His words trembled but didn't break. "She's the one I wanted. The one I felt I could build a life with. You don't get to choose that for me." Another pause, heavy. Then softer, aching. "And I know, Ma—I know I messed up. I should've told you. I should've brought her to you first, asked for your blessing. And I want to regret that, I want to hate myself for it. But put me back in that moment once, a thousand times and I will make the same choice every single time. If you want to be angry, be angry at me. Don't punish her for what I did."

Silence. For a moment, I thought maybe it was over. But then his voice cracked open again, raw.

"She came from a home where nobody wanted her. Where they made her feel like she was a burden. I took her away from that. I promised her safety and I will not—Wallahi, Ma—I will not let her feel that again. Not in this house. Not from you. Not from anyone." His voice caught, breaking for a second. "I'd rather we leave than watch her be treated like she doesn't belong. I won't let that happen to her again. I can't."

Every word landed like a blow. My heart ached at his defense, gratitude swelling—yet at the same time, guilt gnawed at me. He was bleeding for me, fighting his own family because of me. And all I could think was: I'm tearing them apart.

"I'll find another place for us to live as soon as I can," he continued, quieter now but weighted with exhaustion. "But while we're here, I'm begging you—please. Stop behaving this way. If you don't want to talk to her, fine. But don't poison the rest of the house against her. That's not right."

Then his voice shifted again, laced with disappointment that stung sharper than anger.

"Hana... I expected better from you."

The silence that followed pressed heavy against my chest. My throat burned.

Then came the sound of his footsteps returning. I shrank back instinctively, unable to lift my head. My guilt felt too large, filling the room like smoke. I came in here and tore this family apart.

"Come on." His voice was softer now, meant only for me. I looked up, and emotion surged so strongly I had to bite it down. I couldn't cry again—not here, not now. But the way he stood for me... it cracked something deep inside.

He reached for my hand, warm and steady, pulling me to my feet.

"Do you have your keys with you?" he asked Zain.

"They're by the door," Zain said slowly, hesitant. "Are you... really leaving?"

"We'll go for a drive." Badr's voice left no room for question. Then, to me, gently, "Let's go."

I followed him, head low, every step heavy with shame. I couldn't face anyone.

He paused at the entryway, snatching the keys from a glass bowl with a sharp clink, and then our coats from the rack and led me out. The

165

night air met me cool and damp, brushing my skin like a reminder of how exposed I was.

He unlocked a silver Honda civic, opening the passenger door for me. I slid in quickly, fastening the seatbelt with trembling fingers while he rounded the hood and got in.

The engine hummed to life, headlights cutting through the darkness. He didn't speak, and neither did I. Only the sound of tires on gravel filled the silence as he pulled out of the driveway—carrying us away from the house, from the battlefield we'd left behind.

The heater hummed softly as the car cut through the snowy streets, tires crunching against the ice-packed road. A faint fog clung to the windows, blurring the glow of streetlamps and the passing shapes of bare trees.

"I'm sorry," I said at last. Badr turned his head toward me, then chuckled. I blinked at him, dumbfounded. "What's funny?"

"Yesterday, I was accusing you of having a messed-up family and dragging you away from them. Now here I am—taking you away from mine."

I couldn't help laughing too, shaking my head. "Seems I'm not the only one with a dramatic family."

He smirked, fingers drumming lightly on the steering wheel. "What's a traditional family without a bit of drama, right?… But your family still takes the cake. I mean seriously? The classic tough grandpa obsessed with reputation, and the salty grandmother who hates basically everyone."

"Oh, don't forget the bratty granddaughter who wants everything done for her," I added, Khadijah's image flashing in my mind.

"Seriously? She did seem entitled," he said.

"Where do I even begin?" I rolled my eyes, leaning back into the seat. "Gogo pampered her just to spite me, to make me feel left out. Over time Khadijah grew into her entitlement." I caught myself mid-rant and pressed my lips together. "Astaghfirullah. We should stop. I'm sure this counts as *ghiba*."

The wipers squeaked across the glass, sweeping away a scatter of snowflakes as silence fell between us. Talking about them left a sour taste in my mouth, and I hated the thought of earning sin for people who already despised me.

"I have to ask, why do they hate you so much? Especially this... Gogo. How could anyone hate their grandchild?"

I smiled faintly, unsure how to explain. My voice softened. "Baba doesn't. He's just... too strict. Gogo just never wanted Baba to take me in, but he did anyway."

"Take you in how? He's your grandfather."

"Yeah," I said with a small shrug, "but she's not my grandmother. My grandfather had two wives. One of them was my grandmother— she had my dad, her only child. Gogo had three children, including Khadijah's mother. Gogo hated my grandmother, who was the second wife. Eventually my grandma got sick and passed away."

Badr's grip tightened briefly on the wheel. "Innâ lillahi wa innâ ilayhi râji'ûn"

I smiled. "I didn't know her. But everyone says she was a good woman."

Beside me, he made a sound, almost like he wanted to speak but held himself back. I turned my head just in time to see the faint crease on his forehead, his eyes fixed ahead. He only shifted when he felt my gaze on him.

"Can I ask," he said carefully, "if you don't mind?"

I nodded, bracing myself.

He asked quietly. "What happened to your parents? I know they passed away, but how?"

I knew that question was coming. I'd tried my best to avoid it, but maybe it was time. It was always going to come to this.

"Accident," I said, my voice low. "Same accident as Halifa and Ji'dah. We were all in it, I was the sole survivor."

I had already told him long ago that I once had siblings, Halifa and Ji'dah but they were gone. I never spoke about my parents—never directly said they had passed—but I hinted at it. My private life always stayed locked at home. Once, in a weak moment, I slipped. I told him about my siblings' deaths, about how much I hated Gogo. But that was only once. It never happened again.

His head snapped toward me, shock etched into his features. "You lost them all at once?"

I nodded.

"That's terrible, Habiba." His voice softened, and I caught that flicker of pity in his eyes—the look I hated most. But for once, telling it didn't feel like oversharing. For once, the weight of it left me lighter.

"They didn't all… die at once," I murmured. My fingers picked at the seam of my coat. "Abba and Ji'dah died on sight. Mama held on for one more day in the hospital. I got to speak to her. But she couldn't… she couldn't take the news of Abba and Ji'dah." My throat tightened, the memory clawing back. "Halifa woke up. He was alive. But he didn't make it through surgery."

The words scraped raw in my chest, but when I finished, I let out a sigh, like finally setting down something I'd been carrying too long.

The car slowed, then pulled to the side of the road. The faint hum of the heater filled the silence. "You can't tell me all of that," he said, voice steady but gentle, "and expect me not to hug you. I think you need it."

I blinked, stunned.

A hug.

It was a simple thing. Harmless. Human. But for me it felt dangerous. My body tensed, torn between yes and no. Between wanting to collapse into it, and the louder voice screaming that I shouldn't. That I

168

couldn't. That this was still the man I swore I couldn't stand just days ago.

I didn't say any of that out loud. I didn't have to. He must have seen it in my eyes.

But before I could stop him, he leaned across the console and wrapped his arms around me—slowly, gently, but with certainty. Like he already knew I wouldn't move.

His hand rested against the back of my head, guiding it to his shoulder. My breath caught, shallow and uneven.

"You think too much," he whispered, as though he had read the line straight from my mind. "Don't stress yourself trying to figure out the right way. If you want to reach for me, do it. If you want to lean in, do it."

He pulled back just enough to look at me, his eyes warm, steady.

"That's what I'm here for."

Something inside me gave way. My shoulders loosened, my eyes watered, but I didn't sob. I just stayed there, letting myself absorb what Allah had blessed me with.

Two hugs in one day. I barely even had one a year back then. Things really were changing. He tapped my back softly before leaning back into his seat, starting the car again.

For some reason, I felt open, like a locked chest had cracked. Maybe it was the hug, maybe the silence pressing against us, but I wanted to share more.

"When the accident happened, I was sent to live with Baba and Gogo. Gogo hated the idea, so they sent me to my maternal grandmother in Nigeria. But she was already sick... she passed away after a year." I chuckled bitterly at what I was about to say next. "After that, no one wanted to take me in. They said I was cursed."

Badr's sharp gaze snapped to me. "Cursed?"

"Mhm." I nodded, still smiling faintly. "They said everyone I lived with ended up dying. So clearly, I must be cursed. I was a child, I believed it. I thought if I just accepted it, if I just kept asking Allah for forgiveness, the curse would lift. When Gogo made me work endlessly, I figured that was part of the payment, so I never complained. I just... endured. Eventually, I grew older and realized it wasn't me. It was just *qadar*."

His knuckles whitened around the steering wheel. "God. I can't imagine how much that scarred you."

I gave a small shrug. "It did, but... Alhamdulillah Baba put me in Islamic studies for a while, that helped me reshape my mentality."

He let out a breath, eyes fixed on the snowy road. "But once you got the job and everything... why didn't you just leave? Get your own place?"

I chuckled, shaking my head. "Not in my household. If I had left, he would've married me off in an instant. That's what people do when they think you're slipping out of line. If the community found out he let his granddaughter move into her own apartment unmarried..." I sighed. "It would've been chaos. For him, for me. So despite everything... I was better off staying." My words drifted, soft against the hum of the engine. "I'm sorry. I talk too much."

For some reason, his lips curved into a smile. He wasn't even looking at me, just ahead, but the smile made me smile too. Then he turned, his gaze lingering on me with a softness that melted something in my chest.

"Years ago, I was really into poetry" he said, "I came across this little one-line poem. At the time, I thought it just sounded nice, nothing deep. It went: لا تختصر أحب تفاصيلك. Which means, 'Don't shorten your speech. I love your details.'"

He paused, breath fogging faintly against the cold window.

"I never really thought much about it until now. But suddenly... I get it. I get why it was beautiful."

His smile lingered, quiet and warm.

I turned toward the frosted window quickly, pretending to check something outside. But the truth was that I couldn't handle the way my chest swelled at those words.

No one had ever told me my words were beautiful. No one had ever asked me to keep talking. I bit the inside of my cheek and nodded, like his words hadn't just disarmed me completely.

This man was doing things to my heart I didn't have a map for.

The car slowed, pulling into the glow of a shawarma restaurant. He parked neatly, engine purring low. "Wait here, I'll order," he said.

"Wait, we're eating shawarma?" I blinked.

"Yeah. You don't like it?"

"There's food at home," I protested.

He grinned, already reaching for the door handle. "Yeah, but I'm punishing Hana and Ma."

"By not eating their food?" I raised a brow.

"Yes, ma'am. That's the plan." He smirked, stepping out into the cold. "Spicy or not?"

"Spicy," I said quickly.

He gave me a small nod before shutting the door.

Through the windshield, I watched him walk across the lot, his back straight, coat pulled tight against the biting wind. The restaurant lights glowed against the snow, making his figure stand out.

And I smiled. Wide. Too wide.

I had to shut my eyes tight because of the strange, swelling feeling in my chest. Something I didn't recognize, but it pushed up against my ribs, warm and insistent.

It made me whisper, almost without thinking. "Alhamdulillah."

16

BADR

مَا كُنتُ أَعلَمُ قَبلَ بَادِرَةِ النَّوَى
أَنَّ الأُسُودَ فَرَائِسُ الغِزلانِ

Before love's first arrow struck, I did not know
That lions could be prey for gentle gazelle.

- محمود سامي البارودي

Having Habiba as a wife was something that never once crossed my mind. Sure, back then I admit, there might have been a time when I had a little crush on her. It was completely innocent and it died quickly. She was just so unique, interesting, quiet but fierce. Mysterious.

With time I started to enjoy rivalling her with a side of friendship, it was fun. But now, the more layers I uncover, the more I find myself grateful for every decision that brought me here.

There's this instinct in me that wants nothing more than to protect her. Not just from harm, but from the weight of people's words, from the silent battles she carries. I want to see her smiling, carefree, unafraid of the world.

I caught myself smiling, lost in thought, while the smell of sizzling meat and toasted flatbread filled the air like a warm embrace. The little shop was alive: metal spatulas clanged against hot grills, the low hum of Arabic radio wove through the chatter, and laughter burst from the back where someone poured steaming cups of tea. It felt grounding, almost domestic, an odd comfort in the middle of my spiraling thoughts.

Then, a sudden clap rang out, sharp against the cozy noise, pulling me back to the present.

"Yallah! Share it with us so we can smile too!" Habib grinned from behind the counter, palm still hovering in the air like a satisfied cymbal player. His voice was rough from years of yelling over hot grills, but there was nothing but joy in it.

I blinked, a little embarrassed to find all four of them—Habib, Nazif, Hamza, and Mounir—watching me with raised brows and mischievous smirks.

I laughed under my breath and stepped forward, reaching to shake hands, one by one. Habib's grip was firm and warm, Nazif's fingers still dusted with cumin, Mounir wiped his on his apron before offering his, and Hamza—as always—just slapped me on the shoulder like we were cousins reunited at a wedding.

"How are you doing, *akhi*?" Nazif asked, handing a wrapped order to a customer without even glancing.

"Alhamdulillah. How are you all? How's the family?"

"All good, alhamdulillah," they chorused like a choir, nodding as though rehearsed.

"I'm telling you," Hamza said, pointing a finger at my chest, "this one is in love. Look at him. Eyes like he just left Jannah."

The others chuckled. I tried not to blush.

Love?

Could it be that simple? I was enjoying this, enjoying being married to her, the closeness, being able to touch her, feel the softness of her skin, the comfort of her presence. But there was the weight too, heavier than any moment of pleasure—guilt.

She didn't know why I married her, not fully. She didn't know the ways I had depended on her presence, how it had kept me steady, how selfishly I'd used the excuse of my duty to her to anchor myself.

And yet... some selfish part of me wanted more. Wanted this to turn into something real, something deeper than obligation or guilt. Wanted to let myself fall in love with her, even if it was dangerous, even if it meant confronting feelings I wasn't sure I deserved. Could I? Could

I truly love her and still honor her trust, protect her, and not let my mistakes define the space between us?

"What are you hiding from us, Badr?" Kareem leaned on the counter, chin on his fist. "Who's the lucky girl, eh? Some model from Tangier? A poet from Fez?"

I scratched my jaw, unsure. I wasn't ashamed, but Habiba had asked to keep it quiet at the office. This wasn't the office, but still. She was figuring things out. Maybe we both were.

But something in me didn't want to reduce her to a 'maybe'. Not here. Not to these people who celebrated even the smallest joys as if they were their own.

"Nikah is done. Alhamdulillah," I said, quietly proud.

There was a beat of silence before the place erupted.

"La ilaha illallah!" Habib roared, rounding the counter first. "Our brother is a married man!"

They swarmed me. Hugs, cheek kisses, back slaps. Even the guy from the back who usually only came out for quick salams joined in. Someone kissed my forehead. Someone else kissed my hand.

SubhanAllah. I barely knew some of them by name, but they cheered like family.

"El-asad bta'na la'a labweto akhiran!" *Our lion finally found his lioness!* Hamza bellowed. "You're done for, habibi. May Allah bless your marriage with a thousand babies!"

"Ameen," everyone echoed.

I laughed through the heat crawling up my neck. "Thank you, wallahi. Thank you all."

Their joy was so genuine, it made the moment feel… heavier. More meaningful. I hadn't even told my extended family yet. But here I was, getting celebrated in a shawarma shop like I'd just won a Nobel Prize.

"Well, can I order now?" I teased once the chaos settled.

174

"Of course! Seven shawarmas—three spicy, four normal," Hamza said, already halfway behind the counter.

"Just two spicy," I corrected, raising a finger.

They froze. Then they all howled again, laughing like a pack of teenagers.

"Aha! One for you, one for your wife!" Nazif grinned. "She's Moroccan? Egyptian? Wait Canadian? Maybe Sudanese?"

I shook my head, lips twitching. "You'll never guess."

"Bring her here next time!" Habib insisted. "We must make her eat the very spicy one. If she can handle that, she can handle you."

They laughed again, and I joined them. As much as I hated being the center of attention, I didn't mind it now. Not with them. Not today.

"With fries inside, please," I added once the noise faded again.

Hamza nodded solemnly. "Of course, fries. What kind of man do you think I am?"

I thought about heading to the car, but I knew better. If I left, they'd follow me and bombard Habiba with salaam's and wild questions. She'd probably never speak to me again.

So I waited inside, soaking in the smoky scent, the low drone of Arabic, and the warmth of being surrounded by men who didn't need to know you deeply to love you loudly. It felt grounding, even as my thoughts kept drifting to her.

When I glanced out the window, the glass was fogged over, hiding her from view. I wondered what was going through her mind.

She's shy. She tries to hide it, but I see it anyway. And me? I'm trying my hardest to make everything feel normal when it isn't. Yes, arranged marriages happen every day, but this... this feels different. Faster. Stranger.

How do I make it easier? How do I help her breathe inside this new life? I can't let us live in this tight, awkward silence forever. If anyone has to step up, it's me. I have to make her feel comfortable, help her

175

soften into it without overwhelming her like I almost did earlier at the office.

I thought by having her get closer to me by tying my tie or by checking in and offering to drop her off everywhere I was helping, but that did nothing but overwhelm her. I can be too forceful sometimes.

I was in the middle of figuring it out when my order was finally called. After more congratulations and promises I'd return soon, I collected the food and escaped outside.

Sure enough, when I reached the car, I saw the men peeking out the shop window, craning their necks to catch one last glimpse. At least they didn't come running out. I waved at them, a small smile tugging at my mouth, before sliding behind the wheel.

"You're about to taste the best shawarma ever," I said, holding up the bag.

"Isn't that what they all say?" she teased, reaching for it.

"Wait." I grinned. "Let's eat it over a nice view."

She raised a brow. "You're quite the romantic, aren't you?"

"Oh, forgive me for trying to impress a lady." I joked, starting the engine.

It didn't take long—five minutes, maybe—to reach the overlook. My family comes here often, caravanning in two cars to this same spot. Even with other vehicles parked nearby, there was enough distance to make it feel private.

We stepped out of the car, the cold night air brushing our faces. Habiba looked around, her grin wide, genuine. "I like this. It's pretty."

She looked different here, lighter. Less stiff, more herself.

"You've never been here?" I asked, locking the car.

"I've barely been anywhere, to be honest. Always at home, too much to do."

Something in me pinched. Every time she opened her mouth, I felt that urge again, to shield her, to wrap her in every good thing she'd

176

ever been denied. I wanted to show her how much love the world has to offer.

"Well," I said quietly, "get ready. Someday, I'll show you the world."

She looked at me, her smile softening. "InshaAllah."

I smiled back. "InshaAllah."

"Hop on." I patted the trunk of the car and held out my hand.

She looked at it like it was some sort of test, but placed her hand in mine anyway. Despite the hesitation, she held on.

For the few seconds it took to steady her onto the trunk, I memorized everything: the softness of her palm, the way her slender fingers reached just past my pinky, the warmth lingering against my skin. Most of all, the way it fit so naturally, perfectly into mine.

Once she was settled, I climbed up beside her and unwrapped the shawarma, handing her one.

"Thanks," she said softly. I unwrapped mine too, but I didn't take a bite. I waited. I wanted to see her reaction first.

She took one, chewed, then nodded with approval. "Okay… this didn't disappoint. I can't tell if I'm just starving or if it's actually that good."

I gave her a flat, unimpressed look. "It is that good. I know it. I have amazing taste."

She smirked. "Hmm, sure. If you hadn't given me those pastries, I'd be asking for more proof."

I brushed invisible dust off my shoulder with exaggerated pride. "Please. I'm a man of excellent choices."

She laughed and then, to my surprise, shoved me lightly. It was the first time she touched me willingly. Not because she had to. I had to swallow back the rush that came with it, had to keep my face steady. If she could hear half the things running through my head right now, she'd think I was insane.

"You're so weird," she chuckled, taking another bite.

"You married me anyway," I shot back.

She was quick. "I don't remember having a better choice."

"Oooh—wow. Ouch." I clutched my chest in mock injury. "So if you had another option, you wouldn't have picked me?"

She glanced at me, then looked away just as fast, a secret smile tugging at her lips. "Too early to tell."

"Fair enough," I said, grinning.

We ate in silence, and I spent the whole time racking my brain for something to say. Every attempt felt hollow, every joke too light, every comment too heavy with the weight of what I'd hidden. And then, finally, a thought came, and without overthinking it, I said it.

"Let's go on a date," I blurted out.

Even as the words left my mouth, my mind raced. Why not? We're here. Allah put us here, together. Right now, in this exact moment. I don't need to dwell on what's been, on my past mistakes, on the guilt that has clung to me like a second skin. All that matters is now and her.

Maybe it's reckless, maybe it's foolish, but what if forgetting was the way forward? What if I could just let everything be exactly as it is, without pretending, without hiding, and just experience it? Just love it, all the way, fully, without dragging the shadows of the past along?

I looked at her, hoping she'd see the sincerity behind my words, the small, quiet decision I was making in that instant: to start fresh, to let us start fresh, and to just... let this be real.

She turned her head slowly, staring at me like I'd lost my mind. "...Ok?"

"Think about it," I said, leaning forward. "We got married so suddenly, and now—just like that—we're bound together. It makes sense that things feel awkward. I know you feel it too. So... what if we start over? Build something from the ground up. Get to know each other. Be better friends first."

She didn't answer right away, but the thoughtful look on her face told me she wasn't against the idea. That was enough encouragement for me. I hopped off the trunk and stood in front of her dramatically.

"Habiba Mukhtar," I said, bowing slightly, "would you do me the honor of going on a date with me?"

She burst into laughter, shaking her head. "Nope. Sorry, I'm married."

I grinned. "So am I. But they don't have to know. It'll be our little secret." I stepped closer.

She pressed her finger against my chest, pushing me back. "I don't know about you, but my husband is a very big man with very big muscles. He might beat you up."

I laughed, dropping my voice. "My wife is a mean, grumpy lady. But I don't think she would mind sharing."

Her brows lifted. "I'll have you know that I don't like to share. I can get very possessive."

"Lucky for you," I said, smirking, "you won't be sharing. You're just borrowing what's already yours."

She laughed, eyes sparkling. "Ok, that was a good one. I'll say yes for that line alone."

"I'm quite good with my words," I said, feigning pride.

"Mhm," she hummed, tilting her head. "I can tell."

We held each other's gaze. Even in the dark, her eyes glimmered, pulling me in deeper than I was ready for. I looked away first. I can't believe I looked away first. This woman was doing things to me I couldn't explain.

I hopped back onto the trunk beside her, pretending like nothing happened, and returned to my shawarma.

She was smiling wider now, genuinely smiling. I knew bringing her out tonight was the right call. Staying home would've only eaten at her, made her feel guilty about my fight with my family. I didn't want her carrying that weight.

Our marriage might not have been born from love, but it didn't change the fact that she was my wife. And my parents raised me to protect, not just my siblings, but my wife too. Always.

"I really am sorry, Habiba," I said quietly.

She turned to me, brows slightly furrowed.

"For the way they treated you," I continued. "It was my fault. I shouldn't have just sat there, expecting you to tolerate it until they were ready to accept you. It wasn't even your job to win them over, and you still tried. I'm sorry."

I don't know what I thought would happen.

Maybe I believed things would just... settle. That if I gave it time, my mother and sister would come around. That Habiba would somehow bridge the gap all on her own.

But now that I think about it, really think about it, how cruel was that?

I brought her into that house but never made sure she felt like a wife. I stood by, watched them ignore her, speak around her, act like she was furniture and I did nothing.

What kind of man does that?

I told myself I married her to protect her, to give her a better life. But how is this better? What good is a roof if the people under it make you feel invisible.

She deserved someone who'd stand beside her . And I owe her more. So much more.

She let out a long, exhausted sigh, her gaze fixed somewhere.

"You know," she said, "I wished I was back home... I told myself I'd rather be somewhere I was hated but noticed, than in a place where I was simply invisible."

That hurt. A lot. Because I promised her better. I told her this marriage would be a way out, not a detour back into pain.

But then she turned toward me, softer now, her lips pulled into a thin smile, "But truthfully Badr, I have smiled these two days more than I have in an entire year."

She laughed lightly, the sound like the wind brushing her heart.

"What I'm about to say might sound selfish..." she hesitated, adjusting her hijab, "but, at first I wanted this to work just so I wouldn't prove my grandfather right. I didn't want him to say I told you so. But now... I want this to work because when I saw the way your family loves—the way you love—I wanted to learn how to love like that too."

Her eyes lifted to mine, steady but vulnerable.

"Maybe this marriage is a blessing in disguise. Maybe Allah put me here for a reason. And I suddenly don't want to leave just like that, Badr. I want to fight for this. I believe one day you and I will learn to love each other. But even if we don't, at least we'll part knowing we tried."

A slow smile spread across my face. The tension in my chest eased, like a weight I hadn't realized I'd been carrying had lifted. Air returned to my lungs. Relief. Hope. Maybe we could just... start over. Pretend the past hadn't clawed at me so violently, forget the shadows that had followed me here. If she was willing to try, then I was too.

I reached out, brushing my thumb along the back of her hand. "Then let's build it," I said. "A home. One where you'll never question your place again."

And I meant every word. I felt it was possible to move forward without guilt, without fear—just us, here and now, starting fresh.

By the time Habiba and I got home, it was way past midnight. We talked for so long that neither of us realized how quickly the hours slipped away.

Going to bed didn't feel awkward—not even a little. I didn't feel like I was lying beside a stranger anymore. Habiba seemed more comfortable too. She smiled the entire time, and when she laughed, she leaned into me without hesitation. It's only been a single day, yet I could already see so much progress between us.

The next morning was a weekend. Normally, I would've gone downstairs for breakfast, but this time I refused. I wanted Ma and Hana to understand that I wasn't going to let things slide anymore. If they wanted my respect, they had to respect my wife first.

When I left my room, I walked straight to Ba's. I could hear Ma's voice drifting from the kitchen, so I knew she wasn't with him.

I stepped inside. Ba was sitting on the bed, a book open across his lap, pen in hand. He glanced up at me through his reading glasses before returning to his notes.

"Rani jit nsalem 'lik," *I came to greet you.* I greeted softly.

"Kidayr?" *How are you?* he replied without looking up.

"'Hamdulilllah." I walked over, took his hand, and kissed it before letting him return to his writing. Then I stood by his leg, lowering my head. "Ba… I'm sorry. I was very disrespectful yesterday." My voice was low. I had to ask for forgiveness. I'd reacted in a way I never had before. And even though Ba had kept quiet, saying nothing, I knew I was wrong.

He stopped writing. Slowly, he looked up at me. But instead of the disappointment I expected, I found a small smile tugging at his lips as he set his glasses aside.

"Badr…" His voice was calm. "I want you to know—I'm proud of the man you've become."

I had to close my eyes for a moment, just to absorb his words. My father had praised me many times in my life, but this was the greatest compliment I had ever received from him.

"Standing up for your wife, even against your own family, was the right thing to do," he continued. "As much as I disliked what happened yesterday, I'm proud of the way you reacted. I'm happy you stood by the truth."

"Allah ykhalik lia, Ba," *May Allah protect you for me, Ba.* I grinned. "I'm glad you understood. But like I said yesterday, I'm going to start looking for a new place for us."

"You should," he nodded firmly. "You're a married man now. You're on your way to starting your own family. If you hadn't said it yourself, I would have kicked you out."

I chuckled under my breath.

"Wallah," he said, shaking his head with a smile, "I always complained to your mother about how she pampers you boys. I feared you'd grow into Mama's boys, unable to do anything without her. But after seeing how you and Zain reacted yesterday... I know we raised you right."

"Shoukran, Ba," I smiled, warmth filling my chest. "Ana ghadi nkhalik tkammel" *I'll leave you to finish.*

I turned toward the door, but before I could leave, his voice stopped me. "Tsam7 m'a mmk, a Badr." *Apologize to your mother, Badr.*

I turned back.

"Like I said," Ba continued, his gaze steady, "you did the right thing defending Habiba. But the way you spoke to your mother was wrong. Don't ever repeat that. Because if it does happen again, I will stand up for my wife the same way you did for yours." His tone was pointed, sharp with warning.

"I will. I'm sorry again," I replied earnestly, then stepped out.

I arrived back in my room with a smile tugging at my lips, phone in hand as I texted Ayaan to meet later. I still didn't tell him, and I knew he'd be furious. If the roles were reversed, I'd be mad too.

Habiba had gone back to sleep after Fajr and hasn't woken up since. It was frustrating. I wanted to talk to her but she was still curled up, breathing softly. Maybe I didn't have anything to say yet, but when she woke up, I'd find something.

Last night's conversation played in my head on repeat. It gave me hope, made me believe in what could grow between two people who chose to stand beside each other. I made a promise to myself: no more dragging the past into this. No more guilt gnawing at the edges of our life. That was behind us.

From now on, I would simply try to be present, try to protect her peace, try to build something good with her. Every thought, every intention, would be for the future we were shaping together. Her past and mine were just that: past. What mattered now was us, here, and the life we could carve out from this moment forward.

After showering, I toweled off, slipped into my boxers and pajama pants, and stood before the mirror. My gaze landed on my muscles and I couldn't stop the grin spreading across my face. I flexed, slowly, turning a little, admiring the cut of my shoulders and the way the steam glistened on my skin.

She thinks I'm strong.

I started working out for my own sanity, to keep my mind in check. But hearing Habiba acknowledge it yesterday was the most rewarding moment I'd had with my body. Her words replayed like a song, each note sweet and dangerous.

I looked at the shirt hanging on the rack. I could put it on... or I could take my chances. Pretend to step out casually, just to see if she noticed. Maybe flex, but subtly. Realistically.

I counted down at the door—three, two, one—then twisted the knob, stepping into the room, chest loose but deliberate, eyes lowered. Every muscle just tense enough to show.

I glanced at the bed.

Nothing.

Habiba was still curled up beneath the duvet, face soft, lips parted, her breathing steady. She looked peaceful. Untouchable. Beautiful.

I cleared my throat. Nothing. I cracked my neck, loud. Still nothing.

I "dropped" my phone. It clattered on the floor. I bent slowly, letting every movement roll across my back and arms. If she opened her eyes now—Nothing.

I straightened, sighing, running a hand over my chest and through my wet curls.

"Wah," I muttered under my breath, chuckling. "Ana li kunt n7sab l'hub huwa tchaf... daba kanflexi l'wahda 3inaha mghamdin. Ya Rab, wach tab lit?" *I thought love was found in the gaze, but here I am flexing for the one whose eyes stay closed. Oh Lord, is this my test?*

I couldn't help the grin tugging at my mouth. I shook my head.

"What has this woman done to me?" I whispered.

I wasn't used to this. Wanting someone to look at me.

I stood by the bed, waiting like a fool. Five minutes later, I sighed and walked to the mirror. Ruffling my hair, rubbing deodorant under my arms.

That's when I heard it.

"Astagfirullah... Astagfirullah..." muttered under the duvet.

I turned, caught off guard, only to see Habiba hiding beneath the blanket, covers pulled over her face.

Of course. The last time she'd seen me shirtless, she'd practically sprayed Astagfirullahs at me like bullets. Realizing how stupid I'd been, I grabbed my shirt and pulled it on before stepping back to the mirror to fix my curls.

"Habiba?" I said softly.

"Hmm?" She peeked one eye out, saw I was dressed, and finally uncovered herself, smiling. "Good morning."

"What's so good about the morning?" I grumbled.

Her neck was bare, only her scarf around her head. I'd seen necks all my life, but somehow hers felt... different. Wrong to notice, yet good.

Maybe I should start firing Astaghfirullahs back at her every time her neck shows. Let's see how she likes it.

She got off the bed, chuckling as she walked to the wardrobe.

"That doesn't sound like Badr, should I be worri-" The door suddenly burst open.

I was used to it, but Habiba wasn't. She got startled, grabbing the nearest cloth to cover herself. In a flash, I was at the door, blocking it before it swung wider. Ahmed froze on the other side, wide-eyed at my sudden movement.

"Ahmed," I softened, crouching to his level. "Good morning."

"Good morning," he yawned, rubbing his eyes.

"You slept in today, hmm?" I ruffled his hair.

"Yeah. I watched Fast and Furious with Ba yesterday. I was gonna call you but you were not home." he grinned.

"I'll watch with you next time, ok?" I smiled. He nodded. Then I hesitated, not wanting to sound harsh, but needing to draw the line. "Ahmed... you know how Habiba is here now? We're married, remember?"

He nodded, unbothered.

"Well... now it's not just me in the room. So before you come in, you need to knock. Always." My tone softened, but I fixed him with a serious look to make sure it landed.

"Ok," he said quickly, hugging me before darting off.

When I turned back, Habiba was by the wardrobe, watching quietly. "You shouldn't have done that," she sighed, hand pressed to her forehead.

"Why?" I frowned, walking closer.

"Your mother and Hana already hate me. I don't need him hating me too."

"You don't need to sacrifice your privacy to be loved by them," I said firmly. "If they're going to love you, they'll do it while respecting the boundaries you set. Promise me you won't compromise your comfort for their approval."

Her eyes dropped, lips pressed tight. She looked away, face

caught between annoyance and contemplation.

"Habiba, look at me," I said, quieter than usual but still firm. She did, reluctantly, like it pained her to obey me. Her eyes met mine, suspicious, soft, stubborn.

"Promise me."

There was a flicker in her eyes. It took a few seconds, maybe longer than it should've, but she gave a small, reluctant nod.

I smiled.

17

ما يَلْبَثُ الحُبُّ أَن تَبدو شَواهِدُه
مِن الْمُحِبِّ وَإِن لَم يُبْدِهِ أَبَدا

Love's essence, despite every effort to hide,
Will inevitably surface, with nowhere to bide.

- الأحوص الأنصاري

When I got out of the bathroom fully dressed and showered, Badr was sprawled on the bed, laptop balanced on his thighs. "Habiba, come look at this," he called without looking up.

I walked over and sat beside him, leaving the usual safe distance between us. Though, for the first time, a part of me wanted to close it, to lean in, maybe even breathe in his scent. Strange. Yesterday, I'd never felt more comfortable with Badr.

Sharing shawarma in the cold, talking about everything and nothing while the snow drifted down around us, felt almost magical. When it grew too chilly, we moved into the car and kept talking, but I found myself wishing the night would never end. It all went by too quickly.

Enjoying Badr's company had always been effortless; he had a way of making people feel at ease. I meant every word I said to him. I wanted to try, not for my grandfather anymore, not out of duty, but simply because I wanted to.

I craned my neck to peek at the screen. Apartments. Rows and rows of listings. "You were serious about moving?" I frowned.

"Of course. Why not?"

"Because of yesterday? It's past, Badr. It won't happen again.

I was just... overwhelmed." My words came quickly, almost rushed, I didn't want to be the reason he left his family's home.

He sighed, set the laptop between us, and turned toward me. His gaze softened but carried weight.

"I know you think I'm doing this because of you. But it's more than that. We're married now. Our life, yours and mine, needs its own space."

I bit my lip. "I know, it's just... so fast. The marriage was fast, everything was fast. If we move out now, it will only prove to your mother that I did Blackmagic on you, that I'm taking you away."

"It doesn't matter." His eyes didn't waver from mine. "My priority shifts now. It's about giving you the space and security you deserve. And I can't do that in a house where my father holds the authority, not me."

"But I'm sure he wouldn't mind—"

"It's not about him minding." His tone firmed. "It's about me being fair to you. If someone says something to you, I might hesitate to answer out of respect, out of fear of crossing a line. I can't be your shield in a house where the roof doesn't belong to me."

I stayed quiet. He was right. But it still left a weight in my chest.

"My family will always be my family. I'll never abandon them," he continued. "But I refuse to put you in a place where I'd have to pick between my father's authority and your peace. I want to be a husband who protects you, not one who stands silently."

His words were steady, deliberate. Realistically, I knew he was right, we were meant to move elsewhere.

"Islam honors parents, yes," he added gently, "but it also encourages a man to start something new with his wife, a space where the rules we follow are ours."

I sighed and nodded, though in my chest I whispered a prayer that his mother wouldn't stab me in my sleep once she heard the news.

"Ok?" he asked, studying me for signs of doubt.

189

I forced a small smile and nodded.

"Good. Look at this." He pushed the laptop toward me.

The apartment on the screen was cute, modern, the kind of place with glossy floors and clean lines but the price tag made my eyes widen.

"We're trying to move into a home, not go broke," I muttered.

He huffed, closed the laptop, and reached for his phone. A message came through, and instantly, his face lit up in a wide grin. The brightness of it pulled my lips into a smile before I even knew why.

"I have to go to the gym. With Ayaan," he said, but it sounded more like a question.

"Okay."

"Great," he clapped his hands together, boyish excitement flickering across his face. "Do you want to go anywhere? I can drop you off."

I shook my head. My weekends are usually quiet, I'd clean, then take the kids to see their father. The thought of Baba flickered too, and I wondered if he'd finally cooled down. He couldn't stay angry forever.

Badr snapped open a tub of protein powder, scooped some into a shaker with water, twisted the lid on, then handed it to me with a grin.

"Here. Shake this for me while I pack."

I blinked at the bottle, then at him. "Seriously?"

"Seriously." He was already pulling clothes from the closet.

I stood dead center in the room, gripping the shaker, and began shaking it stiffly, like I was starting a generator.

Badr glanced back, chuckled. "Harder. Give it your best."

I squinted at him. Once the bag was packed, he walked over, plucked the shaker from my hands, opened it, and peered inside.

"There's still clumps," he announced, tilting it so I could see. "Look."

"Then shake it yourself," I muttered.

He laughed, snapped the lid back on. "You're not holding it

right." He took my hand gently, guiding my fingers around the cap. His palm was warm, steady. "You press here, or it'll fly off and hit me in the face."

"That's tempting," I said under my breath.

His grin deepened. With his hand still over mine, he gave the shaker a few firm shakes. His forearm flexed close to my face. A vein rose with the movement, and I instantly turned away.

"Astagfirullah," I whispered.

He raised a brow but said nothing, handing the shaker back. I tried again, but my grip was smaller. The bottle slipped. He caught it mid-air, laughing. "Big temper, tiny fists. SubhanAllah."

"Are you mocking me?" I glared at him.

"Relax, Lalla Habiba," he teased, voice low, almost playful. "You can be the storm. I'll be right behind you to throw the punches."

Then, with one hand, he ruffled my head like I was a child and grabbed his gym bag with the other.

I froze, stunned.

Did he just... pat my head?

I stared at the door long after it closed, my scarf crooked, dignity slightly bruised.

"Ya Rab," I muttered, tilting my face upward. With a deep sigh, I began tidying. I cleaned the room before turning to the wardrobe.

His wardrobe was immaculate—ties lined up in one drawer, cufflinks in another, shirts pressed and hanging on one side, suits on the other. The smaller drawers held watches, six of them, all neatly arranged, gleaming with the kind of quiet arrogance only high-end pieces carry. Another cupboard revealed rows of shoes—ten rows, five pairs each— every shelf softly backlit like a boutique display.

I'd always known Badr to be a man of taste—expensive shoes, tailored suits, the kind of shirts that whispered money but I hadn't realized it ran this deep.

Shaking my head with a soft chuckle, I began.

The clothes were scattered across the floor like fallen leaves when a knock sounded at the door. I had already tied my scarf into a quick kallabi, so at least I didn't have to scramble for modesty.

The door creaked open. Hana stepped inside, her gaze sweeping over the mess before landing on me. Her jaw tightened. She turned on her heel, already halfway back out.

"Hana!" My voice was firmer than I intended. She froze for a heartbeat, then kept walking. Desperation nudged me. "Hana, please. Please, can we talk?" This time, my tone was softer, pleading.

Her shoulders rose and fell with a deep sigh before she shut the door behind her. She faced me, arms crossed tight over her chest, chin tilted like a shield. I opened my mouth to speak, but she beat me to it, words rushing out like fire, sharp and hot.

"I don't have a problem with you, Habiba. I'm sorry for making you cry yesterday. You seem like a good person. But I hate how things have been between Badr and me ever since you came here. If it's going to stay like that, then I don't want you here." Her voice trembled with heat, though her eyes betrayed something else, hurt.

"That's fair," I said gently, forcing a smile. "I'm sorry things changed between you and your brother because of me. I promise, I never wanted to make things weird. If I could—"

She cut me off, her voice rising again. "Why couldn't you just wait? He could've done things the right way. Brought you home, introduced you, had a proper wedding! But you rushed him—"

This time, I cut her off, steady but firm.

"Badr was forced into marrying me, but not by me." My throat tightened, but I pushed through. "I admit, I should've fought harder when my grandfather suggested it. But I'm only human. We're all selfish sometimes. My choices were to marry a man twice my age or marry Badr—someone I already knew. Allah gave me a way out, and I took it. I didn't plan for this to happen, but if I had the chance again, I'd still make the same choice."

Her glare faltered. She blinked, lips parting as if to speak, but no words came. The anger in her posture wavered, her arms loosening ever so slightly at her sides.

I stood, walking toward her until I was directly in front of her. My voice softened. "I'm sorry, Hana. For the way things have been with you and Badr. He doesn't like it either, but we can make it easier for him… and for ourselves. Even if we can't be close, we can at least be civil."

Her frown lingered, but her shoulders slumped. A sigh slipped out of her. "I didn't mean to make you cry," she murmured, voice smaller now.

I rubbed the back of my neck, smiling sheepishly. "I know. I just… So much happened the past few days, so much changed, I got overwhelmed. Your family is so beautiful, and I wanted to be part of it. But then I realized maybe I'd never be accepted, and it hurt. That's why I broke down."

Hana's brows pinched. She lifted her gaze to mine, softer this time. "Your family sounds mean," she said bluntly. "I can't imagine what that must be like."

"It's complicated," I whispered.

"It sounds worse than complicated," she muttered, lips twitching as if she wanted to frown and smile at the same time.

I chuckled, then held out my hand. "Friends?"

She stared at it for a long moment before her own mouth curved upward. Slowly, she shook my hand. "Sure. If it makes Badr stop ignoring me, then yes."

"I'll talk to him," I promised, relief warming my chest.

She nodded and turned toward the door. I thought she'd leave, but she lingered there, hand resting on the knob. Her body was still, head tilted slightly like she was wrestling with a thought. Finally, she turned back, shy but earnest.

"Would you… like some help with that? I don't have anything to do right now."

My first instinct was to decline, I could finish it myself. But then I realized this was an opportunity, a fragile bridge offered to me. I smiled. "I'd love that."

Hana's lips tugged upward just a little as she walked over, picking her way between the piles of fabric until she sank down beside me.

"You have nice clothes," she said, running her hand over the fabric. "Is this how you dress back home?"

"Yeah, this is Atampa," I said, holding up a skirt-and-blouse set. "And this is Lapaya." I lifted another. "I barely wear most of them. If you like anything, I can have it fixed to fit you."

Her eyes lit up for a fleeting second before she masked it, quickly pulling out something to fold.

"So, I hear you like to read," I said, trying to nudge us into lighter conversation.

"Yeah," she said with a small shrug. "My room is full. Books are piled on the ground now."

"What kind?"

"Romance. Fantasy. Anything good, really."

"That sounds nice."

"Not really," she muttered, cheeks puffing. "Between all these brothers spoiling me and reading too much romance, my standards are way too high."

A laugh escaped me. "Well, as long as men like your brothers and father exist, you should be fine."

That earned a giggle from her, quiet but genuine.

We spent the next few minutes folding together, our movements syncing, small talk filling the space. The tension that once hung between us had thinned, replaced with something gentler. By the time the last garment was tucked neatly away, I realized the room felt lighter—so did my chest.

18

BADR

وَما نَظَرَت عيني إلى ذي بَشاشَة
من النّاسِ إلّا أنتِ في العَيْنِ أُمْلَحُ

Whenever my eyes behold a face lit with gentleness,
You are the one who shines more beautifully in their view.

- كُثير عزّة

Ayaan is not clingy, he keeps to himself. But when it comes to the people he cares about, he likes to be involved. Him not knowing I got married would absolutely sting him. So when I showed up to his house, I didn't say a thing. He is rich, like embarrassingly rich. Generational-wealth rich. Which is why we don't buy gym memberships, we just use the gym in his villa.

I let the usual warm-up routine play out. It was biceps day. We've been training together for over ten years; what began as a pastime has turned into maintenance. Once we hit the size we wanted, we focused on holding it. Now we push heavy until our muscles say otherwise.

I spotted him on the bench press first, helping him place the bar back when he reached his limit, then it was my turn. He grinned at me like a man with a plan. "Make it 175," he suggested.

"Why?" I frowned. "I always do 150."

"Spice it up," he said, that cheeky smile curling. I shrugged. If I did what he wanted today, maybe he'd be less furious once I told him.

He loaded the plates. I lay back, palms finding the cold knurl of the bar. I adjusted my grip until it felt right, focused, ready. The first reps felt like warm-up, the bar moving luxuriously under my hands. Midset, between breaths, Ayaan's voice cut through.

"You've been awfully quiet and willing today," he said. I didn't answer. I pushed. Another rep. "You doing something that I don't know about?" he pressed.

"What makes you say that?" I grunted, forcing the bar up.

"Years of friendship, man. You look guilty." He watched me like he was reading the fine print.

Sweat threaded down my neck. The room hummed metal, the distant sound of football playing on the tv, the sound of us breathing. This was probably the best time to speak. I had nowhere to hide, and maybe seeing me in a vulnerable situation would make him feel bad for me.

"I went to Habiba's," I started, forcing the bar up, voice tight with effort. "To help."

"Oh yeah, how did that go?" He asked, leaning forward, his hands ready to help me as I was beginning to reach my limit.

"Terrible..." I said, pushing the bar up once more. "One thing led to another and—agh!" The weight screamed in my arms.

He didn't help yet, but his hands still hovered, ready to help. "What did you do?" he asked.

I pushed, teeth bared, the bar trembling under me. The word tore out of me—half scream, half confession. "I married her."

For a beat the gym narrowed to knurling and lactic fire. Then the space above me emptied. Ayaan left.

Time slowed. My arms shook. The bar dipped as my grip weakened. Instinct screamed for him to be there, to steady the lift, to slap it back onto the rack when I failed. Instead I had to find the strength to do it myself. Somewhere under the burn and the shock I dug up one more reserve. I heaved, hips and shoulders driving together, and slid the bar back onto the hooks with the kind of clatter that wakes sleeping dogs.

"Dude!" I barked, scrambling to my feet, sweat stinging my eyes. "You left me for dead?"

He kept walking, towel slung, back turned, footsteps heavy down the hall. I grabbed a towel too and chased him out of the gym, the echo of my own footsteps catching up to his.

"Can we talk?" I followed him into the hall. He ducked into the shower area and slammed the stall closed.

In hind sight, maybe confessing on a bench press was not my most tactical move.

I got into another one of the stalls and ran the water while trying to speak to him, to explain that everything happened so fast, that I didn't have the chance to meet him. We both showered and changed but he still refused to respond to me.

It was only when we reached the dining table and Ayaan had finally eaten that he seemed to realize he needed to respond. He froze, fork mid-air, eyes wide. "I still can't believe you got married and didn't tell me," he said, voice half-grumble, half-laugh. "We literally met at Jum'a yesterday. That was a choice, not circumstances!"

"We were both in a hurry to get back to work," I explained, "and I didn't want the conversation to get cut short, so I decided to wait until we could meet for coffee that same day. But then Ma and Hana made Habiba cry, and I had to take her away to cool off."

He just stared at me, disbelief written across his face.

"All that happened, and I'm only finding out now?!" He jabbed the last pieces of fries with his fork. "I'm gonna go to your place and side with Ma just to spite you!"

"Please don't do that!" I groaned, dragging my palm over my face. "I need this to settle. She's been through enough already. I don't want to pile on her."

He chewed his lip, jaw moving. "You sound like… a husband," he muttered, incredulous.

I chuckled, slipping a piece of lettuce into my mouth. "I *am* a husband," I whispered, the words catching slightly in my throat.

"Crap! Man, you're married!" He dropped his fork and lunged at me, grabbing my hair in mock horror. "Just like that! To the same woman I was hoping you'd marry! Oh my god!"

He pushed out of his chair, shock morphing into a huge, uncontrollable grin. I stood too, reaching to pat his back, but before I could, he wrapped me in a bear hug.

"Congratulations, man! Allahumma Barik!" He patted my back repeatedly. "I'm so freaking happy for you!"

When we pulled apart, he was still shaking his head, trying to process it all.

"We can't just leave it like this, we have to plan a nikah, something proper!" he insisted, eyes sparkling.

I sighed, a little regretful. "Unfortunately, her grandfather wants nothing to do with it," I said, shrugging. "I think we'll just do a *walima*."

"What?!" He plopped back into his chair. "Wait start from the beginning. Tell me everything all over again."

By the time I got home, it was past lunch. I dropped the grocery bags on the kitchen counter. Hana was already there, rifling through them like a scavenger on the hunt—she knew I always came back with snacks and loved being the first to claim them.

Ma, on the other hand, pretended I didn't exist. She stood at the counter, chopping onions, lips pressed tight.

I did what I usually do, I walked over, kissed her head, and wrapped her in a hug. Nothing. Not even a twitch.

"Ma?" I said softly. She didn't stop cutting. "Ma?" I reached for her hand to still the knife. She swatted my hand away.

I glanced at Hana. She giggled but offered no help, of course.

"Ma—"

"Badr, leave me alone. Just leave me." Her voice was sharp, cutting deeper than the knife in her hand.

But I didn't back down. "Can you please talk to me? I'm sorry

199

about yesterday. But Ma, you have to understand, you raised me, all of us, to stand up for what's right. And you weren't. I shouldn't have raised my voice, I know. Wallahi, it hurt me to speak to you like that. I'm sorry."

Her knife slowed. She exhaled heavily. "I forgive you," she said at last, though her tone was reluctant. "Now go sort the groceries."

"Ma..." I caught her gaze, holding it. "Please, go easy on her. She's been through a lot. Really, you can't even imagine. And you always liked to remind us, so let me remind you today that Allah said in the quran—Wa laa tusa'-'ir khaddaka linnaasi wa laa tamshi fil ardi maarahan innal laaha laa yuhibbu kulla mukhtaalin fakhoor." *And do not turn your nose up to people, nor walk pridefully upon the earth. Surely God does not like whoever is arrogant, boastful.*

I held her hand until I saw the familiar softness return to her eyes, that warmth I always loved. Relief washed over me. But then she shook her head again, disappointment etching across her face. "You're right, I shouldn't have been mad at her, I should have been mad at you." She reached over and slapped me on the head "Have you lost your mind? Is there nothing in there?"

"I said I'm sorry," I mumbled, rubbing the spot. She reached to do it again but I dodged it and pulled her into a side hug. "I'm sorry."

She tried to glare, but I could see it, she had forgiven me. No matter how mad she got, Ma was always soft at heart.

Once I finished in the kitchen, I headed upstairs. Habiba was on her computer, typing quickly, but she looked up when I came in.

"You're back," she said.

I smiled. "I am. What are you doing?"

"I still have some work from the office so I'm finishing up" She responded, making me freeze in my tracks.

"You're doing office work at home?" I asked, raising a brow.

"Yeah..." She said but it sounded more like a question "It's a nice pass time, don't you?"

"No, rule number one, never bring work home. That's an unspoken rule in this house." I reached to shut her computer, which to my surprise she didn't protest.

"Forget that," She said, placing the laptop on her side table, then she angled her body to me, her face lit. "I spoke to Hana today."

"You did?" I sat down beside her on the bed, slipping off my watch.

"Mmhmm." She nodded eagerly. "She came to see you, but I stopped her. We talked. I think she likes me."

The way her eyes shimmered, the glow in her smile, the lightness in her voice made my heart swell. I knew I should respond, but all I could do was watch her, struck by the simple beauty of her joy.

MashaAllah.

"You look happy," I said at last, smiling too.

"I am. I thought it would take years to get them to like me. It's only my third day, I'm so happy" She giggled.

God, I loved that sound. Her giggle. What was happening to me? "Adhakallahu Sinaki."

She smiled, seemingly proud of herself. If Habiba and I were a normal couple, this would be a time when I would pull her in and kiss her forehead, but I'm not sure how appropriate that would be.

"How did it go with Ayaan?" she asked.

I sighed. "I should've taken you with me. Maybe he wouldn't have been so dramatic."

Her brows arched, playful. "Why? Was he mad?"

"Yeah. But it's okay. He still loves me."

"Voluntarily?" she teased, eyes mischievous. "No blackmail involved?"

I grinned. "Just a sprinkle of guilt trip and an Espresso Shot of Charm. He doesn't play hard to get."

She laughed, and I got up, tugged my sweater over my head,

accidentally pulling my T-shirt halfway with it. By the time I fixed it, Habiba was already muttering "Astaghfirullah" like she always did whenever I was shirtless.

It used to be funny, cute even. Now it was getting under my skin. I had to say something.

"Can you stop saying 'Astaghfirullah' every time you see me shirtless? It's starting to get offensive."

She shot back without missing a beat, sparing me only a glance. "What's offensive is you walking around like that, giving Shaytan ideas."

"Shaytan?" I scoffed. "Sayyidati, those ideas are all yours. Shaytan can sit this one out." I turned to the wardrobe, then added over my shoulder, "We're married, remember?"

She made a face and turned the other way. "Please. Your muscles aren't distracting anyone… except maybe you."

I chuckled, rummaging through the wardrobe. "That's not what your stare said last time."

"I was zoning out. You just happened to be in the way," she huffed.

I pulled out a hoodie and walked over to her, grinning. I attempted to pat her head but she very efficiently swatted my hand away.

"I'll move closer next time," I teased. "Just in case you zone out again."

。❀ حب ❀ 。

Habiba helped with dinner today—Hana dragged her into the kitchen. I hovered close at first, ready to step in if anyone so much as frowned at her. But Hana was kind, Ma was still hesitant, but she wasn't rude.

I could tell from the way Habiba smiled while setting the table that she was happy. I caught her eye across the room and gave her a secret thumbs-up. Her smile widened instantly.

When the table was set, Habiba slid into the chair beside me, and after *Bismillah*, the usual chatter filled the table.

"Badr," Ba said between bites, "have you started looking for a place?"

Ma sighed deeply, her disapproval heavy enough to silence the air.

"Yeah, but nothing good." I admitted. "I was thinking of getting an agent. It'll be faster."

Ba nodded. "Find one as soon as possible. You two have been together three days and we still haven't done the *Walima*. Once you have a place, we'll prepare, invite people, and make it official. It's not right to be married quietly, best to announce it."

I nodded. "We'll visit the agency on Monday after work, *InshaAllah*."

Approval flashed across his face before Hana piped up, eyes gleaming. "Will we have a wedding party?"

"No party."

"Why not?" she groaned. "We want a party."

"We can have a party with no music or *you* can have a party of your own but it will have no association to my marriage. I don't want my marriage to start with music and haram."

She glared but dropped it, retreating into her food. Ba and Ma went on discussing having to inform our extended family. Ma's disapproval still lingered, but she couldn't fight what was already done. As much as I love her, I wasn't going to divorce Habiba to please anyone.

Dinner passed quickly. Zain and I handled the dishes, and afterward I climbed upstairs, expecting to find Habiba waiting. She wasn't in the room.

I didn't have to wonder. When I reached Hana's door and heard laughter inside, I stopped, smiling to myself. Of course. Hana could be overwhelming when she liked someone, she would latch on, over-chat, but I was glad it was Habiba this time. Despite that, I wanted my wife back.

I knocked and pushed the door open. Hana sat cross-legged on the carpet while Habiba perched on the bed, braiding her hair. Both turned and smiled at me.

"Badr, look! She's braiding my hair like hers!" Hana chirped.

Habiba's scarf was tied loosely, her neck fully exposed—something I was slowly getting used to.

"I can see that," I said, lowering myself to the ground beside Hana. She tried to kick me, but I caught her leg and tossed it away, laughing.

I stayed quiet, watching as Habiba finished the last two cornrows. Hana darted to the mirror, squealing. She would've kept Habiba there all night if I let her. But I was fading fast, my body heavy, eyes dragging. I sent them both to bed.

By the time Habiba and I returned to our room, I was yawning. She disappeared into the bathroom to change while I hurried through mine, then collapsed onto the mattress with a long, bone-deep sigh.

"So… Hana got to see your hair before me?" I muttered once she joined me.

"Are you going to cry about it?" she teased.

"Maybe. You leave me no choice," I said, my voice low and tired.

Her comeback was cut short by a soft knock. Both our heads turned. It could only be Ahmed.

"Come in," I called.

He slipped in, sheepish. I forced myself out of bed, smiling at him.

"*Ustadhi!*" I ruffled his hair. "What's up? Didn't I already tuck you in?"

"The lamp stopped again," he complained. "I hit it like you said."

The poor kid still struggled with darkness. That lamp Ba bought him years ago was too old now, flickering out whenever it pleased. On any other night, I'd have let him sleep beside me. But with Habiba there, it wasn't an option.

I exhaled slowly. "Seems I've been summoned to your room for the night. Go lie down, I'm coming."

His grin stretched ear to ear before he darted off.

I turned back to Habiba with a sheepish smile.

"Poor you," she said softly, pouting. "You look so tired."

"Well, at least he falls asleep quickly," I murmured, grabbing my pillow and phone. "I should've just left you with Hana. My bad."

She waved it off. "Go on. Don't keep him waiting." Her smile was warm, understanding.

I slipped down the hall. Ahmed was curled in bed already. His mattress was small, so I sat on the ground, propped my pillow on the edge, and rested my head there.

I kept quiet, hoping silence would help, but it still took him half an hour. My body ached, my eyelids burned. I probably shouldn't be doing this anymore, he needs to learn to sleep in the dark. Ba would scold me if he knew. But watching him struggle? He's only twelve. Let him have this a little longer.

When his breathing finally evened out into soft snores, I got up and tiptoed back, pillow in hand.

Pushing open the bedroom door, I found Habiba still awake. She was sitting cross-legged on the bed, her Qur'an open in her lap, the overhead lamp casting a warm halo over her. She looked peaceful, glowing.

"Tabaarak Allah..." I whispered.

Her gaze lifted, eyes lazy and warm. "You're back."

I rubbed the back of my neck and smiled, exhaustion heavy in my bones. "He took forever to fall asleep." She nodded, her expression soft. "You're still up?"

She flipped the page and said lightly, "I decided to read the Qur'an while waiting for you."

I paused by the edge of the bed, heart tugging just a little. "You stayed up for me?"

She glared playfully "You're not the only one who wants barakah."

"Allah yjazik bl'khir," *May Allah reward you.* I murmured and I sat down beside her, the mattress dipping slightly under my weight. I leaned in with a grin, voice low. "Are you sure you didn't just miss me?"

She didn't even turn, just raised a brow and shot me that long, withering glare she always gave when she didn't have the patience to humor my nonsense.

I laughed, holding up both hands. "Alright, alright—mashaAllah '3la niyetk. I won't ruin your barakah-chasing moment."

She exhaled, lips twitching in the smallest of smiles, and started to close the Qur'an.

"Wait." I placed my hand gently on hers. "Don't stop."

She looked at me, confused.

"I wanna listen to you recite," I said. "Just… keep going. Loud enough for me to hear."

She narrowed her eyes. "You want me to recite while you fall asleep?"

I laid back on the bed, arm under my head, looking up at her.

"No, until you feel sleepy. Come on, *khayr* on top of *khayr*. You get the reward of reciting, I get the reward of listening." I winked. "We'll both wake up angels."

She shook her head, but I saw the smile on her lips before she looked back down at the page.

And when her voice filled the room again, soft and steady, I felt something settle in me. A kind of peace that didn't need to be explained.

Just her voice, the Qur'an, the quiet and me, lying beside it like the luckiest man alive.

19
BADR

وَإِذَا خَاطَبَكَ السَّفِيهُ فَلَا تُجِبْهُ
فَخَيْرٌ مِنْ إِجَابَتِهِ السُّكُوتُ
فَإِنْ كَلَّمْتَهُ فَرَّجْتَ عَنْهُ
وَإِنْ خَلَّيْتَهُ كَمَدًا يَمُوتُ

If a fool addresses you, do not respond,
For silence is a better choice, by far beyond.
If you speak to him, you'll ease his inner plight,
But if you leave him, grief will take his light.

- الإمام الشافعي

Ma came to me in the morning saying that she truly wanted to apologize to Habiba, but she still couldn't make sense of it all. She couldn't believe that Habiba's grandfather would just marry her off to me like that, without any regard for his granddaughter's safety. She said she wanted to meet the man, to understand why he'd do such a thing. She needed to be sure Habiba wasn't secretly a bad person, that her grandfather wasn't trying to get rid of her and dump her on us.

I tried to argue, but Ba stopped me. He said it would be best for her to speak to him herself.

And to be fair to Ma, something like that had happened in the family before. My cousin married a girl he swore was perfect. The families met, everything seemed fine. Even I met her, she was sweet, polite, the picture of good manners. But SubhanAllah, the marriage barely lasted five months. She drained him, emotionally and financially, and even his parents suffered from the fallout. I guess Ma's just trying to avoid a repeat of that.

The three of us stepped into the hallway, and the house seemed to exhale its gloom over us. Khadijah shut the door behind us. "Salam alaykum," my mother and father said in unison, their tones careful, deferential.

He was sitting on the armchair. He didn't rise. Didn't even attempt to. He folded his newspaper slowly, smoothing its edges as though the paper deserved more care than we did. When his voice came, it was colder than the air in the room. "You should know," he said, setting the paper aside, "it's inappropriate to show up at someone's house uninvited."

I stayed silent. I had greeted this man enough times in the past, and he had made it perfectly clear my words were wasted on him.

Baba's eyes flicked up, a spark of hope lighting them, maybe he expected to see Habiba but when his gaze found nothing, it dimmed, a shadow of disappointment passing over his features. Then it hardened. "Habiba isn't with you," he said flatly. "You better not be here to convince me to take her back into this house."

Heat flared in my chest. The way he spoke of her, like she was a burden he'd cast off with generosity, burned through me.

My father, ever the diplomat, leaned forward as he lowered himself onto the couch opposite. "Habiba is a sweet girl," he said gently. "She's been a blessing to the family."

My mother sat beside him, spine rigid, eyes hard as stone. "I insisted we come," she said. "Because I cannot understand how a grandfather can put his own granddaughter in such a position. How can you hate your own child?"

I winced inwardly. Ma's fire was unrestrained. Habiba would never have wanted this, she didn't even know we were here.

Baba didn't flinch. "Habiba went through so much in her life. She lost both her parents and her siblings in the blink of an eye. I took her in after the tragedy—"

"Don't try to make it sound like a favor," Ma snapped, her voice sharp as glass. "Once her parents were gone, she became your responsibility. To keep her safe. To keep her fed. As her grandfather, it was your duty to care. Not your charity, it was Allah's command upon you."

He leaned back, one thick hand gripping the arm of the couch. "I stopped caring," he said, "the day she disrespected me."

Every muscle in me coiled. Disrespected him? The Habiba who could barely raise her voice? The Habiba who prayed for his health after every insult? The words nearly tore out of me, but Ma's squared shoulders warned me not to interfere.

"She refused a forced marriage," Ma said coldly. "That isn't disrespect. And you should be proud to have a granddaughter who stands for her rights."

He laughed. Low at first, then swelling until it filled the room. He wiped at his eyes, shaking his head. We exchanged glances, me rolling my eyes toward the ceiling and Ma, shooting me a look that screamed: Is he serious?

He gestured toward me. "I see where he gets it. It runs in the blood, the disease of thinking you know better than everyone."

Heat crawled up my neck. "We're not pretending to know better," I snapped. "We're telling the truth. Habiba was wronged. She lost her family in one moment, she never even had the chance for a wedding like any other bride, and—" my voice shook. "you're making her rebuild her life on top of your pride."

His lip curled. "Just because the man was older doesn't make it wrong. He was capable of giving her a good life. I can't say the same about you."

My fists clenched. "Nothing would have been wrong if you had asked for her consent. But you didn't."

"I did what was good for her," he barked. "That house was perfect for her. My only mistake was giving her too much freedom, letting her waste her time designing buildings." He spat the word. "Give me a damn paper and I'll design a masterpiece right now."

"Go ahead then," I shot back. "Draw up a masterpiece."

"You're standing in it." He smirked.

"Funny," I said, my voice venomous. "I don't see reporters lined up outside your door. Habiba has been featured in magazines, her designs are seen across the world and look at you."

"Anyone can publish on paper these days," he dismissed.

"Yeah, sure."

"Badr," my father cut in sharply. "Show some respect."

I bit down hard, grinding the words in my throat.

Baba leaned back, smug. "Maybe you should go home and teach your son manners before coming here to tell me how to run my house."

"SubhanAllah," Ma breathed, shaking her head. Her voice rose, sharp with disbelief. "You act like a man of honor, yet starving your granddaughter of love is what you call leadership?"

"Why do you assume I don't love her?" he finally snapped, as if her words stroked a nerve.

"You're not proving otherwise," I shot back.

"I don't have to prove myself to you. She is my granddaughter, my blood, you can't claim to love her more than I do. I secured a future for her, which your son ruined. And now you're here, preaching"

My father raised his hand, trying to cut in. "I admit, Badr's approach wasn't right. But neither was yours. Your ego was bruised, and you rushed her into marriage."

"What if Badr hadn't been a good man?" Ma cut in, "Would you have just handed her off to anyone? Did you even know his name? His character?"

"I knew the name and the character of the man she was supposed to marry, I knew-"

"Except she didn't want to marry him. Then you could have looked for someone else."

"Alright, enough," my father said firmly, raising his palm as though to settle the storm. "This isn't getting us anywhere. What matters is moving forward. At the very least, we should all come together to plan properly—to plan a wedding or at least all be at the walima. It would mean the world to Habiba."

Baba sighed, deep and dismissive. "I'm not attending anything. I didn't approve of that wedding, and I still don't. I'll speak to Habiba when I see fit. For now, leave my house."

"Tfu." Ma spat the word like poison, pushing to her feet. Her eyes burned into him as she jabbed a finger his way. "Just because she was unfortunate enough to grow up in this house doesn't mean you get to chain her to its misery forever. You failed her as a grandfather, but I will treat her like a daughter, the way you should have."

She turned sharply, only to find Khadijah lingering in the doorway.

"If I were you, I'd pack my bags and run before this man poisons the rest of your life too."

"Have a good day," my father said stiffly, rising to his feet as if Ma's words hadn't scorched the air.

I didn't even glance back. We walked out, the weight of that house pressing against our backs until Ba's voice followed, low and steady, the kind that cut deeper than shouting.

"Badr," he said, placing a hand on my shoulder, "don't forget that this is your wife's family. By marrying her, they became yours. And the Qur'an warns us not to cut ties of kinship."

I kept my eyes on the ground, jaw tight. "I wasn't disrespectful."

"You don't have to shout for it to be disrespect," Ba pressed, his gaze sharp. "A cold face, a careless word, it's enough. The Prophetﷺ said, '*The one who cuts ties of kinship will not enter Paradise.*' Do you want that written against you over a look or a tone of voice?"

I swallowed, heat creeping up my neck. But I wasn't going to let that sit unchallenged.

"With all due respect, Ba," I said, my voice low but steady, "the Prophet☙ also taught us boundaries. He never said we must chain ourselves to people who wound us. He showed mercy, yes, but he never told us to stand still and let the blade keep cutting—family or not. Protecting myself, protecting my household, that isn't disobedience. That's responsibility."

Ba's eyes narrowed, the silence between us stretching taut.

"That's true," he said, his voice firm but not unkind, "but, it's not your decision to make. It's her grandfather. It's her family. And whether she chooses to keep him in her life or not, that's her choice. Not yours. Your duty, Badr, is to respect her choice, and stand beside her in it."

When we got home, Ma went straight to Habiba. I wasn't worried. My mother hated nothing more than the thought of wrongfully hurting someone. She often reminded us of *al-Maqãssah*—the Day of Reckoning—when even the smallest injustice will be repaid. "On that day," she'd say, *"if you've taken someone's right, even with words, you'll have to pay them back with your good deeds until nothing remains."*

That fear of standing before Allah empty-handed has always guided her. So when she realized that Habiba wasn't at fault, that her assumptions had been unfair, I knew it must have crushed her. My mother's temper burns fast, but her remorse burns longer.

I didn't join them. I gave them space. This was between the two of them, one seeking forgiveness, the other giving it. I waited in the hallway, half-praying, half-listening for raised voices, but none came.

When they finally came out, Habiba's eyes were red and swollen, and for a moment my heart sank. But then she smiled, softly, shyly, and I knew everything would be okay.

20

HABIBA

إنَّ القلوب حينَ تُحِبُّ تُضاءُ

Hearts, when they love, are illuminated.

- ابن الفارض

A week went by, and Hana had practically adopted me as her sister. Every evening she pulled me into her world—school gossip, movies, even make-up sessions like teenagers at a sleepover. Loud and animated, she filled the house with life, and for the first time in years, I felt like I had something to look forward to.

Even Badr seemed lighter these days. He'd been nothing but kind, and though I trusted his sweetness, I couldn't help but wonder how long before it faded? Before he wanted someone else? I caught myself hoping he'd admire me, maybe even stay. I didn't know if it was love, but I wanted this to last.

Things were shifting with his family too. His mother had softened since her apology, inviting me into conversations, letting me help. It was still awkward, but she had accepted me, and that was enough for now.

Hana insisted that I join her and her mother's weekly girls' night—a tradition of cooking, movies, and laughter. I was nervous, but hopeful.

At the office, life was quieter. Badr stayed professional, no random visits, only meetings about work. But every time we spoke, I found myself respecting him more. Wanting more. Which was dangerous.

Later, after we wrapped up with the office, Badr drove us to the agency to start searching for our apartment.

The office was neat and smelled faintly of coffee. We were greeted by a middle-aged man whose hair was so aggressively gelled back I worried about flammable hazards. He shook Badr's hand, offered us coffee or tea which we declined, then he sat us down.

"So, Mr. and Mrs. El-Idrissi," he said smoothly, glancing at the file. "Tell me about yourselves."

I let Badr do the talking while I nodded politely. He explained preferences, location near his home, nothing too far.

"How many bedrooms?" the agent asked, pen poised.

"Preferably three," Badr answered smoothly, "but two would be fine too."

I snapped my head toward him so fast I almost gave myself whiplash. He must have felt my eyes burning into the side of his skull because he glanced at me.

"What?"

"What do we need three bedrooms for?"

He hesitated. "In case of… you know. Guests." His cheeks went a shade darker.

I narrowed my eyes. "So, two bedrooms. How many guests do we need on a daily basis?"

"One is for guests," he insisted. "And the other is like… I don't know. For—" he thought—"future expansion."

I stared at him. Future expansion? What was he, a start-up company?

"What's future expansion?" I asked, dead serious.

He groaned. "Habiba, you're irritating me. You can't be that slow. Figure it out."

The agent cleared his throat, fighting back a smile. "Newlyweds, I take it?" We both nodded. He leaned forward. "He means children. Future children. You're planning on having those, right?"

The realization hit, and I burst out laughing. Not a ladylike giggle—no, full-blown, stomach-hurting laughter.

"I'm sorry," I gasped, clutching my stomach, "but why couldn't you just say that?"

Badr sighed dramatically. "I didn't know if you wanted kids. Can we just move on?" He gave me a look that screamed drop it.

"Fine, fine." I turned to the agent, still grinning. "One or two bedrooms is fine. We'll move when the… 'expansion' happens."

The agent chuckled.

Badr turned to me, his eyes searching. "Are you sure? I've seen my parents move with kids, it's not easy."

"It feels pointless to take three bedrooms now when we're barely around ourselves," I said.

Badr studied me for a moment before finally nodding. "One or two," he told the agent firmly.

The man scribbled notes. "Flexible move-in dates, or are you in a rush?"

"Flexible," Badr shrugged.

"Modern or classic style?"

"Doesn't matter."

We ran through a few more details. The agent even prodded me into answering so he could get to know us both. He promised to send us listings by the next day.

And just like that, we were officially hunting for our first home. With or without future expansion.

Once we were done, we got into the car and Badr started it, driving us home.

"So, clearly we need to talk…" I said.

"About what?" he asked, glancing at me briefly.

"Likes, dislikes, kids, no kids," I said lightly, smiling to myself.

"Oh…" his brows lifted, "yeah, I figured the same. Maybe it's time we go on that date. What do you think?"

"Sure…" I agreed.

Truth was, we could learn everything about each other just at home. But still… going somewhere together, just the two of us, felt different.

"Well, it's settled then," he said. "Be ready by 7 p.m. I'll make the arrangements."

"7 p.m.? But I was supposed to go shopping with Hana for tomorrow night!" I pouted.

"Hmm, that's important." He thought for a moment. "How about tomorrow after work, we'll pick them up from school and go straight there."

I nodded—fairer solution, and honestly smarter.

It was 6 when we got home. Ahmed and Hana were already back, Zain was sprawled in the living room surrounded by papers. Ma and Ba were out having dinner with friends.

"Badr! Ma said to tell you to call Rina," Hana called as we headed upstairs. "Something's wrong with a machine at the bakery. She'll explain."

"Okay!" he answered.

I leaned closer as we climbed the stairs. "Which bakery?"

"Oh, Ma has one. Ba opened it for her years ago. She makes amazing baked goods. Used to run it full-time. Zain and Hana help sometimes." He shrugged. "It's not really my thing, I only go when something breaks. I'll take you there sometime."

Upstairs, I dropped my bag and sat on the carpet, back against the bed, scrolling on my phone. The floor always grounded me better than the bed. When Badr stepped out of the bathroom, he frowned at me.

"Why are you sitting there?"

"I just felt like it," I said honestly.

He shook his head with a small smile, then went on with his business.

By the time I finished freshening up, Badr was praying. I slipped out to Hana's room.

She beamed the second I entered. I adored that, her excitement every time she saw me. This family, this pure love… I still couldn't believe I'd found myself in it.

"I have to cancel today," I said sheepishly.

"Oh, why?" she pouted.

"I'm going out with Badr."

"Where are you going?"

"I have no idea," I admitted.

Her pout flipped into a grin. "Ooooh, a date. What are you wearing?"

I smiled awkwardly. "Probably the usual."

"No! Wear something pretty! That pink dress you have!" She grabbed my hand, bouncing. "Bring your clothes here and get ready in my room. Then he can come call you, and you'll look so pretty he'll faint."

I laughed. "I'm sure Badr and I are way past that."

"Please, Romance doesn't die," she said, serious as a sage. "Even Ma dresses up for Ba sometimes. Take it from me, I read romance novels."

I didn't argue.

I snuck my clothes into Hana's room. She made me try on all the options before we settled on a soft pink silk dress I'd bought for a work event but never worn. It draped smoothly against my skin, catching light with every movement. Hana paired it with her maroon scarf, then insisted on helping with my face.

She didn't use much, just clear brow gel, a swipe of kohl, mascara and lipstick. Simple, but when I looked in the mirror, my grin widened. The silk draped over my body softly, and the scarf deepened the color of my skin.

The hour flew by between laughter and chatting.

At 7 sharp, my phone pinged, a text from Badr. I told him I was in Hana's room. A moment later, there was a knock.

Hana practically sprinted to the door, flinging it open with theatrical flair. "I present to you... your wife!"

My stomach twisted. Nervous. Ridiculously nervous. Why?

I forced myself to look up.

He stood in the doorway, a black shirt buttoned all the way up, black suit pants, hair combed back so his curls looked sharper, more deliberate. The color black clung to him like it belonged there. His smile was small at first, then widened as his eyes locked on me.

I couldn't hold his gaze. I looked away too fast, my cheeks hot.

"Oh my God, I just witnessed a fairytale moment!" Hana squealed, rushing to my side. She tugged me closer to him until I was almost pressed against him. His eyes didn't leave mine.

"Picture! Picture!" she cried, fumbling for her instant camera.

Badr slipped an arm over my shoulder, pulling me gently into him. He leaned slightly forward, peering at my face like he was studying it. The warmth of his chest brushed my cheek, and my breath caught.

I glanced up, startled, and he was already smiling. The kind of smile that reached his eyes. My lips mirrored his before I even realized it.

Flash. The moment was frozen in film.

"Perfect!" Hana squealed, fanning the photo as it cured. She grinned so wide her cheeks could've cracked.

Before I could even peek at the picture, she shoved us both out of the room, squealing, "Have fun!"

The hallway was quiet. Too quiet. My pulse thudded in my ears as I turned toward the stairs, desperate to move. But before I could, arms slipped around my waist and pulled me back.

I nearly squeaked. "Wait. Your shoes."

He crouched, steadying me with a hand on my calf, his other hand guiding mine to his shoulder. My breath hitched at the casual intimacy of it. He fastened the ankle strap carefully, then the other, his fingers brushing my skin just enough to make me shiver.

When he stood again, his hand lifted to the edge of my scarf. He straightened it gently, fingers grazing my jaw. My instinct was to lean back, shy, terrified someone would see.

But he didn't move away. He just looked at me. Really looked. His eyes softened, drinking me in like I was something fragile and precious. At first I tensed, too aware of his nearness. But then my shoulders eased, and all my attention narrowed to the way he was staring at me like I was the only thing in the room.

"I think we're going to have to get you checked out," I whispered, breaking the tension. "This staring thing is going a little too far."

His lips curved into a deeper smile. "I'm just… mesmerized. Never thought I'd see the day Habiba Mukhtar dressed up for me."

Heat flared across my face. "Who says it's for you—"

The sudden sound of a door shutting jolted us apart. My heart nearly leapt into my throat.

Footsteps approached, and Zain appeared, smirking. "Sorry, not sorry. Hallways belong to everyone. Get a room."

Before I could die of embarrassment, Badr smacked the back of his head. Zain stumbled forward dramatically, groaning.

I clapped my hand over my mouth, shocked and mortified.

Zain glared from the ground. "I'll tell Ba you were romancing in the hallway."

"Habiba, let's go." Badr extended his hand.

I didn't think twice. I took it, and he led me down the stairs.

When I glanced back, Zain was still on the ground, grinning wickedly as he made a heart with his fingers. I laughed under my breath, shaking my head, then followed Badr out.

Luckily, the hallways were empty. He opened the car door for me without letting go of my hand, guiding me inside.

As we pulled out into the evening, I thought about asking where we were going. But I stopped myself. The night breeze filtered through the crack of the window, cool against my skin, and I let myself enjoy the surprise.

#

21

القلب يُدرك مالا عين تدركه
والحُسْنُ ما استحسنته النفس لا البصر

The heart perceives what the eye cannot see,
And true beauty is what the soul admires, not just what the sight can be

عبد الله بن سليمان النحوي

Badr slowed the car in front of a restaurant. Frankie's.

The building glowed against the evening streets, warm mood lighting spilling through the windows. It looked elegant, sophisticated, definitely not the kind of place I had expected. I silently thanked Allah that I had let Hana dress me up. If I had come casual, I would've stuck out completely.

I reached for the handle, but Badr stopped me with a raised hand. "Will you let me open the door for you, please?"

I raised a brow, smiling. "You're really going all out with this date, aren't you?"

"Well… it's not every day I take my wife on her first date. I figured I'd better try to impress you before you remember you're stuck with me forever."

I threw my head back in laughter. He chuckled too, a quiet rumble, before stepping out quickly and circling to my side. As promised, I waited for him. He opened the door with a little flourish, and I stepped out, catching the faint whiff of his cologne.

He shut the door and, to my surprise, offered me his elbow. I blinked at it, then at him. "That's way too cheesy," I giggled.

"Come on," he urged, eyes glinting with amusement.

I rolled my eyes but slipped my hand into the crook of his arm anyway. His arm was firm under my touch, steady, grounding. And though I tried to play it cool, my heart was beating faster as he led us inside.

He had already made a reservation, and soon we were guided to a table by the window with a sweeping view of the city glittering beneath the night sky. The lights reflected faintly in the glass, framing us in a quiet little world of our own. Badr pulled my chair out for me—I sat, and he slipped into the seat across from mine.

The waiter came, handing us menus bound in sleek leather. The dishes looked refined, expensive. My nerves eased a little when Badr smiled at my expression, like he was enjoying watching me process all of this.

After we finally ordered and the waiter left, it was just the two of us, silence stretching. His gaze caught mine across the table, steady and unflinching.

"So…" Badr leaned forward slightly. "Tell me about Habiba Mukhtar."

"You already know about Habiba Mukhtar," I said, tilting my head, smiling faintly.

He shook his head. "Tell me about young Habiba. I want to know what you were like… before everything."

The question caught me off guard. It touched something in me because ever since the incident, I'd buried that girl. Locked her away. I hadn't revisited her in years.

I stared past him for a moment, searching my memory, and finally smiled softly. "Wild," I admitted, almost shyly. "Free. I used to live for roller coasters. I was always trying new things, too social—way too social. Honestly? I was the troublemaker of my class. A complete handful. Terrible student. I was supposed to go skydiving."

I laughed at his expression—half shock, half amusement.

223

"Yeah, my dad promised me that on my twentieth birthday, I'll get to skydive." The memory warmed me, then dimmed a little. "Young Habiba probably had a few screws loose."

"A few?" he teased. "How about all of them?".

"She was happy," I said quietly, almost to myself. "She lived life to the fullest."

"And now?" His voice softened.

I shrugged, eyes lowering. "Now... Alhamdulillah."

When I looked up, he was watching me carefully, almost like he was trying to read between the cracks in my words. I wasn't ready to stay in that space, though. So I tilted my head at him.

"Tell me about Badr El Idrisi. Tell me about your life."

He smiled knowingly, but didn't push. "Badr El Idrisi..." He leaned back, fingers toying with his glass. "He was born in Morocco."

"Really? I thought you were born here."

"Nope. Born and raised in Morocco. Zain was born there too, he was five and I was nine when we moved here. Hana and Ahmed were born here, in Canada."

I listened, absorbed, as he told me about his family's journey, the move, his father's sacrifices, his mother's bakery, and the way he had quietly taken on responsibilities when money was tight. His words painted pictures: a younger Badr, balancing school with babysitting, working, filling the gaps whenever he could.

His voice held both pride and humility as he said, "That's why Ahmed is so attached to me. I practically raised him in his early years." His laugh was warm, boyish. "Eventually things got easier. Ba and I finished the construction in our current house, he got promoted, life settled. Not rich, but Alhamdulillah. And that... is the life of Badr El Idrisi."

I couldn't help the smile tugging at my lips. "Your story helps me understand you so much better."

"How?"

I searched for the right words. "I don't know. You're just… loving. Openly loving. It's like you need everyone you care about to know it."

"I wasn't always like that." His eyes grew serious. "It changed when I started Islamic studies, a lot changed actually. There was this hadith I heard…"

He told me then of the man who told the Prophetﷺ that he loved another for the sake of Allah, and how the Prophet instructed him to go and say it. He recited the exchange in Arabic, and though my tongue didn't match the fluency of his, the words reached me. They lingered in the air between us, soft but powerful.

When he finished, I whispered, "That's… beautiful."

"Yeah." He smiled faintly. "Love shouldn't be hidden. It softens the heart. Builds trust, and strengthens ties. Life's too short to assume people know."

"Even if they already know?"

"Then it's just a reminder."

My chest felt warm, unexpectedly tender. I found myself smiling back at him.

I wondered—would I ever hear him tell me he loved me? Would I ever be able to say it back? To feel it, really feel it? Right now, I wasn't sure. What I knew was that I appreciated him. I appreciated the way he made me feel safe, seen, and appreciated. I could see myself living a comfortable life with him. But love?

I didn't even know what that felt like.

"So what about Badr?" I asked, leaning forward as I rested my chin on my intertwined hands. "Why Badr? What does it mean?"

He grinned. "Full moon."

I raised my brows, surprised.

"I was born at night, in a tent, back in the village," he explained. "Ma had a traditional midwife with her."

"Interesting," I said, a little smile tugging at my lips. "I always

225

thought it was an interesting name."

"It is, I guess," he smiled, then tilted his head. "What about Habiba? Why did they name you that?"

I shrugged. "I never thought to ask… never even checked the meaning."

His smile deepened. "Habiba means 'beloved.'"

"Really?" My voice shot up, genuine surprise warming my chest.

"Yeah… beloved." His tone softened as if the word itself was fragile in his mouth. "I've always liked the name… Habiba." He breathed it like a secret, almost to himself, then chuckled. "I'd never even heard of it as a name until I met you. But I remember it so clearly when the teacher called your name for the first time. *Habiba*. It caught my attention instantly. Then you stood up…"

His eyes drifted, a faraway look softening his expression, like he was watching the memory replay before him.

"I remember being so fascinated by your accent. It's still the most beautiful accent I've ever heard," he murmured.

"Sounds to me like you've been mesmerized since the first day you saw me," I teased, lips curving. "One could mistake that you might actually be in love with me." I added, turning his words back on him.

"Obviously."

The word slipped from his mouth—quiet, almost thoughtless.

My smile faltered. For a second, I wasn't sure I'd heard him right. His gaze was still distant, lost in some place between memory and confession. Then realization dawned on his face, his pupils sharpening as if he'd just snapped out of a trance.

"What?" I breathed, half-laughing, half-stunned.

"I mean—" He cleared his throat hard, his hand twitching against the tablecloth. "Obviously anyone would mistake that for love." His voice was too quick, too deliberate. "But only Allah knows what it was."

He looked straight at me when he said it, and for a heartbeat, I couldn't move. The air between us felt too still, too heavy—like the silence that follows a storm.

My pulse thudded somewhere in my throat. Heat crawled up my skin, and I was suddenly thankful for my darker complexion—it masked the blush that was rapidly rising. I forced my gaze down, pretending to inspect the table setting, my breath catching somewhere between a laugh and a sigh.

Then, mercifully, the waiter appeared with our plates and cutlery. The tension snapped.

Badr leaned back a little too quickly, mumbling a thanks. I murmured one too. But when he left, it was just Badr and me again.

I don't like feeling small beneath someone's gaze... yet, with him, it feels good. "So... expenses?" I grinned, trying to shift the mood.

Badr glanced at me, brow knitting. "What's there to talk about?"

"You know... how much I'll be contributing. If it's fifty-fifty or something else."

He didn't miss a beat. "Allah already settled that. I'll be a hundred percent responsible—" his lips curved in that confident, maddening way. "and you just be my *barakah*."

The corners of my lips betrayed me before I could stop them. I looked down quickly, hoping he didn't notice. But of course, he did. The waiter set down plates that looked elegant, steam curled upward, carrying scents of saffron and citrus. He placed my dish in front of me, pan-seared salmon resting on a bed of saffron risotto, garnished with delicate microgreens and a drizzle of lemon-butter reduction that caught the light like liquid gold. The fish flaked perfectly under my fork, crisped on the outside yet soft within, the risotto glowing with creamy richness.

Badr's plate was no less impressive: herb-crusted rack of lamb served with roasted root vegetables, a swirl of velvety date-infused jus, and a side of truffle mashed potatoes.

"Today I'm the one eating the potato." Badr teased after his first bite, his voice low, satisfied.

"I wanted to be unpredictable today," I admitted, cutting into the chicken.

He glanced at me, amused. "Want to try mine?"

I hesitated, then smiled and nodded. I expected him to push the plate forward or hand me the fork. Instead, he scooped himself and held it out. The spoon hovered between us. I stared at it a moment too long before deciding I wasn't going to make it awkward. I leaned forward and took the bite. The flavor exploded on my tongue—sweet, smoky, tart. I chewed, swallowed, and finally let myself smile.

"It's… really good," I said, a little too softly.

He leaned back, satisfied, and returned to his plate. Out of courtesy, I mirrored him, lifting a piece of my fish onto my fork and offering it across the table. His gaze flicked from the fork to my face before he leaned forward and accepted it without hesitation.

"Mm," he nodded appreciatively. "Yours might actually beat mine."

A silent laugh escaped me as I turned back to my plate. Our conversation over dinner drifted across safe, shallow waters until I grew tired of the current. Setting my fork down with a quiet clink, I fixed him with a thoughtful gaze before I spoke.

"I wanna ask you a question. Don't get offended, okay?" I started carefully, playing with my fork to buy time.

"I'm already offended, pass." He flicked his hand dismissively, then broke into a crooked smile that softened his face. "Kidding. Shoot." He set his fork down with a deliberate clink against the porcelain, shoulders angling toward me as though giving me his undivided attention.

"Polygamy."

His smile faltered. For a moment he looked stunned, even

choking slightly as he reached for a tissue to cough into before speaking. "I'm pretty sure polygamy is illegal in Canada."

"That doesn't answer my question."

"You didn't ask a question." His retort was quick, sharp, but not unkind. He rested his elbow on the table, leaning in closer, his brows lifted in expectation. "Ask."

"What do you think about having more than one wife?"

He exhaled slowly, shoulders dropping with it. "I think if a man takes that step and manages it with honesty and fairness and he truly keeps all his wives content, then good for him. That's not an easy thing to do."

"You're evading," I said, spearing another bite of my dish.

"Ask me a direct question and I'll give you a direct answer." His tone shifted, edged with challenge.

I mirrored his stance, my elbows brushing the linen. "Are you planning on getting a second wife?"

"No."

"Why did it take you so long to just say that?"

"Because you never asked me directly."

"But you knew what I meant."

"I wanted to hear you say it."

I tilted my head. "It looks like the question made you uncomfortable."

"It did."

"Why?"

His smile returned, but differently this time—smaller, quieter, something that deepened at the corners as though shaped by thought rather than humor. He leaned back in his chair, fingers drumming lightly against the stem of his glass. "Because ever since I married you, I've had an answer to everything. I've rehearsed every question you might throw at me. But this one?" He shook his head, bemused. "This never even crossed my mind."

"Why not?"

"I don't know." He shrugged, but it wasn't careless; it was weighted, sincere. "Having more than one wife never crossed my mind, It's never happened in my family. And I've never looked at more than one woman like that. For me, it was never an option."

I narrowed my eyes. "Why should I believe you? What if one day you meet someone amazing, and you decide you want to marry her too?"

His voice dropped, steady but certain. "I would never do that to you."

"Why should I believe that?"

This time, his smile deepened again, but it carried a different kind of gravity. "Because you mean more to me than I let on. I wouldn't even be here if I hadn't met you. And as much as you think I did you a favor…" He paused, his gaze locking with mine, "…you did a bigger one for me. For my family too. So no, I wouldn't do that to you."

Now I was hooked. "What exactly did I do for you?"

His eyes flickered, guarded. "You saved me from myself. That's all I'm comfortable saying." I nodded, respecting the line he drew. "Did I pass the interrogation?"

"Sort of. That's all I'm comfortable saying." I smirked, leaning back. "So… Future expansion." His laugh broke the heaviness between us.

The rest of the evening flowed with laughter, smiles, and stories—everything I didn't even know I had been craving. Maybe it was because I was finally seeing Badr beyond who I knew before, beyond the man I married by mistake, beyond my colleague, beyond just the man who saved me from my family.

A quiet wish settled over me: that my parents could have known him. My mother would have been so pleased, her heart warmed to see me with a man like this. And I would have loved to witness the dynamic with my father. I suspect their talks would have been rich, full of the kind of depth he would have appreciated.

The house was still when we came in, shadows stretching long across the hallway. Everyone was asleep. We tiptoed up the stairs like two kids sneaking in past curfew, muffling our laughter, careful not to make the floorboards creak. My heart raced from the nearness of him.

We reached the bedroom door, and Badr stopped. He turned toward me, his grin mischievous even in the dim light. He leaned close, voice dropping into a whisper that sent a shiver through me.

"So," he said, "do I get points for walking you all the way to your door?"

I chuckled, too soft, afraid it would carry. "Are you trying to rack up a perfect score on a first date?"

His grin widened, devilish. "Of course. I mean, opened your door, made you laugh, drove you home, brought you to the door… that's the entire checklist. Only one box left." His brows lifted, teasing.

My cheeks flamed. I wanted to swat at him, to break the tension with some joke, but the words tangled in my throat. Still, I managed to whisper back, "Well… for that box you might need a second date. Tonight you'll only get invited in for tea."

"Tea?" he whispered back, pretending to look wounded. His hand pressed over his heart in mock despair. "Cruel." Then, softer, his eyes glinting with laughter, "But fine… I'll take what I can get."

He reached for the handle, easing the door open, and we slipped into the bedroom together, chuckling under our breath, our shoulders brushing as though sharing a secret.

22

HABIBA

إلى محياك ضوء البدر يعتذر
وفي مَحَبَّتكَ العُشَّاقُ قد عُذِرُوا
وجنة الحسن في خديك موثقة
ونار حبّك لا تبقي ولا تذر

Before your face, even the light of the full moon offers an apology.
And in loving you, lovers are fully excused.
The paradise of beauty is bound within your cheeks,
And the fire of your love leaves nothing behind, sparing no one.

- صفي الدين الحلي

As Badr promised, we picked Hana and Ahmed up from school. The trick was convincing Terrence we were headed to the Franklin Site. Which, technically, wasn't a lie considering we had stopped by an hour earlier to finish some documentation before leaving for the pickup.

Hana chose most of the snacks. I just nodded along to everything she suggested, since I didn't eat much of that stuff myself. The only time I ever had snacks was when Hadi or Jamila insisted on sharing theirs, which they often did. Though, to be fair, I never let them have too many, so it wasn't really that often.

Muhammed had texted me, and initially, I wanted nothing to do with him, wasn't willing to respond to him but after Badr convinced me, I finally responded. He apologized for everything. Truthfully, by then, I wasn't angry anymore. In the end, things had worked out for me. Better than I could've imagined.

Now I stood at the counter beside Hana, struggling to tear open a stubborn bag of Doritos. Next to me, her mother moved with effortless grace, slicing fruit into perfect little pieces. Her scarf was tied snugly around her head, her hands precise but unhurried.

The kitchen smelled of Popcorn, mingling with the sweet, tangy scent of the strawberries she was slicing. The light above the counter cast a soft golden glow, turning the polished granite a warm shade of honey. Hana leaned against the counter, pouring caramel into the popcorn while talking about a funny incident at school while I wrestled with the stubborn packet.

No matter how hard I pulled, the thing refused to open. My hands were starting to ache, and instead of tearing, the plastic just stretched like it was mocking me.

"Why do they make these things impossible to open?" I muttered under my breath, trying to keep up with Hana's story.

My phone buzzed on the counter. I wiped my hands on my pajama pants and picked it up, half expecting a random notification. Instead, it was a message from Badr.

Badr: Look at the door.

I frowned, then glanced up so fast my neck almost cracked with the speed of it.

And there he was.

Half of his face and one shoulder peeking from around the doorway, the rest of him hidden. The kitchen light spilled across his face, casting deep shadows under his cheekbones, making him look like a ghost caught mid-haunting. His brows were raised in mock urgency, his lips twitching like he was trying not to laugh.

I widened my eyes at him. *What are you doing?*

I didn't want his mother to see him there. As soon as the time hit 10pm, she sent everyone to their bedrooms, declaring that only the girls were allowed down. It was a no boys night, so Badr coming down for me will only likely get me in trouble.

He jerked his chin, motioning for me to come closer.

I subtly shook my head, mouthing, Go away.

He shook his head right back, like this was non-negotiable, and beckoned again, this time more dramatically, curling his fingers toward himself.

I sighed, thinking fast. "Ugh this is so hard," I said aloud, stepping toward the drawer near the door.

Badr's grin widened like he'd just won. I moved slowly, keeping his lurking figure in the corner of my vision. As soon as I was close enough, I mouthed, *What are you doing here?*

He pointed at the Doritos in my hand.

I shook my head again. *No.*

He pointed harder, his face pulling into an exaggerated look of disbelief that I could even resist this offer.

Behind me, his mother's voice interrupted. "Look for scissors Habiba, they are in the lower drawer."

I froze, heart thumping. When I dared to glance back, she was still slicing strawberries.

I swallowed and bent toward the drawer, my fingers brushing the cool steel handle. Before I could react, Badr's hand shot out, snatching the Doritos from my grip. In one swift, practiced motion, he ripped the bag open with a smug ease, stole a piece, shoved it back into my hands, and tip-toed down the hall like a kid escaping trouble.

I stood there for a second, dumbfounded.

When I turned around, Hana was watching me, her expression completely innocent. "You opened it," she said, like it was the most normal thing in the world.

I let out an awkward laugh. "Yes... yes, I did."

I dumped the chips into the big glass bowl, the salty, cheesy smell puffing up into the air. Then, as I turned toward the counter again, I caught sight of him in the hallway, half-hidden, grinning like a fool, giving me a triumphant thumbs-up.

I tried to glare at him, but my lips betrayed me, curving into a smile I couldn't quite suppress.

Once the Doritos were set and the fruits were sliced, we

assembled the snacks together—popcorn drizzled with melted caramel, sliced mango and strawberries, bowls of doritos.

I was about to follow Hana upstairs when my name was called. "Habiba," Her mother spoke in that gentle, unhurried way of hers, "do you know how to make tea?"

"Yes," I answered instantly. Too instantly.

"Seriously?" She asked, shocked.

"Of course, how could I not?" I chuckled, a bit offended. I was thinking of my kind of tea, the lazy kind.

She smiled as if satisfied, then began pulling out... not a mug, not a teabag, but something she called a *berrad*, long and elegant with a little curved spout. Alongside it, she set a bunch of fresh mint still wrapped in a damp cloth, loose tea leaves in a tin, and a bag of sugar. Three small glass cups followed, each thin enough to make the tea inside glow.

"I don't like it too sweet," she said as she turned toward the hallway. I was left staring at the silver pot like it had personally betrayed me.

I picked it up and felt its weight. Was it just for boiling water? But then why was there also a kettle on the counter? I'd seen videos of Moroccan tea making before but those were quick Instagram reels, not actual instructions. The mint lay on the cutting board like it knew I was about to disrespect it.

I hesitated, glancing toward the hall in case she came back, but it stayed quiet.

And then I heard tap-tap.

I turned so sharply I nearly dropped the *berrad*.

Badr was standing in the doorway like some shadowy burglar who'd been caught mid-heist. The effect was... unsettlingly dramatic. Like a ghost who'd shown up just to scare me into drinking more water.

He raised a finger to his lips, his mouth twitching like he was holding back a laugh. His hair was a little messy, hoodie sleeves shoved up to his elbows, and there was this restless, mischievous energy about him that made me instantly suspicious.

"What are you doing here?" I hissed.

"What are you doing with the *berrad*?" His voice was low and teasing, like this was a game.

I gestured helplessly at the counter. "She asked me to make tea."

"And you... don't know how."

I frowned. "I do. I just... don't know this tea."

He fully stepped into the kitchen without asking, and quietly shut the door behind him.

"Badr—" I started, but he was already scanning the counter like he owned the place which, technically, he sort of did.

"Alright," he said, rolling up his sleeves further, "you prep the mint and cups. I'll handle the rest."

There was something disarming about the way he took over so smoothly, like we'd done this a hundred times. I put the mint under running water, the leaves were cool and fragrant against my fingertips, scent sharp and refreshing. Beside me, he measured out the tea leaves, his movements confident and unhurried.

The water began to boil, and the scent of the tea unfurled into the air—rich, earthy, with that slight bite that promised sweetness. The kitchen suddenly felt smaller. Or maybe it was just him leaning towards me, close enough that I could hear the sound of his breath.

When the tea was ready, he lifted the berrad high above the first glass and poured, the amber stream catching the light. Then he poured it back into the pot and repeated the motion, higher each time until a froth formed at the top.

"Try it," he said, holding out the glass.

I took a sip. Sweet, bright, with that perfect mint coolness cutting through. Before I could say anything, he took the glass from my hands and drank from it, right where my lips had been. This isn't the first time he's done this, back in university he would finish my drinks without so much of a thought. But watching him do it now made heat shoot through me so quickly I almost coughed.

"You like?"

Then footsteps.

He froze, eyes darting toward the hall. "Someone's coming," he whispered.

He placed the cup down and made a run for the door, but I grabbed his wrist without thinking. "You can't! They'll see you!" I hissed.

His gaze swept the room like he was calculating escape routes. He darted toward the narrow gap between the fridge and the counter.

"You're not fitting there," I whispered urgently before I yanked his sleeve and pulled him toward the store room.

We slipped inside just as the footsteps entered the kitchen. I eased the door almost shut, leaving only a sliver for air.

The store room was small and dim, shelves crammed with jars of spices, sacks of rice, and boxes of cereal stacked like haphazard towers. It smelled faintly of cinnamon, mint, and cleaning soap.

We stood so close our shoulders touched, his hoodie warm against my arm. I could feel his breath on the side of my face, slow and steady, and it made the air feel heavier.

"This is ridiculous," I murmured.

His voice was low, amused. "You dragged me in here."

"You were about to wedge yourself behind the fridge like an idiot."

"That's better than being trapped with you in a cupboard," he said, but his eyes even in the dim light were smiling.

Somewhere in the kitchen, the tea bubbled over with a hiss.

His mother's voice followed, mild but sharp-edged with disapproval. "Aish!"

I tensed.

"She's going to find us," I whispered.

He leaned in slightly, and I felt the heat radiating off his body. "Only if you keep talking."

I wanted to glare at him, but the narrowness of the space made it impossible not to be aware of how close we were. His scent was clean, with a trace of something warm and woody mixed with the sharper notes of mint.

I shifted my foot to move closer to the door, but something rolled under my heel. A bottle cap, maybe. My balance tipped, and before I could stop myself, both my hands shot forward, landing squarely on Badr's chest.

His reflexes were faster than mine. His arms closed around my waist, steadying me before I could stumble into the shelf behind us.

For a split second, everything froze. His chest was warm under my palms, solid, steady, and his breath was too close to my face. My heart thudded painfully loud in my ears.

I looked up, and our eyes met. Big mistake. Heat rushed straight to my face, and I snatched my hands back like I'd been burned. His grip loosened too, though not before I felt the strength of his hold and how natural it was for him to catch me.

"Habiba," his mother's voice rang out from the kitchen.

I nearly jumped out of my skin. Shoving at the door, I slipped out, plastering a nervous smile on my face as if I hadn't just been caught in the most compromising position of my life.

"What were you doing in there? The tea was overflowing," she said, already reaching for the rag on the counter.

"I—uh—" My brain scrambled. "I was looking for… some… cheese."

Her eyebrows arched.

"Yeah! Cheese. I just remembered cheese goes well with Doritos,"

I blurted, practically diving toward the teapot, lifting the lid as if that could erase the heat climbing up my neck.

She gave me a long, knowing look. "You were looking for cheese… in the store?"

I froze, then slapped my forehead dramatically. "You're right! I'm so stupid." I snatched the rag from her hands. "Here, let me do it."

She didn't insist, just gave me one of those quiet stares that saw through too much. "I don't think you're stupid," she said calmly, "but you might have company that is stupid."

I laughed nervously, too loudly. "Ha—ha—"

She wiped her hands and added casually, "I went to your room earlier. Your husband wasn't there."

My heart stopped for a second. I forced a chuckle. "Really? Maybe he went for a drive. He likes… night drives." My voice cracked on the last word.

"Hmm." She set the berrad neatly on the tray with three cups, then looked at me, her gaze sliding deliberately toward the storeroom door. "When you see him, tell him he's not very good at hiding."

And with that, she left, her footsteps fading down the hall.

I dropped the rag onto the counter and exhaled so hard it almost hurt. When I turned, Badr was leaning lazily against the storeroom doorframe, scratching the back of his head like a guilty teenager.

"I think she knows I was here," he muttered.

"No kidding," I smacked his chest lightly.

He caught my hand before I could pull back.

"Hey, I helped you make perfect tea," he said with a grin.

I glared, "Go to bed, Badr."

He released me, stepping past me, his smile light. "Sweet dreams,"

Hana's bedroom was exactly as one might imagine: pink walls softened by strings of fairy lights, a shelf overflowing with books, tiny potted plants lined neatly along the windowsill. The bed was an explosion of mismatched pillows, and the faint scent of strawberry lotion lingered in the air.

"We make the bed like this for movie nights," Hana announced, throwing herself onto the mattress and patting the spot beside her. The covers were gone, replaced by a small foldable table in the middle. Three blankets lay folded at the foot of the bed—two matching, and one in a different color, which I guessed was mine. Their thoughtfulness made me smile.

Her mother took the bag of s'mores from my hands and set it on the table. Drinks had already been poured into sippy water bottles, a clever way to avoid spills. Hana plopped the popcorn down, flicked on the fairy lights, and turned off the main one.

She sprawled in the middle, me on one side, her mother on the other. The room instantly felt warmer, the golden fairy lights softening everything. Then Hana switched on the projector, the movie flickering to life on a white sheet Badr had helped her tie up.

We agreed on a comedy—what better way to start than with laughter?

At first, I was stiff, cautious with my chuckles. But by the second ridiculous scene, all three of us were laughing so hard we had to pause. Hana leaned against me like we'd been friends forever. Her mother covered her mouth with her hand, tears of laughter sparkling at the corners of her eyes.

Something inside me loosened.

I tried not to spoil my mood, but every burst of laughter, every high-five, every shared groan about how good the s'mores were pulled my thoughts back to my own family. To my sister. To my mother. We never really sat together like this, we were all too caught up in our own worlds. I couldn't remember the last time the three of us had watched a movie in the same room.

My heart skipped when my hand brushed her mother's as we

both reached for the popcorn, but she didn't even flinch. She didn't seem bothered by me at all. By the time the movie reached its halfway point, I wasn't overthinking anymore. I was just... enjoying it.

When the film ended, Hana hopped off the bed and flicked the light on, making us all squint against the sudden brightness. "Hair time!" she declared.

Her mother muttered something under her breath as she slid off the bed too. I grabbed another handful of popcorn before joining them. Hana fetched argan oil, a comb, and a wooden scalp massager.

Her mother settled herself against the bedframe, then tossed a throw pillow onto the floor between her knees. "Come sit here, Hana," she said, pointing to the space.

I grabbed another pillow and set it on the floor a few inches from them. Sitting cross-legged, I tucked my knees under and tried to relax.

She uncapped the bottle, and the smell hit me—earthy, rich, the kind of scent that clings to you for days. Warming the oil between her palms, she began massaging it into Hana's scalp, her fingers practiced and sure.

"Take out your braids so she can do yours after," Hana suggested.

"No need," I brushed it off quickly. "My hair is literally impossible to handle."

"Open it, let me see," her mother insisted.

That's when I realized that she's never actually seen my hair. A sudden wave of self-consciousness rose in me. The braids were old, overdue for a redo. Still, I tried not to show my nerves as I slipped off my scarf.

"Zwaina," *Beautiful.* she murmured. One of the few words I had picked up this past few weeks.

I smiled, muttering a shy thank you. She motioned for me to scoot closer, and when I did, she rubbed a bit of oil into my scalp and over the ends of my hair.

"It's dry," she observed.

I sighed and nodded. "Yeah, I haven't done it in a while."

Truth was, I could have oiled my hair alone, in the bathroom or when Badr was out. But I didn't want the smell to linger in his room. I was used to it but I wasn't sure how he'd feel.

"Keep the braids, I'll oil it after I finish with her," she said firmly, returning to Hana's hair. "Do you always braid it yourself?"

"Yeah," I admitted. "My mother used to do it for me, but then I had to learn."

Her eyes softened, and her voice dropped. "Badr told me about the accident with your family. I'm sorry, *binti*. I can't imagine how hard that must have been."

A sad smile tugged at my lips. "Yeah, it was hard. But… I had my grandfather."

Her expression shifted instantly. "That mean old man?!" she exclaimed, eyes wide. "I still can't believe he wanted to get you married off like that." She shook her head, her words slipping into Darija at the end, which sent Hana into a fit of giggles.

I couldn't help but laugh too.

"Seriously, when I met him it took everything in me not to pull his eyes out. How can someone be that ignorant of their own family?" Hana's mother said, fingers moving deftly through her daughter's hair.

I sighed. "He wasn't always like that. He used to be kind. They say it's just old age."

"Old age or not, he was ready to ruin your life. That's not something a caring person does."

"I know…" My voice softened. "But when the accident happened, he was the one who stayed with me after the hospital discharged me. He didn't leave me alone for days. He brought me food, woke me up every morning and made sure I showered. He never left my side."

Hana cracked one eye open. "Then why would he force you into marriage?"

I shrugged. "Khadijah's failed marriage really got to him. He didn't want that for me."

"Who's Khadijah?" Hana asked.

"My step-cousin. She lives with us too."

"Oh, I saw her there. Why does she stay with you? What happened to her parents?"

"Her parents divorced when she was like 10 maybe. Her mother remarried, and the new husband didn't want her around. So Baba took her in."

Ma's hands paused for a moment. She clicked her tongue softly, shaking her head. "SubhanAllah, I can't imagine a mother leaving her child like that."

I nodded, exhaling.

"But to be fair, we don't know what she went through. You never really know someone's struggle until you're in their shoes." She added.

"Yeah," I smiled faintly. "We've had a lot of failed marriages in the family. Baba just wanted to protect me from the same fate, so he did what he thought was right."

She made a low, unimpressed sound in her throat, a noise that carried more judgment than words. I only smiled, letting it pass.

"It doesn't matter," Hana piped up suddenly, grinning as she cracked both eyes open. "He's the reason Habiba is here anyway." She poked at my foot, her touch light and teasing.

I laughed, leaning forward to tap her arm in return. Our giggles overlapped, filling the room like a soft ripple of warmth.

23

BADR

للهُ حُسنُك حُسن لا قياسَ لَّه
ما كان لله لم يخضع لمقياس

By God, your beauty is a beauty beyond compare,
What is of God's own making, no earthly measure can ensnare.

- جاسم الصحيح

"Maybe we should just live in a tent," Habiba grumbled.

"At least we'd get to design that ourselves," I replied, earning a reluctant smile from her. "Anyway, I think George is going to drop us if we don't stop being picky."

"Na ga alama," she murmured, almost to herself. Then louder, she translated, "I can see that."

We both went quiet again, drained from the endless apartment hunt. Every place we'd stepped into throughout the week had managed to disappoint us in its own special way. One had a kitchen so cramped I couldn't even stretch both arms out, and another boasted a "modern open plan" that felt more like a glorified hallway. I remember pointing out how the composition of one living room was all wrong, the windows swallowed by a wall that begged to breathe, light blocked where it should've poured in.

In one apartment Habiba leaned in close and muttered that the entire shelving unit was misaligned by a few centimeters, and suddenly I couldn't unsee it. We both stood there, fixated like lunatics on that crooked line while the realtor rambled about "spacious storage." By the third or fourth stop, every flaw seemed to shout at us, and our shared annoyance started to feel like its own private language.

"Let's just take the first one," Habiba suddenly announced.

"Really?"

"It's literally five minutes from here. And we can rip down that trashy wallpaper, add a few of our things, make it feel like home."

I thought it over, then sighed. She was right. Renovating it to our taste wouldn't be an issue. In fact, we'd be doing the landlord a favor.

"It's small, within budget, and easy to redecorate," I said, nodding.

I turned toward her, but she was already watching me. We smiled at the same time. "Well then… I guess I'll text the agent," I said.

She nodded, satisfied.

I did just that. The agent responded immediately, thrilled, said he'd talk to the landlord and start the procedures.

"So, do we fix it up first and then move in, or move in and renovate as we go?" Habiba asked, unclipping her seatbelt.

"I think it's better to fix it first, start fresh. I just hope the landlord allows it."

"Even if she doesn't, we can make temporary changes. Reversible ones. Plenty of ideas out there now," she shrugged.

"Well, Ba will be happy to hear he can finally start planning the *walima*," I said, pulling the keys from the ignition. We both stepped out of the car and headed into the office.

I was in the middle of reviewing drawings when the phone on my desk rang. I grabbed it, frowning.

"Yes?"

"Mr. Idrisi? Could you come to my office, please?" Habiba's voice was firm, professional.

I blinked. She'd been at a site this morning, I didn't even know she was back. A quick check of my phone showed no messages. Pushing that aside, I headed to her office, knocked once, and entered when I heard her response.

245

Habiba sat behind her desk, her posture straight, composed. Beatrice, our structural engineer, stood beside her with a spread of drawings laid across the table.

Beatrice gave me a brief nod. I moved around to stand next to Habiba, my eyes scanning the floorplan.

"It's the Franklin project," Habiba said evenly. "Show him the revisions."

Beatrice began walking me through the drawings, but I stopped her mid-sentence.

"Wait. We set the floor-to-ceiling height at 3.2 meters. Why is this showing 2.95? Where did our height go?"

"We had to raise the slab for the plumbing slope," she replied without hesitation.

I shook my head. "It has to be 3.2."

Her brow arched. "You want working toilets or tall ceilings?"

"I want both," I countered flatly.

"There wasn't enough service space."

I rubbed my temple, irritation flickering. "Then we have to reclaim at least a few centimeters somewhere."

Habiba leaned forward, her voice calm but decisive. "Drop the ground floor level by 150 millimeters."

I considered it, then nodded. "That could work. Let's do that."

Beatrice moved on, tracing the lines of the stair design before halting again. "This tread-to-riser ratio isn't going to pass. The code caps riser height at seven inches. Yours are pushing almost eight."

Habiba folded her arms on the edge of the table, studying the drawing. "We know. The draft looks steep because the landing extension isn't included here. It's a two-part staircase with a mid-level pause to reset the rhythm."

I flipped through the oversized sheets until I found what I wanted. "Here. After the landing, the riser height drops to six-point-seven-five. We compressed the bottom steps slightly to align with the new living room level."

Beatrice leaned over, scanning. She gave a slow nod. "Alright. But your tread depth is still borderline."

Habiba beat me to a response. "We added a twenty-millimeter nosing detail on every step. Brings the effective depth to two-eighty. Perfectly within code."

Beatrice smirked faintly, folding the drawings back into her A4 file. "Fine. But if the inspector so much as blinks at this, I'm pointing fingers at you."

I allowed a small grin. "No problem. We'll even bring an espresso to the inspection."

She chuckled, shaking her head, before gathering her papers and slipping out, the door clicking shut behind her.

I leaned against the edge of the desk, letting my weight settle. With one hand, I spun her chair so she was facing me. She blinked up, startled, but didn't push away.

"You look tired," I said, studying the faint shadows under her eyes.

"Tate is a douche," she muttered, slouching in her chair. "I would pay not to work with shits like him again." The corner of my mouth tugged upward—first time I'd heard her curse. She mumbled a quiet 'Astagfirullah' to herself, the way she always did when she thought she'd overstepped.

"Yeah?" I exhaled, unsure how to help. "I told you to stop taking clients like him."

Her eyes narrowed. "You never told me that. You just dump them on me whenever you don't want them."

I gave her my best sheepish smile because... fair. When I meet a client and get the gut feeling they'll be a headache, I send them to Terrence, knowing they'll somehow land in Habiba's lap, especially the ones with deep pockets. I'm in this job for the craft, not the chaos. She used to think she was winning when one of my clients "transferred" to her. Truth was, I'd sold her the ticket to hell with a bow on top.

"You're the one who takes them anyway," I muttered. "Tell me what happened."

She sighed like the air had been punched out of her lungs, forehead dropping onto the desk.

"First, they wanted the measurements changed, again. Then they argued with me about the color of cement." She lifted her head just enough to glare at me. "Cement, Badr. As if I mix it out myself."

Her hands moved sharply as she spoke, every gesture cut clean with frustration.

"He brought his cousin who dropped out of architecture school in second year. And the man had the audacity to tell me what I was doing wrong." I snorted, pushing off her desk toward her small coffee corner. "Do you know what he said was wrong?" she demanded.

I glanced over my shoulder. "What?"

She gave a bitter laugh. "That I should've made the window three centimeters wider to balance the whole facade."

I couldn't help the chuckle that slipped out, shaking my head. She was already smiling now, the irritation softening as she leaned back.

"And then," she went on, voice catching with disbelief, "he said the corners of the house were too sharp. Too aggressive. That I should've... softened them."

That did it. I doubled over, and she broke right along with me. Her laughter spilled out—free and loud, nothing like the polite, leashed chuckles she usually allowed herself. The warmth of it caught me completely off guard. It made me want to be the reason she never stopped.

"How stupid do you have to be to say that?" she gasped, wiping her eyes. I laughed harder, until the kettle clicked off behind me and we were left catching our breath, small echoes of laughter still curling between us.

"Dealing with stupid clients comes with the job, hbiba dyali," *My Beloved.* I muttered and paused for a second, realizing what I just said. With a scoff and a shake to my head, I reached for the Lipton and added dried mint leaves because it always seemed to loosen the tension in her shoulders.

No sugar. She'd once said it distracted her from the taste. She also hated waiting for it to cool, so I didn't fill the cup all the way, letting it steep just enough before pouring in a touch of cold water.

Her voice rose and fell behind me as she spoke, the cadence more soothing than the words themselves. When the tea was ready, I set it in front of her. She blinked in faint surprise before curling her hands around it like she'd been cold all day.

She took a sip, eyes fluttering just slightly, and the smallest sigh slipped out. "Thanks," she murmured, then groaned. "Sorry... I just... I've never really had anyone to complain to about this. Except Terrence, but he gives me ten minutes before my free trial ends and he's asking if I want another project because I look 'jobless.'"

That earned a quiet laugh from me. "You can complain to me anytime. As long as I get to complain to you too."

"Nope. You don't get to complain, Baddie." She said it softly, peering at me sideways with a grin that knew exactly what it was doing.

I groaned. "Oh my god, did you have to?"

She was already imitating the voice—that voice—"Hey Baddie, how's the project going? Look, I brought muffins. You're working so hard everyday, I have to feed you myself."

Mrs. Raifer. My personal nightmare. I groaned louder; she laughed harder.

"She was smitten with you," Habiba said, throwing her hands up. "She came here every day like she was on payroll."

"She was just… sweet," I defended weakly.

"Sweet? Please. She was ready to have your babies." I made a face, but she kept going, tears of laughter threatening. "Don't pretend!"

The truth? She wasn't wrong. Mrs. Raifer, third divorce, too much time, too much money. She'd stretch the project for months just to have a reason to show up, always with food, always with that ridiculous nickname. When her friends caught wind of me, it was like being drafted into a very unwanted sequel.

"The only reason I put up with it was because I needed the money," I admitted.

She sipped her tea with exaggerated innocence. "Mm-hm."

The room went still except for the low hum of her computer. The tea sat warm in her hand, the faint scent of mint curling up between us. Then her phone buzzed right before mine did.

We both glanced at our screens, then at each other.

"Duty calls," she said lightly, but her voice had that softness to it, like she didn't really want it to.

I nodded, already rising to my feet. But my body betrayed me— betrayed us.

Before my brain registered what I was doing, my hand slipped behind her head, my shoulders dipping toward her. A habit. A reflex I'd done a hundred times with Ma, with Hana, with my brothers.

A forehead kiss.

But this wasn't them.

This was Habiba. My wife.

The one woman I had absolutely no business touching like this unless I meant every ounce of it.

Heat shot through my chest, tightening everything. I froze mid-lean, my lips suspended a breath above her skin. Close enough to catch the soft, warm scent of her. Close enough to see the tiny tremor in her inhale—just enough to know she felt it too.

250

My throat dried. My pulse thudded so hard it shook my balance.

I had exactly three seconds to make a choice.

One: Abort mission. Pull back, pretend I dropped something, laugh it off like an idiot.

Two: Commit. Kiss her forehead, then escape before either of us could unpack what just happened.

Option one would drag us back into that polite, careful distance we'd been tiptoeing around. And I was supposed to be the one closing gaps—not creating new ones.

Her lashes lowered. Just barely.

My hand tightened on the back of her chair. I leaned in.

And I did it. A soft press of my lips to her forehead—light, brief, terrifyingly real. Enough to feel the warmth of her skin and the tiny shiver that went through her.

One heartbeat later, I pushed off the moment like it burned, straightening up so quickly I nearly dropped my phone. I slapped it to my ear.

"Hello!" I announced to Jerry, my contractor, with the enthusiasm of a man who definitely hadn't just kissed his wife for the first time and panicked.

I quickly left her office, shutting the door softly behind me.

The moment it clicked closed, I froze in the hallway. My mind replayed the whole thing in sharp, cinematic detail. I actually did it. I hadn't meant that one to happen yet.

I wanted it to be different. Something slow and deliberate, maybe even somewhere quiet at night, not sandwiched between a contractor call and the smell of printer toner.

I sighed, raking a hand through my hair. And then I looked up.

Terrence. Standing halfway down the corridor, holding a folder, staring at me like I'd just stepped out of a soap opera.

We locked eyes.

"Can I help you?" I asked, shifting the phone against my ear.

From the other end, Jerry's voice came sharp: "Hello? Can you hear me?"

Terrence blinked. "You... good?"

I gave him the barest nod and started toward my office, eyes down. "Hello, Jerry?" I said into the phone, ignoring the fact that Terrence was still staring like he was going to write a tell-all about my life.

#

24

وَالحُبُّ كَاللِّصِّ لَا يُدرِيكَ مَوعَدَهُ
لَكِنَّهُ قَلَّما كالسارق استترا

Love, like a stealthy thief, attacks without a sign or plea,
But hardly ever hides its deed, for all the world to see.

- إيليا أبو ماضي

Badr guided me with one hand over my eyes, the other tugging me along, his palm warm against mine. I had no idea where we were, he'd kept the location a secret all evening and only told me that we are going on a second date.

"Just a few more steps," he murmured near my ear. His voice was calm, steady, but something in the way he gripped my hand made me think he was more nervous than he let on.

I tugged at the blindfold when he finally let go, and the fabric slipped away. My eyes blinked against soft lights that glowed blue and purple across the room, and the second I realized what I was looking at, my jaw dropped.

A pool table. A dartboard. A huge screen with controllers neatly placed beside it. A game room.

My laughter broke out before I could stop it, bubbling and unguarded. I hadn't thought about it in years, but as a girl I used to dream of this exact thing. A game date. Staying up late with someone who actually cared enough to plan it, someone who would play and laugh with me like I mattered. It was the kind of silly wish I'd buried as I grew older. Yet here I was, standing in the middle of it. And it was Badr who made it happen.

"Do you like it?" he asked. His voice was oddly low, almost cautious.

"Are you kidding me? This is so cool." My grin stretched wider than I thought possible, and in that moment, I let myself enjoy it.

He led me to the sitting area, cushions piled against the corner, the console humming softly as he powered it up. He handed me a controller and leaned back, too casual, like he wanted me to believe he wasn't invested in this at all.

"So," he said, "what do you want to play?"

"Anything," I shrugged, pretending indifference even though I wanted to squeal.

"Nope. Tonight's yours. You pick everything."

My lips twitched at the corners. I scrolled the menu, trying not to give myself away, but when I saw the title, I giggled. Need for Speed. A classic. A memory.

I clicked it.

He froze. "You play NFS?"

The expression on his face nearly made me laugh. "Of course. And I'm about to burn you"

The look he gave me said I'd just signed up for a war. "Oh, that's how it is? Alright, then."

Engines roared, the race began, and suddenly I was twelve years old again, hunched over a controller, wide-eyed and unstoppable. I won the first race, and victory surged through me. I shot out of my seat, cheering, fists in the air, my laughter bouncing off the walls.

Badr scowled, but the corner of his mouth twitched. "Best of three."

"Fine," I teased, plopping back down, my grin shameless.

He won the second round, but the third was mine again. This time, I didn't hold back. I whooped and spun toward him, basking in my win, pretending I didn't notice the way he was watching me like I was the only thing in the room.

"You're a loser," I teased.

"And you're annoying."

We kept going, round after round, our laughter tangling together with the sound of revving cars. For once, I wasn't cautious. I wasn't the careful, measured Habiba everyone expected me to be. I was just me— the girl who loved games, the girl who once dreamed of nights exactly like this.

At one point, he got up, rummaged in the fridge, and came back with drinks. "Fanta," he said, handing me the bottle.

Tired of NFS, I scrolled through the games again, feeling a spark of mischief. "Let's play Minecraft!"

He stared like I'd lost my mind. "Minecraft?"

"Yes!" I practically bounced in my seat.

He sighed dramatically, but switched the disk anyway. I knew he didn't care for it, his attention wandered, his body leaning back, shoulders relaxed, but he stayed. And that was enough.

Because it wasn't about the game. It was about this moment. About him. About me finally letting myself enjoy something I thought I'd outgrown.

We played Minecraft for a while—me, practically buzzing as I explained every new feature, gushing about how much I'd missed it, and him… well, trying. He asked questions, nodded at the right times, even threw in the occasional "oh, that's cool," but I could tell the difference. This wasn't like when we played NFS, when his whole body leaned into the game, when his voice was alive with competition. Here, he was humoring me.

A part of me wanted to keep going just to test how long he'd last before cracking, but I decided to put him out of his misery. I set the controller down and stretched, feigning a little yawn.

"I'm tired," I said, glancing at him, "maybe we should play

something else?"

His answer came too quickly. "Let's play billiards."

I shook my head instantly. "No way. I don't even know how."

"I'll teach you." His tone was casual, but his eyes had that glint that usually meant I wasn't getting out of this.

Before I could argue, his fingers wrapped around mine. Warm, firm, pulling me gently toward the table. My lips pressed into a line, pretending reluctance, but I knew deep down that I didn't really want to pull away.

He handed me the cue with the seriousness of a coach, showing me the chalk, the way to hold it, and how to angle the stick. I turned the little blue cube on my cue like it was some alien artifact, then tried to copy the way he stood. My attempt was... not impressive.

"Here, watch." He bent low, cue sliding smoothly between his fingers, and with one sharp, fluid motion, the ball rolled across the table and dropped neatly into the pocket. Easy. Effortless.

When it was my turn, disaster struck. My grip was clumsy, the ball barely moved, and the sound it made was so pitiful it almost hurt. He tried to hold it in, but the laugh broke out of him anyway.

I shot him a glare and swatted his back lightly with the cue. "Don't laugh!"

"Sorry, sorry," he said, though his grin betrayed him. He lifted his hands in mock surrender. "Come on, let me show you properly."

And then he stepped closer. I froze as he guided me to face the table again, his chest brushing my back, his arm sliding over mine. My breath caught, pulse thundering against my ribs. And then his scent wrapped around me.

"Billiards isn't about strength," he whispered near my ear, his voice lower, softer. The sound slid down my spine and I shivered before I could help it.

He felt it. I knew he did. But he didn't move away.

256

His hand covered mine, guiding my fingers into the right grip. His palm was broad, steady, brushing over my knuckles. His other hand hovered at my waist, grounding me, and I wasn't sure if it was to help my balance or his.

I could hardly breathe. I was painfully aware of how close we were, of the warmth radiating from his body even with the AC running. "Focus," he murmured.

I tried. I really did. But all I could focus on was the weight of his chest against my back, the ghost of his breath on my neck, the impossible racing of my own heart.

Together, we pushed the cue forward. The ball rolled smooth and dropped into the pocket with a satisfying click.

We stayed like that for a heartbeat longer than necessary, his chest pressed to me, my hands still under his. The silence between us stretched, thick and charged. I knew I should step away, but I didn't want to.

When he finally pulled back, it felt like breaking the surface after holding my breath underwater. I forced a smile, wide and light, pretending my knees weren't shaking. But he looked at me like he knew. Like he'd felt the same current snapping between us.

"Now give it a shot," he said, smirking as he reset the balls.

I narrowed my eyes, excitement chasing away some of my nerves.

When I attempted again, one of my shots went wild, ricocheting off the table wall, he burst into laughter. "Wow,"

Heat rushed to my face. "I was aiming! That's how they do it in movies."

"No," he said, still laughing, "in movies they actually know how to play."

I swung the cue at him half-heartedly. "Keep laughing and I'll win just to spite you."

"Whatever you say, Lalla," he teased, the nickname soft but

lingering in the air.

I bent down again, forcing myself to concentrate, but my shot was still clumsy. Close, but not enough. When I finally did sink one, though, my whole body jolted with triumph. "Did you see that? I'm improving!"

He gave a dramatic sigh. "Great. I've created a monster."

I laughed, bubbling over with a kind of joy I hadn't felt in so long.

We volleyed shots back and forth, teasing, laughing, the soft hum of music in the background adding to the playful energy. But as the game wore on, something shifted. He leaned in a little closer than necessary, brushing past me, making intense eye contact. My pulse stuttered in my chest.

"You're quick," he said, voice low, eyes glinting. "Almost like you actually paid attention when I taught you."

I grinned, cocking an eyebrow. "Should I be insulted or flattered?"

"Both," he pushed off the table, grabbing his cue.

"Let's play a real game," I challenged, leaning onto my stick as excitement sparked in my chest. "I bet I can beat you now."

He only needed one step forward before he was standing in front of me, smirk deepening. "Game on," he murmured, leaning down so close I felt the warmth of his breath. "I won't be going easy on you."

I rolled my eyes, refusing to let my pulse give me away. "You've been saying that all night, and yet—" I leaned onto the table, struck the cue, and sank the ball cleanly. "—I'm already catching up."

He whistled softly, shaking his head. "Not bad, Habiba. Not bad at all. But don't get cocky." He bent to retrieve the balls, setting them neatly back into the triangle rack.

I grinned, perching on the corner of the table, watching until he finished. When he turned and held up his hand, I hopped down and smacked his palm with a high five, then leaned forward for the break.

258

As I shifted into position, I felt him move behind me, adjusting my arms with careful precision. His hand brushed mine—barely—but the spark it left made my breath hitch.

"Do you always hover over your students this much?" I teased, forcing my focus back to the ball.

"Only the ones who distract me," he whispered. "You've got precision, I'll give you that."

I struck the ball, scattering the rack into chaos. The first few shots were uneventful, but then he started to get bolder.

"Aim a bit higher," he murmured.

My stomach fluttered. "I don't know if I should be taking tips from you or trying to avoid them."

"Take them," he said, his voice dropping an octave. "But focus on the ball, not me."

I missed my shot—whether on purpose or because of him, I couldn't tell—and he chuckled low, the sound curling through me.

"You're cheating," I muttered, more breathless than I meant, turning to face him. But he was so close I had to lean back against the table just to keep from colliding.

Instead of stepping back, he closed the distance, bracing himself over me, eyes glinting. "How am I cheating?" His voice was playful, but the weight beneath it made my pulse stutter.

"You're getting awfully comfortable, Idrisi," I said, trying to sound bold even as my heart hammered.

"Then tell me to stop," he challenged softly. "One word, Habiba, and I'll step away..." His voice dropped, "while I still can."

He knew. He knew I wasn't going to say it. And I hated him for how much I loved his confidence.

His smirk curved. "Have I checked all the boxes?"

I froze. My whole body locked tight, every nerve sparking. This was his game—push and prod until I cracked.

259

I couldn't forget the kiss he'd placed on my forehead in my office. It had been days, yet has been replaying in my mind. He hesitated then, like he hadn't meant to… but he did it anyway. I still didn't know how to feel about it. What if it's the same now? What if he hesitates again? Or worse, what if he doesn't find the courage this time and we're both left standing in that awful, awkward silence? What if he's just joking?

But what if he wasn't?

If I said yes, I'd look desperate. If I said no, I'd be lying. And the truth was worse, part of me had wanted this all along. So I had to find something in between. Not a yes. Not a no. Just enough to keep the moment alive without handing him all the power.

His gaze dipped, lingering on my lips for a heartbeat before flicking back to my eyes.

I swallowed hard. "I did say you needed a second date, didn't I?"

He arched a brow, leaning even closer. "Is that a yes… or a no?"

I held his gaze, nerves and daring tangled together. "It's… whatever you want it to be."

He never took his eyes off mine as his hand slid around my neck, tightening at my hijab, but I didn't care. His thumb rested at the center of my throat, tilting my chin up gently.

My breath caught. Slowly, deliberately, his lips lowered to mine, and the world fell away—the game, the banter, everything. When he pulled away, my gaze lingered on his, longer than I should've let it. My lips were still curved, heart still running wild, and yet I couldn't bring myself to say what was sitting heavy in my chest. So I looked away, fast, back to the balls on the table as if they could save me. I bit down on my lip, hoping it would steady the smile tugging at me, but it didn't. Nothing could.

He suggested a movie break and I immediately agreed to it. My heart was still racing, not from billiards, but from him. From how easy it was to let myself get pulled into this, into him.

In the theater, I don't know how I ended up sitting this close to him, all I knew was that I wanted to be near him.

It scared me, a little, how natural it felt. The games, the laughter, the way he made me forget myself—it had all tugged at something I'd buried years ago. That side of me that used to dream of game dates, the hopeless romantic who once believed her first kiss would happen in some silly, movie-perfect moment.

And now here I was. Living it.

My eyes stayed fixed on the glowing screen, but I wasn't watching a single frame. All I could feel was the steady hum of his presence beside me, the echo of his lips still lingering on mine, and the terrifying, exhilarating truth that I didn't want to move away.

The movie was still playing, but it didn't matter. The real story was happening right here, in the silence between us that no longer existed.

25

 HABIBA

رَأَيْتُكِ يدنيني إِلَيكِ تَباعُدي
فباعَدتُّ نفسي لالتماس التقرب

I saw that my withdrawing drew you closer to my side,
So I withdrew myself more, for nearness to abide.

- العباس بن الأحنف

Ba and Badr carried the groceries and shopping bags inside, placing them on the dining table. Originally, Badr and I had planned to head straight to our apartment to clean and redecorate, but the shopping had taken longer than expected and I was starving.

Badr suggested we grab something to eat, but there wasn't anything appealing nearby. Ma, ever practical, insisted we come home and eat instead. "So much stuff," she muttered, rifling through the bags. "You two are sinking a lot of money into a rental," she added, frowning. "You'll be there maybe a year or two. I doubt it's worth it."

"Ma, one year in an ugly apartment will drive me insane," Badr replied without missing a beat.

"Maybe say *Alhamdulillah* you can rent an apartment at all," his mother shot back sharply, her gaze pinning him.

I bit back a laugh, watching him shrink under her stare.

Pushing their chatter aside, I went upstairs to change into something comfortable so I could help in the kitchen. After praying Asr, I folded the mat and as soon as I placed it in its spot, I felt arms wrap around my waist, spinning me around.

I leaned back to see his grinning face and scowled. "You're really annoying, you know that?" I said, tugging at his grip, knowing full well I wasn't going to break free.

"And you're really cute," he countered, pinching my cheeks.

"Don't do that again," I glared, flicking his chest.

"Or what?" he leaned closer, that teasing, challenging look I'd grown to love. My lips threatened a smile.

Ever since that first kiss, Badr had been relentless, stealing little pieces of me whenever he could, morning, afternoon, night. Pretending to hate it has become my full-time act, but he always knew. Every brush of his lips, every soft nuzzle at my cheek or forehead, made my heart squeeze in ways I couldn't hide.

"Or what?" he murmured again, pressing a soft peck to my cheek. I bit my lip, trying to hold in a laugh, but it escaped, soft at first, then he kissed my other cheek and it bubbled into something full and warm.

He moved to my forehead, trailing gentle kisses down to my temples. Each touch was tender, playful, yet full of an affection I felt deep in my chest. I let my hands rest on his shoulders, leaning into him, surrendering to the warmth of his arms.

Then he pressed tiny, careful kisses along my jawline, my ears, and finally my neck, and I couldn't hold it in any longer—my laughter spilled freely, bright and full. He laughed too, low and happy, wrapping me close so I couldn't escape, but I didn't want to.

I smiled against him, heart racing, feeling more comforted, cherished, and alive than I had in a long time. "You're annoying," I whispered, breathless, but my tone carried no annoyance, only the kind of fond exasperation that comes with being utterly happy with someone.

"And you love it," he murmured against my temple, his lips brushing my hair.

I couldn't help the grin that spread across my face. "Maybe," I giggled softly, letting him hold me a little longer."But I have to stay difficult to keep you on your feet and make sure you don't change your mind," I added, wrapping my arms around him fully, letting my fingers lace over his back.

"What does that mean?" He leaned back slightly to look at me, frowning now, eyes searching.

I bit my lip, realizing what I said before quickly stepping away, "Nothing," But of course, he didn't let me.

His arms held me firm, warm and steady, and I felt a shiver of comfort through me, despite the nervous flutter in my chest.

"It was a joke," I smiled, but he didn't seem convinced at all, so I just aimed for the truth. "I just worry a bit," I admitted softly, letting my forehead rest lightly against his shoulder. "You know how you men are… always chasing excitement. So I worry that you'll get bored."

He didn't answer right away. His silence pressed in, heavy and deliberate, until I swallowed hard and continued.

"You're amazing, Badr. You do everything right and it scares me. It feels too good to be true. I just can't help waiting for the heartbreak, because in everything good, there's always heartbreak. That's just how life works."

When I looked up, his frown deepened, and for a long moment, he simply held me, hands firm at my back. Then he finally spoke, voice low and steady, "I promised you I would stay with you."

"Yeah… so many people promised the same thing. And look where they are now," I said, matter-of-fact, even though the ache in my chest throbbed at the words. His gaze lingered on mine, lost in thought. The silence stretched, heavy and intimate, and I whispered, almost against my will, "Please don't get mad."

He shook his head, drawing me closer again, letting me rest against him. His lips pressed to the top of my head, lingering, and I felt the steady warmth of him grounding me. "Of course I'm not mad. I'm just… thinking."

"About what?" I asked, tilting my head up, letting the tips of my fingers trace the line of his arms.

He exhaled slowly before releasing me, though his hands remained close, brushing the sides of my waist as if to ensure I didn't move too far. "How to be better… If your heart doesn't feel safe with me, then obviously I'm not holding it right as a husband."

I softened immediately, my shoulders relaxing against him, guilt and worry melting into the comfort of his presence. The quiet intensity of him, the way he looked at me, made my chest swell with something unspoken. I felt small and cherished all at once.

I opened my mouth to protest, but he shook his head, not letting me speak.

"Listen, Habiba," his voice was low. "Of course life isn't perfect. Of course things can go wrong. But that's exactly why we put our trust in Allah. Tawakkul isn't about waiting for heartbreak, it's about believing that He will protect you, even from me. That *He* won't let me hurt you, not if I'm meant to be the one *He* preserved for you."

I swallowed hard, his gaze pinning me in place, refusing to let me hide behind my fears.

"If you keep pushing away because you're afraid," he continued, softer now, "then you don't give me the chance to prove that. You don't give me the chance to be the husband you deserve. And that's not fair to either of us."

My throat tightened because deep down I knew he was right.

Slowly, I let myself sink into his arms, guilt curling at the edges of my relief.

"I'm sorry," I murmured, my voice small against him. "You're right. I never thought of it that way. I should've trusted that more."

He gently tipped my chin up, forcing me to meet his eyes. His expression wasn't stern, only steady—like he was holding the weight of both of us.

"You're not wrong for feeling that way," he said firmly. "Doubt is normal. We're human. But I'm telling you now that I'll do whatever it takes to make you trust that I'm not going anywhere. That I'll be with you. Always."

Something in me melted at that, and before I could respond, he leaned closer, his breath brushing mine. His hands held me just so, warm and steady, and I felt the familiar flutter in my chest, the same way it always did when he pressed his lips to mine lightly, a gentle, teasing kiss that wasn't rushed, didn't need words. My pulse stuttered, anticipation and comfort all at once.

We lingered there, forehead to forehead, letting the quiet stretch between us, the small smile tugging at my lips. These little kisses had become our thing—soft, fleeting, but enough to make the world narrow down to just us.

And then a sharp knock rattled against the door, yanking us apart.

"Habiba! Come on, we need to cook!" Hana called cheerfully, her voice slicing through the intimacy.

We straightened, laughing softly at the timing.

At the apartment door, my key scraped in the lock. The hinges groaned as I pushed it open, a faint stale scent slipping out—the stubborn mix of old carpet and damp. I flicked on the light, watching dust motes swim in the sudden glow, and for a second, the silence felt almost physical.

The place was... good. A small one-bedroom tucked into the corner, with an open kitchen bleeding into a boxy living room. The counters were scratched, the maple cabinets faded and begging for a second life. It wasn't perfect, but it felt like a good start for us.

Badr trailed in behind me then went straight to the windows, pushing them open one by one, while I pulled the cleaning supplies from the bag. As soon as I started putting on my gloves, he came up to me, hooking the face mask over my ears and adjusting it at the bridge of my nose until it sat perfectly.

"I don't want your allergies to get bad so don't take it off." he warned, then stepped back. "You can take the bedroom, I'll handle the living room, or whatever you want," he added.

His sleeves were rolled all the way up, muscles taut as he tugged on gloves, and his cap was turned backward, keeping his hair out of his face. "Sure, that works," I muttered with a shrug.

He nodded and picked up the broom. "I'll sweep down the walls. You can wipe the surfaces."

I moved to the bedroom, started wiping down surfaces, then drawers, working my way into the living room and kitchen. We didn't speak, just the rhythm of cleaning and the faint rasp of dust rags on wood.

Every now and then, Badr's voice would break the silence—low, unhurried recitations of random surahs. His tone wasn't performative, just natural, the way some people hum without thinking. But I found myself slowing just to listen. There was a softness in his voice that curled around the words and settled deep in my chest.

I was halfway through scrubbing the counter when his voice came again, not with Qur'an this time, but a question.

"What was your family like?" The suddenness of it made me blink. "If you don't mind talking about them, of course."

"I don't," I said, smiling faintly. My fingers kept moving over the cloth, but my mind had already gone elsewhere. I couldn't remember the last time anyone had asked me that. It was like I'd been holding the answer for years, waiting for someone to care enough to open the door.

Badr didn't fill the silence. He just kept cleaning, but I could feel his attention, the way he'd slowed slightly, making room for my words.

"Abba was… bubbly," I began, the memory tugging a smile from me. "He wanted to open the doors of the world for us. Always pushing us to try new things. He was a software developer."

I glanced over my shoulder. He'd stopped dusting for a second, leaning on the handle of the broom, nodding slowly as if committing every word to memory.

I moved on to the stove, scrubbing at a stubborn grease spot. "Mama was more reserved. She loved her comfort. She was an accountant at Abba's workplace." My smile tilted, teasing. "They tell the same story over and over again about how he fell in love with her at first sight and married her."

His mouth curved into a knowing smile. "Sounds like your father knew exactly what he wanted."

"He did," I said softly. "I was their firstborn, then Halifa, then Ji'dah. Three years between each of us. They planned it that way."

"Smart, I like the way they think." he said, and it made me laugh.

I told him about Halifa wanting to be a footballer, Ji'dah being the little princess who always got her way. For a few moments, it felt warm, light.

"You all grew up here?"

I shook my head. "My dad was born here, but he moved back to Nigeria for work, met my mom, married her, had us there. We only moved here when I was eleven. It was supposed to be for two years. Then… after the accident… I kept going back and forth until I finally stayed."

His hands stilled on the broom handle, he asked. "The accident happened here?"

I nodded, and a shadow slipped over the warmth we'd built. "Abba wanted to take us shopping for a work event." I said quietly. "We stopped at a red light, and when it turned green, he drove forward… another car ran the red from the opposite lane and hit us."

He fell silent, eyes lowered, letting the words settle between us. "What happened to the other car?"

"He died on impact," I murmured. "I was the only one who made it out alive."

"Did you get any bad injuries?"

I nodded. "Mostly emotional, but... a few scars here and there. Cracked ribs, a concussion, a couple of stitches."

He exhaled softly. "I'm sorry you had to go through that." I smiled faintly, unsure how to respond. "Is that why you don't drive?" he asked.

I thought for a moment. "Not really. I did take a few lessons with my dad back then, but after the accident... everything moved so quickly. I never got the chance to go back to the things I used to enjoy. It would be nice, but honestly? I don't think I'll ever get the time."

He nodded, then gave a small, rueful smile, glancing down at himself, dusty, and endearingly disheveled. "I'd hug you, but I'm filthy."

"Yeah... I'm good." I said quickly, wrinkling my nose in mock disgust.

26

 HABIBA

ظَمِئتُ فَلَمْ أَظْمَأ إلى بَرَدِ مَشْرَبٍ
وَلَكِن إلى وَجْهِ الحَبِيبِ ظَمِيتُ

I grew thirsty, yet I did not thirst for the coolness of a drink;
rather, I thirsted for the face of the beloved.

- بشار بن برد

All the seats in the conference room were finally taken. The air smelled like coffee, recycled ambition, and the faint chemical tang of dried glue from the presentation boards in the corner. Badr sat opposite me, flipping through his notes like a man prepping for a Supreme Court trial.

It was our usual Monday meeting and, as usual, most of us didn't want to be there.

Terrence strolled in five minutes late, latte in hand, irony fully intact. He dropped his tablet onto the table with a thud, stood behind his chair like a talk show host about to deliver bad news, and raised his cup. "First of all, congratulations to Theo for wrapping up Villa Sira."

Theo stood, bowed with exaggerated flair, and we clapped.

"And Jannet, for the eco-school in Montreal—keep up the good work, folks." Terrence clapped twice, sat, and sighed like we were already exhausting him. "Okay, who wants to go first? I had a terrible morning. I need good news."

Silence. Then Gabe cleared his throat. "We've finalized the zoning paperwork for the renovation. Still waiting for the green light from the city. In the meantime, our structural engineer thinks—"

"Wonderful," Terrence cut in. "So you're still exactly where you were last week."

Gabe's mouth opened, closed, then he sighed like a man deciding not to die on that hill.

Terrence's gaze slid to Lailah. "Anything new?"

"We will have a one-month delay on the—"

"Thanks for the bad news," Terrence interrupted again. "Badr? Habiba? How's Franklin?"

Badr leaned back, then gestured for me to speak. "We've wrapped up the structural coordination and finalized all the technical drawings," I said. "Got the go-ahead for construction."

Terrence gave a rare approving nod. "Ahead of schedule. Nice."

That's when Gabe, from two seats down, smirked. "Honestly, we all thought the two of you would kill each other before finishing this project. But look at you—suddenly inseparable."

Badr didn't miss a beat. "Yeah. I've already added her to my emergency contacts. Next thing you'll be sending us a wedding gift."

The room chuckled. I glared at Badr because only I knew the irony behind that.

Terrence waved a hand. "As long as you get the job done, you could start a family for all I care."

Badr smiled at me, loudly. "Maybe we should. That's a great idea."

The room laughed. My skin prickled with awkwardness. "Maybe we could keep this conversation away from my reproductive choices? And as tempting as it sounds, I'm not interested in producing more of him."

Badr gave me a look and I smiled sweetly in response, which was my favorite way to irritate him.

"Habiba, personal projects?" Terrence asked.

I flipped open my file. "New project's in design phase—client and I are fine-tuning the concept. Second project's in final construction stage, just finishes left."

He nodded and turned to Badr, "Still in planning phase," Badr said. "Couple of design iterations, client keeps changing their mind. Also working on the Bennets' interior."

Terrence glanced around. "Any more news?"

Gabe piped up about the Trinity presentation. Terrence told him to come to his office after. Then: "Meeting adjourned."

People started packing up, eager to escape. I didn't move, and Badr, noticing, stayed put. Once the door shut behind the last person, I grabbed my notebook, walked around the table, and smacked him on the arm.

"Ow?"

"Stop it," I hissed.

"Stop what?"

"Whatever this is you're doing. You're making it too obvious."

He sighed. "Habiba, they'll be getting an invitation to our nikah next week. What's there to hide?"

"Well until then, behave. We worked too hard to be taken seriously. You think they'll separate your smirk from your talent?"

"You worry too much. Let them think what they want. It's been over a month. I show up, I deliver. So do you. Besides… you're the one who blushes when I look at you too long." He leaned in, that mischievous smile tugging at his lips, aiming to steal a kiss but I caught him with a finger to his chest, pushing him back just enough.

"Yeah. Totally. My skin color really makes that obvious."

He smirked. "Of course, your eyes sparkle," Then, more serious, "But, if it bothers you, I'll be more discreet. I just thought easing them into it was the plan."

I sighed. He was right. "Whatever. Back to work."

Except he caught my hand and kissed my knuckles. He does that a lot. I was mid-eye-roll, lips parting to throw some sarcastic remark at him, when movement at the doorway made me freeze.

Tina.

Her eyes dropped to our hands, lingered, then flicked up to my face, then to his. Back down again. The silence stretched, thick enough to choke on.

Badr's eyes went wide, panic flashing across his features, and he dropped my hand like it burned. My knuckles tingled where his lips had been, suddenly too exposed.

"It's not what it looks like," he blurted, voice cracking with the speed of his defense.

Tina's brows lifted a fraction, her mouth curving into a dry smile. "Yeah. I'm sure it's not."

"You don't understand," Badr spoke, his voice very stable for someone who was probably freaking out on the inside. "It's literally the first time she didn't argue with me. I panicked and got affectionate."

My jaw fell open. That's the excuse he's going with?

"Sure," Tina said slowly, drawing out the word like she was humoring a toddler. "Bet that was terrifying." She extended a file without breaking eye contact. "Approvals for foundation."

Heat crawled up my neck. I snatched the folder just to have something to do with my hands, while Badr—traitor that he is—used the moment to retreat, practically sprinting out of the room and leaving me to suffocate in the awkward silence he'd created.

Tina arched a brow. "So… Badr, huh?"

I played dumb. "What's that supposed to mean?"

"Oh please. You two have been orbiting each other for weeks. Whole office sees it."

"We're just being civil. Promised Terrence we'd behave."

"Yeah. Totally civil. Just two professionals making eyes and kissing hands. What's next, carrying your bag to the car?"

I said nothing.

"Last I checked, you don't even shake hands with men. So why is Badr kissing yours?"

"I don't owe you an explanation," I said, trying to walk past.

"God Habiba! I knew one of you would fall in love, but I didn't think it'd be you, come on girl!"

"I am not in love." I stated before leaving.

News spread fast. I went downstairs to speak to Beatrice, but everyone was staring. Normally, when something like this happened, I'd snap at them to stop gawking, but I had a feeling I knew why I was getting all the attention.

When I glanced down the hall, Tina was at the far end. She looked nervous, eyes darting away the moment I caught her gaze. I didn't bother saying anything to her. But as I was seated in my office, the phone rang.

Terrence. Calling me to his office.

I rubbed my forehead, my whole body scrunching in discomfort, but I grabbed my phone and stepped out anyway. The moment I did, Badr stepped out too. He turned toward me with a smug little smile.

"Where are you going?"

"To Terrence. He called me," I said, already annoyed.

He frowned. "He called me too," I walked past him. "What's going on?"

"I panicked and got affectionate," I quoted, narrowing my eyes. "Seriously? That was the best you could come up with?"

"Hey, I bet you couldn't think of anything better," he said defensively.

"Yes, I can," I whisper-snapped.

"Do it then."

"Well, it's too late now." I threw my hands up in frustration.

We were both standing outside Terrence's office, mid-argument.

"We weren't gonna hide it forever anyway," he shot back.

"You were never even try—"

The door opened, cutting me off.

"Are you coming in, or are you gonna hang around out there like shadows?" Terrence asked, his expression bored.

"Is that a rhetorical question?" I asked dryly.

One look from him had me walking into his office.

27

BADR

وكم أبصرتُ من حَسَن، ولكن
عليك لشقوتي وقع اختياري

I've seen so many lovely sights, this much I can confess,
Yet my heart chose you, my beautiful distress.

- محمد بن وهيب الحميري

I sank into the chair across his desk with a lazy confidence I didn't entirely feel. Best way to handle these situations? Pretend you've been here before.

Habiba… not so confident. She slipped into the seat beside me like she was walking into a courtroom. Her fingers were knotted together, pinching the skin of her thumb over and over. That wasn't her. She was usually the one who stared people down until they broke first.

Terrence leaned back, eyes darting between us like he was trying to solve a puzzle. "I take it you know why I called you here."

"No idea," I said smoothly. For all we knew, he could be calling us in about budgets, deadlines, or the fact that the coffee machine had mysteriously 'disappeared' from the break room last week.

He gave me a slow nod, then sighed like this was the part of his job that aged him. "I've been hearing… inappropriate talk about you two going around."

"Inappropriate?" Habiba said, her voice a little too high, a little too shocked.

"That you two are having… intimate relations." He stressed the word like it tasted sour.

My stomach clenched. Exactly what she was dreading. The

bounce in her leg gave her away instantly. My gaze flicked down, and for a second I had this stupid, protective urge to just lay my hand over her knee, still the movement, tell her it was fine. Instead, I kept my hands to myself.

Terrence kept talking. "I know I encouraged you two to bond, but in case it wasn't obvious enough, I meant professional bonding... You know how the board feels about office romance."

I sighed. "Terrence, I really couldn't care less how the office feels ab—"

"You should care," he cut in sharply. "It's your job on the line."

"Then maybe the board should look at results. Every project we've touched? Done. On time. On budget. Better than half this office produces. We make a good team, so what if we happen to care about each other?"

"It's not about you," he said, voice firm. "It's about the team. About setting a standard. Office romances are messy and complicated."

Ever since Habiba and I got married, I'd done my homework. I knew where the lines were, legally and professionally.

"This isn't about how I feel, Badr," he said. "If HR finds out, they'll complicate it more than it needs to be."

"Well, the board can't do anything about it."

He gave me a short, humorless laugh. "You have no idea, son."

"We're married," I said flatly.

Silence.

Terrence blinked, then looked between us like he was trying to catch the bluff. "You two... you're married? Just like that? No ring, nothing?"

"Our religion doesn't require the use of rings."

The room was quiet long enough to hear the clock tick. Then he leaned back and crossed his arms. "Let me be clear, marriage or not, this changes nothing. The board doesn't want romantic entanglements in the office. It's still a breach of professionalism."

"Actually, it does change something," I countered. "Most workplace romance policies don't apply to married couples, especially when there's no direct line of authority. We're not breaking policy. Legally, we're protected."

"You think being married makes it all go away?"

Habiba's voice cut in, steady now. "I think being married means it's not the company's business unless it affects our work. And since we've consistently delivered, ahead of schedule, and above expectations, we've done our part. We didn't bring this into the office. We kept it private for a reason. We haven't let it affect our teams, our deadlines, or our quality."

The corner of my mouth lifted. There she was. My girl.

The silence that followed was heavy, and then Terrence finally exhaled like he'd lost a round in a fight.

"Fine. You've made your point. But this will go through HR. Full disclosure by end of day. And from now on, separate teams. I will keep you two on the Franklin project for now, but, no bias, no tension. Keep it clean, or I'll find someone who can."

I nodded. "Deal."

We stood. I held the door open for Habiba, and we were halfway out when his voice stopped us.

"Congratulations on your marriage... I wish you both the best."

Habiba gave a small, polite "Thank you," and we stepped into the hall.

We didn't say a word on the way to her office. I could still feel the tension humming off her, like her composure in there had been borrowed and was now overdue.

The thing about Habiba is that I used to think she was made of steel. Always unshakable, always ready to take a hit and give one back. But the last few weeks had shown me something different. Behind the iron was someone doing everything she could to keep her head high—

278

someone who, behind closed doors, just wanted to let it drop for a while.

So I try to be there whenever she needs, to be the person she could lean on when the iron mask got too heavy.

Once the door to her office shut, I half expected Habiba to crumple to the ground from the weight of it all, or to snap at me and tell me it was my fault. Because it was.

She did neither.

Instead, she stepped toward me with sudden urgency. My first instinct was to brace, I thought she might shove me, hit me, something. But her hands came up around my shoulders and then she was holding me, pressing into me like she needed an anchor.

For a split second, I froze. Then instinct took over. I wrapped my arms around her and pulled her closer, feeling the warmth of her body against mine.

"I was so scared," she whispered into my chest.

"I know," I murmured back, my hand sliding up and down her back in slow, steady strokes. "I got you. Don't worry."

I told myself I wanted the motion to calm her down, but the truth was I didn't want it to work too quickly. I wanted her to keep holding on, wanted to feel the weight of her trust. It was rare for her to come to me like this unprompted, and every time she did, it felt like proof I was doing something right.

"I thought we were both going to lose our jobs," she said, voice small.

"Come on," I chuckled softly, trying to lighten her grip on fear. "We basically run this place. They can't afford to lose us."

She huffed, frustrated. "God, they're so annoying with their stupid rules." She pulled away, trying to reassemble her composure.

She was adorable like that.

MashaAllah. Even with fire in her eyes.

Then I remembered why we were here in the first place, because

Tina couldn't keep a secret.

That thought burned through me so fast my pulse went from steady to pounding.

I excused myself from her office and headed down to the hall. The noise was low, until I turned a corner, in search for Tina when I heard her name. My wife's name.

"... couldn't have just switched up in a few days. I'm telling you, he's giving it to her good, softened that cold heart of hers. If she gave me a chance, I bet I could show her what a real man ca—"

He didn't finish. My hand was already in his collar, yanking him around.

For half a second, my fist hovered, my brain flicking through the haram-versus-justice argument. Then his words replayed in my head and my morals stepped aside.

The punch landed with a solid crack. His head snapped sideways, coffee sloshed to the floor.

It was long overdue.

Theo staggered, dazed. Gabe gasped something, but I didn't hear it over my own pulse. I hauled Theo upright again, our faces inches apart. His eyes were wide, skin flushed, breath sharp with panic. I let him see every ounce of intent in mine.

"I'm gonna say this once," I said, my voice low and calm. "Keep my wife's name out of your mouth. You talk about her, look at her wrong, even breathe in her direction, and I won't stop at one punch." I shoved him back, turning my gaze to the rest of the room. "And that goes for all of you."

The silence that followed was thick, heavy enough to press against the walls. Message received.

Then I saw her. Habiba, coming down the stairs, Terrence just behind her. Her face was tight with worry.

I stepped forward, meeting her at the base of the steps then held out my hand. She hesitated, glancing between my face and my fingers. I told her without words that it was okay. She slipped her hand into mine, and that small motion tightened something deep in my chest.

I turned back to the crowd, her hand still in mine. My voice carried.

"Ok," I said, clear enough for every corner to hear, "Habiba Mukhtar and I are married. We've been married a while now but kept it private. But now that it's out, let me make something clear. My job is to protect her peace. And I will. I know she can handle herself with the ladies—" my gaze swept the men, "—but if any of you step out of line, you'll find out just how territorial I can be."

I let my gaze rest on Theo just long enough for the air to thicken again.

Terrence barked. "Get back to work. Badr, Theo—my office."

I knew that was coming. Still worth it.

Theo didn't bother with pleasantries. He launched straight into his complaint, loud and rehearsed. "This is harassment, hostile behavior. I want HR to look into his conduct."

Terrence rubbed his temple and sighed. "Theo, we can talk this through. A fight in the corridor doesn't need a file. Let it go."

Theo's jaw tightened. "So you'll just let him get away with assaulting me?"

I said nothing. I let them dig their trenches. I'd already shut off the part of me that made threats look like promises. I didn't want the circus, I wanted him away from Habiba.

Terrence tried reason, voice low. "You both calm down. We mediate. No HR. No records. This is an architecture firm, not a boxing ring."

I kept my mouth closed until he did the one thing that snapped the tether, a cheap joke about Habiba, the little edge in his voice that made the compliment a weapon.

"The two of them walk around the firm like they own the place. She's a little too full of herself for my taste anyway. They deserve each other."

That was it. I moved before I thought. Only this time, I didn't throw a punch. I just folded my hands on the desk and smile, "You want HR?" I said quietly. "Fine. I'll file first."

Theo blinked. Terrence stiffened.

"I'll file a complaint about your language and your conduct toward a co-worker. If you take this to HR, it doesn't just sit on my record. It sits on yours too. Harassment, creating a hostile environment and threatening your colleagues in the storage room."

Terrence picked it up. He was good at this. He spelled it out clinical and calm. "If this goes to HR, both of you will have notes. One for assault, one for harassment. Both are problems. Theo, are you prepared for that outcome?"

Theo's bravado thinned like ice in sunlight. He swallowed, and then, sharp and quick. "Fine, two weeks unpaid suspension for Idrisi. I walk away. No record."

Terrence nodded and wrote it down. "Two weeks. You accept, Badr?"

I signed the form Terrence pushed across without bothering to read. Two weeks off. No pay check. I didn't care. I didn't care about the job in that moment, I cared about the message. He stays away from Habiba. That was the entire point.

Theo left with his chest puffed and his dignity slightly more brittle. Terrence exhaled, looking at me the way a man looks at someone he knows he can't fully fix.

"You alright?" he asked.

I shrugged, the motion light. "I'm fine. Just don't let him near her."

Terrence gave me a look, half warning, half understanding. I stood, pushed back my chair, and for the first time that day, I felt like I'd done the one thing that mattered.

When I stepped into Habiba's office, she was already waiting.

"You didn't have to create a scene," she said, her voice even but her eyes sharp, like she was searching my face for the part of me I wasn't showing. "You could've spoken to him privately. You know punching anyone in the face is haram."

I leaned casually against her desk, folding my arms. "I did what I had to do," I answered, steady, unyielding. She pushed away from where she'd been standing and crossed the space between us until she stood right before me.

Her lips curved, not with disapproval but with a flash of something dangerously close to mischief. "Well... I'm glad you did. I wish I'd been there to see you land that punch. You should've called me to watch."

A laugh slipped out of me, low and unguarded. My hand brushed against my knuckles, still raw from the impact.

Without asking, she reached for my hand. One palm cradled mine, the other lifted it, and then her lips pressed gently to my bruised knuckles. She stopped there, letting the warmth of her lips soak into my skin, before lowering my hand back down but not letting go.

The gesture went straight through me. Before I could think better of it, I reached out, sliding my hand to the back of her neck. She didn't pull away, not even a little. My thumb brushed against the softness of her skin as I tugged her closer, and when our lips met, the world narrowed to nothing but her. She kissed me back without hesitation, without walls, and for a moment everything else disappeared.

When I finally drew back, her breath mingling with mine, I still held her hand in mine. I gave it a gentle squeeze. "That makes it all better," I murmured.

Her eyes softened, though her voice dropped to almost a whisper.

"Of course it did."

Pushing back from the chair, I muttered something about working on our paper and stepped out, letting the cool air of the hallway calm me.

The rest was easy, forms to fill, our marriage certificate scanned and ready. When Habiba double-checked the details, I submitted them to Terrence.

For the first time, I didn't have to slip out ahead of her like we were strangers. We walked through the door side by side, got into the car together and drove away.

We should have done this months ago. The drama didn't have to happen. I know I caused it, but if I'm honest with myself… I wish I'd claimed this openly a long time ago.

These days, Habiba moves around me differently, more open, less guarded. There's still shyness, yes, but there's trust. Comfort. And that's worth every second of trouble it took to get here.

We even managed to fix the apartment to our liking. Different styles made the process an uphill climb, but at the end of the day, it was ours. And arguing over curtain colors with her somehow felt like winning.

28

BADR

أَضَرَّت بِضَوءِ البَدرِ وَالبَدرُ طَالِع
وَقَامَت مَقامَ البَدرِ لَمّا تَغَيَّبا

She rivaled and outshone the moon, in its most glorious phase,
Then stood as moonlight's substitute, throughout the moonless days.

- البحتري

When I stepped into his office, the air smelled faintly of polished wood and leather—old money and discipline. Sunlight slanted across the shelves lined with books on global markets, gold-lettered spines in perfect order. His desk was a fortress of files, contracts, and a single family portrait, angled away like it wasn't meant to be seen.

He didn't flinch at my entrance. Just adjusted his glasses and kept writing, the pen scratching steady against paper.

I raised my hands. "Before you get mad, I come in peace."

Baba's eyes flicked up, sharp, then down again. "What do you want, Badr?"

"You know my name now? See? That's progress." I joked, which only I seemed to find funny. "I'm here to talk. About Habiba."

"I don't have time for this." He checked his watch.

"Then I'll be quick."

Something in my voice made him pause. With a slow exhale, he gestured toward the chair opposite his desk. Not welcome, but not thrown out either.

I sat, leaning forward. "Habiba has been happy since moving in with me. She's close with my family. Hana treats her like a sister, my brothers love her, my mother... she calls her a daughter."

His pen scratched again. "Is this you bragging? Because I have better things to do."

I ignored the jab. "But none of us can replace you. You're her family. Her blood."

The pen slowed, then stilled. He set it aside and removed his glasses, finally looking at me.

"She checks her phone a lot," I said quietly. "Waiting for a message that never comes. She defends you even when she shouldn't. She tells me how much you've done for her, how you raised her after she lost everything. And she believes you love her. But your silence feels like abandonment. Like she's losing another family member."

Something flickered in his expression. Not regret, but weariness.

He leaned back, hands clasped, voice low. "You think I don't feel the weight of all this? Habiba has always been my favorite. She is the last piece I have of her grandmother. After my wife died, all I had was my son and now without him, Habiba is the only thing that reminded me that I still had something worth protecting."

The words cracked on the edges, the mask slipping.

I seized it. "Then why risk losing her? Why let ego matter more than her happiness? You're willing to lose the last piece of your wife just so you don't have to admit you were wrong?"

His jaw tightened, but he said nothing.

I leaned in, heat rising in my chest. "If you keep going like this, it won't just be Habiba you lose. It'll be the chance to see her children too. To know the family she'll build."

That landed. His eyes fell, shoulders sinking, just for a moment. Then he gave a dry laugh—bitter, half-muttered to himself. "At the rate this family is giving me headaches, I'm not sure I'll live long enough to see that time."

"I came because she loves you more than you deserve, and she invited you to the *walima*. No one else. Just you. All I'm asking is that

286

you show up for her. Just once. Just this one time."

Silence stretched. He looked at me, and for a heartbeat I saw not the stern banker everyone feared, but a tired man haunted by loss, clinging to pride because it was easier than admitting pain.

I stood. "You don't have to answer now. Think about her. Think about what you'll lose if you don't." I offered a quiet salam and turned for the door.

He didn't stop me. Didn't say yes, didn't say no.

Still, I hoped coming here wouldn't be for nothing. More than anything, I wanted him to show up, for Habiba. Seeing her grandfather would light up her entire day in a way nothing else could.

As I pulled out of the parking, I made a mental note not to mention this to Habiba. If he failed to show, it would only deepen the crack in her heart.

A week into the suspension, I realized it wasn't half as bad as I'd thought. I had time to think, to breathe, and to plan the *walima* properly. Invitations, menu, etc. Habiba teased me about being more organized for a dinner than I ever was for a project. Maybe she was right.

The only thing I didn't like about the suspension was her being in the office all day without me. The thought made my chest tighten, not because I didn't trust her, but because I didn't trust them. Especially Theo. But she reassured me that he'd been keeping his distance like a man who finally learned the meaning of "boundaries."

Terrence, to his credit, had been fair. He could've locked me out of everything, but he didn't. He allowed my assistant and Habiba to keep me in the loop. They'd call or send updates every evening about client adjustments, supplier delays, design revisions. I wasn't meeting clients in person, but I was still fixing things from behind the scenes.

Sometimes I dropped by the sites quietly, keeping my distance from the office, pretending I wasn't technically on suspension. And honestly, it worked. The buildings didn't stop taking shape, and neither did my peace of mind.

Overall, it's been good. Great, even. Maybe suspension wasn't punishment, maybe it was just the universe telling me to take a breath before everything changed.

I checked my phone, only to find out that Habiba texted me. She was at a café for a client meeting. She'd sent me the address and asked me to pick her up when I was done. The text was thirty minutes old.

The café wasn't far. When I pulled up, I typed a quick text to Habiba. As I stepped out of the car, my eyes caught the shimmer of a grey hijab through the glass. My lips tugged into a smile. I could spot my Habiba anywhere.

I moved closer. She was speaking with someone, her laptop already closed so their meeting must have been wrapping up. I shifted my angle slightly, just enough to see who sat across from her.

Mr. British Pants.

The man wore his crush on his sleeve every time he looked at her, never bothering to hide it. In his defense, he had no idea she was married, but still. The way his posture leaned in, the way his gaze lingered, it was all too obvious.

Just in case their meeting wasn't officially over, I typed a message: Can I come pick you up?

Her phone lit up on the table. She paused mid-sentence to glance at it. The tiniest twitch curved her lips upward. Just a flicker. But I swear, it sent my heart into a backflip.

Her reply came a second later: Yes.

I didn't wait. Immediately, I pushed the door open and I forced myself calm, smoothing my expression before I reached their table. "Assalamu alaikum," I greeted evenly, my hand extended.

The client glanced up, startled for just a beat before covering it with a grin and shaking my hand. "Mr. Idrisi… I seem to find you everywhere she is."

I pulled out a chair, sliding it firmly beside Habiba before answering, my tone low, deliberate. "She's just better company than most."

His grin faltered, his gaze flicking between me and Habiba and the little space between us, as if recalibrating. "You're a couple, correct?"

Before I could answer, Habiba cut in, her voice smooth, unflinching. "He's my husband."

A slow warmth spread through me at her words but I let it slip in the slight curve tugging at my mouth.

He nodded firmly, "That's too bad."

I scoffed, "Well, that depends… from your side of the table, it might be bad. From mine, not so much."

He forced another smile, though it never reached his eyes. Then his gaze dipped briefly to her bare hand, "I wouldn't be married to someone this beautiful and not have her wearing a ring."

I leaned back, my own smile sharpened to an edge. "The ring is there… but let's be honest, who's going to notice it when she's the one wearing it?"

There is no ring, but he doesn't know that.

His expression flickered. "That I agree with," he smiled, then he rose smoothly, fastening the buttons of his suit jacket. "Well, it was nice chatting with you, Mrs. Mukhtar. I'll be waiting for your updates." His eyes cut to me. "Mr. Idrisi. Always a pleasure."

"Likewise," I said, standing to shake his hand. Only when he walked out the door did I settle back into my seat, draping an arm along the back of Habiba's chair.

"You broke his heart," she said, lips pursed in a pout.

I smirked. "He signed up for a heartbreak the minute he thought he had a chance with you. That's hardly my fault."

"To be fair, he took interest in me before you ever married me. He was just too late."

I raised a brow. "I'm not sure how I feel about knowing he could've been your husband instead of me."

She tilted her head, eyes gleaming with mischief. "For someone who was forced into marriage, you seem awfully happy with the outcome."

"The only thing that would break my spirit is if you weren't happy. And from what I can tell…" I glanced at her, letting the words hang before finishing with a shrug, "…you seem pretty happy to me. So I'm going to relish every second of this." Her lips twitched and I leaned closer, "Shall we?"

She nodded, and we exited the building together. I opened her door, waited until she was settled, then circled back to the driver's side. The car hummed to life.

Without planning it, the words slipped out, "It's time to get you a ring."

Her head turned slowly, curiosity dancing in her eyes. Then she smiled, small but sharp. "Wow, he really bruised your ego back there huh? Were you that jealous?"

"Yes." The answer was out before she finished the question. No hesitation. No shame. Her brows shot up, but I shrugged, allowing myself the smallest smile. "Jealous doesn't even begin to cover it. Mostly I'd prefer to slap a 'do not disturb' sticker on you."

She tried to hold back her grin, "You're ridiculous. In my culture rings aren't even a thing. We don't need them."

I glanced at her, one hand still steady on the wheel. "Well, here they are." my voice dropped, deliberate, "Here, a woman walking around without a ring means she's single. And I can't have people thinking you're single. Too many idiots to fight off."

She chuckled. "That doesn't sound too bad. I could just organize a wrestling match. Whoever wins gets the girl."

"Cute," I grinned. "Or you could just let me buy the ring and save me from arm-wrestling strangers. Same result, fewer bruises."

Her lips curved, sly and amused. "But you're very likely to lose."

I raised a brow. "Aren't you the same person who said her husband is a big man with big muscles? What happened to that man?"

She smirked, leaning back like she had all the time in the world. "Oh, he shows up when I need the groceries carried in. Other than that? Haven't really seen him."

I barked out a laugh, shaking my head at her shameless jab, and she joined in, her laughter warm and unrestrained.

At home I didn't waste time, I dropped her off, asked her to get ready for a third date a went straight to a jewelry shop. The best thing to do would have been to take her with me and have her pick a ring for herself, but knowing Habiba, she would probably pick the simplest things and complain about the price, so I would prefer to pick for her, and besides, I have a pretty good idea of what she likes.

It didn't take too long for me to pick, one out. A silver band with a beautiful flower shaped diamond, perfect like her, florally, simple and beautiful. Size wasn't a problem either because I smuggled one of her rings before leaving and they had her size so I brought it immediately.

At home, I tried to sneak into Hana's room to show her first because if she likes it, then Habiba would definitely like it but obviously they were together, so I went to Zain's room.

He was hunched over his computer, headphones on, fingers flying over the keyboard. "Zain," I said.

He turned his chair halfway, pulling the headphones off one ear. "What?"

"I got something," I said, walking toward him.

His curiosity kicked in immediately. He spun his chair fully, grinning. "What is it?"

I didn't answer. I just handed him the box.

He blinked, then carefully opened it and his jaw dropped. "Woah," he whispered, his grin stretching wide.

I nodded.

He jumped up from his chair, laughing. "You actually bought her a ring?!" he turned the box under the light, admiring it. "You know this was supposed to come like... a month ago right?" He teased.

"Shut up," I playfully slapped his head.

Just then, the door creaked open. We both froze. I snatched the box from his hands, shoving it behind my back, thinking it was Habiba. But it was Ahmed, standing in the doorway holding his game controller.

"What are you hiding?" he asked, narrowing his eyes.

Zain laughed. "Nothing you're supposed to see. Unless you can keep a secret."

Ahmed's curiosity won. I opened my hand slowly, showing him the ring.

His eyes widened. "Whoa. It's shiny."

Zain chuckled. "You have no idea, kid."

Ahmed grinned. "It's pretty. She'll like it."

That simple, honest answer made me smile. "Yeah," I said softly. "I think she will."

Zain nudged me. "Let's go show Ba."

I tucked the box into my pocket and followed them.

We found him in his room, reading. The three of us jumped onto his bed like we used to when we were younger. He eyed us suspiciously. "Ash?" *What?*

I pulled the box out and opened it.

His expression softened instantly. "SubhanAllah," he murmured, reaching to take a closer look. "It's beautiful." He took the box out of my hand and inspected it, smiling. "May Allah bless this gesture, and the one you're giving it to." Then he looked at me seriously. "But you know it's only a symbol right? It doesn't make your bond stronger, nor your love holier. Don't believe what the world tells you about these things. It's bidah."

"I know, Ba," I said, smiling. He nodded, satisfied, and patted my shoulder.

That evening, I took Habiba to a quiet Chinese restaurant. Our third date. I booked a private room, low lights, paper lanterns swaying softly above our heads. We sat on the floor, cross-legged, a spread of sushi and small dishes between us.

She was talking animatedly about work when a bit of sauce clung to the corner of her lip. I reached for a tissue and wiped it gently. She paused, blushed, and smiled.

We laughed. We talked. The world outside disappeared.

When the plates were empty, we leaned back against the wall, sipping our drinks in easy chatter. I set mine down and reached into my pocket.

"I've got something for you," I said.

Her eyes brightened. She put her drink aside. "What is it?"

I smiled and leaned in, brushing my lips softly against hers.

She smiled back, cheeks pink.

My initial plan was to just hand her the ring quietly, without making a fuss. But where's the fun in that? I decided to exaggerate it a little, make a moment out of it. Just for us. Just because I liked seeing her laugh.

"I know it's only our third date," I began, putting on my most serious voice. "But these few days have been enough for me to know that you're the one I want to spend my life with."

Her eyes widened, caught between amusement and disbelief. "Are you about to propose?"

I laughed. "Is that weird?"

She giggled. "Wow, I've always dreamt of some theatrical proposal."

I raised a brow. "Should I get on my knees?"

"No!" she laughed harder. "Just ask me to marry you."

She sat up straighter, still giggling, waiting.

I mirrored her, sitting up straighter, playing along. "Alright then." I pulled out the ring box with unnecessary drama. "Habiba Mukhtar," I said, half-laughing, half-serious. "Will you marry me?"

She laughed so hard she nearly knocked her drink over. "Oh my God, this is so funny!" And before I could react, she leaned forward and kissed me. My heart warmed. It was the first time she'd leaned in herself, the first time I didn't have to.

"Is that a yes?" I murmured when she pulled back.

She smiled, still giggling. "I'm already married to you. I'm saying yes to the ring. It's beautiful."

Her laughter softened into something tender. I slipped the ring onto her finger, thinking how even pretending to propose to her still made my heart race.

"What about your ring?" She pouted slightly.

"We can go get me one together," I whispered as I leaned in to kiss her again.

29

HABIBA

فَإِنَّكَ في عيني لأبهى مِنَ الغِنى
وَإِنَّكَ في قلبي لأحلى مِنَ النصر

For in my eyes, you are more splendid than all wealth untold,
And in my heart, you are far sweeter than a victory.

- أبو فراس الحمداني

On the morning before the *walima*, Badr's mother looked at me and said, "I know this isn't Morocco, but you deserve at least some of the experience." I smiled politely, thinking it would be just a small gesture like a cup of tea and a bit of henna on my palms. But I was wrong.

That same morning, I was swept off like some kind of precious package, tucked into a warm car with two aunties and Hana who hummed traditional songs and fed me dried apricots dipped in orange blossom water. We drove to a hammam that belonged to one of Badr's mother's friends, also from Morocco. From the moment I walked in, I was theirs.

They undressed me of my doubts, scrubbed my skin raw like they were trying to peel away the years I spent being invisible. They wrapped me in rosewater and clay, massaged argan oil into my shoulders, and legs with patience and praise.

Zain drove us to a salon, and for the first time in my life, I let someone other than my mother wash and blow-dry my hair. I sat there quietly, watching it fall in soft coils past my shoulders, reaching almost to the middle of my back. The stylist offered to braid it for me, but I shook my head. My 4A curls didn't need much fussing, I usually braided them myself but today I wanted it loose, free.

I wasn't sure when the thought took root, but the idea of Badr seeing it like this made something stir inside me. The very fact that I wanted him to see it left me shy, almost embarrassed. I kept staring at my reflection, cheeks warm, wondering when I'd started caring what he thought of me and why the thought of his eyes on me suddenly mattered so much.

I tied my hair in a tight bun, and put on my hijab before we left for our next quest.

Badr and I haven't seen each other all day. I had taken the day off work—it's Friday anyway, and site visits could wait. For once, I didn't mind the pause. I didn't feel like I was missing anything.

Because here, in this house, for the first time since my family died, I felt like I belonged somewhere again. Not like a guest, not like an outsider politely tolerated at the edges of a family. But like a daughter. A sister. A bride.

By evening, my henna was finished. The men were sent off to have a sleepover at our tiny apartment, with Ayaan happily joining them.

I didn't always follow their conversations, they slipped in and out of Darija sometimes, but Hana mostly stayed with me, translating when I was lost. Between laughter and teasing, they showered me with advice.

It reminded me of weddings back home in Nigeria. I couldn't help thinking that if my family had been here, I would have experienced both worlds—the Arewa wedding traditions alongside the Moroccan ones. But I had no family to invite. My mother had been an only child, her parents long gone. Baba was still mad. And in Nigeria, there was no one I was close to, no one who would cross an ocean just to attend my Walima.

The ache of that truth lingered in my chest, but it was softened by the warmth around me. We sang, and laughed until we were breathless, every ounce of energy poured into joy.

The older women had taken it upon themselves to shower me

with advices, each word making me wish the floor would open and swallow me whole. I had no idea how to react, how to even arrange my face. Then Aunt Maryam pressed a small bottle of perfume into my hand. "Use it every night before you go to bed," she whispered with a knowing smile. "He won't be able to resist, I promise."

Hana was long gone, having escaped the circle with no interest in their talk. I wished she'd dragged me with her. Ma wasn't any help either, she only sat nearby, smiling politely, too wrapped up in her own conversation to notice how desperately I wanted out.

By the end of the night, we collapsed where we were. They spread themselves across the living room, insisting I take the bedroom. But I couldn't bring myself to sleep alone, not when everyone was gathered here, talking, laughing, creating the kind of togetherness I had long craved.

So they pulled Ahmed's mattress into the living room. I lay down there among them, my heart lighter than it had been in years, wrapped not in blood ties, but in the kind of family that is chosen, built, and gifted by Allah.

The house buzzed with wedding-day energy by midmorning. The event was set for 4pm, but our photoshoot was at 2. After breakfast and a quick shower, I sat for my makeup. I asked for something simple. Soft gold on my lids, a thin black line hugging my lashes, and just enough red to warm my cheeks. No glitter. No drama. Just me, polished.

Then I slipped into the orange takchita Badr had chosen, a warm, vibrant shade that clung to me softly and made my skin look like sunlight. His mother fastened layers of delicate jewelry around my neck and wrists with a kind of quiet pride. I packed my Hausa dress for later and we headed to the wedding studio.

When we arrived, Badr's father was standing by the car, deep in a phone call. He gave me a gentle nod toward the studio. Badr's mother stayed back with him, so I walked in alone, nerves fluttering in my chest like moths.

Inside, the photographer's assistant spotted me first. "Wow," he breathed, grinning wide. "You look amazing. Come in."

Badr was seated in front of a soft white backdrop, dressed in a deep burnt orange robe, traditional and regal. His hair was curled tightly and shorter, a heavy stubble darkened his jaw, trimmed into sharp lines. He looked like the kind of man angels would dress with care.

His eyes dragged over me with something between wonder and disbelief, expression unreadable but intense. The photographer lifted his camera without saying a word and clicked even more.

"God, I love the look of love," he muttered to himself as he studied the preview shots. He was a young Black guy with tight curls and a green shirt tucked into blue jeans, probably no older than thirty. "Join him, please," he said, waving me forward.

I hesitated, fingers tightening on my dress, but Badr stood as soon as I took a step, as if drawn to meet me halfway. I took off my jacket and hung it, then he held out his hand, steady, warm, and I slipped mine into his.

We stood facing each other, eyes locked. The room fell away. My breath stilled.

"Masha Allah," he whispered, brushing his knuckles against my cheek. His eyes held something I couldn't look at too long, like a flame I was scared would burn me if I leaned in. My heart pounded so loud I was sure the camera picked it up.

"Perfect, just like that!" the photographer exclaimed from behind his lens. I had nearly forgotten he was even there.

I turned slightly, and Badr moved behind me, resting his hands gently at my waist. His presence surrounded me like a quiet kind of protection. The flash went off again.

"You look beautiful," he murmured, his breath brushing against my ear.

I smiled without meaning to.

"Yes! That! More of that, Badr. Whatever you're doing, keep it up!" the photographer said, clearly delighted.

I didn't dare turn around, afraid it would break the moment. I just stood there, trying not to melt where I was. Badr made it easier. He kept slipping me small comments, little jokes under his breath that made me laugh even when I was trying not to. He was warm, Gentle.

When we were done with that set, I asked to change. Badr's parents joined us then, and his mother helped me adjust the layers and jewelry.

When I stepped out, all ready for the shoot, Badr was nowhere in sight.

I glanced around, holding the hem of my dress up slightly so it wouldn't drag. The assistant asked me to wait while they set up the lights, but my stomach fluttered for an entirely different reason.

Where was he?

Then he walked in.

And my mouth parted without permission.

He wasn't wearing what he had on before.

He was in a full Hausa outfit—babar riga and all. A pale, regal blue that shimmered just slightly under the studio lights. Embroidered details traced the sleeves, and his cap sat slightly tilted, just enough to be stylish, just enough to make my heart forget how to beat.

"Oh my God," I whispered, barely aware I was saying it aloud.

He grinned as he approached, that playful glint in his eyes. "What do you think?" he asked, doing a slow 360 turn like he was on a runway.

I blinked. "You look so good. MashaAllah."

His smile softened at the edges, losing its teasing bite. "I wanted to match you."

The words hit me like sunlight, warm and golden. I stepped

closer and reached for the folds of his babar riga, fixing the way it draped, smoothing the fabric over his shoulder.

"This part should fall here," I murmured, half to myself, half to him.

He didn't move, didn't even breathe loudly. Just watched me with that look again. Quiet affection. Pride, maybe. That barely-there smirk.

I threw the gele I brought around my body, holding it in place with a practiced hand, then turned to him.

"Ready?" he asked.

I nodded.

And the camera started clicking.

By the time we wrapped up, it was already 4pm. His parents were rushing us. His mother tried helping me out of my dress, but it was stitched so precisely it clung like a second skin. We laughed about it, tugging carefully so the fabric wouldn't tear.

When I finally changed back into my Moroccan *takchita*, we left for the event.

The house smelled like cardamom and roasted almonds.

We had invited an imam from the masjid to come perform the du'a. The living room had been cleared out, the couches pushed back to make space. Cushions were brought out for the elders, and in the center, a small spread of tea, sweets, and traditional snacks greeted every guest who walked in.

It wasn't grand. But it was warm. It felt like home.

Ayaan was everywhere at once, welcoming guests at the door, refilling trays, making sure the tea was hot, reminding the kids not to spill things on the rugs. Badr didn't even need to say anything, Ayaan moved like he already knew what needed to be done.

Zain was right there with him, carrying plates, joking with the younger kids, and directing people toward the washroom like a proper event manager. The two of them were seamless, like they'd done this together a thousand times.

Most of the guests were Badr's people, friends from university, uncles from the masjid, neighbors from years ago, friends from his shawarma restaurant. I held his hand as he guided me through the crowd, whispering names into my ear before introducing me with quiet pride. Most of the faces were strangers to me, yet they smiled like family, kind and easy-going, offering blessings and good wishes without hesitation.

Still, beneath all the smiles, I kept glancing toward the door. Hoping, wishing.

I knew Baba wasn't coming, but a part of me still hoped. Maybe he'd just want to see me happy.

Every time the bell rang I would look desperately, hoping it would be him. I told myself to stop, to let go of the hope that he'd show up. The evening was slipping away, and disappointment had started to nest in my chest.

And then, the bell rang again.

I almost didn't look, almost spared myself the ache of another letdown. But hope is a stubborn thing, it whispers even when it hurts. I lifted my head, breath caught halfway in my throat.

It was him, Baba.

My heart slammed so hard I thought it might give me away, tears burning at the edges of my eyes, but I swallowed them down. Not here. Not now.

Beside me, Badr noticed. Of course he did. His thumb brushed over my knuckles. He leaned in just enough to catch my eye, a soft smile tugging at his lips. And then, without hesitation, he stood and gently pulled me along with him.

We crossed the hall together. My Baba's eyes found mine, crinkling with warmth, but before I could say a word, he shook Badr's hand with a kind smile that surprised me more than anything.

"Thank you for coming," Badr said sincerely, his voice steady.

Baba nodded, "You left me no choice," He responded, smiling, prompting a chuckle out of Badr, then he turned to me. I didn't think, I just threw my arms around him. His laugh rumbled in my ear as he hugged me back, patting my back like I was still his little girl. In that instant, the whole day shifted.

"You look beautiful," he said when I finally stepped back.

I grinned through the tears I refused to let fall. "Thank you."

Then he turned to Badr, mischief dancing in his eyes. "You weren't kidding. The happiness shows on her face."

Badr chuckled, shaking his head with that easy smile. Before I could protest or laugh, Badr's father appeared, extending his hand warmly to Baba. Just like that, the two of them slipped into conversation, voices mingling as if this had been planned all along.

I just stood there, my hand still in Badr's, heart lighter than it had been all night. I took a moment to thank him because somewhere between all that I knew he convinced Baba to come, for me.

In the middle of it all, Badr leaned close and asked, "Wanna switch it up?"

Minutes later, we reappeared wearing our Hausa outfits—his deep blue babar riga matched my shimmering *gele*. It wasn't required, it wasn't part of any official plan—we just wanted to. The cameras came out again. Laughter, compliments, more tea.

Finally, the guests began to leave. One by one, we said our goodbyes. It wasn't until the very end that the mood began to shift.

Hana clung to Badr. Ahmed kept rubbing his eyes, pretending not to cry. Zain had gone quiet.

It hit us all at once, this was it.

He wouldn't be sleeping under the same roof as them anymore. Wouldn't knock on Ahmed's door to say goodnight. Wouldn't sit on the couch drinking tea with Hana curled beside him.

They were losing a brother, and I was gaining a husband.

And I felt guilty. I wanted to say we could stay longer. Just one more night. One more morning. But life had already turned the page.

Badr hugged Hana tight, whispering something to her that made her giggle through her tears. He gave Ahmed his forehead kiss, Zain pulled him in for a long, quiet hug. Then it was time.

We got into the car, waved one last time through the window as the house grew smaller in the rearview mirror.

Our house wasn't far. A short drive away. But the space between that house and ours felt longer than it was. Like we'd crossed some invisible line between what was and what's about to be.

Badr was quiet the whole ride. I could feel it, the weight in his shoulders, the way he gripped the wheel tighter than necessary. He was holding it all in.

When we pulled up to the apartment and the car came to a stop, I turned to him. "Are you okay?" I asked softly.

He sighed, long and heavy, and rubbed at his eyes. He wasn't. I could see it, and I didn't wait for him to admit it. I shifted in my seat and reached for him.

He didn't resist. He leaned forward until his forehead rested on my shoulder, his body slowly relaxing into the contact. "I didn't realize it would be that hard," he murmured.

"I know…" I whispered, rubbing small circles on his back. "I'm sorry."

His head lifted slightly, just enough for me to catch the red around his eyes in the dim car light.

"For what?" he frowned.

"That you had to go through that?"

A ghost of a smile touched his lips. Then he leaned back into me, forehead brushing my collarbone. "Don't worry," he said. "It's worth it."

I smiled quietly to myself, touched in a place too deep for words.

"Well," he sat up with a sigh, blinking the emotion away, "We

303

should head in. Unfortunately, I can't just sit here and cry forever."

"No, you should cry," I teased, pulling out my phone. "Cry loud and ugly, so we can be even."

He chuckled. "Even how?"

"I'm always the one crying. It's your turn now."

"You and I will never be even, Habiba," he said, grabbing the keys. "You're a cry-baby. I'm not."

"I'm not!" I swatted his arm.

"Yes you are. It's cute."

I rolled my eyes, but couldn't help smiling. We unloaded the car and made our way toward the elevator.

That's when it hit me.

The nerves. They crept in quiet and fast, curling in my stomach. We've lived together during all this madness—shared rooms, shared stress—but this was different. This was ours. Our apartment. Our life.

Now, there'll be no Ahmed bursting in, no Hana banging on the door, no one pulling Badr away to help with something. Just me and him. Alone.

I started overthinking. Should I take the aunties' advice after all? Was I supposed to act a certain way now? Dress differently? Was I supposed to walk out with my hair down?

My steps slowed at the door

This wasn't just a wedding anymore. It was a marriage.

And it was real now. Too real.

30

BADR

ما كنت اعلم ما هم و ما جزع
حتى شربت بكاس الحب مغترفا

I never knew what sorrow was, nor what anxiety could be,
Until I drank deep from the cup of love, and truly tasted misery.

- العباس بن الأحنف

I was nervous.

Like, actual, stomach-tightening, breath-shortening nervous.

Which made no sense.

We've been here before—same apartment, same couch, even shared the same bed ever since life got messy. But tonight felt different. Heavier. Like something invisible had shifted between us and now the air itself was holding its breath.

She unlocked the door and stepped inside. The soft click of the lock sounded way too final, like a countdown I hadn't agreed to. I followed behind, arms full—bags of food, drinks, snacks—pretending this was just another normal night.

She flicked on the lights and turned to me with a clap of her hands, a little too bright.

"Well... I guess this is it."

"I guess this is it," I echoed, tossing the keys onto the table like they weighed five kilos and placing everything on the ground.

I took off my cap—the one I'd hunted for like a rare Pokémon. My Congolese friend had a buddy from Lagos who wore these on Eid, and when I asked where I could get one, he'd just handed it to me. I was stupidly grateful. It wasn't just an outfit, it was something I thought she'd notice. Something that said, I see you.

She was by the hallway now, just watching me. Wide-eyed. Curious. The kind of look that could make a man forget his own name.

I stepped closer and placed my palm gently on her head. She didn't move. Didn't even blink. Just looked at me, as if she was trying to work out what I was about to do.

I recited softly, "Allahummainni as'aluka min khayriha wa khayri ma jabaltaha 'alayhi, wa a'udhu bika min sharriha wa sharri ma jabaltaha 'alayhi." *O Allah! I ask You for the good in her and the good that You have endowed her with and I seek your protection from her evil and the evil that You have placed within her.*

"Ameen," she whispered, smiling.

"You understood that?" I asked, a little surprised.

She shook her head, still smiling, that soft, unsure, dangerous smile that made my chest feel too small. "No idea. But I know it must be sweet."

My throat tightened. "It's a sunnah dua a man says to his wife after marriage."

Her smile tilted, almost shy. She bounced once on her toes. "Oh."

I stepped back before I forgot every rule I'd set for myself. "Why don't you go change? I'll bring the food, then we can pray and eat together."

She nodded and disappeared into the bedroom and I exhaled. Deep. Slow.

Was she expecting something from me tonight? Did she even want something from me? Because lately, every glance, every word, every laugh had been feeding something I wasn't sure I could starve anymore.

We weren't here for appearances now. No excuses. Just husband and wife.

I moved to the kitchen, unpacking food like it was a military operation. Ma had gone overboard with the portions, but I wasn't complaining. I chose one big plate instead of two. No need for unnecessary space between us.

I was pouring drinks when her voice suddenly shot down the hallway. Urgent. I dropped everything and ran.

I wasn't ready for the sight waiting in the bedroom.

Habiba was in the middle of the room, flailing like a very graceful moth. Her arms were awkwardly above her head, her dress halfway off, the tulle and satin bunched around her shoulders like a stubborn cloud.

"Badr, please help me," she said, voice muffled. "I'm going to die. I'm actually going to die in this dress." I froze, my brain processing this in delayed frames. "I'm not joking, Badr, I'm stuck. I'm claustrophobic. I can't breathe—"

That snapped me into gear. "Okay, okay, breathe. I've got you. Just... stop spinning before you take out a lamp."

I stepped in behind her and brushed my hand against the fabric, careful not to crease it. The tailoring was precise, scandalously close to her waist. I'd never seen her in anything like this before. Habiba's wardrobe was always soft fabrics that skimmed rather than clung, silhouettes that left everything to the imagination. This... this was different. It stole the breath from my chest and filled in the blank I'd only begun to wonder about since our marriage.

"Is there a zipper?" I asked.

"I already took it off, I'm not stupid," she snapped through the fabric.

I bit back a grin. "Could've fooled me."

The dress didn't budge at first, so I braced and gave it a stronger pull. It creaked, like actual seams protesting life decisions, but it moved an inch. Then another. And then—*fwump*—it came free in one smooth motion.

And I was suddenly holding her dress.

While she was... not wearing it.

Bare shoulders. The graceful dip of her back. The elegant curve of her waist.

Every neuron in my head screamed look away, and I did so fast that I might've strained something. "I'm sorry—I didn't—" My voice cracked. I cleared my throat and stared at the curtain like it had personally wronged me. "I didn't know you weren't wearing... uh."

"Pretend you didn't see that," she blurted, clutching the dress tight to her chest.

My pulse was a mess, my thoughts worse. But before I could stop myself—the words slipped out, low. "Too late, sayyidati... I'm completely flustered and it's honestly unfair how easily you do that to me."

I felt it before I heard it—her breath catching, the room tightening around us. My stomach turned hard, a twist that climbed all the way to my chest.

I cleared my throat, stiff, painfully awkward. "Well—uh—you're free now," I said, still refusing to look at her

But I could *feel* her silence behind me. Like a hand pressing against my back. Like gravity. And it only made the ache in my chest worse.

I took a step back, forcing space between us, but the ache stayed, impossible to ignore, and completely her fault.

"Yeah," she mumbled. "But emotionally scarred."

That made me laugh for real. Which made her laugh. And suddenly the tension shifted, still there, still humming, but lighter.

Without looking, I handed her a towel from the chair. "You good?"

She wrapped it around herself. "I am now."

She slipped into the bathroom, and I... well, I went straight to the living room, sat down, and made the longest dua of my life.

Once I'd gotten a grip on myself and poured the drinks, I shoved the food into the microwave and headed for the bedroom to change. I stopped at the door, hand on the frame. Took a breath, the kind you take before plunging into cold water.

When I pushed it open, Habiba was in front of the mirror.

She jumped, the comb slipping from her hand. We both froze. Her reflection blinked. I blinked. Neither of us moved.

Her hair was thick. Long, dark waves falling below her shoulders, nothing like I'd pictured. This… was something else. She wore a dark green *djellaba*, simple but elegant, flowing down to her toes, sleeves brushing just above her elbows. It was modest, but nothing about what I was feeling was.

I'd never seen her wear it before. There was something about her in a piece of our tradition that hit different. When she wore the *takchita*, my heart did a backflip, but this? This was quieter. Simpler. Somehow more dangerous.

I realized I was just standing there staring like an idiot. I needed to say something before it got weird.

"Wow… I was ready to embarrass myself with tears if that's what it took… but this works too." I stepped toward her, though every part of me wanted to stay rooted in the doorway.

She grinned. "Don't tempt me, I can still take it back and make you work for it."

"Too late." I reached out before I could think better of it and touched a strand. Softer than I imagined. "You've ruined me already, there's no going back," I murmured.

She giggled, twirling a few strands with her finger. "Careful. First it's one touch, then it's an addiction and withdrawals aren't pretty."

I froze.

I wanted to lean in and kiss her. She was expecting it too, I could see it in the way her gaze lifted to mine, her lips parting ever so slightly. For a heartbeat, it felt so easy. So natural.

But I knew things weren't going to end with just a kiss. Then her words echoed again: addiction… withdrawal.

My chest tightened. She didn't know. She didn't know the man she was standing across from, the one she was slowly giving her trust to. She thought she did, but she didn't. And if she found out the truth, what I used to be, would she believe that any of this, what I felt now, was real? Or would it all just look like another lie?

I couldn't do it. Not like this.

She murmured, "You should've given me five minutes. I would've made it prettier."

"It can get prettier than this?" I asked, voice tight.

She laughed softly, bending to pick up the comb. Her hand brushed my waist for balance. That tiny touch set every nerve in me on fire. And that was it. My brain short-circuited.

I backed away before I did something I couldn't take back, snatching my pajamas from the wardrobe. "I'm gonna change," I muttered, my voice rough, and all but fled into the bathroom.

The door clicked shut and I leaned my forehead against it, groaning quietly. What is she doing to me?

I turned on the tap for noise, splashed cold water on my face, forcing myself to breathe. I made wudu, dragging each movement out as if the water could wash away the weight pressing on my chest.

But no matter how much I rinsed, the truth clung like poison. I'm a liar, I deceived her.

When I came out, the room was different. Prayer mats laid out. Food set neatly on the dresser. Habiba had her hijab on, scrolling her phone, but the second she saw me, she put it aside and stood.

I threw on my *jilbab*, joined her, and we prayed.

She stood a few inches behind me. I focused on my recitation, my posture, anything that would keep me grounded. But my body ached. Not metaphorically. It was real, a pull in my chest, heat coiled in my gut. I stayed in sujood longer than usual, whispering to Allah for clarity, for control.

When we finished, I turned to her. She smiled. I smiled back. Then we raised our hands for du'a, and when I was done, I playfully brushed my palms gently over her face, sealing the prayer. She did the same to me, and I couldn't help but chuckle.

"Let's eat," I said.

She took off her hijab and walked to get the plate, and my eyes almost followed before I forced them away. I straightened the mats and got the drinks. I'd planned one plate between us, a small gesture to make it feel intimate. Now it felt like a trap I'd set for myself.

We ate mostly in silence. She sat cross-legged, humming softly, completely unaware.

Her perfume was new. It clung to the air, to my clothes, to my thoughts. I reached for water twice and didn't drink either time. My hands stayed in my lap, clenched.

I tried to start the conversation where I tell her the truth, but instead, I made a dumb joke about the rice tasting better than at the event. She smiled politely, but her mind was now somewhere else.

I kept glancing at her, the flecks of gold in her eyes, the curl of her lashes.

My wife.

And yet, I didn't know how to ask the questions clawing at my chest.

Are you expecting something from me? Are you doing this on purpose?

I said none of it. I couldn't. The last thing I wanted was to make her feel pressured.

When we finished eating, she carried the plates to the sink. I stayed behind, folding the mats and lowering myself onto the bed, my head dropping into my hands.

Shit.

This was either love or temptation. And if it was just temptation, then what? I'd get what I wanted, and the fire would burn out, leaving her with nothing. Would that be fair to her?

I rubbed my face hard, trying to quiet the war in my head.

What if tonight leads where I think it will? What if she gives me everything, and later she finds out the truth from someone else? That I used to do drugs, that I dragged myself clean on the back of her kindness without her even knowing?

I could almost see it, her looking at me differently, her heart cracking under the weight of a secret I should've told her first. And then what? She'd regret me. Regret us.

I couldn't be the reason she regretted her marriage.

If we were going to build something real, it had to be on honesty. And I hadn't given her that.

But what if telling her was the end? What if honesty was the very thing that drove her away?

The walls pressed in around me. My chest was tight, my thoughts circling like vultures.

I need air.

I stood too quickly, my steps brisk, almost frantic. Snatching my keys off the counter, I barely registered the sound of her rinsing her hands at the sink.

"Where are you going?"

"Just… for a drive," I said, not meeting her eyes.

"A drive? It's past eleven."

"I know. I just need to… clear my head."

She paused. I heard the faint hitch in her breath, and it killed me.

"Okay," she said.

When I looked up, the hurt was there. She tried to hide it with a smile, but I saw it. She thought I was leaving because of her. I wanted to explain, that I was walking away from myself, not her. That I didn't trust the line between patience and pressure tonight. But I didn't know how.

So I just said, "I'll be back soon."

She dropped her gaze to the empty plate.

Out in the night air, I gripped the steering wheel like it was the only thing keeping me grounded. I drove without thinking and ended up outside Ayaan's building.

The guard let me in. I called Ayaan from the door.

"Buzz me in."

"What?"

"I'm outside. Just... buzz me in."

The door clicked open. Ayaan stood there, arms crossed, jaw tight, looking like he'd personally descended from Mount Judgment. "Please don't tell me you had a fight," he barked, voice sharp with disappointment.

I walked past him, letting my feet carry me into the house, and flopped onto the couch.

"Badr, what's going on?" His tone had the kind of edge that made glass tremble.

I blinked, blankly, like he'd asked me how many grains of sand were in the desert. My brain refused to cooperate.

"Dude! What are you doing outside your home at this hour?" Ayaan's voice cracked between exasperation and fury.

I rubbed my palms on my lap, staring at a spot on the carpet as if it contained the secrets of the universe. "Wallah... I don't know..." My words stumbled over themselves, my mind circling endlessly, looping on thoughts I couldn't speak aloud.

Ayaan groaned, pinching the bridge of his nose. "It's like ever since you got married, you've lost the remaining brain cells you've had left. Why do you keep making such ridiculous choices?"

I closed my eyes for a fraction of a second, thinking of how to explain. But nothing in English felt right. And he didn't understand Darija. So I said it in the one language that I could express and he could understand. "أشعر أن قلبي يسير إليها دون إذني." *I feel like my heart is walking toward her without my permission.*

That didn't seem to help him at all, it just made him more confused. He ran a hand through his hair and crouched in front of me, watching me like I had lost all of my marbles.

"Let me get this straight… You left your wife on your wedding night to come to my home and tell me you think you're in love with her?"

The way he said it, laying it out like that, made me feel utterly stupid. I could already imagine the headlines, Husband of the year, Badr, genius, leaving his wife to confess his feelings for her to his best friend. Totally normal.

"Badr, I swear to God, I'm going to punch you if you don't start talking properly."

That finally got me speaking. I knew when Ayaan swore like that, he meant it. When he swore to do something, he followed through. I didn't want to go back to Habiba with a bruise—I'm pretty sure that wouldn't look good.

"I never told her about the pills," I admitted.

Ayaan stared at me, his silence stretching before he finally asked, "Why?"

I exhaled, staring at the floor. "I don't know. I couldn't. I can't imagine the way she'd look at me once she finds out."

His jaw clenched. "Badr… are you still on drugs?"

"No. Of course not."

"Then why are you making this such a big deal? Habiba's not going to hate you for taking something years ago to help you cope. Leaving her alone on the night that is supposed to be your wedding is far worse."

I opened my mouth to argue, but the main light clicked on. Heavy footsteps creaked down the stairs. Ayaan's father.

"What's going on here?" His voice was stern, commanding.

Both Ayaan and I froze. No one—not even my parents—knew about the pills. We'd managed to keep that secret buried all these years.

His father's gaze cut into me. "Badr, if I'm not mistaken, you just got married today. So tell me why you are sitting here with your friend instead of your wife?"

Before I could speak, Ayaan jumped in. "He's overthinking things." He waved a hand, half-annoyed, half-protective. Then, with a groan, he launched into complaining about me, how I was being stupid and always got in my own way until finally, his father grabbed my shoulders and forced me back down onto the seat.

I hesitated at first, but then I told him the truth, that Habiba and I didn't marry out of love but now, maybe I was falling for her, but I wasn't sure. I didn't say more. I didn't mention the pills, the secret I'd carried for years. I couldn't risk anyone else finding out. If I was going to tell anyone, it would be Habiba. Only her. Whether she decided to stay or walk away.

His father studied me for a long moment, his expression unreadable. Then his features softened. An almost fragile smile broke through. He leaned forward, resting his elbows on his knees. "Badr," he said, his voice warm, almost amused, "do you have any idea what you've been blessed with?"

I frowned, caught off guard.

He leaned forward slightly, lowering his voice like he was sharing a secret. "The kind of love you and Habiba were given... it's the kind the prophets themselves will envy on the Day of Judgment. A love that begins with sincerity and grows for the sake of Allah. What you feel, it's not just temptation. It's a man's heart softening, learning to love because

Allah placed someone worthy in front of him."

My chest burned, I wanted to tell him that our love didn't begin with sincerity but I pushed that aside and just tacked the next problem eating at me. "What if I'm confusing desire for love?" I asked quietly. "What if it's just... the moment?"

"Desire without discipline is obsession," he said. "But you left your wife tonight to protect her from yourself. That's not obsession. That's self-control. That's love with a conscience."

I swallowed hard.

He asked gently. "Is she kind to you?"

I nodded. "She is."

"Does she remind you of Allah?"

I didn't even have to respond to that, my smile answered it for me.

He nodded. "Then don't let Shaytan convince you this is something cheap. Attraction is a part of love. Love comes in many forms. Sometimes it's slow. Sometimes it's sudden. And sometimes... it looks like a young man sitting in his friend's living room at midnight, unsure if he's good enough."

I chuckled lightly.

"But listen to me well. Leaving her tonight was the worst thing you could have done. Women, they think, they wonder, they spiral. No wife wants her husband to walk out on their wedding night. She will ask herself questions you'll never have answers to. Don't put that weight on her."

His eyes softened again, voice lowering.

"Guard her dignity, yes. Hold back your desires, yes. But don't abandon her. Sit with her. Speak with her. Even silence is better if it means she knows you stayed."

The air felt lighter somehow, though my chest still ached. "I'm so stupid."

"Wow, really? Could have fooled me" Ayaan muttered from behind him. "Go back to your wife, man. Stop acting like a coward," he added, hurling a pillow at me.

31

أَشْكُوكَ أَمْ أَشْكُو إِلَيْكِ صَبَابَتِي
أَنتِ الدَّوَاءُ وَمِنكِ كَانَ الدَّاءُ

Shall I complain of you, or to you, of my passion's flame?
You are the cure, yet from you alone the sickness came.

– لسان الدين بن الخطيب

I chose to sleep.

Or at least, I tried.

When Badr left, the hollow ache in my chest felt like it had been carved out with something sharp. I couldn't remember the last time I'd felt that particular kind of hurt, quiet enough to sit with me in the dark.

I shouldn't have worn that stupid dress. If I hadn't gotten stuck in it, he wouldn't have seen me like that. He wouldn't have seen my body.

It had never occurred to me before that maybe he wasn't physically attracted to me. I'd always thought of attraction as a given. That it was just something that would be there because, well, we were married. But now the thought dug in sharp: what if he saw me and felt nothing? What if I looked fragile to him? Malnourished? Less woman than he imagined?

After he saw me in nothing but underwear, he'd shut down. He didn't even attempt to kiss me again. Badr is very touchy and clingy, stealing kisses from me at any given time, I thought that by moving here, being here, just us, that his affection will only increase, but man was I wrong.

It was like watching someone move behind glass, avoiding my eyes, moving through the space without his usual ease, without the offhand jokes that used to slip out of him naturally.

Maybe it was the perfume the aunties gave me. I'd used it just like they said—dab on the neck, behind the ears, a little on the wrists. Maybe it was too strong. Maybe it irritated him.

I opened the windows, hoping the smell would drift out, but the winter air was cruel and sharp; after five minutes my fingertips were stiff, and I slammed them shut.

I told myself I should be happy. This buys me more time. More space. But the truth sat there like an ugly stone in my chest: it hurt.

I paced the apartment until I felt the thoughts eating holes in me, then finally crawled into bed and closed my eyes. Sleep came in thin, jagged pieces.

When I woke the next morning, the space beside me was cold. I didn't check the living room. I didn't want to. I took my time in the shower, dressed in the long-sleeved cotton pajamas and matching pants. It was one of the new sets they gifted me. When we were preparing for the *walima*, we didn't tell the others that we'd already been married for over a month. We let them believe last night was our first night together.

When I stepped out of the bathroom, he was sitting on the edge of the bed. He held roses and a box of chocolates.

"You're back," I said, my voice flat as I moved to the wardrobe, pretending I didn't feel that sudden pull in my stomach.

He stood, his footsteps slow but sure. I could feel him getting closer before I turned.

"I'm sorry," he said, holding the flowers out.

"You're a grown man, Badr. You're free to do and feel whatever you want. I'm not sure what this is," I replied, referring to the roses and chocolate before side stepping toward the dresser to pick up my comb.

"Habiba…" He sets the flowers and chocolates on the bed like an offering, then comes to me the way he always does when he's careful— slow, as if speed might break something fragile. He grabs the comb from

319

my hand then he lays it down and gives me space. I can feel the distance like an ache.

"I know it doesn't excuse leaving," he begins, voice low. "But I…. I got stressed."

"For both of us?" I say before I can stop myself. The words sting sharper than I meant. "Didn't it occur to you that I might have been stressed too?"

He flinches, like the admission hurts him. "I know." His jaw works. "I have no excuse. I'm not trying to make one. I just—" He looks at the floor, then back at me, all the easy charm stripped away. "I couldn't do this to you, ok? I couldn't take another step into this relationship without being completely transparent with you"

"What does that mean?" My voice is tighter than I want, there's an edge to it now.

"I walked out because I was scared," he says, voice raw. "Scared of what I felt. Scared of the line between love and temptation blurring, and of me crossing it without thinking of you."

My chest tightens. I want to say something clever, to put him in his place, but the heat behind my eyes makes my lip tremble. "You could've stayed," I say instead, softer. "We could've just talked."

"I couldn't talk," he says. "I didn't want to talk because I was terrified I'd say the wrong thing. I—" His mouth opens, closes. He inhales. "I went to Ayaan's."

The name hits me with the force of the rest. Ayaan. I blink. "You went to Ayaan's?"

He nods, and watching him fumble the admission is worse than the words. "I left and I went to Ayaan's house. I—"

I was already walking away before he could even finish.

He left me last night, left me thinking of all sorts of things, worried, irritated, cold, to go to Ayaan, to hang out with his best friend, to talk to his best friend about the things that we should be talking about, together.

"Habiba, please, let me explain." He tried to stop me, but I pushed his hands away, storming out of the room. Of course, he followed. "Please—"

"I don't wanna hear it!" I sighed, heading for the kitchen. But his hand caught mine, firm, unyielding. He spun me around.

"Just give me a minute," he breathed.

"Badr, I don't want to hear your excuses!" I twisted against his grip, but he didn't let go.

"Come on, Habiba. You owe it to me to at least let me explain."

I scoffed, baffled by his audacity. "I don't owe you anything."

"Fine. Not me. But you owe it to our relationship to hear me out."

"I don't!" I yanked my hand free, standing my ground instead of walking away. "I don't have to listen to you. I get to decide not to. You don't get to control everything, ok? You don't get to leave and I'm expected to wait, then you return and I'm expected to listen. Believe it or not, I have rights here too—"

A sound cut through my words.

Crying. Faint, muffled, a child.

We froze, startled.

I lowered my voice. "In fact, you know what? I'm going to make myself breakfast, and you can go back to Ayaan. He could feed you for all I care. And then I'll go to Ma, because I don't want to see your face."

Petty. Ridiculous. I knew it. But he didn't get to walk away from me.

"No," he said firmly. "No one's going to Ma. No one's leaving this room. We'll sit here and resolve this." His jaw was set, his lips a tight line.

"Wow." I clapped once, sharp. "Look at you commanding me."

He caught my hands again, pressing my palms together to stop

321

me from clapping.

"I'm not commanding you. I just don't want Ma knowing we're fighting. If we go there, she'll see it all over our faces. I don't want that."

"Well, you already involved Ayaan."

"I know," he admitted quickly. "That was stupid. I'm very stupid."

"Yeah, you can say that again." I tried to sidestep him, but before I could take more than a step, he lifted me clean off the ground.

I gasped, legs kicking, but he didn't flinch. He carried me to the kitchen counter and set me down firmly, caging me in with his hands braced on either side.

My pulse jumped. Too close. Too solid. Too much. I wanted to fight, really, I did. But my stomach fluttered traitorously, heat licking under my skin.

He leaned in, his voice low, steady, unyielding. "You will sit here, and you will listen to what I have to say."

I swallowed, arms folding stubbornly across my chest, trying to mask the way my heart was hammering.

Because the truth? I probably liked being commanded more than I cared to admit.

"Once I'm done speaking," he continued, eyes locked on mine, "whatever you want to do after is up to you. You can leave, you can scream, you can hate me. I won't stop you."

He held my gaze a beat longer, making sure I wasn't about to bolt, then finally straightened.

And he spoke.

To be honest, all I heard was blah blah blah and then my brain ran off into nonsense—his hand veins, his stupidly pink lips, the way his hair looks when he runs his fingers through it.

But I swear, I got the picture. I get what he was trying to say.

And when he finally went quiet, I realized he wasn't just staring at me. He was waiting. His eyes hopeful and sad at the same time were begging me for an answer.

I looked away, shaking my head in disappointment.

He spoke again, quieter than before—like he was afraid the words themselves might shatter. "I know I told you you're free to hate me. That I'd let you walk away if that's what you wanted." He swallowed. "But please... don't."

Deciding to put the man out of his misery, I spoke. "So let me get this straight..." My voice came out steadier than I expected. "You used to do drugs because you were juggling too much, you needed a push. Then you decided to stop, which wasn't easy. But then you met me, and I gave you some sort of 'electrical' feeling you couldn't explain..." I even air-quoted the word "so you started chasing that feeling. And by extension, you chased me."

"And then when you saw me in trouble, it was the perfect opportunity to repay me for something I didn't even know I'd done, and finally get rid of the guilt that had been eating you alive. But then you decided to just be happy and build a marriage with me anyway. But when you finally did, the guilt came back last night and now you feel like you're betraying me, so you left instead of just telling me the truth. Did I miss anything?" I lifted my eyes to his, steady now.

He thought for a moment, then shook his head. "No. That... about sums it up."

I gave a slow nod. "And you've decided that now is the time to tell me, rather than, I don't know, two months ago?"

"I know," he muttered. "I just didn't want to risk you getting mad and leaving."

"But now you're fine risking that?"

"No!" he groaned, dragging a hand through his hair before dropping it onto his thighs, then pacing across the room like a man on trial. I caught the muttering under his breath.

"Badr," I said slowly, "you literally just confessed that from the very beginning you were using me, then you decided I should be mad, then you left because apparently that was the noble thing to do. Did it ever occur to you that you don't get to decide how I feel?"

"I wasn't trying to decide how you feel," he said, turning back to me.

"You and I didn't even marry out of love. What makes you think I'd be mad that you married me to repay a debt from years ago? Or that you once took drugs? That was your past. Unless you're still doing them, why would that even matter now?"

He was quick to respond. "It matters! It matters because I know the pain it caused my loved ones." His voice was low, rough. "Look… all I know is—that part of my life is what I regret most. I buried it for years. Only the people involved and Ayaan knew about it. And now you do. Because I owe it to you to give you a choice."

He took a step closer, his hands finding my waist as naturally as breath. My skin remembered that touch, and I wanted to tremble.

"Habiba, despite everything, I know that when I married you, I did it for the sake of Allah. I stood by you, protected you, tried to treat you with patience—all for Him. Somewhere along the way, I started to love you. Still for Him." He paused, swallowing hard. "But now… I think my nafs is getting involved. Because now, I love you simply because I want to. And that terrifies me."

The air between us felt thinner. I could hear my own breathing. His confession unraveled something in me I hadn't realized was wound so tightly.

"The idea of my past coming out to you from somebody else terrifies me and I can't claim to love you," he murmured, "when I know I haven't been fully honest with you."

There was salt at the edge of my voice when I spoke. I tried to laugh, but it came out small and raw. "You sound like you rehearsed that line."

He let out a quiet, humorless breath, then leaned his forehead against mine. The contact was both electric and ordinary, a simple, human closeness that said more than words could.

I closed my eyes as he lifted his head to kiss my forehead. His lips were warm against my skin, his stubble rasping gently across my brow—the touch of a man who had been both my trial and my comfort.

"The same love that began with so much guilt and sadness has grown into something I can't afford to throw away." His voice breaks on the last syllable. "I am ashamed that I left. I didn't want to touch you without knowing that you gave me your consent with full knowledge of my past and transparency. I thought I was protecting you by running, but I only hurt you. And I'm not telling you this to pressure you into anything," he murmurs. "I had to say it out loud. I needed you to know I wasn't careless. I was cowardly."

I wanted to rage at him, at myself, at the way my body answers to him. Instead my voice comes out thin. "You made me feel unwanted."

The words break free, the nonchalance I'd been practicing crumbles into the admission I'd been holding back.

"I changed my perfume, I let some woman at the salon touch my hair, I wore things I wouldn't normally wear, I listened when people gave me tips… I did it because I wanted to prove I could be wanted. And then you left. It felt like I wasn't enough."

He flinches as if struck. His hands tighten at my waist. The room is suddenly too small, our breaths too loud. My voice catches and I hate the sound of it.

"I didn't know when it started," I add, the confession tumbling out faster now that the dam has cracked. "At first it was just for the sake of Allah, because he wouldn't make me your wife for no reason, so I was just doing my best to do it right, to be a good wife, to get my barakah. But then it stopped being just that. I wanted you to like me, I wanted you

325

to actually want me. And you leaving felt like… like rejection."

He doesn't try to erase the words; he lets them land. Then he folds me into him as if he can hold the pieces together with his chest. I let him because his arms are always, always safe.

"I'm sorry," he says again, softer, this time with a weight that makes my tears come hot and sudden. He presses his lips to my temple. "I'm sorry I hurt you."

He hugs me tighter, and there is no performative grandness here—no dramatic gesture, no speech. Just the honest weight of his body over mine.

He pulls back enough to look at me, eyes glossy, earnest. My lips find his, tentative at first, a question pressed into his mouth. He answers with a softness that starts at the base of my skull and works its way down into my bones. His hands cradle my face, then settle on my waist, anchoring me.

The kiss deepens, steady and true, like the slow setting of mortar.

I close my eyes and let the world reorder itself around that apology. The room hums with ordinary life—traffic, a distant siren—but inside his arms everything rearranges into the place I'd been aching for. I don't know the shape of what comes next, only that for the first time since we said our vows I believe we can find it together.

32

BADR

و تراه في جبر الخواطر ساعيا
و فؤاده متصدع مكسور

And you see him striving to mend the hearts of others,
While his own heart is shattered and broken.

Past

My head throbbed from the two hours of sleep I'd managed after staying up all night finishing my school project. I've already taken one pill before class, another before work. They'd carried me through the day, kept me upright, helped me smile when all I wanted was to crash.

By the time I got home around five pm, Ma was already halfway out the door. She had errands to run, and Ahmed, my 4 months old brother needed a check-up. That meant I was in charge. Again.

The moment the door shut, the silence hit. I rummaged through my bag, hoping I'd somehow missed one last pill. Nothing. My chest tightened. I pulled out my phone and called George.

"Bro," I said, trying to keep my voice steady, "can you link me?"

Music blasted on his end. I could hear laughter and clinking glasses. I had to wait for him to go out before he finally heard me and responded. "Nah. I'm downtown for the weekend."

"Shit man, I've got a long day ahead, is there no one you can send?"

He was silent for a while then spoke. "Your mom got some meds, right? Her doc probably hooked her up with something strong."

I froze. "Are you insane?"

He laughed. "That's all I can think of, but suit yourself, man.

You sound wrecked." Then the line went dead.

I tossed the phone aside and sighed. Hana was asking for cereal. Zain wanted to go to the park. I made them cereal, half-watching them, half-counting the hours until I could sleep.

"Can we go now?" Zain tugged at my sleeve, eyes wide.

"No," I said automatically. "The park's full. It's almost dark. I can't—"

He frowned, his face falling in that way that always broke me. I exhaled. "Fine. Get your shoes."

I can't take them out, not when I can barely focus enough to keep them safe. It's already evening, I can't risk something happening, can't risk losing them. I have to do this, for their sake.

While they scrambled to get ready, I went into Ma's room. The smell of baby powder and lotion clung to the air. I opened the drawer on her nightstand and stared at the pill bottles. There were so many. I just needed one. Something to keep me going.

I picked the one that looked most like mine, same white coating, same size. My fingers trembled as I held it. I was about to swallow when I remembered my friends saying sniffing it worked faster. I always avoided that, no matter how much they insisted that I try, but today I had to. Not for me. For them.

I hesitated, then ran to the kitchen where I grabbed a piece of paper from the counter and crushed the tablet inside. The sound made my stomach turn. I unwrapped it, lined the powder up like I'd seen them do.

"Just one time," I muttered.

I held one nostril closed and inhaled.

The burn was instant. White-hot pain shot up my nose, into my head. My throat seized. I coughed, gagged, tears spilling from my eyes. It felt like fire had crawled under my skin. I fell to the floor, clutching my face.

Then I caught movement at the door.

Zain.

His little body frozen in the doorway, eyes wide, staring.

My heart stopped. "Zain—" I scrambled up, slammed the door shut, leaning my forehead against it as my nose throbbed and my stomach churned.

I stayed there for what felt like forever. Maybe minutes. Maybe hours. I don't remember. The world blurred, and the next thing I knew, I was waking up to the sound of screaming.

My head snapped up. The kitchen was dark. My throat was dry.

"Hana?" My voice cracked.

The screaming grew louder. I pulled the door open and stumbled toward it, and then I saw blood.

Zain on the floor, clutching his chest. Hana crying beside him. An old door, one we'd taken off its hinges, was tipped over. A nail jutted out, red.

Everything inside me went cold.

I dropped to my knees, pressing my hands over his wound, yelling his name, fumbling for my phone. "It's okay! It's okay! You're ok." My voice shook.

He screamed again, smaller this time.

I called 911, voice breaking, and when they asked what happened, I couldn't answer. Because I didn't know which part to confess first, the accident, or the fact that I hadn't been sober enough to stop it.

33

HABIRA

اطمئني ليس في القلب سواك
قطع الشك يقيني في هواك
لست انسى رعشة الحب
التي غمرتنا و شعور الارتباك

Be at peace, for in my heart there is none but you
My doubt has turned to certainty in my love so true.
I still recall love's tremor that washed over our soul,
And that sweet, bewildering feeling that made us whole.

- إبراهيم ناجي

Present

"Stop, we'll get late," I giggled, pushing his teasing hands away, still laughing under my breath. Badr let out a reluctant groan of his own but finally shoved the covers off.

A week went by in a blink. Two, actually—but it feels shorter. Living alone together is a completely different world from living in the family house.

Or maybe it just feels different because we finally move like a married couple. Long stretches of bed rotting, quiet evenings, conversations that start with something sensible and end with us laughing over nothing. Terrence giving us a week off as a wedding gift only made it worse, or better, depending on who you ask.

One thing I've learned quickly, Badr has his rhythm, and I've started timing myself around it.

The moment he's out of bed, he sits up on the edge, murmurs his morning dua, and then heads straight to the bathroom for a shower. I've joined him a couple of times, enough to notice that even in there, he has a pattern. Shampoo, body scrub, quick rinse, and then he lingers under the hot water for exactly as long as it takes for the mirror to fog.

He trims his beard every other day, runs a towel over his curls until they're damp but not dripping, and then wanders around shirtless.

Sometimes he calls Ayaan, and whatever they talk about is an unholy mix of Arabic, English, and French, mostly nonsense.

I genuinely don't enjoy morning conversations but Badr is very chatty day and night, so having Ayaan take him off my back in the morning is like a blessing.

When he's done showering, it's my turn. By the time I step out of the bathroom wrapped in my robe, he's usually combing his hair.

That's when I head to the kitchen.

It's an unspoken part of our morning: I put the kettle on and head back to the room, then while I'm changing, I hear the kettle shut off. That's usually his cue to get coffee. He goes to the kitchen, then the familiar whir of the coffee machine as he drops in a capsule for himself and sets another mug beside it for my mint tea.

By the time I'm dressed, the kitchen smells like him mixed with warm coffee, that sharp edge of fresh mint, and the faint musk of his perfume. He's by the counter, sliding my cup toward me without looking up, like muscle memory.

I take a sip, the mint wrapping around my tongue, and pull out the last of Zain's cookies from the box on the counter. He made enough for a month, but we've been eating through them at a dangerously steady pace.

Badr leans against the counter with his own mug—the mug. The one I used to wash every night and set in the cupboard but it will somehow magically appear on the table again.

At first, I thought it was laziness—leaving it on the table instead of the sink—until I realized it was deliberate. He had the same habit back home, keeping his coffee cup close like it was an old friend. Without it, he forgets to drink coffee, and when that happens... well, let's just say the entire day tilts off balance. Now, it's part of my routine too: wash it, dry it, put it back on the same spot.

He normally keeps it dirty then washes it the next morning

before starting the coffee machine, but by washing it, I make the routine one step easier for him.

Also because I hate dirty dishes lying around.

We eat quietly, speaking in fragments.

Through the walls, a child's laughter filters in—Naeem.

Keys jingle in the hallway, and I'm already halfway to the door before the lock clicks. Sanaa is turning her key when she looks up, her bright smile lighting her face. She's Pakistani, with warm brown skin, a soft round face framed by her neatly pinned hijab.

Naeem spots me instantly, his whole face glowing as he throws his arms wide. "Habiba!" he squeals.

"My little baby!" I got down to his level and pressed a kiss to his warm cheek. "How are you?" I ask.

"I'm okay," he giggles, squirming.

"Naeem!" Badr's voice calls from inside, and Naeem's joy bursts like fireworks. He wriggles out of my arms and all but dives toward Badr.

I pout at the betrayal. Sanaa watches, her smile full of fond amusement.

We met her by accident. Though she lived next door, we never spoke until one evening I found her in the hallway, juggling grocery bags and a toddler balanced on her hip. Since then, she's become a friend. On nights when Badr is out with Ayaan, I often find myself in her kitchen, sipping tea while Naeem, her 6 year old babbles around us.

"How are you?" I hug her tightly.

"I'm good, how are you?" she asks, voice warm but hurried as her eyes flick to her watch.

"Alhamdulillah." I smile.

When I glance back, Badr has Naeem upside down over his shoulders, the boy shrieking with laughter. Noticing our attention, Badr quickly rights him and sets him on his feet. "Come on, big boy, don't give your mom too much trouble," he says, tapping Naeem's shoulder.

Naeem hugs both our legs in turn before toddling into the elevator with Sanaa.

I turn to Badr, eyebrows raised in a silent, *Should we head out too?* He nods, and we gather our things.

Lately, the office felt more boring than ever. But I push through the day, doing what was expected of me.

My client came in and we spent the next 30 minutes to an hour discussing corrections and changes to the plan of his villa, then once he finally left, I got up and wandered into Badr's office.

He stood by the wide window, phone in hand, voice low and steady. His posture was relaxed, but his words had an edge sharp enough to cut.

"Yes, Damon. I just find it so…" his tone almost warm. "Impressive, really, how you manage to consistently misinterpret straightforward instructions. A rare talent, really."

My brows lifted. Ouch.

I hovered near the door, not wanting to interrupt. But then his gaze flicked to me, and his eyes softened instantly. He gave the smallest tilt of his head as if to say come here.

I crossed the room. Without breaking stride in his conversation, he slid an arm around my waist, pulling me against him. His hand moved in slow, grounding circles on my back.

"Yes, I'm aware it's the third time this quarter," Badr continued, calm as ever. "One might think repetition would lead to improvement, but you seem determined to challenge that theory."

I bit back a laugh, hiding my face against his chest. He kissed the top of my head, subtle, almost invisible, but I felt it.

"Here's what we'll do. You'll fix this by tomorrow morning. And if it happens again, Damon, I'll have to assume you're testing the limits of my patience which, unfortunately for you, isn't infinite." A pause. A clipped, "Good."

Then he ended the call.

Only then did he turn to me fully, tilting my chin up. "What brings you here, Hayati?"

"I just wanted to see you." I murmured. A sigh slipped out of me before I could hold it back. "I wish I could stay here forever,"

His chin brushed the top of my head as he whispered, "I would like that."

I smiled softly, tilting my face up to him. "My office makes me lazy. But whenever I see you..." I hesitated, shaking my head at how ridiculous it sounded. "I get this energy, it's like a splash of water that wakes me up."

The crease between his brows told me he didn't quite follow. I chuckled, brushing it away with my hand.

"Never mind. It's weird."

He lowered his head slightly, voice gentler. "Then stay here a little longer. Or better yet..." His lips curved. "Come work in here with me whenever you want."

I shook my head quickly, though my smile betrayed me. "I won't be able to focus with you sitting right in front of me."

That earned me a low laugh. "Then maybe this will make it worse." His hand cupped my jaw, pulling me up into a kiss but just as he tilted his head, a sharp knock rattled the door.

We jumped apart. My heart pounded as his assistant stepped inside, clipboard in hand. Her eyes flicked to me for the briefest second before she smiled.

"Good Morning," she greeted warmly.

I straightened, smoothing down my hijab. "Good morning," I returned, before slipping past her and back to my office.

Just that time with him gave me enough dopamine to push through. I managed to get myself back on schedule. When the clock finally hit closing time, I let out a long, heavy sigh, excited to go home.

At some point, our apartment felt too quiet—too still. We missed the noise. So we started spending more evenings at his family's house. Most nights, we had dinner there, and helping Ma in the kitchen always lifted my mood.

We went to Hana's room, the evening folding softly around us. I was seated between Ma's legs like I'd done many times before. Hana darted across the room to grab her bonnet, slipping it over her curls.

Ma's hands moved through my hair with a gentle tug. Then a pause. "Your hair is dry, Habiba."

I winced a little. "I know. I washed it this morning, but then I had to rush to work. Didn't get to oil it."

Normally, I'm meticulous about it—wash, dry, oil, wrap—but today was a weekday, and oiling my hair was not a part of my weekday routine.

She clicked her tongue. "Hana, pass me the jojoba."

Hana tossed it over, and Ma worked the oil into my scalp with warm, practiced fingers. The room went quiet, only the soft hum of the fan and the sound of her fingers moving rhythmically in my hair.

Then she asked, casually, "Did you and Badr talk about kids?"

My eyes snapped open. "What?"

"What's your plan?"

I hesitated, then nodded slowly. "We're planning to wait. We just want to find balance first. I want to feel... ready."

She hummed in understanding, fingers moving again.

"Kids are just—" I sighed. "—terrifying. You're raising a whole human. If you fail, you're not just hurting them, you're affecting everyone they'll interact with. A badly raised person doesn't stay in their lane; they ripple out into society."

Ma chuckled softly, rubbing the back of my head. "It is scary."

I smiled, then added, more seriously, "I think about you and Ba a lot. MashaAllah, you raised such incredible kids. They're grounded.

Kind. Honest. And I wonder how I'd even begin to do that. I worry I won't be able."

There was a silence. Then, she spoke gently, "Habiba, you won't raise them alone. You'll have Badr, insha'Allah. And you'll have us."

I swallowed the lump forming in my throat. There was something in her voice that made me feel held.

"Can I give you some advice?" she said, pausing her fingers.

I tilted my head back slightly to look at her. "Of course."

"Long before I got married, my mother told me something I never forgot: Don't just pray for your future. Pray for your bloodline. Pray for good children. Pious children. It's easy to forget, but it matters. It really, really matters."

She tapped the back of my head lightly with the tail of her comb. I laughed under my breath and nodded.

"Don't let anyone pressure you into motherhood. Let it be your choice. On your terms."

That stunned me. I'd expected pressure by now, if I'm being honest.

She noticed my silence and added, "Our society rushes couples into parenthood before they've even unpacked their wedding clothes. I was barely figuring out how to be a wife when I had Badr. I have no regrets, but I know the struggle. So take your time. But remember, having children isn't just personal. It's spiritual. It's worship. Raising a child with love and *La ilaha illa Allah* in their heart is sadaqah jariyah. That's your legacy. But only if you're ready. Only if you choose it with intention."

I nodded slowly. "I'll keep that in mind."

She turned to Hana. "You should keep that in mind too."

Hana made a face. "Nope, I'm not having kids." She dropped a pillow beside me and flopped down.

"What do you mean you're not having kids?" I said, nudging her.

"I will not be reproducing, that's what I mean, and I will only marry someone who doesn't want kids." She stated. I expected Ma to protest, but she said nothing, just shook her head, smiling. Hana turned to me and shoved her phone in my face. "Look at this one!"

She was hunting for a dress for her school event, and we've been scrolling options for days. I took the phone and studied the picture, then raised it for Ma to see.

"I don't like it," Ma said flatly.

Hana gasped. "What? It's so flowy!"

"It's dull," I agreed, shaking my head.

Hana groaned dramatically and collapsed onto the floor, clutching the phone like some tragic heroine. I laughed, and Ma gently resumed working oil through my scalp, until the sound of voices drifted up from downstairs. All of us froze, our eyes drawing to the door.

Ma, already wearing a scarf, rose first and stepped out. Hana and I hurried to cover our hair with loose wraps in case there were guests. I followed next, pausing halfway down the stairs where Ma was already descending. From the rail, I saw them—Badr and Zain—standing face-to-face, their anger practically sparking between them.

"Zain, I'm not going to stand here and argue with you. Go to your room!" Badr's voice thundered as he jabbed a finger toward the stairs.

"You're overreacting!" Zain shot back, just as loud.

"Overreacting?" Badr scoffed, his chest rising with fury. "That's all you've got to say? That I'm overreacting?"

"HEY! HEY!" Ba appeared from his study, his voice calm but commanding. "Don't raise your voices in my house. What's going on?"

The brothers glared at each other, neither backing down, until Badr finally spoke. "I caught him with a cigarette."

A stunned silence fell over us. Ba's expression hardened, his eyes drilling into Zain.

"Ba, wallahi, I didn't smoke it!" Zain blurted, hands lifted in

337

defense.

Ba pinched the bridge of his nose with a sigh. Hana shrank back. I hovered near the wall, unsure whether to step closer or vanish.

"I keep telling him that I wasn't going to smoke it, but he won't believe me!" Zain groaned, frustration heavy in his voice.

"I said it doesn't matter," Badr snapped. "You didn't smoke it, so let's end it now."

"Yeah, but you don't believe me! You still think that if you hadn't shown up, I would've done it, but that's not true!" Zain's voice cracked. "He asked me to hold it for him, I was just—"

"And you held it?" Badr barked, cutting him off. "You thought it was okay to even touch it?"

"Badr." Ba's warning was sharp. He turned to Zain. "Tell me the truth. Were you going to smoke it?"

"Of course not!" Zain's voice broke as he shouted. "No one ever believes me! It's like you all want me to be the screw-up!"

"Don't raise your voice at Ba. Respect—" Badr's tone dropped, low and dangerous.

"Oh, please." Zain scoffed, turning on him. "Spare me the perfect older brother act. We get it. You're flawless. The advice-giver, the wisest kid. Do you ever get tired of acting like a second dad?"

Badr's face froze as though the words had landed like a slap. He stepped forward, his hand gripping Zain's arm—not with violence, but with desperation. "I'm trying to protect you. Do you even understand what it would do to this family if you went down that path?"

"Leave me alone!" Zain yanked his arm free, eyes blazing. "Just because you made a careless choice once doesn't mean I will."

The room went still. The weight of his words sucked the air out of us all.

Ba stepped forward at last, his voice quiet but absolute. "That's enough. Both of you."

Zain's jaw worked furiously as he blinked hard, then turned and stormed past us up the stairs. The door to his room didn't slam, but the silence it left behind felt louder than any echo. Seconds later the door opened again and Ahmed stumbled out, sad. He ran straight to his mother.

Hana looked at me, eyes glassy. Badr stared for a long, aching second. His chest rose and fell like he was swallowing a thousand words. He turned away without looking at anyone and walked up the stairs, past me and into his old room.

I didn't follow. Not yet. I just stood there, heart heavy. It was only when Ma gestured for me to go and check on him that I moved.

He was in the room, on the floor, back against the bed, legs stretched out, head tilted back like he'd been holding his breath for hours.

I knocked gently. He didn't look at me, but he didn't tell me to leave either. So I stepped in, closing the door behind me. "Badr?"

He rubbed his face with both hands, then let out a shaky laugh. "You should go back. I'm fine."

"I think you need someone to talk to," I said, inching closer. "And I happen to be married to you."

He sighed. "That was so bad." His voice was raw as I crossed the room and sank down beside him.

"It was," I agreed softly.

"I can't believe he fell for something like that. I would've expected it from him years ago, but not now. He never used to hang out with the wrong crowd or even go near things like that."

"Yeah, well... he's still young. Twenty-one is the peak of life—"

"He should be smart enough not to fall for things like that."

"Badr..." I touched his arm. "Not everyone grows at the same pace. Yes, he's legally an adult. But emotionally? Maybe halfway there. You matured early because life forced you to. Zain's just getting there on his own terms. He still has time to make mistakes and learn. That doesn't

339

mean he's broken. It just means he's human."

A bitter chuckle slipped from his lips, his head shaking slowly. "So you think so too."

"Think what?"

"That I act perfect."

I smiled faintly. "Of course I think you're perfect. I'm married to you, aren't I?" I kissed his bicep, hoping to draw a smile, but his face stayed unreadable. His whole body was tense, coiled like a spring. "He didn't mean it," I added softly.

"He did." His voice was barely above a whisper. "And it hurts more because he knows I'm not. He probably thinks I'm a hypocrite."

My brow creased. "What do you mean?"

He scratched his jaw, eyes drifting toward the corner of the room as if he were watching something play out there, something he didn't want to relive.

"Have you ever seen the scar on Zain's neck?" he asked, voice low, careful.

I nodded.

"My life was a mess back then—the drugs, the job, everything. Hana was three, Zain nine, and Ma had just had Ahmed. I'd go to school, then go to work and then come home and take over babysitting. It was always one pill a day, just one, to get through it."

Silence stretched between us—heavy, waiting. Then he finally told me the story of Zain's scar. The story only he and Ayaan knew.

All this time, I thought his guilt was about a mistake, an accidental drug use from years ago. But it wasn't. It was about a memory. Because only he remembers how bad it was. Only he carries the image, the sound, the guilt. To me, it was just a story. To him, it was a wound that never healed.

His eyes lifted to meet mine, red-rimmed but steady, and I could tell that he was being haunted by what he could never forgive himself for.

340

"Ma and Ba never blamed me. They said I was overworked, that it was their fault for putting so much on me. They even apologized." He let out a humourless laugh. "But they didn't know the truth. I was high. I wasn't paying attention… I thought he'd forget, he was only nine. Kids forget things." His voice trembled, cracking softly. "But what he said downstairs… he didn't forget. Not a single thing. I'd rather he had hit me. At least that would've been easier than remembering."

I reached for his hand, squeezing gently. "That doesn't make you a bad person," I said quietly. "You were just—"

"—Careless," he finished for me. "And it almost cost me my brother." He dragged a hand through his hair, eyes glassy with exhaustion. "The only good thing that came out of it was that it woke me up. I stopped that day. Cold. Never touched a pill again."

He finally looked at me then, eyes shadowed. "You remember when I told you that you saved me from myself?"

I nodded.

"That was three days later," he said quietly. "I had been clean for three days, but that day… the withdrawals were brutal. I couldn't take it. I had one last pill in my bag. I should've thrown it away, but I didn't. I told myself it would be the last time, that I just needed it to get through the day." His voice faltered, softening to a whisper. "I was so close."

He smiled faintly.

"And then Allah sent you—to bump into me."

I smiled too, unsure what to say. I couldn't remember that day the way he did, not with the same weight. But clearly, for him, it changed everything.

He exhaled deeply. "I saw myself in him. And I hated it."

"That doesn't make you a hypocrite, Badr. It makes you human."

He stared down at our joined hands. "It doesn't feel that way."

"You just shouldn't have yelled at him in front of everyone," I said gently. "If you'd spoken to him privately, it might've gone differently.

But this isn't something you can't fix."

He huffed a dry laugh. "And how do I do that? Another perfect speech about how perfect I'm supposed to be?"

"With love," I said simply. "And transparency. You've carried them your whole life like they're your children, not your siblings. Maybe it's time to let them see the real you, not the version that never makes mistakes."

He exhaled slowly, some of the tightness leaving his shoulders. "Yeah... I was just blinded by rage."

I tilted my head, studying him. "Then go unblind yourself."

He smiled weakly at that, the smallest spark returning to his eyes.

The air at home stayed thick after that. Ba told everyone to give Zain space. He had a habit of locking up his anger, and tonight, there was already too much tension to breathe through.

We drove back to our apartment in silence. When we arrived, Badr went straight inside while I turned toward Sanaa's apartment.

Her apartment was the same size as ours, but older. The tiles faded, the paint chipping, the cupboards warped with age. Yet stepping inside, it didn't feel tired. It smelled faintly of musk, of the spices she must've used earlier in the kitchen, and beneath it all, that trace of something that was just her. It felt like a home.

"Where's he?" I asked.

"You missed him by like 10 minutes." she pouted, throwing the scarf onto the couch "I'm so sorry it's a mess in here" She began shuffling around.

Badr and I help her as much as we can, but there is only so much we can do. "Please" I scoffed. "Let me help you clean up, then I'll leave" I said.

"No no, you just got home, go rest please." She tried to stop me from taking off my jacket.

"I literally did nothing to be tired, you on the other hand clearly had a rough day. Let me help." I insisted.

She didn't argue, she just sighed before taking my jacket to the side for me.

"How are you?" I asked, putting the toys in their place.

"Better than my fridge is holding up."

"It stopped again!?" I frowned.

"I had to throw away so much. I didn't realize it had stopped." she rubbed her temple, cleaning in an aggressive manner.

I sighed, my heart aching. "I'll have Badr come and take a look at it." I said.

She stopped and turned to me, "Can he do that? I literally cannot afford another repair now and I don't want to ask my brother for money again."

I nodded, my smile sad. Every time I see Sanaa, my heart aches, with everything she's going through, I wish I could take the pressure of life off her shoulders but there is nothing I can do. The only thing I could do for her is pray and help as much as I can.

I cheered her up a little and helped her clean the house before leaving after she gave me one of the biggest hugs ever.

When I got back to the apartment, Badr was in the kitchen, sleeves rolled to his elbows, brow creased in focus as he stirred something gently on the stove.

He turned when he heard me, offering a small, easy smile. "I'm making dessert" he said, as if that were just an ordinary thing. As if I hadn't just returned from watching a woman carry the weight of her life like it cost her pieces of herself. "I'd appreciate it if you pretend to like it," he added, grinning.

I didn't respond. I walked over and before I got to him, he had his arms open, ready for me. I wrapped my arms around him. He was warm and solid, smelling faintly of ginger. He held me like he didn't need a reason. "Habiba?" he asked, brushing his hand over my head. "What's wrong?"

"Nothing," I said, my voice tight. "I'm going to pray."

I turned, but he caught my wrist gently and pulled my body back to him, then kissed my temple and bumped his nose to mine before letting me go.

I made my wudu, laid out the prayer mat, and prayed to Allah for what He gave me.

A few months ago, it was just me. Alone. Carrying myself. And now I had this warmth, this home. It hasn't even been long, but already that old life feels like a distant echo.

I thought of Sanaa. What she was going through. What I saw.

And when I finished praying, I stayed on the mat. I made dua—not just gratitude for the gift I'd been given, but a plea. A plea to preserve it. To never let it slip from my hands. And to give Sanaa something just as good. Something whole.

Because our Prophetﷺ said: "None of you truly believes until he loves for his brother what he loves for himself."

And I love this. So I asked for her to have it too.

The prayer mat was still warm beneath me when I finally whispered my last *Ameen*. I stayed seated for a while longer, palms still open, heart still soft. Gratitude is heavier than grief sometimes, it fills you in a way that makes you ache, gently.

"You've been here long," Badr said, leaning against the doorway, eyes soft and sleepy. "Should I be worried?"

I smiled, but didn't respond.

He crossed the room in three quiet steps and lowered himself to the floor, resting his head on my lap with a long exhale. "I missed you."

I laughed softly and ran my fingers through his hair, gently untangling a curl behind his ear. He closed his eyes and hummed at the touch.

344

"What were you praying for?" he asked again, without opening them.

"Why should I tell you?" I teased.

He opened one eye, squinting at me with mock offense. "Wow. Keeping secrets from your husband now? After everything we've been through? I let you steal my fries last week and this is how you repay me?"

I laughed again, leaned down, and pressed a kiss to the bridge of his nose.

He smiled, eyes closed now, completely relaxed. "Fine. Don't tell me. I'll just assume you were praying for me to get even more handsome and irresistible."

I rolled my eyes but didn't respond right away. Instead, I stared down at him, at the way his brow relaxed when I touched him, at the softness of his eyelashes, the peace he carried when he was near me.

"There are certain men in the world," I began quietly, "men who are… rare. Gentle, responsible, God-conscious. Not perfect, but patient."

His eyes opened slowly, watching me now.

"And for the longest time," I continued, my voice barely above a whisper, "I came to terms with the fact that men like that were only written for certain women. Women with a special kind of light in their hearts. The ones who were chosen. And I always wondered what my mother did to be one of them."

I paused, fingers still moving through his hair.

"I never saw myself as one of them. I didn't think I was special enough… or whole enough. Not after everything. But… I realized I must have been wrong. Because He gave me you. And that means… somehow, in all the places I fell short, He still saw me as worthy."

He didn't speak. He just listened.

"So, I had to sit down… and thank Allah, for you."

His eyes glistened, not dramatically, not tearfully, but in that way his always did when his heart softened and he didn't know what to say.

He lifted my hand from his hair and brought it to his lips, kissed it once, and whispered, "Alhamdulillah."

I just smiled, and whispered it back.

"Now can we go eat?"

34

BADR

قالوا جُننتَ بِمَن تَهوى فَقُلتُ لَهُم
مَا لِذَّةُ العَيش إلا لِلمَجانين

They said, "You are mad for the one you adore."
I said, "Life's true sweetness is for madmen, nothing more."

- قيس بن الملوح

"Thank you so much for doing this, Badr. I'm sorry you had to look back there. I know it's disgusting," Sanaa apologized.

"You apologize too much," I said with a grin as I turned the fridge around. "Go sit down, relax."

She walked over to Naeem, who was busy with his toy, leaving me to do what I came for.

Habiba was still asleep when I slipped over here. I was making coffee when I heard Naeem cry, which told me that Sanaa was awake, so I offered to check the fridge because I was leaving for an expo and I didn't want to go without making sure she and Naeem will be fine.

The wiring was loose, that was the main problem. I tied it up and managed to get it running again, but I knew it wouldn't last. It was only a temporary fix.

I hated the way they were living. It pained me more than I could admit, because her situation unlocked a fear I didn't even know I had. Losing her husband while raising a child alone. The thought of Habiba ever being in Sanaa's place, it made my chest ache. The fear gnawed at me until it felt like my own.

"I managed to get it working for now but I don't think it'll last long to be honest." I explained as I peeled the gloves and set them aside.

"But, I have a friend who can bring you a new fridge. It's old, he doesn't need it anymore, but it's in good shape." I suggested.

It wasn't a full lie. Ayaan did have a fridge that he planned to sell. I'll buy it off him. Sanaa never accepted help directly from Habiba or me, so it was best she didn't know.

She nodded, gratitude in her eyes, though her exhaustion bled through.

I turned to grab my toolbox when I felt a tug at my pant leg. "Badr," Naeem called out.

His curls were wild, hands sticky, clutching a battered plastic truck that looked like it had survived a war. He stared up at me wide-eyed, as if I were the most fascinating thing in the room.

"You coming to say goodbye?" I asked, crouching down.

He didn't answer. Instead, he pressed the toy into my hand, like an offering. "For you."

"For me?" My lips curved into a smile. "That's a big responsibility, Naeem."

He giggled, then lifted his arms. "Up, up!"

I chuckled, scooping him up under my arms before swinging him over my shoulder the way I always did. His laughter filled the room, loud and bright, until I spun him around and set him down, crouching again to meet his eyes.

"You're a brave little man, you know that?" I whispered.

He only grinned. "Mama said we can go to the park today."

"Really?" I glanced at Sanaa. She didn't say anything, just watched us quietly, lips pressed together.

"Yeah! Come!" Naeem asked.

"Sorry, buddy. I've got work," I say with a playful groan, ruffling his curls before pressing a kiss to his temple. "I'll make it up to you someday. Take care of your mama for me, okay?"

He nods solemnly and follows me all the way to the main door.

348

When I came, I left the door ajar on purpose. Not because I forgot, but because I am a man in another woman's home, and there is no reason to close a door that doesn't need closing. An open door costs me nothing and gives her peace of mind. It keeps things clear, uncomplicated, exactly where they should be.

Once I said my salaams, I left.

When I walked into our room, Habiba was awake, scrolling on her phone. The second she saw me, she dropped it and spread her arms wide. I practically tossed my toolkit aside and dove onto the bed, my head landing against her chest.

When Habiba gives her heart, she gives all of it. She's clingier than I am, claiming every corner of the bed, and no matter how far I move, if she wakes up and finds us not skin to skin, she'll pull me back until we are.

So I make it a point to meet her halfway, to pull her close before she stirs—so she never feels she has to chase me.

Sometimes, when I watch the way she talks more than she needs to, how she rushes to clean up after me like she's trying to earn her place, it hurts me because she grew up in loneliness. Not just silence, but the kind that convinces you love is something you have to work for. I don't blame her. I know it'll take time for her to believe that I'm not going anywhere. That she doesn't need to prove herself. She already has me. All of me.

"How are you?" she asked softly, kissing my forehead.

"I missed you," I murmured.

"Aww, poor baby." She pouted. "But you're leaving me."

"Come with me," I offered, for what felt like the hundredth time. "We'll make it a little holiday. Stay an extra day."

"It's a three-hour drive," she groaned. "Just ask them to ship it."

"They won't ship samples. And this finish is exclusive, I can't risk someone else snatching it before I see it. If it fits the villa, I'll order it on the spot." I kissed her hand, reaching to pull her phone that was poking me on my chest.

The video playing wasn't one I'd seen before. She had dozens—old clips with her siblings that she replayed whenever she missed them. In this one, she and her little sister were messing with a filter when her brother barged in, blocking the camera with his face. Both girls immediately smacked his arms before shoving him off screen.

I chuckled. "Ah, so it's genetic. Planning to pass it down to our kid?"

"Yeah," she shot back with a grin. "So if anyone annoys her, she can smack them too."

"Her…" I arched a brow. "So you want a girl?"

"I want whatever Allah gives us," she said softly, smiling.

"Well," I teased, wiggling my eyebrows, "I'm ready whenever you are."

Without warning, she shoved my face away and slipped out of the sheets. "Go get ready and hit the road. I don't want you driving at night. It's already 11 a.m."

I groaned but dragged myself up. The faster I went, the faster it would be over. I showered quickly, stuffed a change of clothes into my bag, and had breakfast with Habiba.

I dreaded leaving. Since our marriage, we hadn't been apart for more than twelve hours. Now I was leaving for twenty-four.

She was standing by the sink, wiping the surface like she couldn't hear me hovering behind her.

"Think about it," I said, leaning casually against the counter, "Three hours in the car, scenic route, gas station snacks, maybe a fight over the AUX cord. Romantic stuff."

She didn't look up. "Sounds like a punishment."

"Some people pay good money for a road trip with someone like me."

"Some people have poor judgment."

I chuckled and took a step closer. Circling my arms around her waist, I shifted her braids to the side and trailed kisses from her neck down to her shoulder. "Come with me." I whispered.

"No."

"Come on." I groaned, turning her to face me. "It's one day. We'll stop for real coffee, not that fake syrupy stuff you like."

"No." She narrowed her eyes at me with that stubborn glint I enjoy a little too much.

"Habiba—"

"No," she said slowly. "Read my lips: no."

I blinked, pretending to squint. "That's weird. I hear you saying no, but when I read your lips, they're screaming kiss me, kiss me."

Before she could get a comeback in, I closed the space between us and kissed her—light at first, just teasing. But then her fingers caught the fabric of my shirt and I couldn't help it. I kissed her properly.

I pulled back a little, breath caught somewhere in my throat. Her eyes were soft, dazed, maybe a little annoyed at me for pulling back.

"I shouldn't be kissing you like that when I'm supposed to be leaving," I said quietly, my voice rougher than intended.

"Then don't leave," she whispered.

I swallowed, forehead resting against hers. "You keep saying things like that and I might just cancel the whole trip."

She let out a quiet laugh and started smoothing the front of my shirt like it mattered. "Drive safe, okay?" she murmured.

I nodded then kissed her forehead and bumped my nose to hers, lingering there. "Always. And you? Stay out of trouble. Keep your phone near."

She smirked, already walking back toward the couch like the moment didn't just rearrange my soul. "Read my lips: bye."

I grinned, shaking my head as I grabbed my keys.

Yeah. I am completely gone for her.

Before hitting the road, I stopped by home to let Ma and Ba know I was heading out of town for the day. Hana was still asleep, but Zain was in the kitchen, alone, baking something.

When he saw me come in, he looked up and quickly looked away. His face tightened. He didn't greet me, didn't smile. He just went back to wiping the counter, his movements a little too sharp, too tense.

I closed the kitchen door gently behind me to give us privacy. I could already tell something deeper was weighing on him.

"Can we talk?" I asked.

He nodded, washed his hands, then leaned against the counter, his eyes fixed on a spot on the floor. He didn't even glance at me.

I leaned against the island to face him, trying to think of the right words, but before I could say anything, he spoke.

"I wasn't going to do it, Badr," he said quietly. "I wasn't going to smoke it."

He still didn't look at me, but the hurt in his voice was clear. He wasn't lying. It was eating at him too much for it to be a lie. I felt the guilt hit my chest like a rock. I'd assumed the worst of him, and snapped.

"I'm sorry," I said. "I should've believed you."

"Why didn't you?" he finally looked at me, and I wished he hadn't—the hurt in his eyes was unbearable. "I've always been honest with you. Why didn't you believe me when it mattered? You could've at least given me the benefit of the doubt."

I dropped my gaze. "I projected," I admitted. "I assumed you might make the same mistake I di—"

"Yeah. Of course," he snapped. "Because I'm the one who always screws up, right? That's the expectation. I make dumb choices."

I frowned. "Why are you so convinced that we think you're a disappointment, Zain? What makes you feel like we see you that way?"

He looked away again, jaw clenched.

"You want to tell me what's really going on?"

A long silence passed before he answered, voice low and fragile. "I just feel invisible sometimes."

I didn't interrupt. I wanted him to get it all out.

"Every time something happens, Ma says, 'Call Badr.' When Ba needs advice, it's, 'Ask Badr.' Even Ahmed doesn't think of me when he needs help. You don't live here anymore and you're still the first person they call. Last week, you weren't picking up, and instead of asking me, Ba called Ayaan. Can you imagine that?"

I said nothing. The truth stung because it was real.

"I want to be asked too," he continued. "I want to feel like their son, not just someone they see at dinner. Hana's always with Ma. Ahmed's the baby. Me? I'm just… there. Not the favorite, not the baby, not the only daughter. Just Zain."

His voice cracked.

"You don't even hang out with me unless we're playing basketball. And now you're married. You're busier than ever, but you always make time for Ayaan. Not me."

I pushed off the island and pulled him into a hug. "I'm sorry," I whispered. It felt pathetic compared to what he needed to hear, but it was the truth. I had no excuses.

"I just assumed you preferred your friends."

"Still," he mumbled, stepping back slightly. His eyes were glassy, red at the corners, but he blinked back the tears. "Sometimes I want to be with family too."

My throat tightened. "How long have you felt this way?"

He gave a small shrug.

I reached for his shoulder. "When I get back tomorrow, we're picking something to do, just the two of us, every week. Also…" I smirked, nudging his arm, "it's about time you join Ayaan and me at the gym."

He looked at me, surprised. "Seriously? Same gym as you?"

I nodded, and the way his face lit up shattered me. That little bit of excitement—it told me everything I needed to know. This kid hadn't been asking for much. Just a few hours. A few words. A little space in someone's world.

My mind flashed back to a week ago. He'd asked me to come with him to buy new parts for his PC. I said I'd come. Then I canceled last-minute, caught up with other things. He never brought it up again.

I pulled him back into a hug and held him tighter this time. His shoulders were still stiff at first... but then slowly, I felt him melt into it.

When we pulled apart, I exhaled deeply. "Can I give you some advice?"

He nodded.

"You remember when we were kids, and Ma would ask you to clean something or help carry groceries?"

"Yeah," he muttered.

"You'd sigh. Roll your eyes. Say you were tired. It didn't seem like a big deal then... but to them, it wasn't just a sigh. It was rejection. It hurt them more than they ever said. So after a while, they just stopped asking. Not because they don't love you, but because they love you too much to hear 'no' again."

He looked down. "I didn't mean to do that. I don't even remember half of it."

"I know. You didn't mean it. But if you want them to think of you again, then show up again. Don't wait to be asked. Step in. Be present. And be gentle. I never had the option to just say no, when you were all young, I was old enough to start making better choices, so I did."

Zain nodded slowly. "I'm sorry about what I said earlier. About you thinking you're perfect."

I grinned. "Are you kidding? I *am* perfect."

He laughed, finally.

"It's alright," I said softly. "Things were said, but I didn't take any of it to heart. And about what you saw back then—"

"I'm so sorry for bringing that up!" he blurted, cutting me off.

I placed a hand on his shoulder—gentle, but firm.

"It's fine. I made a stupid choice back then. But I realized quickly... and I'm sorry. For not being there when you needed me most, for letting you fall." My gaze lingered on the small part of his scar that peeked through his collar.

"Are you kidding? All the ladies think it's cool," he said with a grin. I managed a small smile, but he must've noticed the shift in my face, because he straightened up. "I know you would've been there if you... could." he said quietly, exhaling. "But why did you...?"

"Life," I answered simply. "Things were hard then, really hard. I was juggling too much, and I fell into the wrong hands. They told me it would help, that it'd make things easier..." I sighed. "That's why I'm so against you hanging around that kind of crowd. Because no matter how smart we think we are, someone can always plant a seed in our heads... That incident was exactly the wake-up call I needed and I promise you, from that day on, I never touched drugs again."

He smiled, smaller this time, softer. "I'm glad."

I glanced at my watch, pushing off the counter. "I've got a three-hour drive ahead. I'll see you tomorrow, InShaAllah."

"Wait ten minutes," he said, perking up. "The cupcakes will be ready. I'm bringing them for Habiba, but she won't mind if you have two."

I smiled. "Make it three and I'll call it forgiveness."

He rolled his eyes, but he was smiling too. This time, it reached his eyes.

The trip went by smoothly, *Alhamdulillah*. I called Habiba to let her know that I had arrived then headed straight to the expo. The air buzzed with voices, deals being made, people rushing from booth to booth like bees in a hive. It didn't take me long to find what I came for, a supplier willing to lock in a batch of the product I'd been chasing for weeks. Contacts exchanged, hands shaken.

35

HABIBA

أأنت ناديت أم صوت يُخَيَّلُ لي
فلي إليك بأذن الوهم إصغاء

Was that your voice I heard, or my desire's sweet deceit?
For I am listening with the ear that fancy made complete.

- إبراهيم ناجي

Once Badr left, I showered and tidied up the house until Zain arrived with a box of carrot cupcakes I had shamelessly begged him for.

I hadn't expected a message from him this morning, telling me he'd already baked them. After everything between him and Badr, I thought he might avoid me too. But he said they'd talked. Cleared the air.

We carried the cupcakes to Sanaa's and had lunch there as we waited because Badr told us that Ayaan would be dropping off a fridge for her. He also mentioned that Sanaa didn't know the fridge was meant for sale. He and I would pay Ayaan for it, but she wasn't to know.

When Ayaan arrived, he texted Zain, and they brought it up together. I stood by the door as they appeared, carrying the fridge with another man's help. Once they set it down, Ayaan paid the helper and turned to me, smiling.

"Habiba, how are you?" he asked warmly, brushing his palms against his jeans.

"I'm good," I said, smiling back and stepping aside.

"SalamuAlaikum," Ayaan greeted as he stepped inside, most of his attention on getting the fridge to its place safely. His short sleeves clung to his arms, muscles flexing under the weight, sweat glistening on his skin.

He didn't seem to be struggling nearly as much as Zain, though, whose forehead vein looked ready to explode. Once the fridge was inside, all they needed to do was nudge it into position because we'd already cleared the space.

As they worked, I drifted toward Sanaa, who sat on a sunken chair with Naeem curled in her lap. She bounced her knee, making him giggle.

"That's a very fancy fridge," she whispered.

I laughed softly. "It is."

"And he's just giving it away?"

Technically, we were paying him. But I only nodded vaguely. "Allah does the most beautiful things, doesn't He?" I smiled then turned back toward the fridge and froze.

Ayaan was crouched by the fridge door, a shelf in hand, but he wasn't moving. He wasn't even looking at the fridge anymore. He was looking at Sanaa.

And not casually.

He looked at her like a man memorizing something he knew he might never see again. Not creepy, not intense, just still. Quiet. A little stunned.

Zain caught it too. His eyes flicked from Ayaan, to Sanaa, then to me. He raised his brows knowingly and smirked.

I choked back a laugh.

"Where does this one go?" Zain asked loudly, snapping Ayaan out of it.

Ayaan blinked, cleared his throat, and looked back at the fridge like it had suddenly become a puzzle. "This shelf is broken," he muttered. "Couldn't find a replacement. I'll look online, see if I can track one down."

Sanaa rose, gently placing Naeem down. "You don't have to do that." she said softly, walking closer. "This fridge is already huge, I can't

358

believe you're just giving it away."

He looked at her again. Closer this time. And for a moment, he seemed to forget how to speak. His lips parted slightly, like he meant to say something but nothing came out. Four long, quiet beats.

Zain, merciful as ever, bumped him on the shoulder.

Ayaan blinked hard, cleared his throat again, and turned away. "Don't worry about it. It's no big deal." He glanced at his watch. "I have to go."

He clapped Zain's shoulder and headed for the door. As he knelt to put on his shoes, Sanaa called after him, "At least let me give you something to eat. Or water, just water?"

He shook his head too quickly. "That won't be necessary. Thanks for offering."

And just like that, he was out the door, hitting the elevator button multiple times until it opened. I slipped out, closing the door behind me. "Wait," I called. "I didn't give you the money."

"You know that's not necessary, Habiba." His voice had softened again.

"Your friend insisted. Just take it, so he doesn't eat my head."

He smiled and entered the elevator. "I'll call him. It's an old fridge anyway. Please. Don't worry about it."

And then he was gone.

I stood there for a moment, smiling to myself.

Maybe I was reaching. But maybe I wasn't. And if I wasn't, then Ayaan just saw something beautiful. And Badr is going to have a field day with this.

Later that day, I dreaded climbing into bed. The mattress felt cavernous without Badr, the sheets too cold, the silence too sharp. I'd told myself one night apart wouldn't matter, but lying there proved me wrong. Every shift, every sigh, reminded me of his absence.

As if he could sense it, my phone lit up. His name. His voice. He was already in bed too, speaking in that low, tired drawl I loved. I wanted to tell him about Ayaan and Sanaa, about the little moments I'd been saving for him, but instead we let the conversation drift aimlessly until sleep tugged me under with his voice still in my ear.

It didn't fill the space beside me, but it dulled the ache.

I woke more than once, hand searching blindly across the sheets, half-expecting him there, half-forgetting he wasn't. My chest hollowed each time my fingers met nothing but cool cotton.

Then morning.

This time, when I stirred awake, there was warmth. A solid weight against my back. An arm cinched firmly around my waist. Slow, steady breaths grazing the curve of my neck.

For a moment, I didn't dare move. I thought maybe I'd dreamt him, conjured his presence out of longing. My heart pounded with the fragile, terrifying hope that if I blinked, the illusion would vanish.

But I shifted slightly, and like always, his grip loosened just enough to let me turn, then tightened again once I'd nestled into him. His lips brushed the crown of my head, real and tender.

"You're back," I whispered, my voice thick with sleep, breaking somewhere between dream and prayer.

"I am." His voice was just as rough, gravelly from the night, and it made my chest ache.

"I missed you."

"That's why I'm back."

I pouted, tilting my face up to him. His hair was messy, sticking in every direction, eyes rimmed with exhaustion, but he still smiled down at me like I was worth it. His thumb brushed lazily across my cheek.

"I couldn't sleep, so I came back."

I blinked, my sleep-fogged brain catching up. "You drove here last night?"

"I was awake until three. So I packed up and left." He said it with a shrug, like it was nothing.

My frown deepened. "I told you not to drive in the dark—"

Before I could finish, he caught me, flipping us easily so that I was beneath him. My protest dissolved into a gasp as his mouth found mine, warm and insistent. He kissed me like he needed me to breathe, and just as my heart leapt into my throat, the alarm split the air.

He groaned against my mouth, forehead falling to mine. "Your timing is cruel," he muttered, voice ragged.

I chuckled but pushed him off me anyway. I had a morning meeting.

I tried persuading Badr to stay home, at least sleep in, take the morning slow but he was stubborn. He insisted on coming to the office, and once he'd made up his mind, there was no shaking him.

After my shower, I slipped into a green and black patterned gown. While I dressed, Badr ran downstairs to grab a coffee and snacks, since we'd run out of capsules. By the time I came down, he was already in the car.

After work, we freshened up before heading to his parents' house, where I helped with dinner. Once we got home, we prayed Isha.

Badr was already in bed, flipping through a catalogue. After tying my bonnet and rubbing cream onto my legs, I slipped into bed beside him.

He put the catalogue down and opened his arms for me. I settled against his chest, my head resting on his shoulder. His warmth pressed against my back, arms circling me, steady and protective.

Then his voice, low against my skin. "How did it go with Ayaan? Did he drop off the fridge?"

Then the memory of Ayaan hit me like a spark. I pulled out of the hug, excitement spilling out as I told Badr the whole story—the way Ayaan froze when he saw Sanaa, the look in his eyes. I did my best to mimic it, much to Badr's amusement.

"So you think he likes her?" His brows drew together.

"I think so," I said quietly.

"From what I saw… it was kind of obvious."

"Hm." He reached for his phone on the side table and turned it on. The screen lit his face briefly. "That explains," he murmured, more to himself than to me.

"Explains what?"

He sighed and set the phone back down. "He hasn't responded to me all day."

I frowned. "What does that have to do with Sanaa?"

He hesitated, choosing his words carefully. "Ayaan didn't have the… cleanest history with women. Of course, when he took his *shahada*, he knew Allah forgave him—but you know how guilt works, it never really goes away."

I stayed quiet, listening.

"He's very scared of falling into that path again and when something threatens that," he continued, "he spirals. He either disappears completely, overthinks until he exhausts himself… or gets reckless." His jaw tightened. "Pushing limits. Anything to drown the noise in his head."

I shifted closer and rested my head against his shoulder. "So liking someone would mess with his head?"

He nodded. "Especially when he's spent years convincing himself he's better off alone."

"So you think he's not okay?" I asked softly.

There was a pause before he answered. "I think he's probably out there doing something he'll regret in the morning."

I sighed, letting the silence stretch between us. Then I glanced up at him. "Do you want to go check on him?"

He nodded slowly, but then he looked at me and I saw the guilt cloud his face. "I really don't wanna leave you, I just want to make sure he's-"

"Go check on him," I said gently, patting his chest. "I'll be right here when you get back."

He smiled, then leaned down and kissed the top of my head. "Every time I look at you, I feel like Allah gave me more than I deserve."

I smacked his chest lightly. "Don't be silly. Allah knows exactly what He gives and why. And if He gave you me, then you absolutely deserve me."

I pressed my lips to his—just long enough to steal his breath—then nudged him away.

"Now go check on him."

36

BADR

وَالنَّفْسُ مَا لَمْ تَرْتَقِبكَ كَثِيبَةٌ
وَالطَّرْفُ مَا لَمْ يَلْتَمِحكَ كَلِيلُ

The soul, when not in wait for you, is but a barren dune,
The eye, unless it glimpses you, is dim as a sickly moon.

- ابن خفاجة

When I left the house, my mind ran through every possible scenario.

Ayaan has a habit of choosing the worst coping mechanisms when he was overwhelmed, so I found myself silently bargaining, hoping he wasn't spiraling in one of the ways I knew too well.

I called him once.

No answer.

I called again.

Still nothing.

Each unanswered ring tightened something in my chest.

When I finally arrived, I asked the gatekeeper if Ayaan was home. When he said yes, relief washed over me. "He's at the gym," the man added.

I frowned—but the relief stayed. Of all his habits, this was the least destructive. Better sweat than speed.

I headed straight for the gym. Through the glass door, I spotted him immediately. He was mid-deadlift. And it was too much weight.

I have trained with Ayaan for years so I knew his limits. This wasn't strength—it was punishment. His back trembled, face strained, jaw clenched so hard I could see the tension from where I stood.

I pushed the door open. "Dude." My voice snapped through the room.

He dropped the bar instantly and collapsed onto the floor, chest heaving, breath ragged. I crossed the room, grabbed his water bottle, and held it out to him before sitting on the bench nearby.

He took it from me with a trembling hand and drank like he'd been stranded in the desert—too fast, careless. Water spilled down his chin, soaked onto his gym shirt, darkening the fabric as it clung to his chest. When he lifted his arm to wipe his mouth, the sleeve rode up just enough for me to see the flash of ink along his bicep, partially hidden, partially exposed.

A tattoo he pretends doesn't exist. One he goes out of his way to keep covered—long sleeves, careful movements, the kind of awareness that comes from regret rather than pride. He hates seeing it reflected back at him, hates the reminder of who he was when he thought permanence meant nothing.

I looked away before he could notice. Not because I disapproved, but because I knew how much it bothered him. How much control it took for him to keep it buried, like if he ignored it long enough, it might fade on its own.

His breathing slowly steadied, then he sat up—only to slump back against the opposite bench.

"Are you okay?" I asked.

He nodded.

"Why would you do that?" I pressed. "You could've snapped something."

He didn't answer. Just drank more water, so I waited.

Finally, he glanced at me. "What are you doing here?"

"You haven't responded to a single text," I said. "What did you expect?"

He rubbed his temple. "I was busy all day."

I gave him a look. "What?" he muttered. "It's true."

"Habiba told me about Sanaa." He froze—just for a fraction of a second—before slipping back into casual deflection.

"Who's Sanaa?" I didn't respond. I didn't need to. The look on my face said enough. "Ah! your neighbor?" he tried. "I don't know what Habiba told you, but I'm fine. I don't even know what you're talking about."

I let it go.

I knew better.

Pushing Ayaan only made him retreat further, and that was the last thing I wanted. So I changed the subject.

I didn't leave until he'd showered, changed, and looked steady enough to sleep.

I didn't fix anything, but I distracted him. I kept him company and pulled him back from the edge, even if only for a moment. And sometimes, for someone like Ayaan, that was enough.

When I got home, Habiba was asleep, the Qur'an still open in her hands. My heart softened instantly. I kissed her fingers, then her forehead, before sliding the book away and setting it on the nightstand.

She stirred as I adjusted her, but before she could wake fully, I slipped behind her, pulling her body into mine. Her warmth, her breathing melted everything else away.

The week passed quietly, but Habiba's words lingered in my mind, how she preferred being in the same room as me, how my presence somehow boosted her productivity.

It reminded me of the way she makes me feel, how a little dose of her was my everything. It didn't make sense to me why she would feel that way now, when she never used to. But it didn't need to. What mattered was that it made sense to her. And if being near me made her days easier, then I'd do whatever it took to give her that comfort.

When we got to the office, after greeting everyone, I walked her all the way to her door. She threw me a sidelong glance, suspicion glinting in her eyes. I didn't usually escort her this far.

Standing in front of her office, she turned, mischief curling on her lips. "So, now I get walked to my door? Are you gonna carry my bag next?"

I leaned closer, smiling back. "I'd carry your bag any day."

She arched a brow, teasing. "Hmm, then everyone will say you're whipped."

"Are you kidding?" I chuckled. "I *am* whipped."

Her laugh made something loosen in my chest. She finally turned the knob and walked in. For a moment, she didn't notice. Her eyes went straight to her desk as she placed her bag. But when she finally looked up—She froze.

Her gaze landed on the frosted glass wall that hadn't been there before, framed with heavy curtains, a second door connecting her office to mine. The faux wall between us was gone.

I stepped in and quietly shut the door behind me, watching. Her wide eyes softened, a slow smile tugging at her lips then, they filled with tears. By the time I reached her, her arms were already open, wrapping tightly around me.

I kissed the crown of her head, breathing in the faint trace of her. My hand rubbed soothing circles against her back.

"You didn't have to do that," she whispered, voice thick.

"I wanted to," I murmured. "Do you like it?"

She pulled back just enough to meet my eyes, cheeks damp but glowing with that small, genuine smile I loved. "I love it."

Over the weekend, I had arranged everything in secret.

Contractors had replaced the wall with a curtain glass partition and door. Frosted, for privacy. Curtains, for discretion during client meetings. But at its heart, it was simple: a way for her to know I was there.

Her fingers lingered against my chest as she said softly, "Thank you… How did Terrence agree to this?"

I scratched my temple. "I got tossed into a threequel with Ms. Raifer."

Her mouth dropped open in shock. "Seriously?"

I nodded. He's been trying to get me to take her new villa project, and I've avoided it for as long as I could. I was ready to do anything to never come in contact with that woman again—but for Habiba's comfort, it was a no-brainer. He knew exactly what he was doing.

"It's okay, I'm here now. I'll bring you muffins before she does," Habiba giggled, looking up at me with that mischievous grin of hers.

"As long as you don't bake them, I'll eat them," I teased, kissing her nose.

She frowned, pouting. "But wait—what if you get tired of me coming into your office? A little distance is good for couples, you know."

I shook my head, "Habiba, if I wanted distance, I wouldn't have torn down a wall for you."

Her lips curved, half-smile, half-grimace, the kind she wore when her heart was caught between joy and disbelief. "You always hear me," she whispered. "That means more than you know."

I did know. I noticed it even at home, how she drifted into whichever room I was in, almost unconsciously. Sometimes I'd wander into the bedroom for something, only to get distracted with something else, and minutes later she'd appear too—settling on the bed, a chair, the floor—just being there. It wasn't about watching me. It was about not being alone.

Now, in the office, the glass wall gave her that same reassurance: a line of sight, a door, the knowledge that at any moment she could step into my space—or I into hers.

I kissed her forehead and tightened my arms around her. "I want you to agree to something for me today," I murmured.

Her brows drew together. "What?"

"You'll see. Just promise me you'll try it for me."

She frowned, but she nodded. That was enough.

Soon, I slipped into my office through the door I'd added, closing it gently behind me. From there, I could still see her shadow moving in the next room. As she went to make herself a cup of tea, I brewed my coffee, and only then finally settled down to work.

The day passed quietly, almost effortlessly. I wandered into Habiba's office a few times, and she came into mine. It was easier now.

When we got home and changed, I told her we weren't staying in. We were going somewhere else. She didn't protest, just freshened up and got ready without question.

But when we arrived, that changed. She shook her head, refused, kept whispering no. It took time, soft words, and a lot of patience before she finally gave in. The place was exactly as I wanted it for her—no cars, no people, nothing but an endless stretch of dirt and sky. No eyes. No pressure, just us.

"Relax," I murmured, reaching over to rub her back.

Her nod was stiff, her gaze locked on the wheel as if she were afraid it might spin out of her hands. Her fingers were curled so tight, her nails dug crescents into the leather.

A part of me smiled. If those marks stayed, I wouldn't mind. This car could carry her imprint in the smallest details, and I'd welcome every reminder.

"Yeah," she whispered, though her voice trembled like a thin sheet of glass.

I drove us to this empty field myself, parked, and switched places with her. This was supposed to be step one. Small, safe. A start.

I stayed silent, letting her gather herself. She closed her eyes, lips moving with words too quiet for me to catch. A prayer maybe, or a bargain with herself. When her eyes opened again, she turned the key, shifted the gear, and slowly, the car lurched forward.

My chest tightened. My heart thudded with hers. I knew I wasn't the one holding the wheel, but I couldn't breathe any easier than she could.

The car crawled ahead. Ten kilometers an hour, maybe less. Still, it moved, steady, sure.

I glanced at her, tears had blurred her eyes. My hand darted across to wipe them so she could see clearly.

"I'm doing it," she cried, voice breaking.

"You are," I whispered back, my throat thick. "I'm so proud of you."

The car was slow, but to me it felt monumental. She leaned forward in concentration, every muscle tense, refusing to blink away from the road. I had expected jerks, false starts, maybe even a stall. But no, she kept it smooth, driving in careful circles, one after another.

And then, braver this time, she pressed the pedal a little deeper. Fifteen kilometers. Twenty, twenty five. The air rushed faintly through the half-cracked window, the field stretching wide around us, her hijab trembling in the breeze.

20 minutes passed like that. She was no longer whispering, no longer shaking. Just breathing, driving in circles. Remembering.

When she finally eased the car to a stop, she turned to me with a grin so wide, it looked like her whole face had been lit from the inside out. My chest ached just looking at her.

"I am so proud of you," I teased, cupping her face.

Her grin only widened, then suddenly, she flung the door open.

I blinked as she leapt out, spinning and jumping in the middle of the field, her laughter carried by the wind. "I did it!" she screamed, and her voice echoed against the open sky.

I got out and leaned against the car, arms crossed, just watching. Letting her joy wash over me.

Then she spun, eyes wild with triumph, and bolted toward me. I barely had time to steady myself before she threw herself into my arms. I caught her easily, lifting her clear off the ground as she wrapped her arms around my neck. Her laughter burst warm against my ear.

"Thank you, thank you, thank you!" she said between hugs, squeezing me so tight I almost lost breath. When I set her down, she tilted her face up, eyes shimmering. "Thank you," she whispered again, softer now, as though the words themselves were too small for what she felt.

Her excitement lit something in me I couldn't hide. Tears pricked at the corners of my own eyes.

"I didn't think I could ever do this again," she said, voice breaking.

"Well, you did it. And you were perfect." I corrected.

She pulled back a little, spread her arms wide to the wind, then rushed right back into me, hugging again. "I loved it!"

"Soon you'll be driving me around." I tapped her nose.

That earned me a closed-lip smile, her face hovering just inches from mine. Her eyes softened. "I love you," she whispered.

The words landed deep, rattling through me.

"I love you so much," she repeated, before leaning in and pressing her lips to mine.

I pulled her closer, one hand firm at the back of her head. The wind rushed around us, the scent of grass and earth heavy in the air, but all I felt was her, her warmth, her fire, her surrender.

When we finally broke apart, breathless, we returned to the car. She was still buzzing, her joy radiating like the sun.

By the time I drove us home, Habiba practically skipped into the living room. Ma and Ba were chatting, Ahmed lounging nearby. She burst in with a grin that split her face.

"I drove!" she announced, her grin so wide I thought her face might split. "Ba, Ma! I actually drove!" She repeated, almost bouncing on her toes.

They all looked up, smiling as she chattered away, recounting every detail. I stood back, just watching.

This—this was what I loved. The way she was already part of my family. The way she could sit with them, chatting like she'd known them all her life. I loved walking into a room and hearing her voice tangled with theirs.

And though a part of me thought she should've kept today private, that this was just the beginning, just a field, and the road ahead would be so much harder, I couldn't bring myself to dim her fire.

#

37

وَكُلُّ جِرَاحَةٍ فَلَهَا دَوَاء
وسوء الخُلُقِ لَيسَ لَهُ دَوَاء

Every wound has a cure,
But a bad character has no remedy.

- علي بن أبي طالب

Baba called Badr and me over to meet him at home. Badr insisted I tell him to arrange it at his office instead, he didn't want me anywhere near Gogo and Khadijah. But I convinced him I'd be fine.

Truthfully, I wanted to see for myself what state they were in—mostly Khadijah. She had been so thrilled to see me leave, and I was curious how well she was handling the house now. Especially since Muhammed told me she'd changed. Back then, she would rather die than let him have his own kids for more than two days a week. And now suddenly he had four days with them. Clearly, she wasn't managing as well as she thought she could.

Khadijah opened the door, Jamila trailing right behind her. The little one broke into a grin and launched herself at me. I scooped her up without hesitation, her tiny arms curling around my neck.

"How are you, my little baby?" I cooed, swaying her a little.

"Ok," she grinned, dimples flashing.

Muhammed and Khadijah had agreed for him to have the kids 4 days a week rather than just the weekends and so one of those days, I get to meet them. They cried when they saw me again after so long but the more we met, the more everything started to normalize for them. At first, Badr wasn't comfortable with me spending time with them and

Muhammed, knowing very well that he had feelings for me, but he never really made a big deal out of it.

"You look so cute," I pinched her cheek, earning that sweet giggle of hers before I passed her to Badr. He gladly took her, bouncing her in his arms, whispering nonsense that made her giggle even harder.

"Where's Hadi?" he asked, still playing with her.

I let my gaze shift past them to Khadijah. One look and I knew. Her clothes weren't crisp and perfectly pressed the way they used to be, instead, they hung wrinkled and tired on her frame. Shadows dragged under her eyes. Life had been pressing hard on her, that much was clear. But when her eyes landed on me, irritation replaced exhaustion.

I shut the door myself. "SalamuAlaikum."

No reply.

"Come, Jamila." She reached for her daughter, and Badr gently set the child down. Khadijah grabbed her and disappeared toward the kitchen without another word.

I glanced at Badr. He raised his brows in that *you see what I mean?* kind of way. We sat on the rug in the living room, waiting for Baba. Instead, Gogo came down first.

"Khadijah wa ya zo—?" *Khadijah who came?* she started, only to stop dead when she spotted us. "Kai!" she snapped, groaning as if my very existence exhausted her. "La hawla wa la quwwata illa billah."

That old, familiar heaviness settled over me like a storm cloud. Being in her presence always dragged me back into it. Still, I opened my mouth to at least greet her but, she spoke first.

"Wallahi na tsani ganin wannan yarinyar," *I swear, I hate seeing this girl.* She spat, turning to Khadijah who stood at the kitchen door. "Yadda kika san an yi kashi an ajiye a tsakar gida, haka nake ji kullun idan na gan ta." *As if someone pooped and left it in the middle of the courtyard, that's exactly how I feel every time I see her.*

It should've stung. Maybe once upon a time, it would have.

Now, I almost wanted to laugh at the ridiculousness of it. But I pressed it down. I wasn't here for her. I was here for Baba.

"Toh, che maki akayi sai kin ganta?" *So who said you must see her?* Baba's voice cut sharp from upstairs. He was descending, his tone like thunder. "Go back upstairs, sit there. You don't have to look at her." He waved her away, scowling.

With a hiss under her breath, Gogo retreated upstairs.

"Ina yini Baba," *Hello Baba.* I said quickly, standing to greet him with a side hug.

"Yauwa," he patted my head, his touch softening the weight of his voice. "How are you?" I nodded. He turned to Badr and grinned, extending a hand. "Architect."

They shook firmly.

Badr chuckled, patting Baba's shoulder. "Hope you're well."

"I am, thank you. Sit, please."

We sank back onto the rug as Baba settled in. Then, with the same unfiltered directness he always carried, he said, "You've been married long enough to stop walking around without your gele."

My body warmed to his comment and I nodded "I'll keep that in mind." I responded.

"Badr El-Idrissi," Baba said, leaning back into his chair. Badr looked up, smiling kindly. "You're doing a good job, you know. She looks happier every time I see her."

"I'm hoping to do better," Badr replied.

Baba let out one of his deep, rumbling chuckles before leaning forward, his gaze steady. "Well, I called you both here because I was hoping to ask you for something."

Badr frowned, confused. His eyes flicked briefly to me before returning to Baba.

"Every year, we organize a food donation event in the name of her parents, siblings, and grandmother," Baba continued. "Habiba and I usually travel to Nigeria together to oversee it. But now that she's married, I thought it might be more appropriate to send you both—if you're comfortable with that, of course. I can still go with her if you'd prefer."

"Of course," Badr said at once. "I'd be honored." He turned to me, checking my expression, then back to Baba. "I'd also like to contribute to the donations, if that's alright."

Baba gave a small, approving nod, then looked at me. "Can you have your kids assist you this year?"

"Maryam and Ismail, most likely," I said. "But Danko's sick. I just sent for his medication last week, so I doubt he'll be able to come. The rest will help as usual."

Baba nodded again, thoughtful. "Alright then. Let me know if you need anything. I have to travel to Washington tonight for work, so you'll have to handle the arrangements yourselves."

"Alright," I said with a smile.

We sat in silence for a few seconds before Baba spoke again. "I hear you two are designing the resort for Franklin Starr."

I tried not to grin, but the pride pressed at the corners of my mouth. I hadn't expected him to find out so soon—certainly not before the final stage.

"Yes. We're still in the first stages."

"It's good," he said, nodding slowly. "It's good," he repeated, still nodding. His leg bounced slightly, a telltale sign of excitement. "I heard it from Baban Hafsah, the HD. He told me to wish you luck."

"Thank you, " I murmured, meeting his eyes briefly. His smile was faint, but it carried a weight I wasn't used to. Maybe it was pathetic, but I didn't expect more than this from him. He wasn't the type to show affection. The only time I'd truly seen his softer side was after the accident, when he took care of me.

"So do you finally understand that our job isn't just scribbles on paper?" Badr teased, though his tone edged toward hostile.

"Badr—" I started.

"No, no, it's alright. He's right," Baba cut me off. He exhaled, then turned toward Badr. "And, yes. I did my research. As long as the job makes her happy, I don't care. I realize I need to start focusing more on that girl over there." He jerked his chin toward the back, meaning Khadijah.

I chuckled softly.

"Wallahi, when you left, the house was a disaster. I had to force her to do something. Not only did she do it badly, but she complained the whole time. I told her that was what you did for years without complaint. She stood right there—" he pointed at the floor, his voice rising. "right there, crying, throwing tantrums. Now suddenly she wants to go back to work. The same job she once refused because it was 'too hard.'"His eyes flicked behind us. "Yes, you. I'm talking about you." He pointed directly at Khadijah, who must have been standing in the kitchen doorway. I didn't bother turning. I didn't care to see her face.

The conversation lightened after that, we laughed and stayed until he announced that he had to prepare for his trip.

In all my years with Baba, I had never felt happier sitting with him. My eyes stung as I walked to the door.

As a child, I used to hear him speak harshly to my mother. I'd tell her I didn't like him because he was so rude. She would only smile and say:

"Your grandfather's heart is hard, but it isn't stone. When you meet his sharpness with sharpness, you only break yourself. Some people you don't win with arguments, you win with time, patience, and prayer. You never know, maybe someday my kindness and prayers for him will be all worth it and will help us."

And it did, because after she was gone, it was that same man who took me in. Kindness leaves a seed even in soil that looks barren.

In the car, Badr glanced at me before asking, "What kids was he talking about?"

I frowned, confused.

"He asked you if you'd be involving your kids in the donation."

"Oh, right. My orphans," I said. "My parents used to take care of orphans in Nigeria. Covering their expenses, medical bills, clothing, everything. When I grew older, I took over. Usually it's just until they can stand on their own feet, or I help them start a business. Sometimes they help with the donations because we could end up feeding over 300 people and it gets quite messy."

He nodded in understanding. "MashaAllah… maybe I should start something like that in Morocco."

"You should. It's a beautiful thing. My mom used to say, 'You can't change the world, but you can always start from home.'"

He reached for my hand, kissed it lightly, then turned his eyes back to the road. "In fact, you know what? What if we make a trip out of this?" He glanced at me, a spark in his eyes. "I'll come with you to Nigeria. From there, we head to Morocco, maybe set up some kind of donation. You meet my family, I meet yours."

I grinned, instantly in love with the idea. "What if we plan it around Hajj? Have you ever been?"

He shook his head.

"Then let's do it! It's so close, and I've been dreaming of a chance to go."

His grin matched mine. "Sounds perfect."

And that's exactly what we did. Within a month, we had our Hajj tickets booked, along with the trips to Nigeria and Morocco. When the time came, we left—hearts light, plans set, and something bigger than both of us waiting ahead.

38

HABIBA

يا بدرُ كم سهرت عليك نواظرٌ
ويا غصنٍ، كم ناحت عليك بلابلُ
البدرُ يكمل كل شهرٍ مرةً
وهلالُ وجهك كل يوم كاملُ

O full moon, how many eyes have stayed awake for you!
O branch, how many nightingales have lamented for you.
The full moon becomes completes its circle once every month,
But the crescent of your face is complete every single day.

- طرفة بن العبد

The year slipped by in a breeze, then another. Badr and I had been moving through milestones like stepping stones across a river—the six-month mark, the first fight, first apartment together, first anniversary.

We fought like any couple would, but not once, not even in the heat of an argument did I question whether I had chosen the right man. That doubt never touched me.

Our lives had settled into a rhythm, a routine that felt safe and comfortable. We didn't need to orbit each other constantly anymore, and that was okay. I still loved him, deeply. As long as he came home to me at night, he was free to move in his own space, breathe in his own world.

Badr was still Badr—unchanged, unapologetically himself. Which is why it wasn't surprising when he lifted me onto the bathroom counter, as though I weighed nothing. The cold marble bit at the back of my thighs, but I barely noticed. He stepped between my legs, close.

And we just stared. Smiling like fools.

The little stick sat in my hand, upside down, its secret still hidden. The alarm buzzed on the sink, sharp and insistent, telling us that two minutes had passed. The results were ready.

My heart hammered. I was about to flip it when his hand caught mine. He cupped my face, tilting me toward him, and kissed me softly, firmly, like he couldn't let the moment pass without claiming it.

I pulled back, eyebrows furrowing. "What was that for?"

He smiled in that maddening, devastating way of his. "Because I already know what it's going to say."

I blinked at him. "How?"

"Because," he whispered, his nose lightly bumping mine, "I love you."

I couldn't hold back my own grin as I flipped the test.

Two lines.

Positive.

A laugh slipped out of me, half sob, half squeal, and I threw my arms around his neck, hugging him so tightly I thought I might never let go. He wrapped me in his warmth, his hold secure, then lifted me straight off the counter and walked us out of the bathroom, into our bedroom where he spun me around, my laughter mixing with his, until he set me down gently on the bed.

He pulled me close again, his lips brushing my temple as he whispered, voice trembling with conviction, "I will forever thank Allah for making you my wife."

And then something caught my eye.

I gasped, wriggling free, and darted to the window. My grin stretched wider than I thought possible. "Look—it's snowing!"

The first snow after summer, falling soft and slow, blanketing the world outside. He laughed with me, his voice thick with wonder. "SubhanAllah," he whispered, his smile radiant.

We stepped outside, letting the snow dust our shoulders and faces. The cold bit at my cheeks, but I didn't care. Badr didn't look at the sky or the city, he only looked at me. He stood there watching me spin and laugh, his gaze soft and unblinking, like I was the only thing worth seeing.

By the time we got back into the house, Badr was full of wild ideas about how to tell our families, each one more ridiculous than the last. I teased him, making him promise we'd start with the hospital first, just to be sure.

He slipped into full care mode, warming tea while I did my skincare, lying on my side of the bed to warm the sheets for me, like he always did in winter. He offered to massage my legs, but I waved him off. In the end, we simply curled into each other, our bodies warm and steady.

"Are you nervous?" I asked softly, tracing my fingers across his chest.

"Very." His breath came out deep and ragged. "It's a whole new chapter. So much to do." His voice was husky with exhaustion.

"Yeah…" I whispered.

"We need to move," he said suddenly. "This place won't be big enough."

"We could stay until the baby needs its own room," I murmured, running my nails through his beard, knowing how much he loved the feeling.

He shook his head. "No. Better to move now. It's easier before the baby comes. You don't want to do it with a child." His fingers drew slow circles on my shoulder.

I nodded and rested my head against him. Silence settled, deep and soft. His hand slowed, then stilled as he drifted to sleep. Eventually, I followed, my last thought a quiet prayer of gratitude. For him, for us, for the tiny miracle now growing between us.

It took us a full week to put the plan together, the right place, the right moment to tell them.

The doctor said I was six weeks along. Well, seven now. We booked a private room at a restaurant and invited everyone.

Baba patted my head as he took a seat next to Ba. The two of them are kind of friends now, though Ma still says he carried a "rotten ego"—her words, not mine.

I sat between Hana and Badr. Nothing looked suspicious; after all, Zain had just graduated, and tonight was supposed to be his celebration. We agreed to wait until the end to share our news.

The table filled with chatter, menus flipping, laughter weaving through conversations about which drinks to order. Badr took everyone's choices, passed the menus to the waiter, and ordered two family platters for the table.

My heart raced each time someone's eyes lingered on me. They didn't know, of course, but what if they could tell?

Badr slipped his hand under the table, fingers closing around mine. His thumb brushed over my knuckles, steadying me without a word. I glanced at him, managed a smile, then turned back to the others.

The drinks arrived, followed by steaming plates of food. Laughter swelled around me, Hana angling her phone for selfies, Ahmed hunched over his game, Zain smiling at some text he clearly didn't want us to see.

When the meal slowed, Badr lifted his glass. "Before we go any further, a toast. To Zain, for graduating. We're all proud of you. Welcome to the real world."

Glasses lifted, voices rang, and Zain ducked his head, that shy grin on his face. Then Badr glanced at me, his eyes asking. I nodded.

He grinned, squeezed my hand beneath the table, and said clearly, "Habiba and I have an announcement."

Silence fell. Every face turned toward us, curious, expectant. Ma already wore that soft, knowing smile. She knew. She had to know.

"We're having a baby," Badr said.

The room erupted—shock, then joy, then chairs scraping back as hugs and congratulations poured over us. Hana wrapped her arms around me first, kissing my cheek, I hugged Ba and Baba too while Ahmed and Zain hovered close, beaming.

"I wish I could give you a hug," Zain pouted.

I smiled gently. "I know."

Hana squeezed me tighter. "I'll hug her for you."

Ahmed lit up. "Is it going to be a boy or a girl?"

"We don't know yet," Badr answered.

"I hope it's a boy," Ahmed declared, determined. "I'll teach him how to play Call of Duty."

"And if it's a girl?" Badr challenged.

Ahmed sighed dramatically. "Then I guess I won't mind watching Barbie together." That earned another round of laughter.

The warmth of family filled the space, wrapping me tighter than any blanket. I hugged Ma, who pinched my cheek and rubbed my stomach. "I knew it," she teased. "The glow gave you away."

I laughed, burying myself in her arms again.

The evening carried on with soft teasing, hugs, and endless conversation about names, features, and futures. Baba quietly slipped away and paid the bill, insisting it was his gift for the good news.

When it was time to leave, I walked beside Baba. "Ina patan mijin ki ze bar ni in ga gikoki na." *I hope your husband will let me see my grandkids.*

I laughed. "Ya za aye ya qi? Ni da kai na zan kawo su." *How could he refuse? I will bring them to you myself.* He chuckled, "I don't want Gogo or Khadijah to know," I admitted softly.

I didn't want them involved—not their ill wishes, not their energy. Especially not Gogo. She has a long-standing habit of visiting *bokas*, men who work with black magic back in Nigeria. I know that as long as I have Allah, nothing she does can harm me or my family, but still, I wanted peace.

He chuckled. "Do you take me for a fool? They won't hear a word from me." I laughed and thanked him. Badr joined us, Baba patted his shoulder, told him to take care of me, then disappeared into the night.

By the time we got home, exhaustion weighed on me. Once in bed, Badr offered me a massage, and I didn't refuse. His hands moved gently across my back, loosening knots of tension.

"Speaking to your grandfather gave me an idea," he murmured.

I hummed, half-asleep. "Which is?"

"What if we started our own firm?" I opened my eyes, surprised. He hurried to add, "I know it sounds crazy. But when he spoke about building something of your own, it stirred something in me. What if we did that—for us, for the baby?" He paused, his hands stilling. "It would give us flexibility, more time with the child. We wouldn't be chained to anyone's schedule."

I thought about it, then nodded. "True."

He smiled faintly. "We already have the clients, the experience. It'll be hard at first, but I believe in us."

I rolled onto my side, meeting his gaze. "Whatever you want, I'll give you my full support."

He bent, kissing me softly, then pressed one to my temple.

When I offered to massage him, he shook his head, slipping off the bed to wash his hands. I pulled my gown on and settled under the covers.

"I don't think Terrence will be pleased though," I called out loud enough for him to hear over the running tap.

He didn't respond to me until he stepped out, and murmured his dua.

"Terrence won't be with us for long," he said as he reached for his hand cream.

I frowned. "What do you mean?"

"He's thinking of moving to Italy, to be closer to his daughter. He's not sure yet, but..."

I nodded slowly, my dhikr soft against my lips as I waited for him to join me. When he did, I rested my head against his chest. He opened the Qur'an and began to recite, his voice calm and steady, filling the room with peace.

And just like that, the noise of the evening melted away. It was only us and our small world.

39

BADR

لأنتِ منى قلبي، وغاية بُغْيَتي
وأقصى مرادي، واختياري، وخيرتي

For you are my heart's utmost desire and plea,
The end I seek, my final wish, my chosen destiny.

- ابن الفارض

I knew the test would be positive, something felt different. She felt different. For the longest time, she even smelled different, sweeter, softer, like something had shifted in her very skin.

I figured maybe she'd just changed her diet. She was pickier with food, but she was still my Habiba.

I was ready. It had always been at the back of my mind. I even knew exactly which neighborhood we'd move to if we managed to get an apartment there. I'd saved enough over the years. I was never the type to chase a lavish lifestyle—except maybe for the shoes, the watches, the suits, the ties. But those came with the job.

I wanted us settled before the baby arrived. I saw what my parents went through—moving countries with me as a kid and Zain still in diapers. It wasn't easy. Habiba and I wouldn't be moving that far, but I knew how fast things piled up. Cribs, clothes, toys, every little thing would only make the move harder.

Now she's nineteen weeks, starting to show and only getting more beautiful. She stands in the mirror admiring her little bump, and I just stand behind her, admiring her. She has that glow, the pregnancy glow. I brought a camera simply to document the whole journey.

Her hormones are all over the place, but I'm not scared of

hormones. She'll yell at me first thing in the morning, then all she needs is tea or sometimes just space. Rarely a hug anymore, she doesn't like to be touched now.

At first, it crushed me. I'd reach for her instinctively, only for her to pull away. I thought I did something wrong. But I realized it wasn't me, it was just her body, and she needed room. Even with Ma and Hana, she keeps her distance. We've all learned to give her that.

She's stopped taking clients, stays home more. Only goes in when she has a meeting but she does her work from home and site visits, which I prefer to take her myself in order to avoid accidents. She prefers her own quiet world.

I walked in with groceries, and the smell of *barrouk* filled the air, as usual. She'd been cooking it all week, and the scent was thick. I wondered how she could even stand it. I cracked open a window, then headed to the bedroom.

There she was, sitting cross-legged on the carpet, fanning herself while reading Qur'an.

I came closer and gently touched her hand to take the fan, accidentally startling her. "You're back," she said, smiling as she let me take over fanning her.

"I am," I leaned down to kiss her forehead. "Why didn't you just open the window?"

She shrugged, slipped a bookmark into the Qur'an, and set it aside.

"Don't you think it's too much? The barrouk?" I asked as I got up to nudge the bedroom window open.

"Badr." Her voice pulled me back. I turned. Her eyes were wide, almost nervous. "Do you think I stink?"

I froze. "What kind of question is that?"

"Answer it."

"Of course not. My love, you don't stink." I reached for her face,

387

but she stopped my hand.

"You're lying. You're just saying that so you don't hurt my feelings. I never stop smelling. I just showered, yet I stink right now." Her eyes dropped. "I can't use deodorant, I can't use perfume, I can't use anything…" Her voice cracked.

"Habiba, you don't smell bad." I stepped closer. She stepped back.

"I smell bad. I know I do. I can smell it." Her lips trembled, tears welling up.

"Habiba, look at me." She did. "Wallah you don't stink. Not to me. If anything, you smell amazing to me. You smell like roses."

She sighed, but doubt still lingered.

"But maybe that's just you," she whispered. "What if Ma and Hana think I stink?"

"They don't. I promise."

"Yes they do,"

"They don't."

"Ask Ma. Call her."

"Habiba-"

"Don't tell her I'm here, just ask, like you're asking for yourself. That way she'll answer honestly."

I grimaced. "I don't…"

"Please." She grabbed my hand, pleading.

And that was that. Moments later, I was dialing Ma.

"Salam'alaykum, Ma."

"Wa 'alaykum salam, Badr. Labas 'lik?" *Are you ok?*

"Labas, alhamdulillah. Ma… can I ask you something?"

A pause. "Hm?"

I lowered my voice. "Do you ever feel like… Habiba smells bad? You know, since she can't use deodorant now with the pregnancy and all…"

388

Silence. Then she snapped.

"Hayawan!" *Animal!* Ma's voice exploded through the phone. "Hayawan! Shame on you, Badr! If you think she stinks, bring her to me—I'll take care of her myself! She doesn't need you! SubhanAllah, useless, selfish boy!"

"Ma—"

"Ma 7chemtich?" *Aren't you ashamed?* "Tfu, tfu, tfu! She's carrying your child, and instead of giving her love, you're thinking about her smell? Wallah, I'll tell your father, and I hope he beats some sense into you!"

I pinched the bridge of my nose. "Ma, Thadni shwiya. Please, calm down."

"Tfu!" she spat one last time before switching into English. "Disgusting."

I glanced at Habiba. She was sitting right beside me, laughing. Laughing so hard she had to cover her mouth. I glared at her. I knew Ma would react this way.

"Ma, listen," I tried again. "I never said she smells bad. I just wanted to know if you think so. That's all."

"Why else would you ask such a stupid question? You're the reason she keeps showering? You're making her feel bad?"

"No, Ma, wallah! I didn't say anything to her. I don't even think she smells bad. It hadn't even crossed my mind."

She sighed on the other end, muttered something about me being stupid, then finally said, "She doesn't smell bad. I don't know why we're even talking about this. You've ruined my mood." Then she hung up.

I dragged a hand through my hair and turned to Habiba, who was now looking sheepish.

"That went well," I muttered.

"At least now we know," she said softly. "I'm sorry." She leaned

389

forward for a hug.

I considered being mad for a little while longer. But I've never been able to stay mad at her. I'm weak for affection.

So I hugged her back, and later we went to the kitchen to cook. She seemed calmer, though she still kept sniffing herself every so often.

There wasn't much more I could do about that. But I did call Ma again later to ask her to book a private hammam session for Habiba. Just her, a safe temperature, no harsh scrubbing.

If anyone could care for her better than me, it was Ma.

Habiba has been easing back into herself these past weeks. She doesn't shy away from my touch anymore, doesn't stiffen when I hug her from behind or curl myself around her. At night she cuddles into me like she used to before, her small body pressed trustingly against mine. Sometimes, when she's too tired, I hold her belly up just to give her back a break. She always sighs with relief when I do that—and I swear it makes me feel ten feet tall, like I've actually done something useful.

We'd spent the last two weeks packing, boxing up two years of our lives. I'll miss the comfort of this little place, but not the paper-thin walls. Nobody needs to hear their neighbors argue, or worse, hear us argue.

It's our last night here. Everything's moved out, except that I forgot to buy new sheets for the new apartment. Habiba insists she won't set foot in the new place until we buy new sheets, green ones, specifically. I couldn't care less what color we sleep on as long as she's sleeping next to me.

Now, my head rests carefully on her stomach. The doctor says it's fine, but I still can't bring myself to put my full weight. The thought of hurting them—even by mistake—makes my chest seize. She's reciting Qur'an softly, her voice filling the room the way it always does, calm and grounding. But then, mid-ayah, she veers off into casual chatter about the baby's room, her tone so easy, so domestic it warms me all over.

"I told him to use the heart stickers," she says, her hand rubbing her belly, "but your Abba brought the star shaped stickers and now we're stuck with stars."

"La, la." I shook my head. "In my defense, when I brought that little heart-shaped pillow, your Umma threw it at me and declared no hearts."

"That was a pink pillow," she counters, indignant. "We agreed everything would be gender neutral—"

She doesn't get to finish. Something taps softly against my head. It almost didn't happen but I felt it. My head jerks up instantly, fear lancing through me that I'd pressed too hard. But then I see her face, shock, followed by a slow, radiant grin.

"You felt that?" she breathes, her palm smoothing over her stomach.

I blink, still not fully processing. "What was that?"

"The first kick!" She chuckles, eyes bright.

"Seriously?" My voice cracks. I got on my knees, eyes wide. My hands hover, unsure where to touch. Then, gently, I rest my ears on her belly. "Hi, baby," I whisper. "Kick again for Abba?"

We freeze, waiting. Nothing.

I laugh, giddy anyway, and lift my head to kiss Habiba's temple, whispering against her skin, "That was so beautiful. You're doing wonders."

She frowns in confusion. "What did I do?"

"You grew a miracle inside you," I say, unable to keep the wonder from my voice. "Habiba, I literally just felt our baby kick my face." I'm half laughing, half on the verge of tears.

She grins, scratching her head. "Okay… I think you kicked your Abba's brain a little too hard, baby. He's gone crazy now."

I chuckle, but when I lay my head back, all I hear is the soft nothingness of her body at work, growing life. And I love her more than I know how to say.

Sometimes I catch myself just watching her sleep, whispering Alhamdulillah. It's still surreal to me that she's carrying our child. Every new curve of her body, every inch she grows, I find myself prouder of her, more in awe. She's sacrificing her comfort, her ease, everything, for this. For us.

"You're the cutest," she says suddenly, pinching my cheek. "Now go get me some cheesecake, and maybe I'll convince the baby to kick again for you."

My jaw drops. "Cheesecake? Habiba, it's 2 a.m.!"

She gaves me a warning look, hand on her belly. "Hey! Blame yourself, not me. The baby clearly inherited your cheesecake addiction. Time to take responsibility for your actions."

I groan dramatically, but there's no escaping it. I've already learned: when Habiba craves something, Allah Himself seems to guide me right to it, no matter the hour. I slip my shoes on, heart still light from the kick, tongue moving in dhikr the way she taught me. Lately, my most constant one has been:

Allahumma rahmataka arju, fala takilni ila nafsi tarfata 'ayn, wa aslih li sha'ni kullah, la ilaha illa ant. *Oh Allah, I hope only for Your mercy. Don't leave me to myself for even the blink of an eye. Rectify all my affairs. There is no god but You.*

I carry it with me everywhere now—this prayer, her, and the tiny miracle that just made its presence known.

I kissed her belly, then kissed her lips, before leaving the house, my phone and keys in hand. Sitting in the car, I drummed my fingers on the steering wheel, racking my brain about which café in the city would be mad enough to still be open at 2 a.m. and have cheesecake. None came to mind.

Then it hit me! I had something better than cafés. I had a brother who bakes and a mother who owned a bakery.

I tipped my head back, staring up at the quiet night sky. "Ya Allah," I whispered, "please let there be cheesecake at the bakery."

Then I dialed Zain.

The phone rang so long I thought he wouldn't pick up, but finally his hoarse voice came through, heavy with sleep. "Why are you calling me at 2 a.m.?"

"Kidayr?" I greeted, but he only grumbled something I didn't quite catch "Wallah, Habiba said she wants cheesecake."

A long, tortured sigh. I could almost see him rubbing his face. "Badr... I can't make cheesecake at 2 a.m. It doesn't work like that."

"Isn't there any left at the bakery?" I asked, hopefully.

"We're usually cleaned out before closing," he muttered, followed by a yawn so big I heard it through the phone. "I didn't even go in today, but maybe there's some cream cheese filling. I can ask Ma—"

"No, don't wake her up," I cut in quickly. I pictured my mother storming into my apartment in slippers at this hour. That wasn't worth it.

There was silence. Then, against all odds, Zain sighed again. "I'll meet you at the bakery. I'll whip up something for her—close enough to cheesecake."

"Seriously? I owe you one."

"You owe me ten," he grumbled before hanging up.

I ran back upstairs, practically bouncing. Habiba was back to reading the Qur'an, but she immediately glanced up when she saw me. Her eyes darted to my empty hands, narrowing.

"Where's the cheesecake?"

I grinned, "I have a better idea."

Ten minutes later, thanks to the empty roads, we pulled up at the bakery. The warm glow of the lights spilled out onto the street, almost welcoming. Inside, Zain was already in the kitchen, hair sticking up like he'd just fought a pillow and lost. He waved weakly.

"Hi, Habiba."

The kitchen smelled faintly of sugar and cinnamon. It was a typical kitchen—stainless steel counters polished but still scarred from knives, mixers lined up like loyal soldiers, shelves crammed with piping bags, cookie cutters, and jars of sprinkles. Big fridges hummed in the background, and trays leaned against the wall like tired bakers themselves.

Habiba frowned at me. "You dragged him out of bed to do your job?"

"Hey, you wanted cheesecake. I'm delivering. Besides, he offered." I ruffled Zain's hair as I passed.

Zain ignored us, slipping on gloves. He pulled a small crust from the fridge, setting it down on the counter he'd just wiped. "At least when the baby is born," he muttered, "he or she will never hear the end of this from me."

I chuckled, then grabbed Habiba by the waist and lifted her onto the counter so she could watch. Pulling on my own gloves, I turned to my brother. "So, what's next?"

"Get the filling from that fridge."

I did, plopping the piping bag onto the table. Zain grabbed it, ready to pipe into the crust—but Habiba suddenly stopped him.

"Wait, wait, no!"

She held out her arms, attempting to slide off the high countertop, but her legs weren't exactly tall enough to touch the ground. I quickly rounded the table and grabbed her by the waist, placing her down softly myself.

She padded straight to the cupboards, ignoring both of us, and pulled out a plate. Then, with the confidence of someone who knew exactly what she wanted, she opened a container of shortbread biscuits,

394

set them down, and piped the filling directly onto the shortcakes.

Zain and I froze, stepping back like soldiers giving space to a queen. She took a bite, and let out a blissful sigh. "Can she do that?" Zain asked under his breath.

"Are you gonna stop her?" I asked.

He shook his head immediately. That was the end of that.

Honestly, it didn't look bad. I grabbed a biscuit, piped, tasted. My eyes widened, it was incredible. Zain caught my reaction, grabbed one himself, and the three of us stood around the counter like conspirators, devouring biscuits at 2:30 a.m.

Between bites, I announced proudly, "The baby kicked for the first time tonight."

Zain's jaw dropped. "WHAT? Why didn't you start with that?!" He spun to Habiba, suddenly fully awake. "From now on, you get cheesecake, carrot cake, shortbread—name it, it's yours. Call me any time."

Habiba smirked, still focused on her plate. "I like him better than I like you," she told me.

I scowled, halfway through my fifth shortbread when my phone buzzed.

Ma: Imagine getting a motion alert in your bakery. You check the camera, and it's three idiots stealing your shortbread.

I burst out laughing and showed the screen to the other two. We all turned to the camera and waved like guilty children caught red-handed.

40

BADR

وأنا الذي مهما نظرتُ إلى جَمالكِ لا أمل
وإذا ضحكت يَفُوحُ في الأجواء نسرين وفل

I am he who, at the sight of your beauty, knows no fatigue or dread,
And when you laugh, the very air blooms with jasmine in its space.

- أبين العتوم

When we told Terrence we'd be starting our own firm, his face fell. He was disappointed, very disappointed, but still encouraging. He admitted he wasn't planning to stick around much longer himself, but he had hoped one of us might someday become the face of the company. Still, he gave us a list of his contacts, wished us well, and told us his door would always be open if we needed guidance.

Of course, it wouldn't be easy. Running a firm isn't just sketching pretty buildings on paper. It's contracts, insurance, sleepless nights, clients who don't pay, mistakes that drain money faster than you can count it. But we were ready.

I asked Zain to design a website for us. He built a clean portfolio page and even started an Instagram, though Habiba took the reins there. The plan was to prepare everything now, launch after she delivered. I've saved enough to keep us afloat even if clients were slow at first.

The truth was, I wanted more time for the baby. Working under someone else meant endless deadlines. Owning a firm wouldn't make life easier, but at least it would give me flexibility. And despite everyone at home ready to help Habiba, despite knowing that she wouldn't have to carry the weight alone, I wanted to be there, every moment, every step.

Alhamdulillah, we already had two clients lined up through

connections, projects set to begin right after our launch. Things were falling into place. But for now, all I could think about was the matter at hand—finding out the gender.

At first, we thought of waiting until delivery to find out the gender, but in the end, the doctor handed us an envelope and we agreed not to open it until the whole family was there.

When we walked in, the house was alive in its usual organized chaos.

Ayaan and Ahmed were hunched over the chessboard, their faces scrunched in concentration. Ma and Zain were setting the table, voices overlapping in quiet chatter. Ba had the news on and Hana was on the rug, trying to keep Naeem from chewing on one of her pens.

Habiba went straight to Ma, her voice light and warm as she greeted her. I joined the boys, leaning against the back of the couch to watch Ayaan make a risky move that Ahmed immediately punished with a grin.

Then the bell rang.

Being the only jobless one in the room, I went to get it. Baba stood at the door, his presence as commanding as ever, his smile softer than usual. "Assalamu alaikum," he greeted, stepping in.

"Wa alaikum salam," I replied, shaking his hand.

He made his rounds, greeting everyone before joining Ba in the living room.

By the time Sanaa arrived, the aroma from the kitchen had taken over the house—warm, rich, and familiar. Ma's voice floated in from the dining room, calling everyone to the table.

I looked up just as Habiba stepped out of the kitchen, her headscarf slightly loose, a few strands of hair escaping around her face. She wore a soft green maternity gown patterned with tiny pink flowers—the color made her skin glow. She looked like peace personified. My peace.

"MashaAllah," I murmured under my breath, smiling like a fool.

She caught me staring and frowned. "What?"

"Nothing." I shrugged, offering her my hand, though the grin refused to leave my face.

"Why are you smiling like that?" she asked, sliding her hand into mine. The moment our palms met, something in me settled. No matter how many times I hold her hand, that quiet rush never fades.

I leaned closer, lowering my voice so only she could hear. "You were waddling."

Her eyes widened. "I was not."

I laughed softly, earning a light smack on the chest. She tried to look offended, but her lips twitched. "Habiba," I murmured, pressing a kiss to her temple before whispering, "you kind of were."

She rolled her eyes but smiled anyway.

Dinner went on with the usual laughter, teasing, and overlapping conversations. Then, halfway through her plate, Habiba cleared her throat. "We have the gender of the baby," she said, holding up the sealed envelope.

The entire table froze. Then came the gasps. Ahmed, who's somehow almost as tall as me and Zain now, jumped up and snatched the paper. "Do you know what's written inside?"

We both shook our heads.

"Let's all guess," he said, grinning.

Hana, Ayaan, Ma, and Sanaa said "girl."

Baba, Ahmed, Ba, and Naeem—who didn't even know what was happening but copied Ba—voted "boy."

Habiba and I just smiled. Boy or girl, our hearts were full.

Ahmed tore the envelope open dramatically, his expression changing as he read. He turned to us, eyes wide, grin spreading. "It's a girl!"

The room erupted in cheers. Ma covered her mouth, Sanaa

squealed, and Ba threw his hands out in excitement. Habiba's eyes shone, and I found myself grinning so hard my cheeks ached.

One by one, hugs went around. When I reached Ayaan, he was smiling through damp eyes. We met in a tight embrace, his hand firm against my back. "We're having a baby girl," he whispered, voice shaking.

I scoffed softly. "My baby girl, Ayaan. Don't get carried away."

He barked a laugh against my shoulder, and we pulled back quickly, both swiping at our eyes before anyone noticed.

The rest of the night blurred into joy. We talked names, colors, plans—Ayaan and Hana were already arguing over who'd get to hold her first.

When dinner was cleared and the smell of mint tea filled the house, I slipped my jacket on and stepped outside. The air was sharp against my skin, the night alive with distant hums. I leaned against the railing, staring at the cracked driveway glistening faintly under the porch light.

I looked up at the sky and smiled, heart swelling in my chest.

A girl.

SubhanAllah.

A daughter.

At the creak of the door, I turned. "Architect," Baba began, then corrected himself with a warm chuckle, his hand a firm weight on my shoulder. "No. I should call you Baba now." I shook my head, a breath of laughter escaping me, utterly adrift in a swell of joy. "How are you feeling?" he asked, his voice gentler now.

I exhaled, eyes fixed on the dark. "It feels unreal," I admitted. "She isn't even here yet, but already... I feel like I have to protect her. Both of them. Like I could wrap them in bubble wrap and never let them out."

He took the space next to me, his arm firm, his voice low and heavy with memory. "You know," he began, his eyes drifting toward the night sky, "the day before you came in with your Prince Charming nonsense and married her, I asked Habiba why she was so against marriage."

I shifted, suddenly interested, turning fully toward him, hanging on to every word.

"She told me, she's not against it. She just wanted to find someone like her father." His lips curved into a smile that trembled with both pride and loss. "I told her men like her father don't come twice. But SubhanAllāh... here you are. With every passing day, I see it clearer: Allah answered her little prayer."

His words cracked something open inside me. I've heard many compliments before, about how I treat Habiba, about the kind of husband I am. But this... this was different. Every time I learned something new about the man who raised her, I found myself loving him too, and now, hearing this, from his father, the man who knew him best, I couldn't hold back.

I threw my arms around Baba and hugged him, my chest tight, eyes stinging with tears of gratitude. "InShaAllāh," I whispered, voice thick, "I will always be that for her."

The door creaked open, and Ma's voice floated out, playful and teasing. "Shuf, shuf... two old men crying outside?" We pulled apart quickly, sheepish, while she stood there with her shawl pulled tight, grinning like she'd caught us red-handed. "Come back inside, have some tea."

I was about to follow her in when Baba placed a hand on my shoulder, his grip surprisingly firm. He leaned closer, whispering with a deadpan expression, "You see that woman?"

I frowned. "My mother?"

"Yes, her. Don't leave me alone with her. I promise you, she'd stab me if she got the chance."

A laugh burst out of me despite myself, and I clapped his back.

"Don't worry. You wouldn't be the first."

Back in the warmth, My eyes found Habiba immediately, and I couldn't stop the smile tugging at my lips.

MashaAllah.

I prayed that Allah would keep her smiling this way, always.

She was seated beside Sanaa, head resting on her shoulder, while Sanaa chatted and played with Naeem, who was busy scattering confetti on the ground. Both of them watched him with quiet amusement.

Those two had grown inseparable. On weekends, they disappeared for hours, leaving me to miss Habiba more than I cared to admit.

Zain distracted me, pulling me into a conversation. I sat with the boys to have tea and talk, each of them excited.

Finally, Habiba's gaze found mine across the room. Relief washed over her face the moment our eyes met, and I didn't hesitate. I crossed the room toward her. As I approached, Sanaa began to rise.

"Please, stay," I said quickly.

She smirked. "I think your wife's tired of my blabber." She stood, and Habiba reached to swat at her playfully, missing as Sanaa slipped away.

I lowered myself into the seat beside her, catching sight of Ayaan moving toward Sanaa. Their body language was unreadable, but my curiosity flickered before I turned back to the only person who mattered.

"Bikhair?" *Are you ok?* I murmured.

She nodded, tired but smiling.

"Let's go home," I whispered.

41

HABIBA

تُريدُ مهذباً لا عَيْبَ فِيهِ
وهل عود يفوح بلا دخان

You seek a refined man with no flaws,
But can Oud emit its scent without smoke?

- الطغرائي

This is harder than I thought it would be. I was so caught up in the fairytale of being a mother—the soft glow, the tiny clothes, the sweet flutter of kicks—that I forgot about everything else that comes with it.

I can't even bend to put on my socks anymore. Badr kneels for me every morning, slipping them over my swollen feet as if it's the most natural thing in the world. Behind the wheel, I hate how the bump steals space from my hands, forcing me to sit stiff and awkward, my ribs pressing tight.

The stretch marks came slowly at first, like faint threads, but now they map across my skin in full bloom. Badr swears he loves them. He kisses them reverently each time he sees my belly, murmuring compliments that make me laugh and roll my eyes. But deep down, I wonder if he only says it to soothe me.

The mood swings… those are another war entirely. At first, he handled them with the patience of a saint, but lately, I catch the fatigue in his sighs. I feel bad for him, he's weathered this pregnancy alongside me, but he doesn't carry the weight in his body. He can still sleep face-down. He doesn't know the ache of rolling from side to side, trying to find air, comfort, rest.

Badr and I are seated in the park of our new apartment, staring at the shrieking in the playground. He often drags me out for a walk, claiming I need the fresh air, and afterward, we sit on the park bench together, watching those children. Each one is a little universe of their own. I watched the girl, no older than six keep jumping from a small ledge and yelling, "Mom! Look!" Her mother clapped every single time, as though each leap were magic.

"Badr?" I said.

"Yeah?"

"I want to have it at home. A home birth."

His head whipped toward me, his expression instantly hardening. "Habiba. No. Absolutely not."

I had braced myself for this, but the firmness still stung. I sat up straighter. "I've done my research. With a trained midwife, it's safe. I want it to be intimate. Just us. Not a hospital full of strangers."

He dragged a hand through his hair, frustration simmering. "This isn't about candles and comfort, it's about life and death. Do you understand? If something goes wrong, if the baby's heart drops, if you start bleeding out, we can't wait for an ambulance! Minutes matter." His voice cracked, sharp with panic.

I clenched my jaw, refusing to flinch. "And what if I go to the hospital and they treat me terribly? Rush me into interventions I don't need? What if they take the birth away from me? I don't want that. I don't want to feel powerless."

I was there, in the room with Khadijah for both of her births. The doctors were awful. They took a moment that was supposed to be special for her and turned it into a nightmare. They forced her into things she didn't want, and ever since then, the thought of giving birth in a hospital has haunted me. I don't want my special moment to feel like that. I don't even like strangers.

His eyes flashed as he leaned forward. "Habiba, you're asking me to gamble with your life. With our child's life. I can't. I won't."

403

I pressed my palm to my belly, the baby shifting beneath my skin. My voice rose without meaning to. "This is my birth. Don't I get to decide how I want it?"

"Your birth, yes. But not just your life. That's my child too. All I want is for you both to survive."

"Listen, I'll only do it with a certified midwife. Someone who knows when to transfer. It's not a gamble, Badr, it's a safe choice. And statistically, healthy women with low-risk pregnancies can do just as well at home. Sometimes even better, because stress is lower."

He laughed bitterly, shaking his head, "Statistics won't comfort me if something happens." then he got up, pacing a few steps away. He stopped, turned back, and his voice came firm, almost pleading. "Habiba, I haven't said no to you once since this pregnancy began and I don't want to start now. Please, just drop it."

My lips pouted on their own, beginning to tremble, so I looked away before he could see. I thought about getting up and leaving, but I'd need his help to stand, so I stayed put, stubborn and silent.

"Habiba." His tone softened. He reached to turn my face toward him, but I swatted his hand away.

He exhaled, then paced again, two quick rounds before stopping in front of me. His eyes closed for a moment, as if steadying himself, then he knelt down, taking my hand in his. His grip was tight.

"Tell you what." His voice was low now, ragged. "We'll go back to the doctor and ask her, then I'll spend the next few days researching. If it feels safe enough… I'll consider it."

That was the closest I was going to get to a yes. Slowly, I turned to look at him. His jaw flexed, as though swallowing back all the protests he wanted to throw at me, but instead, he pulled me into his arms and held me like he couldn't let go.

He got a call, so we headed back inside so he could finish up some work. I drifted into the kitchen, pulling out a pan to start dinner,

404

but before I could even place it on the stove, Badr stepped out of the guestroom he now used as his office.

He wasn't with the firm anymore, but he'd managed to secure a contract that let him work freelance while tying up the projects he'd already started. "Let's order takeout," he said, leaning against the doorframe.

I turned, narrowing my eyes in mock offense. "Do you not like my food anymore?" I teased. This was the fifth time this week we're ordering in.

His smile was soft as he crossed the room toward me. "It's not that. I'd just rather not have you going through the trouble." His hand came to rest against my belly, warm and gentle. "She's getting heavy, and your feet aren't getting any stronger. And I've got a meeting coming up, so… Chinese?"

I opened my mouth to reply, but a sudden movement inside me cut me off. My hand flew to my stomach and I laughed, shaking my head at Badr's raised brows. "She doesn't agree, apparently."

He chuckled, sinking down to his knees so he could address our daughter directly. "Well, we'll eat whatever you want, little one. Just… don't kick too hard, okay? She's precious cargo." His words sent me into another fit of laughter.

When he stood again, his face softened, voice dipping into a whisper meant only for me. "What do you want to eat?"

I glanced around the kitchen, as though the shelves or countertops might offer me an answer. Before I could say anything, the doorbell rang. Both our heads turned at once.

I made a half-hearted attempt to rush toward the bedroom— waddle was more accurate now—while Badr moved toward the door. I was in nothing but a loose maternity gown, no scarf or hijab, so I ducked out of sight and pressed myself against the door. Heart thumping, I listened for a familiar voice.

Sure enough, I heard Zain's. I grinned, loosening a scarf from the hook and wrapping it around myself before stepping into view.

"Habiba! how's my niece doing?"

"Wow, so now you don't even ask how I'm doing anymore? Just using me as a carrier service, huh?" I teased.

"More like VIP transport. You should be charging him per minute," Zain fired back.

Badr's voice cut in smoothly, dry but amused. "Keep talking and I'll start charging you for visitation rights."

The three of us laughed before Zain revealed the reason for his visit—he'd brought food.

Apparently, Ma had sent over masa and spinach stew, a Nigerian dish I'd mentioned craving a few days ago. It had only been a passing thought at the time, I was too tired to cook it myself. I never expected her to actually have it made and sent to me.

The moment I lifted the lid and the familiar scent hit me, tears blurred my vision. I cried openly, not even bothering to wipe them away. I couldn't imagine anyone caring for me that much. And honestly, I couldn't blame this one on the hormones. Even if I weren't pregnant, I'd still cry.

Badr had been wonderful about my cravings all throughout the pregnancy. No matter the hour, he was always willing, up on his feet, out on the streets, making phone calls, hunting something down. Sometimes he even cooked, though his efforts in that department were… let's just say less successful.

He'd learned to stock the fridge with things I could grab when I woke up early for tahajjud. I tried to keep up with eight rakats, but lately, I'd get hungry halfway through and end up making something quick to eat. He always made sure there was food ready—Ma's home-cooked meals, Zain's baked goods, little comforts tucked away just for me. If it wasn't there, he'd go out and get it, no matter the time.

That night, I ate while Badr finished his meeting. Afterward, we curled up together on the couch, the glow of the TV flickering across the room. We half-watched a movie, half-talked about baby names, tossing possibilities back and forth. And still, somehow, we hadn't managed to settle on one.

In the end, Badr agreed. I was having a home birth afterall.

Our doctor signed off on it, we had a wonderful midwife, the birthing pool, all the supplies stacked neatly in the corner. I knew he still wasn't comfortable, I could see it in the way his jaw tightened when the topic came up, but he gave in because he knew how much it mattered to me. I overheard him and Ayaan whispering about having an ambulance waiting outside, just in case. They thought they were being discreet, but I heard.

I didn't care. Let them have their backup plans. All I cared about was that I was going to bring my baby into the world at home. Not in a cold, sterile hospital.

We're in Badr's family home. The living room had been cleared out, transformed. No couch, no clutter, just the pool and the equipment ready for the big moment.

I still had a week and a half left, but I was done. Done with swollen feet, endless bathroom trips, the backaches, the sleepless nights. I was ready to meet my baby. Ma and Ba were away at a friend's wedding, promising to be back in two days.

Zain, Hana, Ahmed, and Ayaan were at our apartment, putting the last touches on the nursery, disinfecting, rearranging, painting little details. It warmed me to think of them all working so hard just so the house would feel new again when we brought the baby home.

Here, in the family house, I kept myself busy. Bouncing on the birthing ball, stretching, clinging to the body pillow Badr had gotten me—which, honestly, deserved its own thank-you note. Since Ma wasn't here, Sanaa decided to stay over so I would still have a woman with me.

But right now, it was just me and Badr. I flushed the toilet, my twentieth trip that day, and yes, I was counting—washed my hands, and padded out with a secret smile tugging my lips. He was at his desk, typing, focused, glasses sliding down the bridge of his nose.

I came up behind him and scratched lightly at the nape of his neck—that one spot that always made him soften. He leaned into my touch instantly, sighing, before catching my hand and pulling me into his lap. His chair squeaked as he pushed it back, creating space for me to settle. I dropped into his embrace, looping my arms around his neck.

"Hi, pretty mama," he murmured with a grin, leaning in.

But the sudden release beneath me, the faint dripping sound, the warmth spreading across my thighs, made my whole body go still.

Badr watched me, amused, waiting for me to meet his eyes—but I couldn't. My face flamed. No, no, no. I did not just pee on him. There was no way.

"Are you okay?" His voice was soft, cautious.

Heat rushed up my chest. "I am so sorry," I whispered, mortified, my heart pounding so hard it hurt.

He chuckled low, nudging me to stand and that's when another gush soaked through, splashing the floor. I stared at the spreading puddle, shocked, breathless. This wasn't normal.

Badr's eyes widened, darting from the floor to me. "Habiba…" he murmured, his voice unsteady. "I don't think that's pee."

"I don't think so either," I admitted, my voice barely audible.

I tried to step forward, awkward and dripping, but he stopped me. "Wait, I don't want you to slip. Here, hold on to me," He leaned down, and I looped my arms around his neck. In one motion, he swept me up, carrying me away from the mess. His arms were steady, careful, like he was afraid I'd break. He set me down gently on the other end of the room before darting off for a rug to contain the water.

"Call Sarah," he said firmly. Sarah is our midwife.

My hands shook as I dialed, and she fired off a dozen questions while I stood there wet and embarrassed. She said it was very likely that my water did break and began instructing me on what to do until she arrived.

When I hung up, Badr wiped my legs for me and then I left the room and stood at the foot of the stairs, glaring at them. Regretting every stubborn decision that had led me to climb up there earlier.

Ma had cleared and prepared the downstairs room just for me, so I wouldn't have to climb the stairs anymore. But while I was asleep, Badr had work to do, so he came upstairs. When I woke and found myself alone, I decided to come up to him.

Five minutes. That's how long it had taken me to drag myself up. And now? Now I had to find a way back down.

"Come on," Badr's voice floated from behind me, calm but laced with urgency. I turned, meeting his eyes, and he gave me that smile—steady, reassuring, but tense at the edges.

He didn't ask. He just scooped me up bridal style, careful not to jostle me, and carried me all the way downstairs. My heart thudded in rhythm with his steps, and when he finally laid me down in the prepared room, reality hit me like a tidal wave.

This was it. Our baby was on the way.

42

BADR

أَثَرُ الفَرَاشَةِ لا يُرَى
أَثَرُ الفَرَاشَةِ لا يَزُولُ

The butterfly's trace cannot be seen,
The butterfly's trace never fades away.

- محمود درويش

I had always thought of myself as strong. I carried the weight of work deadlines, family expectations, and even my own insecurities without breaking. But nothing, absolutely nothing, prepared me for the night Habiba went into labor.

I watched her for months with this mix of admiration and fear—the way her body carried our child, the way she smiled through discomfort, the way she softened whenever she felt the baby kick. And now, suddenly, we're here.

Her hand gripped mine so tightly that I thought my bones might break. The midwife came as soon as we called, her presence steady, but it wasn't enough to calm the storm inside me.

Ma was supposed to be here, but we weren't expecting this today, her due date was over a week ahead so Ba and Ma took a drive out of the city for a wedding. When I told her that Habiba was going into labor, she was very frustrated that they were so far away, then quickly started making the trip back but she wasn't sure if they would make it. I also had to call Sanaa and Zain.

"Breathe with her," the midwife instructed, her tone firm, practiced.

I sat close, pressing my forehead to Habiba's temple, whispering encouragement, inhaling and exhaling with her. Her breaths were ragged, uneven, trembling with pain. And every time she squeezed her eyes shut, every time her face twisted in agony, a knife drove deeper into me.

I wanted to take it from her. To trade places. To carry the burden, the pain, the weight. But all I could do was hold her hand and murmur words that felt so small.

Her body shuddered with another contraction, and she clung to me, almost climbing into my chest. I wrapped both arms around her, pulling her into me as if I could shield her from what her own body was forcing her through. She buried her face against my neck, damp with sweat, and I whispered again, over and over, like a prayer, "I've got you, I've got you."

Time blurred. Minutes felt like hours. The midwife moved around us, checking, preparing, her calm voice occasionally cutting through my haze of fear. I heard instructions. "Support her back. Hold her leg here. Help her lean forward"—and I obeyed every word without hesitation.

At one point she broke, her voice cracking with desperation. "Badr, I can't... I can't do this."

I cupped her face, forcing her to look at me even as sweat and tears blurred her vision. My own eyes stung, but I held steady for her. "You already are. Look at you."

Her sob broke me, but she nodded, collapsing against my chest again.

The midwife kept guiding us. "She needs to change position. Help her kneel, support her from behind."

So I did. Every minute stretched me thinner, shredding me. I wasn't used to being helpless. Her nails dug into my arm as another contraction tore through her body. I could see the sweat dripping down her temple, her lips moving in broken dua. My chest felt like it was being ripped open.

I leaned down, pressing my forehead against hers, breathing her same breath. My voice shook, but I whispered anyway, the verses I had clung to in my own heart.

"Wa dhkur fi al-kitābi Maryam…"

Her eyes squeezed shut, but she gripped the front of my shirt and held me closer, as if my trembling recitation could steady her against the waves of pain.

I whispered the words into her ear, broken by my own tears, praying that just as Allah had sent Maryam relief in her agony, He would grant Habiba mercy in this moment. My lips brushed her damp hair as I finished the verse, and kissed her temple.

The hours crawled until I heard the midwife murmur something I barely caught. And then a new voice entered the room—Sanaa, rushing in, breathless but calm, immediately moving to help the midwife. Relief warred with shame inside me. Relief because I wasn't alone anymore, because Habiba had another hand to hold her, another woman to guide her through what I couldn't fully understand. Shame because even though I was giving everything I had, it still didn't feel like enough.

Her fingers latched onto mine, crushing tight, and I almost winced at the strength of her grip. Then she shook her head frantically at the midwife, tears beading at the corners of her eyes. Finally, she found her voice. "I want the epidural."

The words punched through me. Habiba had insisted she'd be fine, that she didn't need it, that she could endure. I tried to convince her otherwise, but she brushed me off, saying she'd manage. And now, hearing her ask for it, my heart shattered.

I looked at the doctor, expecting movement, urgency, anything. But she wasn't even preparing. She just stayed there, calm, almost hesitant.

"She said she wants the epidural," I snapped, my voice rough, edged with panic. "Why aren't you already administering it?"

The midwife met my glare with steady eyes. "She's fully dilated," she said gently, almost apologetically. "It's too late. It's time to push."

For a moment, I just froze, the words bouncing around my skull. Then I turned back to Habiba. Her face was glistening with sweat, her body trembling from the strain. My hands rose to cup her cheeks, forcing her eyes on me.

"Habiba, listen," I whispered, steadying my voice even as everything inside me shook. "It's time. You've done everything, you've been so strong, but now it's time to push. I'm right here. Every second."

She blinked at me, breaths ragged, then gave the faintest nod. Relief and heartbreak collided in my chest. I kissed her damp forehead, wiping the sweat away with my sleeve.

"Good girl," I murmured, stroking her hair back. "I've got you. You can do this."

And just like that, she braced herself, ready.

The midwife's voice grew more urgent. "With the next contraction, you push."

The midwife leaned forward, hands sure and steady. In one fluid motion, she lifted our baby out of the water, glistening, impossibly small, and placed her gently onto Habiba's chest.

I held my breath. My entire world stilled in that moment as I watched Habiba rub the little one's back, whispering broken prayers through her tears. Then like the most beautiful sound I had ever heard, a sharp, fragile wail cut through the silence.

My lungs collapsed in relief. I hadn't even realized I'd been holding my breath until that cry freed me. The sound filled the room, filled me, filled everything. Habiba sobbed harder, clutching our daughter to her chest as if she could fuse their hearts together.

I stepped aside and got down in sujood, thanking Allah. Then I leaned over her shoulder, staring at the tiny life, at the wrinkled face, the clenched fists, the fragile breaths. My tears fell onto Habiba's hair, Sanaa rushed to the room and came back with a blanket.

I knew I'd never look at her the same way again. She has always been strong in my eyes, stubborn and brilliant. But now? Now she was something beyond words.

I held them both, wrapping my arms around them, swearing silently that I would spend the rest of my life proving worthy of what she had just given me.

The room quieted. The midwife stayed calm, reminding us the work wasn't finished yet. I held Habiba's hand, useless and awestruck, while Sanaa hovered close, steadying her. Within minutes, the midwife guided her through one last effort.

I stared at the blood pooling after the placenta was delivered and the cord was cut, my chest tightening, fingers itching to grab my phone—Ayaan was on standby, ready for anything, but seeing neither the midwife nor Sanaa flinch, I forced myself to take a shaky breath and trust them.

Later, the midwife helped Habiba nurse, gave me quick instructions, and then quietly slipped out, leaving the three of us in the stillness of our home. Sanaa moved about the kitchen, managing to coax a little soup into Habiba between feedings, though her appetite hadn't yet returned. I couldn't bring myself to eat either, my whole focus was on watching Habiba breathe, watching our child's tiny chest rise and fall.

Ma called a few times, her voice thick with emotion, assuring me they were only a few hours away. I told her we were fine, though the truth was I wouldn't feel fine until Habiba was rested and strong again. For now, I sat there in the dim light, heart torn between exhaustion and gratitude, knowing I would spend the rest of my life thanking Allah for the sight before me—my wife and our child, safe.

43

HABIBA

نَصِيبُكَ فِي حَيَاتِكَ مِن حَبِيبٍ
نَصِيبُكَ فِي مَنَامِكَ مِن خَيالِ

*Your share of a beloved in your waking life
is only your share of a dream in your sleep.*

- المتنبي

I woke the next morning to the soft, insistent cries of our baby.
I remembered waking up a few times in the night to feed her, though it
felt dreamlike—uncertain if it had really happened or if my exhausted
mind had imagined it.

Every inch of my body ached, muscles sore and trembling, but
I forced myself upright. Badr was slumped next to me, deep in sleep,
utterly oblivious to the tiny wails.

I tried to hurry, to get to her, but each step sent jolts of pain
through my legs. I leaned heavily on the bed for support, inching my way
to the cradle. Once I reached it, I braced myself, gripping the edge so I
wouldn't collapse. My legs wobbled dangerously, I couldn't risk dropping
her.

Badr's hand rested gently on the cradle. The drawn curtains
filtered sunlight just enough to illuminate our daughter.

I paused, caught in awe. Our baby, our tiny miracle. Her hands
were clenched into fists, face scrunched in protest against the world. Her
skin glowed pink, her cries fierce yet fragile. She was swaddled in the
same blanket Badr and his siblings had been wrapped in. Ma had given it
to me, a thread connecting generations.

I tried to lift her, cradle her, but my body betrayed me. Tears sprang unbidden, warm and helpless, and I began to sob. I wanted so desperately to soothe her, to hold her, but my strength had evaporated.

Badr stirred abruptly, panic in his eyes when he realized I wasn't beside him. Seeing me trembling, only amplified his worry. He was at my side in an instant.

"Habiba, why are you crying?" His voice was taut with fear and concern as he pulled me into his arms. I leaned into him, weight spilling over, muffling my sobs against his chest.

"I want to pick—her up, but I can barely stand... and she's crying," I whispered through shaky breaths.

He exhaled slowly, steadying himself, and scooped me up bridal-style. "Why did you get up, Habibati? You should have woken me." He settled me gently back on the bed, pressing a soft kiss to my temple.

Turning to the cradle, he lifted our daughter with careful reverence. I adjusted, sitting upright, and he placed her gently into my arms. My hands instinctively guided her to my chest, helping her latch. I leaned back, eyes closing against the exhaustion that weighed on me.

I felt him shift beside me, and soon his shoulder was at my back, his warmth a grounding presence. His lips brushed my head. Words floated past my awareness, soft and protective.

The next time I woke, it wasn't to crying but the sound of a burp. I thought it was Badr at first, until I saw him expertly patting her back, a grin lighting up his face.

"You're good at this," I murmured, forcing my voice past fatigue.

He glanced at me, still gentle, still patient, and asked, "How are you feeling?" He inched closer, adjusting so his arm was around me, fingers brushing mine.

"I'm tired," I admitted, resting my head against his shoulder. He leaned back, cradling our daughter with ease, the three of us forming a fragile, perfect little world.

We didn't speak after that. Words were unnecessary. I traced my finger into her tiny, hand, and she curled around it instinctively. A laugh escaped me, light and shaky, and Badr chuckled too, his chest warm against mine.

I closed my eyes, breathing in the quiet intimacy of the moment. I couldn't believe it, we were parents. We made it this far.

Badr asked if I wanted to shower, mentioning that the midwife recommended it, and I nodded. I genuinely felt grimy, every inch of me sore and sticky. He helped me in the shower, patient and gentle, and then showered himself and changed into fresh clothes too. Not long after, Ma arrived. She sent Badr off to rest, and I was quietly grateful for that, he looked very tired.

She changed the sheets, prepared me a small meal, and fed me with careful hands before helping me tend to the baby. The house settled into a quiet rhythm, and evening was nearly upon us by the time Badr finally stirred awake.

Baba came by with Zain, Hana, and Ahmed. Hana made it clear she didn't want anything to do with the birth. She wanted to be as far away as possible, so she was very happy that she didn't have to be there when the birth happened.

She practically leapt onto the bed next to me, hugging me tightly. "You did it!" she exclaimed.

"I did," I grinned, hugging her back, relief and pride mingling in the warmth of the embrace.

She got off the bed and moved to stand beside Zain, both of them staring at the tiny figure in Badr's arms. "Awe, she's so..." Hana began, her coo faltering mid-word, and I caught the hint of insincerity, prompting a soft chuckle from me.

"Beautiful?" Badr offered, voice gentle, full of pride.

"Yeah... that... very... that," she muttered, sounding almost reluctant. Zain smacked her lightly on the head. "What!? She looks exactly how anyone would after marinating in water for nine months.

Give it time—she'll take shape eventually. Ahmed did."

Ahmed side eyed her with a glare, which she chose to ignore. "What's her name?" He asked.

Badr glanced at me, and I simply shrugged. We had a few names we liked, but nothing felt quite right yet.

The week blurred by, with Badr carrying both me and the baby through it all.

He helped me shower, scribbled notes whenever the midwife came by, made sure we both ate, reminded me to stretch, and woke up every single time the baby did. I don't think I would've survived those first days without him.

The night before the *Aqiqah*, we decided to spend the night in our apartment. Everyone would come over in the morning to help.

It was 10 p.m. The baby had just gone back to sleep, and I lay with my head on Badr's bare chest while he leaned against the headboard, his hand softly tracing circles along my arm.

He began reciting Surah Ash-Sharh, his voice low and steady, almost like a hum vibrating through his chest beneath my ear.

"Fa inna ma'al 'usri yusra."

"So, surely with hardship comes ease." I translated, but my voice came out as a breath of relief. It was nice to hear this verse, especially after the past few days we've had.

"Inna ma'al 'usri yusra." He sighed deeply. "Indeed, with hardship comes ease." Then he fell quiet.

I waited, expecting him to continue with the last verses, but he didn't. He never finished speaking so I glanced at him to be sure he was all right, half afraid he'd drifted off—but no. He was awake, his eyes fixed, heavy with thought.

After what felt like forever, he finally spoke again. "What do you think of Yusrah?"

I sat up, needing to see his face. He only stared at me, expression unreadable.

"As a name?" He nodded. A smile spread across my face. "Yusrah," I repeated softly.

I didn't even need to answer aloud. From her cradle, Yusrah let out a gurgle, and Badr and I chuckled quietly, careful not to wake her again.

We hadn't invited many people to the aqiqah, mostly the same faces who'd been at the walima, though a few couldn't make it. Baba had a cow slaughtered for sadaqah back home in Nigeria, and Ba arranged the same in Morocco, while we did ours here in Canada.

The ceremony began at 2 p.m., when the imam arrived. We went door to door in our building, offering meat to every household—some accepted, others politely declined. After about half an hour of Qur'an recitation, when everyone had gathered, we announced her name aloud.

Yusrah.

Once the excitement settled, we shaved her tiny head, weighed the hair, and recorded the weight to donate in silver.

The feast followed, warm and full of joy. Yusrah was passed from arm to arm until, halfway through, she protested loudly enough to make her feelings known. After that, we tucked her away in the bedroom, where she could rest in peace.

After the aqiqah, we spent more than a month living with Badr's family. He had to pour his focus into preparing for the launch of our firm, and he insisted we wouldn't move back to our apartment until I was fully healed. He didn't want me home alone with the baby and no one to care for me, especially now that we no longer lived so close to family.

Once we did move back home, things were still a bit hard, so

Ma sent Hana to stay with us for another month. Having her helped a lot. I didn't have to worry about cooking or cleaning, all I did was feed the baby and rest.

I couldn't stop thanking Allah for making me lucky enough to have all those people around me to help me recover. I knew well that not everyone had that opportunity.

I woke up earlier than usual today because Yusrah decided to turn her entire sleeping schedule upside down. So I made breakfast for everyone.

While Badr was in the shower, I laid out his shirt, suit, and cufflinks—though he still prefers to pick his own shoes. I also placed his keys and wallet on the table by the door.

After his shower, Badr dressed while I waited with Yusrah. I passed her to him briefly so I could fix his tie, but when I tried to take her back, she cried inconsolably until she was returned to his chest. So he kept her there, cradling her as he drank his coffee, played with her tiny fingers, and moved slowly through the house, tending to the last of his morning routine with her along for the ride.

He had a client meeting today, our first since the launch, apart from the ones we had secured long before.

He leaned in to peck my lips just as the handle to Hana's room rattled, startling us both. "Maybe it's time to send her home," he whispered, but kissed me anyway.

I chuckled, just as she appeared, stretching into a yawn. "Good morning."

"Good morning." He dropped a kiss on her forehead. "Pack your bags."

She stopped mid-yawn, eyes darting between us. "What?"

"He's joking," I assured her, chuckling as I headed for the kitchen.

"Oh." She exhaled, palm pressed to her chest. "I was already calculating how to make this permanent." Her gaze slid to Yusrah, nestled in her father's arms. "Hi Yusrah. How's my favourite little girl?" She reached out, and Badr gladly handed her over. "I'll see you later!" he waved, rushing out the door.

"You're up early," Hana said, walking toward me.

"She was up early. She sets the schedule," I replied.

Hana made a face before taking some of the food I prepared and headed to the living room, where she picked up her Kindle and began reading to Yusrah—fully convinced she understood every word.

Epilogue

BADR

وَإِنِّي وَإِيَّاهُ لَعَيْنٌ وَأُخْتُهَا
وَإِنِّي وَإِيَّاهُ لَكَفٌّ وَمِعْصَمُ

Behold, my love and I are as one eye and its twin,
And as the palm and wrist are joined, without and within.

– أبو فراس الحمداني

I stepped out of the bathroom, rubbing a towel over my damp hair, rolling my shoulders until my neck cracked from side to side. The sharp sound echoed through the room, and immediately, two pairs of eyes snapped to me.

My girls.

Yusrah, now five years old, froze mid-jump, her big brown eyes wide, mirroring her mother's expression for half a second before she broke into a fit of giggles. The sound was contagious and it set Habiba laughing too, her shoulders shaking.

"What?" I asked, feigning confusion, though I already knew exactly why. "Why are you laughing at me, huh?"

I took a slow, exaggerated step toward them. Yusrah's laughter turned into a squeal as she scrambled to the far end of the bed, but I caught her easily, scooping her up and spinning her in my arms.

"Why are you laughing at Abba?" I teased, blowing loud raspberries against her tiny stomach.

She screamed louder, that beautiful sound that could cure any bad day.

"Shh, hush!" Habiba hissed.

I froze mid-tickle, both Yusrah and I turning to her like two guilty children.

"You'll wake him," she whispered, nodding toward the bed.

There lay Yasin—our little storm of a 2 year old boy—fast asleep, cheeks puffed, lashes thick against his skin. Not even a thunderclap could wake him. I smiled. Has to be Ba's genes.

Yusrah pressed her finger to her lips, mimicking Habiba, and I did the same, exaggerating the motion until she giggled again—quietly this time. I set her down gently, watching her climb back onto the bed and reach for the Yogurt cup she was happily taking before I interrupted.

She took one spoonful, then lifted another toward me. "Here, Abba," she said through a half grin.

I bent down, pretending to inspect it seriously before taking the spoon she was offering me. "Perfect," I said, mouth full. Her giggle was reward enough.

Then I turned to Habiba. The light brushed her features, softening everything it touched—the curve of her cheek, the faint crease near her eyes when she smiled. I pressed a kiss to that cheek, tasting faint traces of her floral lotion. She blinked, surprised, then gave my back a playful slap.

I chuckled, pulling a clean shirt from the wardrobe and slipping it on.

"Abba! Me too! Me too!" Yusrah called, bouncing on the bed, her hand stretched out.

I turned, catching her hand and cupping her face between my palms. "Of course, my princess," I said before planting an exaggerated kiss on her cheek, then another on her forehead. She squealed, laughing so hard the bed shook.

I leaned over to Yasin next and brushed my lips against his warm, chubby cheek. Not even a twitch.

"Yup," I murmured under my breath, watching his tiny chest rise and fall. "Definitely Ba's genes."

Habiba walked me to the door, her limp still faint but noticeable. She'd sprained her ankle earlier chasing Yasin through the hallway. He thought it was a race, and she refused to lose.

Before she could protest, I scooped her up, earning a soft gasp and a glare that didn't quite reach her eyes. She fit perfectly in my arms like she always had, and I set her down gently once we were outside the apartment and in the hall, shutting the door behind us.

"I could've walked," she murmured, though her voice had that teasing lilt I knew too well.

"I know." I smiled. "But you didn't."

Her lips parted, ready to retort, but I leaned down instead, my hand rising to her chin. My thumb brushed against her jaw as I tilted her face up, feeling the faint hitch in her breath. For a heartbeat, the world felt still, no noise, no time, just her eyes on mine, wide and soft and impossibly familiar.

Then I kissed her, slow, unhurried, the kind of kiss that said I'll miss you even if I'm gone for five minutes.

When I pulled back, she blinked up at me, dazed but smiling. "You're so weird," she muttered, though the warmth in her tone betrayed her.

"Only for you," I said quietly, bumping my nose against hers before stepping back. The gesture had become ours, a wordless I love you without needing to say it.

"Drive safe," she called after me as I pressed the button for the elevator. "And say your duas."

It was routine now—the same words every time I left. But hearing them never stopped warming me. I loved that she cared enough to make it a habit. I loved how we'd grown, how our home had grown with us, how love had turned from something fragile into something that just was.

I whispered my dua as I walked to the car, the night air crisp against my face. The dashboard clock read 9:02—I was cutting it close; the supermarket closes at ten.

At the store, the aisles glowed under harsh lights. I pushed the cart lazily, half on autopilot, tossing in the usual things. When I reached the dairy section, a small smile tugged at my lips. Yogurts.

I'd only bought a few, just to try, but Yusrah and Yasin had devoured them. I grabbed enough pieces for them to have to their hearts content.

When I returned, the house lights were still on. I could hear them before I even stepped inside—laughter, shrieks, Habiba's soft scolding in the background.

Then I rang the bell, followed by the telltale sound.

"Aba!" Yasin's voice, high and wild.

I laughed quietly, already picturing it.

The second the door swung open, I barely made it two steps in before both Yusrah and Yasin came charging at me—a blur of curls, tiny feet, and uncontainable joy. The grocery bags hit the floor with a soft thud as they collided into me, Yusrah yelling my name and Yasin squealing something that only vaguely sounded like Abba!

I scooped them both up, one on each arm, their laughter echoing through the hall.

Once the kids got distracted by their own little adventures, Habiba and I carried the groceries to the kitchen and began sorting through them. I crouched in front of the fridge, stacking juice boxes neatly on the lower shelf when her voice reached me. "Badr... what is this?"

I turned, confused, only to find her standing by the counter, brows slightly furrowed. Her gaze was locked on the yogurt cups piled up in the bag.

"Yogurt," I said simply, closing the fridge door and straightening. "Don't you like them?"

"Yes, but…" She tilted her head, blinking at the heap. "This is a lot."

I followed her gaze properly this time—and yeah, she was right. It looked like I'd bought out half the dairy section. My hand went to the back of my neck, rubbing awkwardly. "I—uh—I saw that you and the kids liked them, so I thought I'd just… you know… get a few extra."

Before I could finish, she let out a laugh—not just a giggle, but that full, unrestrained kind that starts in the chest and spills out before you can stop it. Then she crouched down, holding her stomach, her laughter filling the entire kitchen.

"What's so funny?" I asked, even though I was already smiling like an idiot.

"Badr," she gasped between breaths, her cheeks flushed, "you've become a dad. Don't you see it?"

I frowned, half-laughing. "See what?"

"That thing dads do—" She pointed at the pile through her laughter. "Buying a ridiculous amount of something just because the kids liked it once. You just did exactly that."

It hit me then. The image was so clear—me at the store, proudly throwing yogurt after yogurt into the cart like I'd just discovered gold. I couldn't help it. I started laughing too, the kind that shakes your shoulders and makes it hard to breathe.

We must've looked absurd sitting on the kitchen floor surrounded by groceries, laughing over a pile of yogurt because a few seconds later, Yusrah came running in, eyes wide and curious.

"What's funny?"

She didn't even wait for an answer before joining in, giggling just because we were. Habiba, still smiling, reached for two cups and handed one to her, then another to Yasin, who had toddled in right behind his sister, clutching his yogurt proudly in both hands.

"Go on, take them to the living room," she said softly.

426

Their laughter echoed down the hallway as they disappeared, tiny feet pattering on the floor. Habiba looked at me then, her eyes soft with that quiet affection that always makes my chest ache. "Here," she said, handing me one of the yogurts with a smile that was half amused, half tender. "Go sit down and have one too, Abba."

I laughed, shaking my head as I took it, but I couldn't stop the grin tugging at my lips.

We just finished Maghrib. The kids were mumbling to themselves when I leaned back, letting my head rest in Habiba's lap, like I always did.

Her hand found my hair, gentle and familiar, moving slowly through it. I closed my eyes, listening to the sound of Yusrah playing with her toy on the bed. Yasin was beside her, babbling in his usual gibberish, and somehow she was replying as if she completely understood him.

When I opened my eyes again, I just looked at Habiba.

Her eyes seemed brighter than before, like they carried a little more light every day. Her cheeks—softer, a little puffier now, proof that she's loved and cared for. Her lips were curved upwards as always, and on the days they weren't, I always found a way to make sure they were.

She smiled. "What?" she whispered.

I shook my head. "Say Alhamdulillah," I murmured, my voice barely above a whisper.

"For what?"

"For our peace."

"Alhamdulillah." She whispered.

"For our patience."

"Alhamdulillah."

I smiled. "For you."

She chuckled but whispered again, "Alhamdulillah."

Before my next words came out, a small body crashed onto my chest. I groaned in pain.

"Abba! Look, look! His eyes are woogly!" Yusrah shoved her toy into my face, her giggles filling the room.

Before I could recover, Yasin toddled over and plopped himself right onto Habiba's lap—or rather, half on her, half on my face. I jerked up, holding my breath to avoid inhaling the unmistakable scent of his diapers.

Habiba burst into laughter, the kind that filled the room and made everything feel softer, lighter. She adjusted Yasin on her lap, and he reached up with those tiny hands to pat her face. She caught one, kissed it, and then pressed her lips to his chubby cheek.

While Yusrah is obsessed with her Abba, Yasin can't stand being away from his mother. Every day, I watch them grow more attached to her, falling in love with the same smile, the same warmth, the same woman I fell in love with. Yusrah has her mother's smile and laughter but my eyes; Yasin has her eyes, and sometimes, her patience too.

Watching them is like watching my own heart run around outside my chest. Fragile and fearless. I'd burn the world down before I let anything hurt them.

"For them," I said quietly, watching her, the warmth swelling in my chest.

Her smile softened. Then she whispered back, "Alhamdulillah."

THE END

Acknowledgments

I'd like to start by giving a huge thank you to Abderrazak and Alaa, who I confided in throughout the writing of this book. From the very beginning to the very end, they helped shape this story in more ways than they know.

Thank you for showing as much interest in this book as I did. For the ideas, the late-night conversations, the laughter, the Islamic guidance, and the thoughtful suggestions. This is our final year together, and I don't know if I'll have the two of you to plot future books with me and knowing that makes this book a thousand times more special.

A heartfelt thank you to my parents, who remain my most beautiful and dependable example of a good marriage. And to my siblings for supporting me constantly, no matter how ridiculous the dream. For slapping some sense into me when I needed it, and for always offering real solutions when I needed them most.

And to my readers: thank you for always looking forward to my work, for engaging, encouraging, and showing up every time. The book community has brought some of the kindest, most supportive people into my life, and I am endlessly grateful for that.

This book holds a very special place in my heart, and it always will. Thank you to everyone who loves the story of Badr and Habiba as much as I do.

I would like to end this with a hadith from our Prophetﷺ:

"The example of a good companion and a bad companion is that of a musk seller and a blacksmith. The musk seller will either give you some perfume, or you will buy some from him, or at the very least, you will leave with a pleasant scent."

I am endlessly grateful to Allah for surrounding me with people who, in one way or another, left something beautiful behind.

About The Author

G. M. Asmau

G. M.Asmau is a young writer who used to write stories on Wattpad for fun. After leaving writing for several years and focusing on her Architecture dreams, she found writing again at a hard point in her life. She decided that she's ready to start writing again, this time wanting to share her story beyond just words on her screen, she wanted to feel it on paper.

Today, her dream is to integrate the structured realm of architecture with the whimsical universe of love stories. She dreams of being a successful architect who is also a prolific author, penning novels that captivate readers. She wishes to live a life that drafts between blueprints to scripting love stories.

Connect with me
Instagram: author.gmasmau
Goodreads: G M Asmau
Email: asmaugm@gmail.com

www.ingramcontent.com/pod-product-compliance
Lightning Source LLC
Chambersburg PA
CBHW070901260626

47162CB00007B/2521